Dracula's Death

Dracula's Death

BY

Amaya Tenshi

www.penmorepress.com

Dracula's Death by Amaya Tenshi
Copyright 2024 © Amanda Thoss
Published by Penmore Press LLC

All rights reserved. No part of this book may be used or reproduced by any means without the written permission of the publisher except in the case of brief quotation embodied in critical articles and reviews.

This is a work of fiction. The characters and events in this book are fictitious and any resemblance to persons living or dead is purely coincidental, with the exception of historical personages as described in the Author's Note.

ISBN-13:978-8-957851-42-6 (Paperback)
ISBN-13:978-8-957851-41-9 (e-book)

BISAC Subject Headings:
FIC009060 FICTION / Fantasy / Urban
FIC010000 FICTION / Fairy Tales, Folk Tales, Legends & Mythology
FIC051000 FICTION / Cultural Heritage

Edited by Chris Wozney
Cover Art by Neutronboar

Address all correspondence to:
Penmore Press LLC
920 N Javelina Pl
Tucson AZ 85748 USA

PROLOGUE

One very fine, chill day in early December of 1476, a small force of men on horseback rode in a terrible hurry to Snagov Monastery. The monastery was a fortress, well-hidden by a dense forest, and surrounded by the protective waters of a beautiful lake. It was accessible only by the foot bridge that the voivode, who now rode towards it at the front of his men, had constructed years ago during his previous reign. Vlad Dracula—the voivode who had sat on the throne of Wallachia twice before—had regained it for the third time. He had returned from imprisonment and exile to retake the throne with the aid of his cousin, cousin-in-law, his eldest son, and his own men who had returned to his service. He had been crowned prince just a few days before St. Andrew's Day, the holiday celebrating the patron saint of the country. But an Ottoman force was bearing down on Bucharest at that very moment. With them was the pretender that Vlad Dracula had ousted from the throne of Wallachia a few months prior, who was no doubt eager to regain that seat.

During his previous reign, Dracula had hidden his gold and wealth at this monastery, which had been founded by his grandfather Mircea the Elder, returning from time to time to withdraw gold at need and as he wished. His coins were also minted there. He had even had a prison built on the premises. In the past, he had come and gone quietly, secretly, often in disguise. This time, he arrived dressed for battle, with his son Mihnea and his men likewise prepared to fight. They crossed the wooden bridge and entered the fortified walls, dismounted, and made their way to where the gold was stored. Dracula made no attempt to speak to the monks. He had no time.

His men formed a line and were soon busy moving barrels of gold from hand to hand to throw into the placid lake, while Dracula oversaw the operation. The commotion of so many unannounced visitors and the pounding of hammers on barrels drew the attention of the monks. A good number of them recognized the voivode and respectfully kept their distance. But one monk, with kind, bright eyes in a gaunt yet young-looking face, approached. His cassock was worn, but in good repair. His hands were aged by weather and hard work. He was a priest monk—a clerical position of the Orthodox, as the title suggested, both a priest and a monk. His beard and hair were gray, grayer than seemed appropriate for his apparent age. He was either older than he looked, or wise for his years.

"Your Majesty," the priest monk greeted him, "some of the villagers told me you had come again unto your own country. They were pleased to have you once again on the throne of your grandfather, Mircea the Old."

Dracula, bedecked in fine armor and purple cloth, his sword at his side, nodded his head in small deference, but did not ask for the priest monk's blessing. He hadn't the time, and he was estranged from the Greek Church into which he had been baptized as a boy.

"How is it you were you were released from the prison of His Majesty, Matthias Corvinus?" the priest monk inquired.

"Father," Dracula addressed him. "I am occupied with matters of state. I haven't the time to discuss politics. Some later date, perhaps."

DRACULA'S DEATH

Dracula returned his attention to the task his men were performing. A good deal of gold had already sunk beneath the clear, deep blue waters. Mihnea, now very nearly a man himself, watched the operation quietly. Dracula could ask for no finer son. If only he had been legitimate, as were his younger brothers, still too young to go to war and so left behind in the care of their mother in Hungary. Three living sons. A good number. A blessing.

"Why did you leave the Church of your mother and your country, your Majesty?"

"My father felt warmly toward the Latin faith. I think he would have preferred for me to be baptized into that church. It was only by happenstance that I was baptized in the Greek Church, by servants, during my father's absence."

"Your Majesty surely knows better than that. God does not allow such things to happen without His consent. All that we call happenstance is the hands of God."

"If you mean to lecture me about apostasy, I would remind you and all those here" —Dracula indicated the other monks watching his men at work— "that Orthodox Constantinople has fallen to the rapacious Ottomans, while the Latin Pope gains power. If, as you say, God 'does not allow such things to happen without His consent,' then it follows that the Pope is favored by God, while the once illustrious Greek Church is not. Constantinople lies in ruins now, though I would recover that city for Christendom if it is given to me to do so."

"The Emperor gave his life to defend the city."

"Though he also agreed with the Council of Florence," Dracula pointed out, "and allied with the Pope as well."

"He was not crowned emperor in the way previous emperors were, for the people objected to that alliance. They put their faith and trust in God's aid, not in armies and the riches which can be found in the world. Surely your Majesty does not suppose that God dwelt in the Hagia Sophia and nowhere else?"

"Constantinople," Dracula repeated, "has fallen. There is no strong Christian power now but the Pope. And much good faith alone did the inhabitants of that city. Services were being held when the Turks smashed open the doors of the Hagia Sophia and stormed inside. Those who were not slain outright were sorely abused by the Ottoman lust for flesh and booty. Constantinople has fallen. There is no other stronghold for Christendom now save the Latin Pope."

The priest monk's kind eyes considered the *voivode* before him, his shining armor and purple cloth, his sharp sword, and his band of strong, loyal men; Dracula's intelligent son standing by, listening to the conversation and watching all that transpired.

"What profit is it to a man to gain the whole world, but to lose his soul?" the priest monk gently asked.

"Father, I repeat that I am occupied at the moment. I have done my best to serve God and shall continue to do so, so long as there is breath in my body."

"Your Majesty, have you heard what your cousin, His Majesty Ștefan, was advised by his spiritual father to do in order to succeed against the Ottoman threat?"

Dracula remained silent.

"He was advised to build a church after every battle to thank God. He has been very successful in defending Moldavia against incursions."

"That is thanks to geography, Father. My cousin has the good fortune to rule Moldavia, which has mountains and fewer points of ingress, whereas our country of Wallachia is flat, and the Danube is no real protection against the Turks." Dracula cast his eyes at the walls surrounding the monastery. Originally there had been only a small wooden church; now there was a sizeable structure of brick and stone, its interior lovingly and piously covered with exquisite images of saints, so that one's eyes were gazing through dim windows into heaven itself. "I have made repairs to this monastery, Father," Dracula reminded him. "I have built strong walls around it. It is a fortress." This was more than true, for the monastery presided over its own town, complete with a mint and a residence for the voivode. The sounds of industry from the little town could be heard drifting on the air. Yet tranquility rested on the little church. Or was it the priest monk himself who carried the feeling with him wherever he went?

The more he considered the priest monk, the less certain Dracula was that he had met the man before. It had been many years since Dracula had last set foot on the soil of his country; perhaps the man had come to the monastery in those intervening years. If he had not met this priest monk before, the ascetic was taking a peculiarly familiar attitude with him.

"Why do you throw your wealth into the lake?" the priest monk inquired.

"So that the Ottomans cannot seize it, should they overrun this stronghold, as they have so many others," Dracula answered.

"You would rather your worldly wealth came to nothing than let your enemies have it?"

"Just so, Father. Would you have it otherwise?" The man must have come recently to the monastery, Dracula decided; elsewise he would know of the Son of the Dragon's reputation for cunning, and his demand for respect from one and all, no matter their rank or affiliation. Not even priests were exempt from showing deference. Dracula knew no prince succeeded without strength. If he had shown just a bit more, had things gone just a little differently, he would not have been forced into years of exile and imprisonment. Just a little different...

But he had his throne back, and relations with his neighbors were better than they had ever been. His loyal men were ready to defend their land against the Ottomans. This time would be different. *This time*, he would not fail. *This time*, he would demonstrate, to all his enemies and allies, the sort of man he was and what manner of ruler; he would lead his country to prosperity and win much respect.

Since January, he had fought alongside the Serbian hero and heir to the Serbian throne, Vuk Brankovic—who would be known as *Zmag Ogjeni Vuk*, "The Fiery Wolf Dragon"—defeating Turks in Bosnia. In the summer, they had joined forces with Dracula's cousin, Ștefan. Together, they had driven the Sultan Mehmet and his forces out of Moldavia, which the Ottomans had overrun as far as the capital of Suceava, raiding and pillaging large portions of the country. Dracula had succeeded in ousting from the Wallachian throne the pretender Laiotă Basarab. He had even resumed trade agreements with the Saxons, who had been so quick to slander him in the past, accusing him of allying with the Turks. The boyars had all sworn allegiance to him, and he and his cousin Ștefan had sworn allegiance to each other. These all seemed good signs to him. And *this* time he would be certain to slay the treacherous Laiotă, as he had done with another pretender thorn in his side, all those years ago. He'd beheaded Dan the Third of Wallachia directly into the grave he'd forced the man to dig at sword point.

"You know how to deal with your worldly wealth, your Majesty," said the priest monk. "Would it not be wise to deal with your heavenly wealth with even greater care?"

"I am now, and have always been, loyal to Christendom. Has any other man done more than I have done to defend my country from the Mohammedans? Could even Scanderberg have claimed to have done what I have done?"

The priest monk's kind eyes darkened a little, perhaps with sadness. "No, he could not claim to have done what you have done when he defended his homeland of Albania," he agreed, quietly. He crossed himself and prayed for a space.

Dracula's men had nearly completed their task. Dracula needed time to make preparations, to meet the invading Ottomans on ground of his own choosing, not to be taken unprepared. He wished to show his son how he'd managed to impress the man who had conquered Constantinople—by being crueler than the Ottoman Sultan, Mehmet the Second. All cruel men understood was cruelty; that was their language. Dracula had learned to speak it, and speak it fluently. He wished to show his son how to be a strong lord in the face of overwhelming odds. Yet he had a certain feeling, a foreboding that troubled him...

Dracula cast his eyes on the priest monk, who was still praying. It was the opinion of the Russians who had visited Corvinus' court that Dracula had traded his heavenly crown for an earthly one by converting to the faith of the Latins. But aside from any political motivation—and there had certainly been a great deal: he had agreed to marry Corvinus' cousin before being taken prisoner—there remained the fact that Dracula had not seen much strength from the Greek Church. And now its capital, Constantinople, was fallen. The loss of Constantinople had shaken him—and all of Christendom—to his very bones.

Refugees had poured into his country, fleeing the unthinkable destruction. They had spoken of the doom they had perceived preceding the city's fall, the portents and signs which had warned them: the strange weather; the severe, harsh, pelting hail when they had prayed for help; the dense fog; the glowing in the sky; the eerie fire around the dome of the Hagia Sophia. Worst of all were the accounts of horrifying atrocities that the Turks committed—the capture and rape of innumerable children of both sexes, and of nuns, the razing of homes, the taking of so many slaves, the slaughter. The Divine Services were held even as the doors of the Hagia Sophia were burst open, and the invaders forced the clergy to cease.

The refugees' eyes had been darkened wholly by grief. The fall of Constantinople, the center of civilization with its harbors and markets, the legal court, the university, the hospitals, the libraries, and Hagia Sophia itself, was the end of an era. The end of an age. It had felt like the end of the world itself. He, Dracula, was looking to the next one, the only bright possible future he could see.

"My son," said the priest monk, his voice more gentle than that of any father, so much so that it stirred something in Dracula's very hard heart, so that he could not help but give his attention once more. "My son, victory rests in the hands of God. There is a little time, if you wish to make a confession. I know you are a proud man, and I know you have been taught that pride separates us from God's mercy. Yet I know you have also been taught that God will rush to you, if you turn even a little towards Him. Before you and your men go to battle," — his searching glance took in all the voivode's men, including Dracula's son Mihnea— "will you not take a moment for the sake of your souls?"

The gold was all gone. Any glint from treasure through some poorly made or broken barrel could only shine dimly at the bottom of dark waters, to be covered over by silt and hidden from sight. Perhaps unrecoverable.

"Father, I presume you will pray for our victory and our safe return?" Dracula prompted the priest monk. The wise eyes did not smile. They closed. The priest monk nodded, and raised his hand to bless them.

"Of course," he agreed. "May God bless you and have mercy on you all."

Dracula nodded curtly and passed by, his son following. Some of his men stopped to receive a blessing and to kiss the priest monk's hand, and so trailed a bit behind. There was much to do, and Dracula lacked the force he wished he could bring to bear. The country was not wholly secured, his throne remained precarious—as it always was. But he had the aid of his cousin's men; they should be of help, although they numbered only two-hundred. And the Hungarians sent by Corvinus added several thousand to his numbers. It was more than nothing, but inadequate for what he would likely need.

His small group crossed the small wooden bridge which connected the holy place to the shore—little knowing the bridge would be destroyed in later times, that the monastery itself would fall into disrepair before finally being restored centuries in the future—to rejoin the main force that waited on the other side of a rise. Soon they would all engage in battle. If they rode hard, they might be able to better their odds against Mehmet's much greater force by finding a favorable battleground.

*****

The sun was winking on the horizon, the air turning chill and frosty. His breath fogged around his head. Warmth was running down his back. How cold his fingers had become; he could not feel them as he clawed at the grass and sod to pull himself along. Under darkness, he stood a chance of escaping.

Mihnea had been captured. The Turks would take him to be delivered into Mehmet's hands. Dracula dared not imagine what the Sultan would do to the son of his so-hated enemy. His loyal men had fallen, skewered by blades, pierced by arrows, to be mutilated and plundered by their murderers.

Had he been betrayed? Perhaps. If so, he would avenge himself on whoever had betrayed him. More thoroughly than he had avenged his brother and father all those years ago. Twenty years ago; no, a few years more than that. So long ago as that? Was he really forty-five already? So old as that? His strength was not what it had been. Not only age, but incarceration, imprisonment, and exile had taken their toll, robbing him of youth and strength and vigor. He was an old man.

An old man who had been stabbed in the back, who had become separated from the others in the fighting, who was now crawling for a safe place to hide. If he could but live another day, he could turn this defeat into victory. He would gather more men. He would recover any lost fortresses, rally the peasants who showed him such earnest loyalty, make them victorious over the janissaries and hordes of Turks who would almost certainly return to Wallachia to prevent the Impaler from settling securely once more on that throne...

Had this been a plan of Corvinus'? Had that sly fox thought to himself that Dracula had two young sons who could be raised in Hungary to become heirs to the Wallachian throne? The Hungarians had fled the field of battle so quickly, leaving him exposed. The Moldavian force had been inadequate, but he refused to believe his cousin had betrayed him. No, Ștefan had pushed for Dracula's return to the throne, and the good men Ștefan had sent had died to a man, as far as Dracula knew.

Bitter, bitter, loss and defeat. He had helped both Corvinus and Ștefan to achieve their thrones. Now here he

DRACULA'S DEATH

was, crawling under the safety of darkness, for the Turks did not like to engage at night. Whatever victory or betrayal his allies had intended, all his efforts would come to naught if he did not manage to survive the night.

He heard footsteps breaking fallen twigs and rustling the damp grass. He could not feel his own hands. He needed his hands to draw his sword and gut whoever was coming after him. It was all he could do to crawl. How long had he been bleeding? It was nearly night. Snow lay lightly on the ground, so very cold.

The footfalls were close now. He must slay this assassin himself, there was no help, no ally. He pushed himself from the ground and fumbled for his sword, his head swimming, spinning from cold and exhaustion and blood loss. He could not hear nor see. No! He could not afford to swoon now. He prayed, or tried to. His mind could not pierce the haze....

He felt something curious. An impact to the back of the neck, which passed impossibly through to the front of his throat. Then there was falling. The freezing grass on his face and his cheeks, but not his hands, or his arms, or his legs or his back. He couldn't tell where he was. His head rolled impossibly upside down, onto his crown, the fresh air on his face, and he realized what had just happened.

He had beheaded Dan the Third, had ordered children slain, burned men alive. He had built no churches or monasteries, had confessed too infrequently.

No...

He had to save Mihnea, had to recruit his allies...

Had to pray for forgiveness.

Cold.

The world drifted away from him, and he had a sense of falling, and of black.

*****

Lost.... Wandering.... Hopelessness....

*****

"...delights with me?" a woman's voice asked him in Turkish.

He was standing in a graveyard. The dark of night all around him, though the dark was not impenetrable. He could see forms, outlines, even colors. Perhaps there was a bright moon overhead. He was not cold. He was not warm. He had never been so hungry in his life. Famished did not do the feeling any justice. It was agony, like dying.

There was an open grave before his feet, and an elegant woman with piercing, hungry eyes kneeling before a fresh corpse, stinking from the onset of rot. The scent repulsed and excited him in unequal measure.

The woman's fingernails were long and claw-like.

A ghoul! he realized, and reached for his sword to defend himself from the evil monster. But his sword was not there. He looked down; his armor was gone, but he was dressed in his best clothes, a fine cloak, his jewelry. The clothes were stained from dirt or mud.

"Isn't that why you came?" the ghoul asked, inviting him with an eager smile.

Her smooth skin and her white teeth enticed him as no woman had ever beguiled him before. Her black eyes were singing sweetly to him. He wanted to be lost in her mouth and her hair and give in to the hideous hunger on him. He ached for her, and for things he dared not acknowledge.

To keep her at bay he raised a hand to cross himself... but could not. His fingers refused to obey him. He knew how they should move, but he could not make them.

Dracula's Death

Some evil sorcery, he concluded, and turned to run. Ghouls were quick monsters, but they could be escaped. His feet, at least, obeyed his will. No footsteps followed.

He ran far out of the graveyard, searching for some indication as to his whereabouts and how he came to be here. Had he fainted from exhaustion and been carried to safety? But by whom? And to where? This was not Wallachia in December. The air was warm. He scanned the skies to see what constellations were overhead, to get his bearings. It was a dark moon, yet he could see as clearly as if the moon were full. There were city walls beside him.

The ghoul was long left behind; she had made no effort to chase him. He ought to thank God for his deliverance, and puzzle out what had happened afterwards.

A ghoul speaking Turkish to me? He studied the immense wall of brick and mortar beside him, stretching on and on. The scrub landscape which the wall faced. The scent of sea air.

Constantinople?

Could it be? But how could he have come here? His mind wrestled with questions until another revelation struck him. He had run a great distance, but his lungs did not burn for air. Though he had been afraid of the monster behind him, he had felt no racing of his heart, no blood pounding.

He considered his clothing again. Funereal garb. The best clothing, a purple cloak embroidered with gold.

His blood did not run cold. He began realize it never would again. No heartbeat when his hand pressed to his chest.

No, no, merciful God, no...!

He fell to his knees and screamed.

CHAPTER 1
INTRODUCTIONS

One very dark and very wet day in late April, a moving truck rolled slowly down the narrow streets of Seattle's Capitol Hill until it came to an empty parking spot in front of a little cluster of shops and restaurants. The truck pulled into the open space, and out stepped a group of men wearing long and baggy coats. The driver remained behind the wheel and fingered the bill of his cap. Most of the men looked East Asian, but the leader's brown face, black hair and high cheekbones placed his ethnic origin elsewhere. Over his shoulders he wore what looked like the pelt of a black jaguar, complete with the head dangling between his shoulder-blades, the paws and claws loose beside his hands. The man's gold eyes scanned the storefronts, settling on the sign for a yoga studio. He pointed to it, then nodded to his companions and led the way.

The door tinkled cheerily as the man wearing the jaguar skin let himself inside. The studio was cozy: wooden floors, mirrors across one wall, potted plants, and meditation music playing softly. A forty-something man, his long hair bound in a man bun, was leading the class. He stood up and approached the group as they filed inside. The men in coats stood behind their leader, the largest standing by the door, blocking it.

"Hi there..." the instructor ventured, eying the group confusedly. "My next class is in an hour. There's some coffee shops if you want to wait...."

The gold eyes blazed like embers, and the instructor stepped back when they fixed on him.

"I don't wish to wait," the jaguar man replied. "And if you will all cooperate, I won't take very much of the remaining time allotted to your lives."

"I... I really think you ought to leave," the instructor told him. The gold eyes burned him into silence.

"I wish to know, of the lot of this nest of whores, who among you has any faith?" the jaguar man said to the class. "Real faith. Not the sort that the modern, decadent degenerates you all resemble put on as a fashionable coat."

"You need to leave, or I'm calling the police," the instructor told him. He stepped forward to push past and open the door. The Asian man at the exit opened his coat to reveal an AR-15 hanging at his right side; there was a sword in a scabbard on his left. A noise like a startled kitten makes escaped the instructor's throat.

"I h-have cameras," he stammered, and pointed to one under the big front window. The jaguar man stared at it.

"Does it record sounds also?" he asked. The instructor nodded with all his might. "Out of my way," the jaguar man told him, and pushed him aside to approach the camera. He looked up, and his gold eyes blazed. He spread his hands and bowed, then pointed to the lens. The jaguar paw fell away from his wrist, revealing a tattoo in the outline of what appeared to be the head of Anubis. He swept the gesture down across the class and to the instructor.

"S-so if you don't leave, they'll be able to find you."

"Excellent," said the jaguar man. "In that case, I should offer my introductions. You may call me Ocelotl." He bowed to the class. "And my question still stands. Who among you" —his gold eyes burned them all, one by one by one— "has faith?"

One young woman who crouched near the exit gasped, and his gold eyes fell to her. But she was looking at his wrist. He observed that she must have recognized the tattoo, and he glanced at his companions. He spoke to them in what sounded like Chinese, and one came forward, brandishing a gun, to corral her away from the others.

Protests rose, half-murmured; a palpable panic threaded through the group, but Ocelotl silenced them all with a look. He pointed to one of his companions, who pulled his automatic shotgun from his coat and held it at the ready.

"Again, and for the last time," Ocelotl said. "Who. Has. Faith?"

"You can't do this," the instructor protested. "You can't."

Ocelotl gestured to one of his companions who had not yet acted. The man came forward, glared at the instructor, then turned his attention to a young woman kneeling on the floor in terror. No one had gotten up from their mats yet. The stranger loomed over her, then punched her in the face with such force she flew backwards. A few screams broke loose, and the other men raised their guns in warning. The instructor stared at the injured young woman on the floor as her body began to convulse and shake, but she made no sound. His thin fingers rose to cover his mouth.

"You won't escape your karma," he told Ocelotl.

"Karma. You claim to have faith?"

"I practice Hinduism," the instructor told him. "I studied under a guru. I traveled to India during college—"

Ocelotl stalked towards him. "We shall see," he said.

Dracula's Death

The instructor dropped to the floor in a cross-legged position. "I won't fight you. I'm a pacifist."

"You are a coward," Ocelotl corrected. "The faith you claim to follow commands that you bravely resist enemies—and surely you view me as an enemy." He came to a stop before the instructor and seized the man's hair. "My beloved son, I have use for you, especially if your faith should prove genuine. Go." He inclined his head towards his companions, and shoved the man towards them. Once the instructor had been positioned against the wall, Ocelotl returned his attention to the rest.

"Why should we cooperate?" a middle-aged woman with salt-and-pepper hair near the back demanded. "What are you going to do? How do we know you won't harm us?"

"I have made no promise not to harm any of you," Ocelotl told her. "Nor will I. The offer I am making is this: if you lack faith, I can give your life purpose. I can help you to serve a higher cause and calling. To erase your sins, and help erase the sins of others."

"Sins?" a college student in the middle repeated. "What are you, some kind of crazy fundamentalist?"

"Fundamentalist?" Ocelotl gave the word some thought. "I suppose. But not crazy."

"It isn't Christian to treat people like this," a young woman piped up.

"No?"

"No."

"Have *you* any faith?"

"I'm a Christian," she responded.

Ocelotl burst out laughing, and clapped his hands.

"Oh, *very good*. But we shall test that. Rise. Stand there, by him." He indicated the instructor. She stood and timidly made her way over. Ocelotl pointed at her attire, the sports bra and yoga pants. "Is it Christian to dress like a whore?" he asked, and laughed. She glared at him.

"This is completely normal for a yoga class, and you're a bad Christian," she told him. "This isn't what Jesus would do."

"I am not Christian," he told her. "But I intend to find out whether you are, as you claim."

"What will you do to them?" a forty-something woman near the mirrors piped, her voice trembling. She hugged a fourteen-year-old girl with honey-colored blonde hair. Ocelotl gazed at her.

"I shall test whether their faith is real," he said.

The young woman still convulsed in their midst. Another woman was trying to help her with trembling hands. The injured woman was lying in a puddle of her own urine, her feet and hands twitching, her arms shaking.

"As for the rest of you, I have told you that I am here to provide you all a purpose, which faith would have provided if you had any."

"Why?" several of them asked.

"Because the world is sick, and rotten, and full of sin," Ocelotl answered. "And I intend to do my part in setting that right. If you all cooperate, then so shall all of you."

"What do you want us to do?" the college student asked.

"It is very simple," Ocelotl said, and nodded to his companions. The one nearest the woman who had recognized the tattoo singled her out and grabbed her by the arm, wrapping a hand around her mouth to silence her. He made for the door with her in tow. "All I ask from you people is open hearts. Will you give me that much?"

Confused murmurs coursed through the room, rippling across the students. The mother near the mirrors nodded frantically.

DRACULA'S DEATH

"Yes," she gasped with relief. The others echoed her, nodding and agreeing. Ocelotl held up a hand for silence, and nodded to his companions again and spoke to them in Chinese. One of them led the instructor and the Christian girl outside. Ocelotl's gold eyes blazed with hot, yellow light, and he grinned, exposing teeth filed to sharpened points and inset with bits of jade.

"Thank you all," he said to them, and folded his hands over his heart, "for your sacrifice."

*****

Junior police officer Brian Warren drove out to Echo Lake in search of his partner, Felix Akerman. Brian's half-sister, Melissa, had been dating Akerman for several months. Even though he tried to pretend the dating thing wasn't happening, Brian had learned about his work buddy's off duty habits as a result. Akerman liked to give Melissa presents of fresh fish, something she'd found endlessly amusing, and she had decided to try her hand at cooking. Brian refused to admit that what she served up was tastier than restaurant fare. She'd mentioned that Akerman liked to visit Echo Lake when he had downtime. Today it wasn't drizzling or raining; that meant Akerman would be out fishing, since he had the day off. His Shoreline apartment was only about 15 miles from Echo Lake, so not too much of a journey for Brian.

He took an Uber—he didn't want Melissa to find out about this meeting, so he hadn't asked to borrow her car—which dropped him off at the park near the lake.

It had been a tough six months since he'd wound up in the hospital after a very strange series of events. Brian's friend, Cammy, had been kidnapped by "invisible elves", according to a strange woman who'd somehow been involved with all the craziness of that night. Brian had tracked Cammy to the Fremont Troll, only to run into that jerk from the bar who somehow knew about the dead wrestler who had come back to life as a super zombie. The jerk had *turned into a wolf right in front of Brian's eyes.* And Dr. Acula himself, the creep with the fancy mansion in Snolqualmie, had shown up and used some sort of mesmerism on Cammy. After that there was a blank. Brian didn't remember how he'd gotten hurt, but he'd woken up in a hospital with injuries that the doctors chocked up to him getting hit by a car, since he couldn't account for what had happened. He certainly hadn't told them what little he remembered. The nurses had told him that a very petite young woman, wearing a torn shirt and bloodied leggings, had brought him to the hospital, but she'd run off without leaving a name. It had to have been Cammy. She had somehow gotten him into a car—he had no idea whose, or *how*—and driven him there. No one had seen a man matching Dr. Acula's description. She had done it alone, so clearly Mr. "I can't eat garlic" hadn't been interested in helping. So far as Brian could tell, Cammy had somehow saved his life.

If it hadn't been for all of the recovery time and physical therapy, he'd have tracked Akerman down sooner. But broken ribs, a punctured lung, a massive concussion, a broken wrist, and a bad shoulder injury take a while to heal. He'd been going to physical and occupational therapy for months.

Brian wandered around in the brisk morning air, getting the lay of the land, then walked across the grass between a small parking area and the lake. Some geese waddled around under an apple tree. They barely noticed him. There was a little clearing amongst the trees and bushes that surrounded the lake, a steep little incline down to the water. Akerman

DRACULA'S DEATH

was standing on the muddy shore, barefoot, up to his calves in the water, wearing his police academy hoodie. He held a thin fishing rod, already cast into the water.

"Isn't it cold?" Brian asked by way of greeting. Akerman whirled, surprised.

"Warren," he said. "You like to fish?"

"Melissa told me you come here a lot."

Akerman nodded absently. Just behind him on the grass was a cooler, what looked like a small tackle box, and his shoes.

"I wanted to ask you something." Brian didn't step in the water, but he came right up to the edge.

Akerman gave his attention.

"About the Count," Brian added. Akerman shook his head and looked out at the water.

"Leave it be, Warren," he grumped.

"I'm going to kill him."

Akerman's attention snapped back.

"You *what?*"

"I'm going to kill him. I have all his vampire hunting equipment. Been mulling on that for months; still no idea why he had it all, but he's got Cammy."

Akerman shook his head. "She went over there herself. She chose to go, and she chose to stay."

"I don't know that she did!" Brian snapped. Akerman tried to shush him—there were homes across the water visible through the leaves and branches—but he went on, "All I know is something really bad happened about a year ago, then suddenly she's living up there and won't give me straight answers. He hypnotizes her, or something."

"He doesn't...."

"Doesn't what?" Brian glared at him. A year ago, when Brian had arrested Dr. Acula, Mr. Fake-FBI-Guy, after finding his car trunk full of weapons, Akerman had been the one who'd made a phone call that had gotten the creep released, and Brian suspended. And somehow Akerman had known about those shady people who'd asked Brian all those weird questions at the hospital, asking him what he remembered about the zombie wrestler. They hadn't told him their names, only given him a card with a phone number—which he still had, though he'd never called it.

The other mystery out there was the redhead with her weird perfume, but Akerman had never mentioned anyone like her, so Brian didn't know if Akerman knew about her or not. Or what *her* deal was. All Brian knew was she wanted someone to spy on the Count for her, and that she was probably also a vampire. Possibly some sort of turf war or negotiation, or maybe an old flame looking to get back together, or to get revenge. Either way, another unknown element to keep an eye out for.

"Nothing," Akerman finished, glumly, looking away.

"You know a lot more about all this stuff than I do," Brian said. "You owe me. I got in big trouble after that phone call you made, *and* I need your help."

"You want *my help* killing Dracula?" Akerman echoed. "Are you out of your mind?! Yes, I made a phone call to some bad people who want me to do that sort of thing for them, but remember, Rookie, I told you to leave him alone!"

"You didn't have to make the call."

"You don't know everything about me," Akerman grumped. He reeled in his line and cast again.

"Well, now you're dating my sister *and* you owe me. So are you in or out?"

Akerman glared again. It was a little hard to take that baby face seriously, so Brian refused to. Akerman stepped onto the grass, wedged the fishing rod into one of the handles of the cooler, then walked back into the water and

DRACULA'S DEATH

towards a low, overhanging branch. Squatting down, he lowered one hand into the lake.

"Well?"

"You have no idea what you're talking about," Akerman hissed. Brian couldn't quite see what he was doing with his hand; he stepped towards him.

"Don't scare 'im," Akerman whispered.

"What, a fish?"

"No, a mermaid. *Of course* a fish," Akerman snarled.

"Akerman, this is serious. There's an actual vampire, and for all I know he's preying on people. Remember Councilman Wright? The one who was exsanguinated last year?"

Splash. Akerman stood up, a big mouth bass clutched in his hand. Akerman looked it over. "Decent enough," he mumbled to himself.

"The *exsanguinated councilman,* Akerboy," Brian snapped. He knew Akerman resented all the kiddy nicknames that got tossed around at the precinct. Sure enough, he turned to face Brian, scowling.

"I told you to mind your own business. I told you this is a crazy town and crazy things happen," Akerman retorted. He fetched a sharp knife from the fishing tackle box and started gutting the fish right then and there.

"Whoa, man, kill it first!" Brian told him.

"It's dead now," Akerman replied.

"Does Melissa know you go all psychopath on fish?"

Akerman glowered at him, but kept on cleaning the bass.

"People get all hung up on that these days," he grumbled.

"Because it's not the Dark Ages, Akerman! Listen: I could really use your help going after the literal Dracula. The Evil Ed to my Charlie Brewster—you know, like *Fright Night,* but for real. I'm going after the historical madman and current vampire lord, or whatever he is. You know more about what's going on than I do, but if you don't come, then I'll go without you."

Akerman dropped the guts in the lake, then looked up at him.

"You're serious about doing this?"

"Yeah. Cammy's in danger."

"She's been up there a whole year. If she was in danger, wouldn't that show? Has it occurred to you that maybe she's *safer* there than anywhere else?"

Brian stormed into the water and grabbed Akerman's hoodie. He winced a little. Sometimes, if it was cold or wet, or both, his wrist ached. Or his shoulder, or his ribs. Or all of them.

"He's got her up there and no one's giving me a straight answer, and for all I know he's been eating people and he's got her hypnotized or something!" he shouted.

"All right!" Akerman raised his hands. "All right, I get it. But Warren, you have to slow down a second. Slow down." He pried Brian's hands from his hoodie. "I get it. All right? I just..." He clenched his jaw and let out a breath slowly. "You're going to get yourself killed."

"If you have some suggestion on how to *not* get myself dead, I'm all ears," Brian told him. "If you don't want to come, I get it. But give me *something*."

"All right, all right." Akerman rubbed his eyes. "Just... *hold it*." He took some deep breaths. "We all need to cool down, ok?"

"What do you mean 'we all'? You and me?"

"Listen Warren, if you're serious, you need a plan, right?"

"Yeah," Brian agreed. He hated to admit it, but he'd been trying all this time to find a tried-and-true way to kill vampires, but there were too many legends and myths out there. It sounded like staking and beheading were the closest to a sure thing, but if he was wrong… He'd just have to hope that the King of Vampires up there had genuine tools for killing members of his own species, and carried them around in his multi-million dollar vehicles for kicks. Otherwise, Brian was in for a bad time.

"Give me a few days," Akerman told him. "Don't do anything yet. Let me think about it."

"A few days?! But Cammy—"

"If she's been up there this whole time, a few more days will not make a difference. Give me a *few days* to think of something, all right?!"

Brian gritted his teeth, then spoke through them. "Ok, yeah. A few days."

"Just don't do anything stupid in the meanwhile," Akerman told him.

Brian nodded. Having Akerman on board ought to increase his odds of making it out of there alive. Or at least, ending up regular dead if things went south. A few days. That was all the time Dracula had left. Or that Brian and Akerman had.

*****

Cammy was sitting at a small table in a busy downtown café, surreptitiously gazing about her through the hole in the adder stone she wore on a leather thong around her neck. A woman with bat wings and snakes for hair was ordering a low-fat latte with caramel swirl on top. Cammy quickly dropped the adder stone back under her shirt before the woman could see it when she turned away from the cashier. Without the stone, the woman looked like an attractive brunette with the features and figure of a classical Greek statue. Soft face, soft hands, serene expression, tall, stately.

While the woman moved to a table across the room, Cammy busied herself with her phone, calling the only person she could talk to about this development. The man at whose mansion she was living, none other than Dracula himself. She'd moved in a year ago after winding up destitute and homeless. At first, she'd thought she'd learn all about fighting monsters, like a heroine in a tv show, but people had died, and it had been awful, and she'd had to kill her best friend. So instead of becoming a monster slayer she'd focused on school, and work, and avoiding the more dangerous supernaturals who'd also found sanctuary at his vast estate. She still didn't quite understand why Dracula let *satyrs* live there. Even after a year, Cammy had only managed to talk to a handful of the other monsters up there: a shape-changing fox, a tanuki, and their child, as well as a few Icelandic elves, but hadn't yet seen any of the 'vampire ghost women' she was assured were also up there somewhere. She didn't even spend time looking for them anymore, and rarely saw the few friendly monsters, either. These days, the novelty of being surrounded by supernatural creatures she could only *sometimes* see had worn off some. Apparently people really *could* get used to anything. The phone rang four times, the buzz in her ear competing with the café's hum, which she hoped would mask her call.

"Is this important?" was the greeting she got.

"I'm at a café, and there's this woman who's got bat wings and snake hair, like Medusa or something. I mean, she can't be Medusa, no one's turning to stone—"

"What is she doing?" he interrupted her. Was something bothering him?

"Nothing," Cammy confessed. "She's drinking a latte."

"Then leave her be."

"What if she's dangerous?" Cammy persisted. "Shouldn't we do something? What is she?"

Dracula's Death

"If she's dangerous, all the more reason to leave her alone. Don't do anything. I have no idea what she is. Nothing I've seen. I can't talk right now." The line went dead.

Well. She was on her own, then.

What are you doing that's so incredibly important you can't even be civil? she wondered. But what was she thinking? She knew he'd never be *that* terse unless he had reason to be. At least, he'd never been that terse without reason before. So it was just her and a bat-snake woman sitting across from each other in a busy café, and no one else knew what was up.

"Great," she said.

The sun was out for a change, so clearly the woman didn't mind sunlight. She drank coffee, so that meant she could eat regular food.

That was all Cammy could figure out. Time to head to the internet.

She had found nothing online except images and descriptions of Medusa when a young police officer let himself down in the seat across from her. Cammy almost threw her phone over her head in surprise, fumbled with it, and put on a smile she hoped looked natural.

"Hope I'm not too late," said her friend of many years, Brian Warren.

"Hi, no. Not late," Cammy assured him. She glanced at the woman, who was serenely sipping her coffee, bothering no one at all. The sun shone in through the glass windows, brightening the bustling space. Nothing was amiss. And now that Brian was here, Cammy didn't want to risk using the adder stone again to take another look in case there was another monster hiding in plain sight.

"I had to deal with this guy who held up a gas station, and he was high as a kite. Worse, so was the cashier. Neither one of them could tell me anything coherent."

Cammy forced her eyes to focus on Brian's face. His brown hair looked a bit mussed, there was a shadow of stubble on his chin, dark circles under his blue eyes. There was also something dark about his eyes as he swept them across the café. More than suspicion, but Cammy couldn't figure out what.

"Sounds tough," Cammy said. She watched Brian chug the cup of coffee he'd ordered. Her latte art had dissolved. Now that he was here she could finish drinking it.

"Anything new with you?" Brian asked. He licked foam off his lip.

"Not really. Just signing up for classes," Cammy said, wondering what was going on with him.

"You dealing with everything ok?" he asked.

Cammy had figured that's why he'd wanted to meet.

In a few days it would be the anniversary of the death of a mutual friend—Heather—and shortly after that it would be Cammy's birthday. Heather, Brian, and Brian's sister, Melissa, used to celebrate Cammy's birthday all together, but after what had happened last year, Cammy didn't want to celebrate her birthday ever again.

"Yeah, I mean... yeah," Cammy answered, with vigorous nods for emphasis, trying to put on a brave face. Heather had been turned into a vampire, but Brian didn't know that. He also didn't know that Cammy had been the one who had put a stake—a broken broom handle, actually—through Heather's heart to stop her bloodlust-fueled rampage. That wasn't the sort of thing you could just tell people.

Cammy noticed her hands were shaking, and thrust them under the table. She closed her eyes, drew breaths through her nose, squeezed her phone. *Not now. Not the time to have a meltdown!* There was some sort of monster sitting in the café. She didn't know what it was, but she was the only one who could do anything about it. She couldn't let herself go to pieces now. When she opened her eyes, Brian was gazing out the window. Good, maybe he hadn't noticed her moment.

"I saw this girl down at the precinct, and for a moment I thought it was Heather. It was like Heather had started using again, and gotten arrested. Then I remembered...." Brian fingered the cup. "Do you want to... do anything?"

"Hmm?"

"About Heather. I thought we could do something. You know, to remember. Visit the park or something. You and me and Melissa. Unless you want your... *friend* to drive you."

Brian's tone almost always became hostile when he was referring to Dracula. Cammy couldn't blame him for being suspicious, but she wasn't sure she could confide in him.

After Heather went missing and Cammy had been evicted from the dingy apartment they had shared, Dracula had rescued Cammy from the same vampires who'd killed her friend. Then, inexplicably, he'd offered Cammy a place to stay in his weird mansion up past Snoqualmie Falls, with woodland and gardens and *vineyards*. Oh, and resident monsters. Brian didn't know those details, of course. All he knew was that Cammy had moved in with a perfect stranger: a man of considerable wealth, who was enormously eccentric, secretive, and went by the most ludicrous name conceivable.

The world was full of monsters, like in movies or books, but the rules weren't what she'd expected for a magical Masquerade. There wasn't a law set in stone not to talk about the supernatural or the creatures that went bump in the night. The monsters hid because there were humans who hunted them, and humans hunted them because some of the monsters hunted humans. Usually, the hunting happened out of sight, out of mind, but sometimes there was bleed over. Cammy still wanted to find out what was going on more than she'd wanted to be safe, and she'd been able to talk to some of the parties on both sides pretty openly. But she wasn't certain Brian could handle the truth. He had been badly injured by a monster last year. Cammy couldn't be more relieved that he didn't remember what had happened. What would he say if he knew that one of her acquaintances was a werewolf? He already suspected that the man in whose mansion she was living was more than he appeared. Brian was a cop through and through; what would he think, what would he *do* if he found out that there were magical creatures that flitted around the periphery of human society? Some of them committed crimes out of malice, some out of necessity. He'd tried to stop the draugr, and he'd barely come out alive.

"No—I mean, yes. I'd love to come with. When were you thinking?"

"Melissa's free on Thursday, so, evening?" Brian suggested.

"I'll make it work. Midterms are going to start next week, though," she said.

"Can I pick you up at"—Brian gritted his teeth—"your *friend's* house?"

Highly inadvisable. The mansion was guarded by monsters, plus her "*friend*" as Brian called him when he was trying to be polite, didn't like people poking around. She knew that from firsthand experience.

"I'll check," she told him. He snorted derisively and looked away as he sipped more of his coffee. "Hey, it's not my house," Cammy reminded him.

"I know," he grumped. "It's Dr. FBI's summer home."

"Dr. FBI" referred to an incident that had almost lost Brian his career, when he had arrested Dracula for impersonating a federal agent. In fact, Dracula was some sort of agent for a far more secretive government organization. Well, not *agent*. More like... an unwilling contract worker. But the Powers That Be which wanted the supernatural world *dead* weren't keen on letting their greatest weapon get spotlit in the Justice System, where people were bound to ask questions. So they'd pulled some strings, and Brian had paid the price. Cammy still felt guilty about that.

But she had nothing to say in response, so she glanced down at her phone. Brian set down his cup.

"Sorry. I'm on edge. It's been crazy down at the precinct. There's some missing persons reports that have been floating around, and when I hear those I think about Heather—"

"Missing persons?" Cammy interrupted.

"Yeah, a number of people going missing, all a few blocks apart. It might be racially motivated, or some sort of turf war. At any rate, most of them seem to be South Asian. But I'm not sure. I don't work Missing Persons, I just hear chatter."

"Do you know where?" Cammy asked.

The warmth melted right out of Brian's face and eyes.

"Why?" he demanded.

"No reason," Cammy said. He continued to stare, his face unchanged. This was the worst change in him since he became a cop. It was like all he could see in anybody was a criminal just waiting to be caught. Even her.

She averted her eyes. The bat-snake woman was watching the people pass by on the sidewalk outside.

"I gotta go get some rest. It's been a long shift," Brian said. He stood.

"Thanks for meeting up," Cammy told him.

"Yeah." His voice was as cold as his expression. "Take care of yourself."

Cammy watched him stalk out the door, passing right by the bat-snake woman without a second glance, and disappear from sight.

I should just tell him, she thought. *He'd be ok. He could handle it.*

Who was she kidding? The minute she explained what was really going on, Brian would have an aneurysm when he figured out that her *friend's* ridiculous name was not actually ridiculous. If he found out who and what the man actually was, and what had really happened to Heather, he might never forgive Cammy.

She stared at the woman across the café. It was now or never. Cammy forced herself to stand, felt her stomach wobbling inside her. She drew more deep breaths, grabbed her bag, and made her way over. It was busy in the café; the bat-snake woman probably wouldn't want to draw attention to herself in such a public, crowded space. That meant that Cammy could probably run for it if she had to. Probably.

She stopped next to the woman's table, trying to figure out what to say. Being direct might be the best bet, but that was only with friendly or neutral parties. She didn't know about this one.

The woman had noticed Cammy's presence, and turned from the window to study her.

"Can I help you?" the woman asked. Cammy thought she heard a slight accent, but she had no idea what the accent was.

"Um," said Cammy, her stomach vibrating inside her, "What are you?"

The bat-snake woman's expression remained fixed.

"I beg your pardon?" she asked.

"I mean," Cammy glanced around the room, "you know, what *are* you?"

Dracula's Death

The bat-snake lady's little smile melted away the same way Brian's friendliness had.

"Excuse me," a man's voice cut in.

Cammy felt a hand on her shoulder. She looked up, and there was Malcolm at her side. He was addressing the woman very politely.

"Pardon my young friend's rudeness. I'm Malcolm Marrock, with the Order of Ophois."

The woman snorted with amusement. She waved a finger in Cammy's direction.

"Trainee?" she inquired.

"Not exactly," Malcolm told her. "Guest of a friend of mine."

"Well," said the woman, smiling now, "I suppose it's not so strange she doesn't know me. This is only my third trip to the United States."

"May I ask your business?" Malcolm asked, sounding innocent and friendly enough, though Cammy wondered if there was another message hidden under his winning smile. The Order of Ophois was a mercenary group of occultists, consisting partly of humans and partly of werewolves and other human-monster hybrids. They existed in an unhappy middle ground, so neither monsters nor monster hunters particularly liked them. Malcolm didn't like them either.

The woman finished her coffee. "Certainly. Vengeance," she answered, and dabbed at her soft, pink lips with a napkin. "I'm Magaera."

Cammy felt Malcolm's fingers dig into her shoulder. It hurt.

"I see. Thank you for your patience. I'm sorry to have troubled you." Malcolm flashed an irresistible smile full of impossibly white teeth at her, and bowed his head.

"No trouble at all. Good hunting to you, Ophois," said the woman.

Malcolm hurried Cammy out of the café and up the street to his cherry red muscle car. She recognized it by the beautiful mirror-polish wax job. This was the car he liked to remind everyone he had built himself. When they got to the curb, he sucked in a breath and clutched his hair.

"Do you have some sort of death wish?" he demanded. "You are going to get me *killed* one of these days, coming to save you."

"I didn't *ask* you to come."

"No, you didn't, but you know who did." Malcolm ran his fingers through his slick, slightly curly black hair. "Do you have any idea who that was in there?" He pointed back the way they had come.

"Who? Not what?" Cammy asked.

"Oh, she's very much a Who. Magaera. One of the Furies." Malcolm covered his face and swore in every language he knew. Or Cammy guessed he did. It sounded like a mix of Latin and Egyptian and French or whatever. She didn't understand any of them, but he and her host were both polyglots, and she was beginning to occasionally recognize the languages, if not the actual words.

"Furies?" Cammy repeated. She thought those were Greek demi-goddesses of some sort.

"Yeah, horrible spirits of vengeance. You don't *ever* want to get in their way," Malcolm told her. "They're supposed to have bat-wings and snakes for hair and dog heads—"

"She didn't have a dog head," Cammy said. Malcolm shrugged.

"Probably the usual permutations that happen." He shrugged. "Like with satyrs. They all have goat legs now because they've been depicted that way for centuries. They didn't used to, but now they do."

Dracula's Death

Cammy hadn't known that. She'd never be able to look at satyrs the same way again.

"You sure she wasn't just lying? Like she was something else that doesn't normally have a dog head but said she was a Fury to get us to leave her alone?" Cammy asked.

"I don't know," Malcolm snapped, "and I'd really rather not find out."

Cammy crossed her arms. Typical Malcolm. He didn't ever get involved unless he was getting paid to. But he was a mercenary, after all.

A sleek, black, high-performance car pulled up along the sidewalk. The door popped open. The driver inside—Dracula—removed his sunglasses.

"Thank you, Malcolm," he greeted. Malcolm saluted him with a finger.

"Anytime," Malcolm answered flatly, then he stuck his hands under his armpits and leaned very carefully against his car, though he managed to make it look natural. In another walk of life, he'd have made a perfect male model: chiseled chin, high cheekbones, soulful eyes, perfect physique, and always dressed in that "effortless casual" that you saw on magazine covers. Malcolm knew it, too. He worked hard at maintaining appearances. Instead of trying to pass unnoticed, he made himself unforgettable. Cammy could recognize him by the scent of his cologne and hair product alone.

"Cammy," Dracula said, "I've got an assignment. Where do you want to be?"

Cammy nodded goodbye to Malcolm and slid into the passenger seat.

"What assignment?" she asked, closing the door. Dracula waited until she strapped in before he pulled away from the curb. He replaced the sunglasses. The black suit he wore matched the black car. He shifted gear and merged into traffic.

"Some missing people," he said, and she knew immediately that it must be whatever Brian had heard about.

"All around the same area? South Asians?" she prompted.

He glanced toward her.

"Police have wind of this, I take it?" he asked.

"Yeah."

For reasons she couldn't guess, Dracula smirked to himself, then muttered in his native language. At least, she assumed it was his native language. He knew a lot of different ones, even more than Malcolm. "What's going on?" Cammy asked.

"I haven't been told, and I don't know," he said, then looked to her again.

"I'm in," Cammy told him.

"Very well," he said. "That will save me the necessity of driving you back first."

His mansion was tucked up against the Cascades, far from the city, so it took a commute to get there and back. Cammy leaned back in her immaculate leather seat. He drove really nice cars, but this little beauty was his functional one, the one for "working."

The sun glinted off the large ring he wore, its face worn down from literal centuries of use, so she couldn't make out the engraving. Aside from how well dressed he was—he never wore anything but perfectly tailored suits unless a job required dressing down—he didn't look all that special. Not tall, not short; very powerfully muscular but not bulky; well-kempt hair but a gaunt face. Straight, thin nose; dark green, deep-set eyes, darkened over the centuries—or maybe during his life. He looked somewhere north of forty, though it was tricky to guess how far.

Dracula's Death

He looked so little like the popular images of Dracula in pop culture that she wouldn't have believed he was who he said he was if she hadn't seen him in action with that strange sword, that terrible night when twenty vampires had surrounded her. He defied expectations. They didn't matter to him. He used his real name and didn't care who it confused, or whether they might figure out that he was the real deal. It drove Cammy nuts. But she had to concede he was right; it had been his name for centuries before anyone else started using it for their own purposes.

Bram Stoker had picked the name because, by the Victorian Era, its meaning had changed into something that worked for his vampire story. According to Dracula, Stoker hadn't based his vampire on any particular member of the family, either; he'd just liked the name. And that had made all the difference. And Dracula resented every single minute of it.

CHAPTER 2
THE LADT OR THE TIGER

"And how is Officer Warren?" Dracula asked his guest as he navigated his way downtown. He asked not just to be polite, but also because he found Brian's unspoken infatuation with Cammy endlessly entertaining. Something about the modern man that made relationships nearly impossible to launch. Like the Victorian Era all over again.

Cammy crossed her arms. She was almost twenty-two, very slim, her short black hair flipping as she turned to pout out the window. Something about the modern way of life made twenty-somethings more like children than adults. She didn't want to admit how she felt about Brian, either; her reticence was less intelligible to him than Brian's.

"Well?" he pressed.

"We're going to try to do something for... about... to remember Heather. He wants to pick me up."

"When?"

"Thursday evening."

"I'll inform my tenants," he offered. "Have him come up."

He felt Cammy studying him out of the corner of her eye. He knew she didn't know what to make of him, even after almost a full year living in his manor. No matter how many questions she asked, she never seemed to be able to take him at his word. That was the power of the narrative the world had adopted, and he was buried under it. Entombed, if he felt like waxing ironically poetic.

He found a parking spot near an apartment complex. The brick facades were old, dirty, and crumbling; pigeons and crows rimmed the rooftops. Some tenants had their laundry hanging on the balconies, taking full advantage of the beautiful sunlight and unusually clear weather.

"Are you going to stay out of trouble?" he asked Cammy.

"Yeah," Cammy said.

"Are you?" he repeated.

"Yeah."

He knew better. She never stayed out of trouble. That was how they'd stumbled across each other in the first place. He'd eliminated some vermin, and by coincidence—which he knew could have been nothing of the sort—he'd saved her. Then she had tracked him to his home and demanded to know what was going on. So he'd told her.

He exited the vehicle and read the numbers of the top corners of the brick apartments, looking for the correct building. Cammy trotted behind him. She was slender, petite, looking all the smaller in her skinny, high-waisted jeans with a flannel shirt tied around her waist, a loose shirt hanging off one shoulder and her knit bag across the other. Oh, how fashions changed.

Seeing the correct building, he stepped over a puddle, ascended the small flight of rust-stained concrete stairs, and found the apartment he sought. Once he stood in front of the door, he waved Cammy back with one hand and knocked.

An agent from Special Services opened the door a crack. It was policy to secure a location until they had what they needed, or at least until they cleaned it sufficiently to prevent law enforcement or uninformed civilians from stumbling across anything difficult to explain. Usually, Special Services deployed five or more agents per job, if they had the manpower.

Dracula stared at the man. His name was... Neilson? Something like that. His partner had been slaughtered by the *draugr* last year. He looked thinner and more wan than he had when last they'd crossed one another, or at least crossed paths. His shirt was wrinkled, and he had deep, dark circles under his eyes.

The agent swung open the door and Dracula pushed past him. He knocked away the man's drawn gun and waved Cammy in.

"Who is this?" the agent demanded when Cammy entered.

"This is Camellia Lilly, my guest," Dracula explained.

Neilson stared at Cammy, baffled, then looked to Dracula. It took him a few moments to think of a response to her presence.

"You brought a booty call with you?" he demanded.

The man must have been taking notes from the other agents, or from Boese himself. He had been far more demure the last time he and Dracula had spoken.

Cammy glared, her eyes blazing.

"Excuse you!" she said. "Rude! And not true!"

"Who authorized her to be here?" Neilson demanded, ignoring her.

"I did," Dracula told him. "Now be silent. You *are* being very rude."

Cammy sidled up beside Dracula as he took stock of the apartment. Torn curtains that looked more like dishrags, an overturned sofa. There was the usual linoleum floor in the tiny, attached kitchen. The grimy-looking refrigerator door was open. So he went over to the most interesting thing in the small apartment: the dead tiger lying half-hidden behind the overturned couch.

"What is that?" Cammy asked.

"You have my adder stone," he reminded her. "You tell me." He'd lent her the adder stone after she'd moved in, in the hopes that should she see something dangerous she would know to avoid it. So far, it seemed she was using it to *find* creatures and seek them out instead. She pulled out the smooth little stone with a hole worn through the center. She wore it around her neck along with the key he'd given her for her room in his mansion. Cammy held the hole up to her eye and looked at the tiger.

"I don't know. There's some sort of... I've never seen it before. Glow?"

"If you please." He held out his hand. She pulled the stone over her head and passed it to him. When he looked at the tiger's corpse, he saw the faint, wavering haze of magic, but it was fading. It would be gone in an hour or two. He handed the adder stone back to Cammy. She turned in a circle as she put the stone back, her eyes searching for other clues.

"Who lives here?" she wondered.

An excellent question. She was perceptive, when she didn't get in her own way, which was her unfortunate usual habit. Neilson remained silent, so Dracula stared at him unblinking until the man provided an answer.

"Supposed to belong to a woman named Cempaka Sin. Fake name, so far as we can tell."

"The tiger's female," Dracula pointed out.

Cammy and Neilson stared at him.

"You mean, that's the woman?" Cammy ventured, horrified.

"Perhaps," he said. "Unless we find her elsewhere. Or she's *inside* the tiger."

He took the opportunity to look through the other rooms. The bathroom seemed ordinary, except that there was nothing in the medicine cabinet. There were no photos in the apartment at all, not even in the bedroom. The bed had a deep impression in the middle, much too large to fit the small women's clothes that he found in the drawers and closet. Finally, with Cammy following behind, he went into the kitchen. What he would or would not find there ought to clinch the whole thing.

The contents of the refrigerator were still cool enough not to have gone bad. He spotted four cardboard Chinese takeout boxes, a durian fruit sliced in half and wrapped in plastic. In one drawer was unlabeled meat, about thirty pounds' worth, wrapped in sealed plastic bags.

"I would say the tiger is the missing woman," he asserted, picking up one of the bags.

"What makes you think so?" Cammy asked.

"Because this is probably human flesh," he said. Cammy's eyes widened and she covered her mouth.

"Oh, that's *so gross!*"

"Probably?" Neilson demanded pointedly. Dracula gave him his attention.

"Yes, probably. You can check, if you like." He tossed the bag at the agent. Neilson sidestepped it and the bag sailed across the room to splat on the floor.

"*You* can check it," Neilson retorted.

"But I won't." Dracula stood and returned to the tiger.

"What happened?" Cammy wondered.

"Someone came in and stabbed her," he replied.

"Stabbed her?"

"Yes, in the chest. Here." He pointed to five bloody points in the white fur. "But the chest would be hard to reach if she'd been in tiger form. That's why I think she's our missing woman." He turned to Neilson. "This doesn't look like something you need me for. You people cover up scenarios when monsters kill people. You don't care about monsters getting killed."

"But the police think these missing persons are human. They don't find the bodies, so they're missing. We have to get on top of this."

"So there's a monster serial killer?" Cammy sounded amazed at her own observation. "Hunting these tigers, or whatever they are?"

"It appears so," said Dracula. "My guess is the hunter's a human."

"Why?"

"A human seems the likeliest to use a knife, instead of claws or teeth or magic. Another monster would know that Special Services would investigate a series of slain tigers, so there would be no point disguising the weapon they used." Turning to the agent he said, "I don't kill humans for you."

"You do now," said Neilson.

Dracula summoned a malicious smile. He knew it unnerved people. "No, I don't."

"What are *you* being so squeamish about? You killed twenty-thousand people once, and were pretty proud of it."

"Twenty-three thousand, give or take," Dracula corrected. "That's ancient history. I'm not your hitman. Get someone else. Ophois isn't above cold-blooded murder for the right price."

"Director Boese insisted."

"And I'm refusing."

"You can't."

Dracula snorted and pushed past Neilson to get out of the apartment. Cammy trotted behind him.

"You can turn them down like that?" she asked. "I thought you couldn't?"

He didn't answer.

"Twenty-three thousand?" Cammy asked when they got back to his car.

"Yes. I was trying to keep enemies out of my land."

"*Thousands?*" she repeated.

"The Pope seemed pleased," he told her. "For all the good that did me."

She asked no further questions.

That was the part that irritated him the most, although silence—possibly thoughtful silence—was preferable to the mix of ignorance and accusations she had been wont to demonstrate previously. Perhaps she was too afraid to ask for more context, or perhaps she wasn't interested. Ignorance and indifference had been the status quo on and off for centuries.

She slid into the passenger seat as he started up the car.

"We should find out who's killing these tigers," she asserted as soon as she closed the door.

CHAPTER 3
CATCH A TIGER BY THE TAIL

Dracula squinted at her, seemingly annoyed.

"We should," Cammy insisted.

"Should we?"

"It's not like you have lot to do when you're not working," she pointed out. "Besides, if we don't find this person, Boese is going to."

"I'm not in the business of saving people," he told her. "And for your information, I have quite a bit to do when I'm not 'working'."

"You saved me," she reminded him.

He started the engine and looked over his shoulder as he reversed out of the parking space.

"I did no such thing. I slew a group of vampires. Incidentally, they would have killed you if I hadn't killed them first. Saving you was not my goal."

He had stuck to that story from the beginning. Cammy didn't really buy it, since he'd let her stick around afterwards. He went out of his way to see to her safety, but he'd also thrown her out of the mansion when she annoyed him too much, so she wasn't sure to what extent he *truly* worried about her. In fact, she wasn't sure what their actual relationship was. As much as she resented the idea, she often wondered if she wasn't some sort of pet to him. What did other people start looking like to someone who'd been walking the earth for centuries? Gerbils or hamsters maybe? Or maybe he was just an old-fashioned sexist. He was born in the Middle Ages or whenever, after all. He still occasionally kissed women's hands by way of greeting, so that theory wasn't too far-fetched.

"Boese is going to kill whoever is hunting these tigers if we don't get to them first," Cammy said.

"And that is no concern of mine," he told her. "Besides, he's low on manpower. He's much more likely to hire the hunter on."

"Low on manpower?"

Dracula pointed over his shoulder at the apartment complex. "Only one agent assigned to the scene. Not even a second for backup."

They pulled out onto the road.

"Maybe we could befriend this person?" Cammy suggested, elaborately directing her glance out the window. She heard him let out one of his theatrical sighs, but she persisted. "I mean, these tiger monsters eat humans, right? Whoever is killing them is on our side, right? And we don't know that it's a human. It could be, like, a satyr."

He snorted at the idea.

"Well, or something that doesn't have magic or super strength or something, just hands."

"I have no idea what 'side' you think is ours. I have only one side: mine. Where everyone else stands is not my concern."

"But, you take in monsters who need help—"

"If they ask for asylum, and can do me service in exchange without killing humans. For no other reason. I have no particular love for all the creatures who go crawling about in the dark."

She narrowed her eyes at him. *Hypocritical, much?* she thought, but knew better than to voice that aloud.

He kept driving. She put her chin in her hand and stared out the window at the city going by. The good weather was holding up, which was something, she supposed. Maybe it was climate change. It would be nice if there was an upside to that.

What was the point of knowing about the supernatural if you couldn't help people who were in trouble? People like Heather, who had needed help more than anyone. She gritted her teeth. She checked her phone and texted some of her friends. Someone had posted a video of a cat sleeping on a pillow with an iguana and there were the usual shoutouts. She wanted to care about that stuff the way she used to, but it just wasn't the same anymore.

One of her friends, Lindsey, was asking what she wanted to do for her birthday. Cammy stared at the message. The real answer was "nothing," but she couldn't reply with that.

Whatever you want to do, she replied, *but nothing too big, thanks.*

She looked up as the car pulled into the parking lot of another apartment complex.

"Hang on, where are we?"

"First disappearance," Dracula answered.

"The first? Wait, are we looking into this?" she asked, turning to look at him. He wore an expression of pronounced disinterest.

"I didn't have anything else to do today," he said.

She smiled as she got out of the car once more.

This complex seemed nicer than the last one. The bricks were newer, there were trees planted out front, a few kids on tricycles on the sidewalk.

He led the way to a window facing out on the ground floor. Dracula peered in through the window, but when she shaded the glass with her hands to do the same, he walked away.

"What's in there?"

"I doubt there's anything now. I just wanted to make certain," he said. He walked into the complex, passed the door that would have opened to the apartment he had peered into, and on to the next door and knocked on it. There was no answer, but it was morning on a weekday; most people would be at work or school. He backtracked to the door on the other side of the empty apartment.

"What are we doing?" Cammy asked.

"We're finding out if anyone saw anything," he told her.

Well now she just felt stupid. She fingered the strap of her bag and the nerdy pins that she'd accumulated over the years as he knocked on the door.

An older woman answered, shouting through the wood.

"Who is it?"

"Good afternoon, ma'am," Dracula said. "I am with law enforcement. There was an incident at neighboring apartment across from yours some time ago. I was wondering if you had seen anything."

"I don't talk to cops!" she shouted back.

Dracula didn't bother pressing, but moved on to the next apartment. Most of his attempts garnered no response, though he did manage to get a middle-aged woman to actually open her door. She smiled *way* too eagerly at him and kept playing with her hair and rubbing one foot on the back of her other ankle. Cammy rolled her eyes. You met all types, she supposed. Dracula cut the interaction short—probably he figured out she had nothing to say which would be relevant.

Dracula's Death

"How long is this gonna take?" she asked. Dracula frowned at her. She shut up. They were now at the far end of hall from the empty apartment. He knocked at the new door.

A young man opened it. He had a pale face, but his features looked Mediterranean or Levantine, especially with his dark hair and eyes. He was thin, dressed in a long-sleeved shirt, wore glasses, and had delicate fingers. The young man fidgeted in the doorway, blocking it with his body. Dracula shot Cammy a sidelong glance.

"Not very long at all, it seems," he remarked. To the nervous young man he said, "Good morning. Would you happen to know anything about tigers?"

He caught the door as the tenant tried to slam it shut, then forced it open with ease. Dracula stepped into the apartment—he didn't need an invitation like in the movies—and watched the tenant run to the kitchen and return with a huge knife.

"You're one of them!" the young man shouted, waving the knife. Cammy gasped as he rushed them both. When he came close, Dracula grabbed his wrist and tripped him to the ground, disarming him in the process.

"No. But you've drawn attention to yourself. You're in some trouble."

"Don't eat me!" the young man pleaded.

Dracula glanced at Cammy.

"So they do eat people," she said. The young man on the floor looked up at them both, hyperventilating.

"Wait, you didn't know?" he wondered.

"Don't try to attack us or run," Dracula told him, and helped him up. "Tell us what's happening."

"Who are you?" the young man demanded.

Instead of answering, Dracula pointed towards a table with a centerpiece of fake flowers and wooden chairs set on three sides. Wide-eyed, the young man set himself down in one. He stared first at Dracula, then Cammy, then back. His breath hissed through his teeth.

"Hi, I'm Cammy," she said, holding out a hand and smiling. She knew what that sort of fear felt like. Not knowing what was going on, thinking you were about to die. You were never the same afterwards. Hesitantly, the young man took her hand. She felt him trembling. "I'll get you a glass of water," she told him, and went to the kitchen. When she stepped around the half-wall partition that separated the living space from the kitchen, she spotted the sink. Another large knife lay in it, washed clean, but easily big enough to kill a person. She took a breath herself, searched some cupboards, found a cup, filled it with the filtered water she found in the fridge, and returned to the terrified tenant.

He accepted the glass hesitantly, searching for an ulterior motive in her face before he took a sip. The water trembled in the glass as he wrapped both hands around it. She noticed he wore a pendant that looked like some bearded man who was a bird or something below the waist. The symbol looked sort of familiar, but she couldn't place it.

"From the beginning," she suggested as gently as she could. "Who are you? How'd you find those tigers?"

"I'm Emet," he answered. "I... I couldn't believe it. There must have been at least five of them going into and out of that apartment," he gestured at the wall that separated his from the empty one at the other end of the hall.

"How did you know?" Dracula asked.

"One of my friends," he said. "His girlfriend went missing. The police never found anything. But he" —Emet pointed at the wall again— "something fell out of his trash: a bracelet my friend had bought his girlfriend. I called the police again, but they still didn't find anything. Then he came here, and..." Emet licked his lips and glanced at the kitchen.

DRACULA'S DEATH

"I didn't know what to do, and it was so much worse afterwards. He wasn't even human! I had to have my friends help me to drag the body back to his apartment. I didn't want to tell the police that I had killed a man who turned into a tiger. I thought if I just left the corpse there they would investigate and perhaps solve the mystery, but they never did! And then... then the others came snooping around." He shivered.

"How many?" Dracula asked.

"Five so far, but six came to visit when he was alive. I copied their license plates to track them down. I finally found all five, I think. There's only one left. Of *those* ones."

"Hmm," said Dracula, a knuckle on his chin.

"What is the matter with you both? There are tigers who look like people! Am I crazy? Have I been killing perfectly normal, innocent people? Am I delusional? This is crazy!" He gasped and clutched at the cup of water, spilling its contents on his hands. Cammy sat in the chair beside him and touched his arm.

"It's ok," she told him, "I went through the same thing. There are some things out there I didn't believe were real."

"There are actually tigers that can disguise themselves as humans?" Emet shouted. "That is so much worse than me being crazy!" He let out a high-pitched squeal.

Cammy had never thought of it that way. But yeah, that actually *was* much worse. She looked around the apartment. There were food wrappers kicked into corners, crumbs ground into the carpet. Dust on the top of the TV, the coffee table. This poor young man was a wreck.

"They're actually rare," Cammy assured him. "We've never even seen one before, isn't that right?"

Dracula answered with a small, dismissive shrug.

"Really?" Emet asked, gasping for breath.

"Yeah, I mean, otherwise everyone would know about them," Cammy assured him. That probably wasn't true. It was much likelier that there were more than the six, but the others were better at hiding.

"How would we know? They could be *anyone*," Emet whispered.

Cammy thought about the adder stone. But she couldn't go walking around everywhere staring at people through a hole in a stone.

"See here, you tell us where the last one is and we'll take care of it," Dracula told him. Emet's eyebrows knitted together.

"You'll what? Why? Who are you?"

"Don't worry about that. Where is the last one?"

Emet stared at Dracula as though trying to size him up. Then he reached into his pocket for his phone. He pulled up an address and showed Cammy and Dracula. Cammy put it into her own phone.

"Leave that one to us," Dracula told him. "But beware: you've drawn the attention of a powerful group of people who will no doubt find you soon. If you don't want them to bury you, or worse, I'd recommend you run as fast and as far as you can."

"What?" Emet breathed.

"Unless you want to spend the rest of your life hunting monsters, in which case they may offer to hire you," Dracula added, then nodded at Cammy to come with him.

"Sorry," Cammy said to Emet. "Um, take care." She followed Dracula out of the apartment.

"We're going to leave him like that?" she asked.

"What else would we do?"

"Help him?"

"I believe we just did."

Dracula's Death

"But Boese is going to hunt him down?"

"I told him to run," Dracula explained, slowly, as if to an idiot, "or to work for him. Those are his options at this point."

"What about me?"

"What about you?"

They had returned to the car. She stared at him over the top of the vehicle.

"Well, I didn't have to work for your boss or run," she pointed out.

"You made your own choice," he told her. "To do neither, and once again you're making me regret taking you in."

Another trip. They spent this one in silence, except for her occasionally navigating via her phone. This time, they parked as close to the building as possible, in a shaded spot behind a van which partly hid the vehicle from sight. Dracula opened the trunk. Inside was a small arsenal of weaponry ranging from wooden stakes to metal knives, swords, axes, grenades, and so forth—and numerous guns. There were a few wooden crosses tucked to one side.

He selected a small handgun and held it out for her to take.

"I don't do guns," she reminded him.

"I'm not having this argument again. Either you're armed or you're not coming in."

"You can't keep me out here," she said.

"I can lock you in this trunk until I'm done," he told her.

"With all the guns?"

"If you don't 'do' guns, then there isn't any risk you'll use one in there, is there?" he pointed out. "In addition, this vehicle is armored. If you fire one of those in there you'll probably kill yourself."

What a way with words. Truly, he was a big softie. She glared at him, but he continued holding out the gun. She crossed her arms.

"You'd rather fight up close?" he reached into the trunk and pulled out a sword instead.

"Ugh, *fine*," she grumbled, and held out her bag. He tightened his lips but put the gun into it. While he fetched the weapons he wanted, she very gingerly held the bag as far from her body as possible. He had explained that they didn't go off all on their own, but she still didn't trust them. Even so, she'd gotten more used to them over the last six months. Dracula was something of a gun nut—he liked to collect them and had a whole room dedicated to antique weapons in his mansion. And he'd been taking her to a gun range to practice shooting. She'd gotten better at firing them and actually hitting the targets, but that didn't mean she had to like them.

He concealed the sword he'd selected under his coat while she put in the specialty ear plugs he'd bought her for using firearms. She'd heard several guns go off without ear protection, and never wanted to do that again. As he adjusted his coat, she glimpsed the huge Smith & Wesson magnum he wore in a holster. At any given time, he always had a collection of weapons on him.

"You keep behind me," he told her.

"Sure," she said.

"I mean it."

"I know."

As nonchalantly as they could, they crossed the street to the apartment complex. They entered, found an elevator, and rode up to the fourth floor, then made their way to the end of the hall under a flickering fluorescent light. Cammy stood well out of arm's reach, about fourteen feet away in fact, near the stairwell, while Dracula rang the bell.

Dracula's Death

A middle-aged Asian woman answered the door. She wore her dark hair in a low bun, her skin looked golden. She eyed Dracula.

"Good day. I am Vladislav Dracula," he told her. "I'm with the enemy. May I come in?"

That had to be the strangest introduction Cammy had ever heard him make. The standard introduction when you weren't sure where someone stood was to give some sort of name and say the organization you were with, if you were with one. So far as she could tell, it was the supernatural way of showing an empty hand. However, "the enemy" was a new one.

The woman frowned at him, looked him up and down, then tried to slam the door. Once again, he caught it with one hand. She shoved it, and he didn't budge. The whites of her eyes swelled when she realized she couldn't overpower him.

She ran into the apartment, and he followed after her.

"I have no intention of killing you at this moment," he was saying as he passed through the doorway. Cammy slunk behind to peer inside. In the living room crouched a snarling tiger, with Dracula blocking the only way in or out.

"*Vetala*," the tiger snarled at him.

"I have no idea what that means," he answered. "But I do wish to talk. Tell me about your kind."

The tiger bared its teeth at him, but he did not move. At last, it sat back on its haunches, though its ears remained pinned back and its eyes were wide with fear. Dracula turned to Cammy and waved her inside. She entered and shut the door behind her in case anyone happened by.

"There are hardly any of us left," the tiger said. "I'm not sure what my family should call ourselves any more. We've had to breed with other creatures, so I could hardly say which bloodline is the strongest."

"I see," said Dracula. "What brings you to Seattle?"

"It was safe. No one knows what we are here," said the tiger. "Or so we thought. We were wrong."

"Your friends?"

"Someone has killed them."

"Apparently you kill and eat humans."

The tiger's yellow eyes darted back and forth, avoiding his green ones.

"Is that not true?" he asked.

"What do you want?"

"It is not my habit to hunt monsters indiscriminately. That would be a touch hypocritical of me," he explained. "I'm certainly willing to turn a blind eye to the ones that can live peacefully alongside humanity."

"We can peacefully coexist," said the tiger. "Some of us must eat human flesh to attain human shape, but we don't need to consume more once we've achieved that form."

"Wonderful news. In that case, would you mind if I searched your apartment to make certain that you have nothing stored in here that would contradict your story?"

The tiger crouched, frozen. Cammy knew the violence was coming before the tiger ever moved. Then the tiger leaped forward, snarling in rage, claws white and sharp. Dracula stepped backward, drawing his sword, and took its head clean off. Cammy couldn't see what happened next, but suddenly he turned and ducked, the sword in his hand flashed, and she saw that the blade was buried to his hand in the chest of a middle-aged man who must have come from a back room. He was of similar complexion as the tiger-woman. The man dropped his own sword, gasped once, then turned into an enormous tiger. Dracula pushed the body off his sword's blade, then he began searching the floor.

Cammy gasped in horror. The tiger man must have been awfully fast, because she could now see that he had

DRACULA'S DEATH

succeeded in slicing part of Dracula's head clean off. She turned to a wall and tried not to retch.

"That was careless of me," Dracula grumbled.

She clenched her fists, gritted her teeth, and forced herself to turn back around. He had found the missing section of his head and was now picking up the strands of his hair that had been severed. Blood oozed down one side of his face and his neck.

"You're bleeding," she told him.

"There is nothing I can do about that," he responded.

He finished searching the floor and put the strands of hair into his pocket. He stood and surveyed the apartment, the detached piece of his head in one hand. Without a word, he stepped over the two dead tigers and went to the fridge. He opened it.

"As I thought," he said.

"Is it like the other one?"

"Yes."

Cammy shivered. She didn't want to see.

Dracula was mumbling to himself.

"What are you doing?"

"Saying a prayer for them. For whatever good it will do."

"Can saying a prayer help?"

"From me? I doubt it. But there is nothing more I can do."

"What will Boese do... with them?"

Dracula looked up. She gulped at the dreadful sight.

"Do you think Boese is going to alert their families and give them a proper burial?" Dracula said, staring at her with part of his stupid head missing. "Or do you think he's going to take all this meat and feed it to some of his lab experiments?"

She knew Boese's department did experiments, but Dracula had never explained exactly what that entailed. She feared to think what that would mean if Boese got his hands on a pile of dead people.

"Can we do anything about it?"

"You mean to ask whether we can bury them ourselves?"

Cammy hadn't really thought of it. But was there any other way to stop Boese from doing...whatever he would do?

"I... I don't know," she confessed.

Dracula considered the fridge.

"I know of no legal way to see to their burial."

Cammy played with her fingers.

"What about the elves at your mansion?"

Dracula grunted.

"*Elves...*" he murmured. "I suppose even a heretical burial might be better than none at all, and removing the remains would be better than letting Boese find them. Very well. We will need a cooler."

Cammy gagged at the idea.

"Would you prefer carrying these bags as they are, then?"

She glared at him. He glared back. She couldn't stand seeing his open head like that. She looked away.

She looked down at the two dead tigers. He'd killed both of them. These were undoubtedly monsters. They killed and ate people, but she couldn't help thinking about what the tiger lady had said, that some of them could peacefully coexist. Maybe that was true. If so, it was a shame that they were all getting hunted to extinction. She doubted Boese and his goons were going to split hairs about which tiger creature was friendly. As far as she could tell, all monsters were on their chopping block, even cute, harmless ones. Why they used Dracula to hunt some of the monsters was something she still didn't fully understand, given how clear he made it that he hated the department, and how much Boese seemed to hate him back.

Dracula's Death

"I'll go get a cooler," she mumbled. "You can't leave here looking like that."

He remained motionless, studying her. She fiddled with the strap of her bag. He reached into his pocket and tossed her his keys.

"You know where to find me," he said.

CHAPTER 4

BE IN THE HUNT

When Cammy returned, Dracula was sitting in an easy chair in the corner of the room with the two dead tigers at his feet, like those animal skin rugs in movies. Only this was far more demented.

"I forgot I had that gun in my bag," she grumbled. "I almost screamed when I went to pay."

She set down the large Styrofoam cooler, opened it, and retrieved the bandages she had purchased. Carefully, she tiptoed around the dead tigers and dropped the bandages into his open hand without touching him. He had warned her very strongly against coming into contact with his blood.

He said nothing, just unrolled the bandage and clearly gave some thought to what he was going to do about his head. At last, he did his best to stick the severed bit in place and wrapped the bandages around it. His shirt was sticky with blood, but hard to tell at a glance because it was black, like the rest of his clothes. Maybe that was why he wore black. No stains to speak of.

"I got the cooler," she said, "but I can't do the fridge, I'm sorry."

"That's all right," he said. "But before we proceed, I have to ask something."

"What?"

"Are you trying to get yourself killed?" he asked, meeting her eyes. He didn't look angry now, and the bandage was almost comical. That helped to take the edge off him.

"No." She shook her head a little. He held up his flip phone and waggled it at her. He couldn't use touch screens.

"I just got off the phone with Malcolm. He tells me you tried to confront a Fury in a crowded coffee shop."

"I didn't know she was a Fury. Or even what a Fury was," she admitted.

"And you wanted to waltz in here unarmed as well. If you're not going to take dangerous situations seriously, you can go back to your previous life. I won't take you along with me for any reason. I have been trying to teach you to be careful."

"I *am* serious about this," Cammy insisted.

"No, you're not. You're playing some sort of game. And you're going to get yourself killed." His eyes glinted. "I won't be party to that. You can kill yourself without my help."

"You let me come along! You didn't have to!"

"Sit down." He pointed at the sofa in front of the TV. The tigers had watched TV. The thought of the two of them sitting in front of the television watching shows together almost made her laugh, but then she saw them lying there, lifeless, and she didn't.

"You're not my parents," she told him.

"Sit. Down," he repeated. She did.

"What is troubling you?" he asked.

"Nothing."

He folded his hands together, hiding the bottom of his face. That made his eyes so much more intense.

"You've always been impulsive, but this is absurd," he said. "If the only thing you're going to do with that stone is walk up to every single monster you see and accost them, I'm going to take it away from you."

"I'm not a child," she told him.

"Then don't act like one."

She looked down at the two dead tigers, their unfocused eyes. One's tongue was lolling out almost like a cartoon, and it was so sad.

"I just want to help," she said. "Like with Emet. We should have helped him."

"We did. I warned him about the danger he would face and told him his options. He was wrong about how many of these creatures were here. If he'd come by himself, they would have killed him."

Cammy noticed dark, purplish blood forming pinpoint stains in the bandages. It looked like he was going to keep bleeding until that wound was able to heal. However long that would take.

"You were taken by surprise, too," she pointed out.

"I have less to lose," he said.

"Well, what if he'd taken your whole head off and threw you in the incinerator or something? Wouldn't that have killed you?" She actually wasn't totally sure what would kill him, but he had told her people had tried—and failed—to kill him in the past.

He didn't so much as move; he hardly breathed. Yes, he breathed. He said he didn't need to, but he did it anyway.

"Tell me what happened at the coffee shop," he said.

Cammy sighed.

"I saw her there, ordering coffee, and I thought she might be dangerous. I couldn't just stand by; there were all these people there. She might hurt someone, or worse."

Dracula's Death

"I told you to leave her alone *because* she might be dangerous. I thought you would understand that. I had to get off the phone and didn't have time to talk."

"Why not? What were you doing?"

He tapped his thumbs together. "Boese was calling at the same time."

Oh. "Well, you know me," she said. "I'm impulsive, remember?"

"That's why I sent Malcolm. I also contacted the department and the Orders I know. They will assess the situation. If it's something I can handle, no doubt they'll inform me."

"What can Ophois or the department do about her?"

"If she is a Fury? I imagine nothing at all. I am certainly not equipped to fight something that strong. The department might want to, but I can't imagine what resources they could possibly bring to bear against so powerful a pagan spirit."

She fiddled with her bag strap. She realized the gun was still in it.

"Well, what am I supposed to do if I see something like that? Just leave it alone?"

"Yes."

"I can't do that. People might be in danger."

His eyes tried to burn holes in her head.

"This is about Heather, isn't it?"

She gritted her teeth and twisted her bag strap, looking down at the floor. The tigers kept pretty good care of the carpet. It had been vacuumed recently.

"Heather needed help. If someone had stepped in, or seen something, maybe..."

"Maybe. Probably they would have been killed, also. You certainly would have been, if not for my unexpected arrival. And when you tried alone, you nearly *were*. And as you may remember, someone else did die, because you interfered."

"I can't do *nothing*," she told him. "And we should have helped Emet."

"I told you, I did."

"It's not like people can just run away! Besides, he killed a lot of these tiger monsters. He'd be a useful ally, right?"

"What should I have done, Cammy? Picked him up and taken him back home with us, like a lost dog?"

Wow. He made the pet comparison all on his own. It was looking worse and worse for her all the time.

"Well, I mean you let me live there—"

"You came charging up to my door all on your own without an invitation," he said. "And the department wanted to take you for their own. I put myself and my entire household at risk to let you stay. What do you think would happen to you and all my tenants if another errant soul set up shop there? I don't have the power to take on the US government. I have to pick and choose my battles."

"What do you care, right? You're almost six hundred years old. Must be hard to care about anybody anymore."

His expression slid towards hateful again.

"You believe that?" he asked.

She wasn't sure. He let her come along with him sometimes even if it was dangerous, but he told her to stay out of the way. When she'd asked for help finding Heather, he'd given it. She wasn't sure how upset he was about his lover who had committed suicide way back when. He didn't want to talk about her, but he didn't want to talk about *anything*.

"Yes, I'm messed up because of Heather. Maybe that's why I'm being impulsive," she admitted. "And something's got you messed up, that's why you're distracted." She met his eyes. "Am I wrong?"

Dracula's Death

He didn't blink. He could do that. No one was ever going to win a staring contest with him if he didn't let them. He glanced down at his hands.

"I mean, you take it personally when people say you're a monster, but you admitted to killing thousands of people."

"*Millions* of people were killed during both World Wars. The world leaders that ordered them have that blood on their hands, but they're not all called monsters. Your atom bombs have killed men, women, and children, as did the Tokyo city fire bombings. Yet there isn't a commonly held narrative that Truman was a monster who dipped his bread in blood, or whatever other nonsense they say about me these days."

"Well, we were at war," Cammy said. He was probably going to catch her here somewhere. He'd actually fought in that war, if she could believe Malcolm, so he'd know much more about World War II than she would. Stupid American education system, always letting her down.

He spread his hands. "There you are."

"Well, being surly all the time doesn't really help your case," she said. "I mean, I don't know what to think half the time because you don't tell me anything."

"You don't want to know," he insisted.

"Yes, I do."

He studied his hands, the one covered in blood and the other one that remained clean. He opened his palms, then stood up.

"I should head back," he said, "before this" —he gestured at himself— "gets more out of hand."

She stewed in the car on the drive back to his mansion. It lay near the foothills of the very edge of the Cascades. The sun faded as clouds rolled in, turning the sky gray. Figured. Sure, Seattle wasn't exactly known for its amazing, sunny weather, but it was just the icing on top that they'd have a silent car ride while clouds rolled in.

The bandage was deep wine red with blood when they arrived. Dracula parked his car outside the garage and stepped out, frowning at the blood dripping down one side of his body. It had pooled on the nice leather seat, dripped down his right hand, soaked his pants. That was the most she'd ever seen him bleed at once. A living human would surely have died from the blood loss alone, not including losing part of their head.

"I'm not bringing that in," she said, and pointed at the cooler in the backseat. He didn't reply, so she turned away and went towards the door.

The mansion was nowhere near as large as modern homes built to house the wealthy, but it was sturdy. Its walls were thick and made of stone, the doors were inches-thick wood. The windows were small, allowing just enough light in during the day. In some ways, the building more closely resembled a fort or a castle trying to masquerade as a house.

Cammy entered through the back door. The front door was for admitting guests or his employers, and he rarely used it. The back door opened into the main hall, its polished stone floors immaculate, the rich dark of the wood paneling and furniture gleaming as though lacquered. She flipped the switch and the electric lights in the overhead chandelier filled the space with warm light. The skeleton wolpertinger—a sort of winged squirrel-rabbit-duck thing—that sat mounted over the fireplace had one paw raised as though waving "Welcome home" to her.

She went up the beautiful staircase, made a right, went to her room. Inside, everything was just as spotless as the rest of the mansion. As a rule, she liked to be organized, but this tidiness had more to do with the servants—or tenants, as

Dracula's Death

Dracula sometimes called them; he seemed to use the words interchangeably—that lived on his estate.

There were house spirits that spent most of their time keeping the place clean: a handful of brownies and a domovoy and his family. The reason she never used the adder stone in the mansion was because Dracula had warned her that the domovoy looked like a hairy, naked old man who crawled around the house invisibly. If she used the stone, she might be able to see him. She definitely did not want to. The brownies were tiny, naked, elf-like beings; she hadn't run into them either. She'd only been told not to give them clothing if she did. Her shoes were always clean these days, but she didn't know how to feel about the fact that they snuck into her room and cleaned her shoes at who knew what hours without her noticing.

Much of the monster world had ridiculous rules to follow. The domovoy, even though he looked after the house, would become angry if you didn't tidy up after yourself, so he wasn't so much a maid service as a reminder to do your chores. When the domovoy was happy, he'd do quite a lot of chores—presumably this was why the mansion was in such good shape despite neither she nor her host dusting and sweeping top to bottom every week. So far, Cammy didn't know what he would do if he was unhappy. She'd only been warned not to upset him. If the brownies were given clothes, they would leave. Weird stuff like that.

So she didn't use the adder stone inside. She dropped her bag—now thankfully gun-free—onto the old-fashioned feather bed with the four posts that she liked more than anything else she'd ever slept in. She opened the dresser where the few clothes she had managed to salvage from the apartment she'd shared with Heather were stored. She found a light sweater she liked and pulled it on. Dracula didn't often heat his home unless she reminded him—temperature didn't bother him, so she guessed he simply didn't notice or forgot that it might bother her. On the other hand, there was always firewood by the fireplace. She figured he'd need some time to deal with the whole "re-attaching part of his head" thing, so a sweater was the go-to.

Her eyes dropped to the nightstand under one of the windows. She had set the great big, ugly mug Heather had bought for her—the one with the dog print on it—on the stand. Well, the pieces. Because it was so big and thick, it had broken into large chunks instead of shattering when it was tossed out of the apartment with the rest of their belongings, so it was the only mug she'd been able to salvage when they'd been evicted. She carefully traced the broken edge of one piece. For months, she'd been meaning to glue them back together, but she couldn't bring herself to do it. It felt like something would be over forever if she did. So the broken pieces lay under the window, holding none of the flowers or herbs she and Heather used to grow in the apartment.

She intentionally turned away and checked the status of the classes she wanted to sign up for, then looked up the professors. She'd be graduating sooner than she'd expected, and still didn't know what to do with her life. At least she'd have a degree in Communications. She turned her tablet off so she couldn't look at college stuff any more, then plugged it into the charger beside the bed. Carefully, she descended the stairs.

Her host was nowhere to be seen, so she slunk back outside. The grounds were extensive, more like a park than anything else. The vineyards were planted along a sloping hillside. There were cows and chickens on the property as well, so there were always fresh milk and eggs. That was actually pretty great. She'd begun to feel a lot better since she'd started eating the food here.

Dracula's Death

She walked past the well which had the most amazing tasting water in it—as well as a water spirit who did not like being looked at. The water spirit was so shy she would fly into a murderous rage if anyone looked at her. Stupid rules.

The car wasn't out on the gravel driveway anymore. The suit Dracula had been wearing was hanging above the small patch of vampire watermelons that grew in the shadiest corner the mansion overlooked. Yes, vampire watermelons. All they did—when they did anything—was roll around on their own and try to bump into ankles. She wasn't entirely certain what turned melons into vampires in the first place; Dracula had explained it was sometimes age, or the moon, or other factors, but in any case, they were pretty harmless. At the moment, the melons just lay there, like regular watermelons. Boring. You'd think living in a mansion with Dracula would be more interesting more often. It was eerie how used to some of the unusual stuff she'd gotten. Or perhaps it was because she still couldn't interact with most of the monsters and supernatural creatures that lived here. It was more like having interesting shadows crawling around at the corners of your vision, but you could never get a good look at them. If that went on long enough, you stopped jumping every time you glimpsed something odd.

Her phone buzzed. It was Lindsey asking about birthday plans again.

How about going to hear Lorelei? She's doing a gig two days before your birthday? Kenzie likes her a lot.

Lorelei was some sort of local performer. Cammy didn't know much about her, but even Brian had mentioned the singer a few times.

Sure, sounds good, Cammy texted back.

The clouds were thicker. Was it even a good idea to go for a walk now? Cammy refused to let the weather daunt her.

She needed a walk, and she was going to get one, end of story.

She hadn't gone far when she stumbled across a girl playing patty cake—or some variant of it—with a little, gray fox out on a path she had discovered about a month ago. The little girl wore her hair in braids, and the small gray fox sat up on its haunches, waving its tiny paws. The girl giggled. A picture of them would have been right at home in some whimsical fairytale book for children.

"Fjola? Ginko?" Cammy called out. The girl jumped to her feet and brushed leaves off her jeans skirt. She looked like a normal girl now that she wasn't wearing the old-world clothes she'd worn when she'd come to America with her older brother. Fjola was an Icelandic elf, while Ginko was a shape-changer, the child of a kitsune and a tanuki with the tongue-twistingly difficult species name of *"tanukitsune"* which both Boese and Dracula managed to say without tripping over, but Cammy still couldn't quite. Cammy had rescued Ginko about a year ago from Boese's laboratory, and she'd persuaded Dracula to take in the elves. But he'd insisted that Fjola and her brother Trausti be Cammy's *slaves* as part of the price for their sanctuary! She wasn't about to forgive him for that. Since she never ordered the children to do anything, it was an "in name only" sort of arrangement; that was the best she could do, since apparently she couldn't just set them free. Stupid rules.

"Good day, Miss Cammy!" Fjola greeted her. "Welcome back!"

Her English was better than her brother's now. She barely had an accent. If no one was listening for it, they'd probably think she was an ordinary American kid. Ginko yapped an adorable, high-pitched yap, shivered all over, then

DRACULA'S DEATH

turned into a little Asian girl who appeared perhaps eight years old. Cammy almost jumped.

"I learned how!" Ginko explained, and waved her arms in excitement. "Fjola goes to school! I want to go to school, too!"

"Oh," Cammy said. "I'd have to figure that out. I still owe Malcolm for the fake IDs he got for Fjola and Trausti. Let me see what I can do, ok?"

Ginko nodded eagerly.

"Were you out for a walk, Miss Lilly?" Fjola asked. She looked up at the sky. Though overcast, there was no drizzle. That counted as good weather, in Seattle.

"Yeah," Cammy said.

"We shall go with you!" Fjola asserted. Ginko nodded eagerly.

So they went along the path. Fjola chattered about her days at school, what she was learning in third grade, and how she'd set a crow to harass a boy who had pulled her hair.

"Um, maybe don't use magic in school," Cammy suggested.

"Why not?" Fjola asked.

"Because..." Cammy didn't want rumors of strange activities in a public school getting back to Boese; on the other hand, she didn't want to terrify Fjola with dire warnings of underground laboratories, "... the boy won't understand that what's happening to him is because he was mean to you. Maybe your brother can show up and warn him to leave you alone. Most bullies are afraid to fight." Cammy really didn't want magical comeuppance to escalate in an elementary school, and she was pretty sure that Trausti could handle a bully.

Fjola stuck out her lip and pouted. Finally, and with a dramatic crossing of her arms, she agreed. "All right. Then if he leaves me alone, I will leave him alone."

They kept along, under the trees along the faint path she had made clearer over the past year. The leaves rustled overhead, alerting her to the presence of some of the creatures that lived on the estate. It was probably the rusalki. Dracula had told them to keep an eye out for her, since those undead female spirits liked women and girls and would protect them. But she hadn't been able to make friends with them; she guessed they were suspicious of her, the only human on the property. Perhaps one day she'd be able to have a real conversation with them.

"Have you seen the lake?" Fjola asked.

"There's a lake? No, I haven't seen that."

"We can show you!" Ginko chimed in, and took Cammy's hand. Cammy supposed the two supernatural creatures wouldn't lead her anywhere dangerous, especially if they were both indebted to her, so she followed them off the path. They made their way through the woods that covered the majority of Dracula's estate. Cammy hadn't explored much of it, for fear of the satyrs. The vineyards the satyrs tended were pretty far away, though, so this ought to be all right.

"Mother goes fishing in the lake!" Ginko was explaining.

"All the rusalki play there," Fjola added.

Cammy was a little excited by the prospect of finally seeing the rusalki she had heard so much about but never set eyes on.

They came to a clearing in the midst of which lay a lake, limpid and clear like a mirror, reflecting the gray clouds above. There were a few women milling about in diaphanous clothing on the far shore. Were they the rusalki?

"Nymphs," Fjola explained.

Cammy took in the scene. It was picture-perfect. The water was as flat and smooth as glass. Something disturbed the surface, creating lovely ripples that glided across the clear surface. Cammy guessed it was a fish. She hadn't heard about any water monsters on the property—except the one that lived in the well.

"Wow, this is really pretty," she breathed. Fjola tugged happily on her hand and Ginko snapped back into fox form and pounced on an errant bug.

Cammy was thinking she could try to do homework out here if it wasn't raining, when the women in diaphanous clothing all melted into the tree line like a school of frightened fish disappearing behind submerged tree roots. A stranger stepped out of the woods to the water's edge and knelt to scoop up some of the clear water to drink.

It was a satyr. Nowhere near the vineyards. He bowed down his head and sipped the water he'd cupped in his hands. It didn't appear that he'd noticed Cammy or Fjola. Cammy gulped, and carefully stepped backwards to retreat. But the movement must have attracted his attention, because he shot upright like his goat legs were springs, and he stared at her.

Fjola hugged Cammy around the waist, but the satyr didn't seem to notice the girl. His eyes remained fixed on Cammy. One cloven hoof kicked just a little in the mud.

"Hi, I'm Dracula's guest," Cammy reminded him. "I'll just be going now, ok?"

The satyr stared at her with eyes that betrayed no understanding. He said, in a thick, foreign accent, "You don't need to go. I won't hurt you."

"That's great," Cammy said. "But it's late, so I'll just head out..."

She stepped backwards, and the satyr stepped forward. Her stomach tightened in terror. Maybe she could call her host? The mansion wasn't too far away. She pulled her phone.

The satyr burst towards her, and she turned to run. Ginko had already darted into the underbrush and all Cammy saw was her little, gray tail disappearing into the foliage. Fjola screamed, and Cammy tried to pull her along.

She heard the satyr shout behind her, and turned to see how close he was. What she saw instead was eight women, some in diaphanous dresses, some in what looked like long, white tunics or old-fashioned nightgowns, and all of them clinging to the satyr and wrestling with him. He shouted and kicked his hooves, but the women managed to overpower him and throw him into the lake. Some of the women laughed, others pounced on him while he flailed in the water and shouted in distress.

Cammy turned and ran for the path, dragging Fjola with her, then up the path to the mansion. She didn't stop until they were across the gravel, inside the house, and the door was slammed. Cammy collapsed to the floor to catch her breath. Fjola twisted her hands and looked worried.

"You ok?" Cammy asked between breaths.

"Yes," Fjola said. "I'm sorry. I hadn't seen one of them over there before."

Lesson learned. No more walks, even if it wasn't near the vineyards. Suppose she bumped into that satyr while walking alone? She didn't even want to think about it, and she resolved not to. She'd go to her room and do normal things, like homework.

"You thirsty?" Cammy asked Fjola. Her own throat felt like the inside of an oven after all that running. Fjola nodded, so Cammy got back on her wobbly feet.

The mansion was quiet as a tomb, but it usually was. Dracula had turned off the lights, so she flicked them back on and trudged to the kitchen. She opened the fridge and screamed. The bags of human flesh were in there.

Dracula's Death

"Are you kidding me?!" she shouted. No response. When he disappeared he really disappeared.

Furious, she stormed past Fjola, who watched her with concern. She stomped past the ornately decorated doors that led down to a cellar where there was a beautifully lacquered black coffin lined with gold. Dracula didn't use it; it was a ruse for any particularly enterprising vampire hunter who might make it up to the property. She found nothing in any of the spare rooms, all spotless, but dark and cold and uninhabited. There was nothing out of the ordinary in the trophy room, just the usual relics and skeletons of weird monsters, like a stuffed griffin and a multi-headed snake thing. The same with the gunroom, with the antique blunderbusses, the cannon, a machine gun from the First World War, some explosives, war axes, and other weapons and paraphernalia. Empty bathrooms she couldn't be certain ever got used, spare bedrooms she *knew* never got used. Just a bunch of wasted, dead space.

The door to an upstairs bathroom was locked, so she banged on it. She heard no response, but pounded again.

"Something the matter?" his voice came from the other side.

"You put the human flesh in the fridge?!" she demanded.

"Where else could it be put?"

"Just leave it in the cooler, maybe? I have to *eat* out of that fridge, you know? I'm going to get hepatitis or something! Also, that's disgusting! Why would you do that?"

"The cooler isn't going to keep cold for long. Surely you know that? The fridge can be cleaned out."

"You could have warned me!" she shouted.

She heard him shuffling around in there, then the door opened. The bandage was gone, so it was just him and his sliced head. Literally. No towel, no nothing. She blinked and aimed her eyes at anything else: the ceiling, the doorjamb, the walls. Then she noticed bloody footprints leading back to the tub, where he must have been sitting, if she could guess by the gore she saw there. That was probably to keep from making a bigger mess. There was a book and his phone on the counter.

"There's human flesh in the fridge," he told her.

"Oh, you're *hilarious*," she hissed.

"You were gone."

"Text me next time!"

"Fine."

He shut the door.

"That's it?" she shouted through the wood.

"I'm not interested in arguing with you," he said.

She made rude gestures at the door.

"Who's arguing? I'm not arguing! I'm just asking for some consideration, is all. Just common courtesy! 'Hey, just so you know, there's a biohazard in the fridge'!"

He opened the door again, this time in a robe.

"I apologize. That was inconsiderate of me," he said.

"Thank you!"

"Now, if you don't mind, I need to manage this injury. If you have nothing urgent to bring to my attention, please stop bothering me until sundown."

She stared at his head. It was one of the grossest things she'd ever seen, and it was still bleeding. How long would it do that?

"Good day." He shut the door again. She heard the lock click this time.

She glared at the door. Just as the words were lining up to leave her mouth, she thought better of mentioning the satyr. Knowing him, he'd get angry with Fjola or Ginko, or else he'd tell her it was her fault for going out there in the first place. She shuffled her feet. She hated him with all her strength.

Dracula's Death

Still, she decided pestering him further wasn't a good idea, so she went downstairs and got some water from the well for Fjola, who accepted it with gratitude. Cammy drank several glasses herself.

Fjola meekly excused herself, leaving Cammy alone to process what had happened and what she intended to do about it. She went to his study. It was unlocked, so she let herself in. In the center presided a huge mahogany desk. An ancient inkwell was situated beside a modern feather pen, probably a novelty item of some kind. There were also ballpoint and expensive ink pens. A ledger lay open in the center of the desk, but she knew she wouldn't be able to read what he wrote in it. She suspected he left that stuff out where she could see it because he knew she couldn't read it. It looked like some sort of accounting, all in neat columns with numbers on one side. Maybe it was for keeping track of his wine.

Antique bookcases lined all the walls. Most of the books were in Latin, but there were some in French, German, and other languages here and there. There was an entire section in English, including a book called *Ancient Legends, Mystic Charms, and Superstitions of Ireland* written by Lady Jane Wilde. She'd looked inside; Lady Jane Wilde had inscribed a message inside the book which read, *"We were terribly sorry to hear about poor Margaret. I do hope that you will visit again. With love."*

Cammy didn't know who Margaret was, but Dracula had explained that he had known Lady Jane Wilde and her son Oscar Wilde during the Victorian Era, and it was through them he had made the acquaintance of Bram Stoker. He didn't talk much about his time in England, only to say that London had been horrible and he'd hated it. He said he'd spent more time in Ireland, though he remained unspecific about dates. He apparently hadn't cared very much for Bram

Stoker, but she wasn't sure if his dislike for the Irishman was a result of his annoyance at the book.

There was an antique record player he'd shown her how to use, so she found a record of music by a singer named Maria Tanase—it didn't matter to Cammy who this was, she just wanted noise—and set down the needle to play it. Then she flipped through Lady Jane's book. Fairytales had always fascinated her, but now that she knew some of them might be real, her childish wonder had been replaced with trepidation. Knowing they could be real put a horrifying spin on some of them.

About twenty minutes after the sun had set, Dracula made a reappearance. She had wandered back upstairs, played a mobile game for a while, done some studying for Midterms, and then made her way back into his study. He walked in on her sitting in his leather chair flipping aimlessly through a book she guessed was in Polish or Russian. Her phone couldn't translate it into anything useful.

His head was all in one piece again, to her relief, though his face was unusually and frighteningly pale, almost corpse-like. At least the bath had gotten all that blood off. His hair was a still little damp. The clean clothes he had put on were the same style: all black, immaculate, pressed shirt and pants.

"Sorry, I guess I freaked out earlier," she told him as he stood in the door, one hand tucked in his pocket. He had a book in his other hand. He said nothing, just crossed the room and put the book away.

"When can we get rid of that stuff so I can clean the fridge and eat something?" she asked.

"The elves haven't taken care of it yet?"

"Were they supposed to?"

Dracula's Death

"Yes."

They both made their way to the kitchen, and found the bags all gone. That was a relief, at least.

"Do you wish to pick up something to eat?" Dracula asked, once they had determined the fridge was clear.

"*Please.* I'm starving."

"Very well, but first I need to...." He opened a cupboard, fetched a loaf of bread and wheel of cheese, and sliced off an enormous chunk of each. He practically inhaled the oversized portions while Cammy prepared a much more reasonably sized open-faced sandwich. Yes, he ate food. He finished the dictionary-sized wedge of bread and cheese before she'd finished her own serving, and immediately prepared another sandwich, just as large as the first. He managed to go through the entire wheel of cheese and the rest of the bread before she was done. She considered his pallid complexion.

"Um, are you ok?" she asked him.

"Famished," he said.

Well, that probably wasn't good. He didn't like to advertise it, but he did need blood. That was one of the first things she'd asked him about, way back when deciding to stay in his mansion. Weirdest conversation *ever*. Apparently a mouthful or two every few days was usually enough. And getting bitten by him wouldn't turn a person into a vampire. Still... yuck.

He'd actually, well, not *bitten* her, but sucked blood out of the back of her hand after the vampire attack he'd saved her from, to verify that she was still human. She rubbed her knuckles at the memory.

She heard a startling rattle against the window. The *rat tat tat* kept getting louder, so she stood and went to see what it was.

"It's hailing," Dracula observed.

"Yeah, a lot," she agreed. Outside the window she could see white balls the size of dimes bouncing on the grass and the driveway. "What's the deal? It was so nice this morning."

She jumped as he came up behind her to peer out at the rattling spheres of ice. He squinted. "That's odd," he muttered.

"Yeah. I haven't seen hail like that... maybe ever."

"Hmmm," was all he said.

They had just reached the door to go get food when Dracula's phone rang.

"Hello?" he answered. Someone's voice buzzed for a few moments, and he "Hmm'ed" periodically, then said, "I'll be there. Have something ready for me when I arrive. My earlier encounter took a lot out of me." He flipped the phone shut.

"Work?" Cammy checked.

"What else?" he said.

CHAPTER 5
UNDER THE WEATHER

To his enormous irritation, he had to use one of his other vehicles, since his work car had not yet been sufficiently cleaned to be safe to use. But he had to head out, and if he didn't eat soon he might become dangerous.

It had been so long he'd all but entirely forgotten what it had felt like to be ravenous while he was alive, but he did have a memory of being beset by this consuming hunger when he first woke up, overwhelmed by how much stronger it was than anything he'd experienced in life. Many physical sensations were all but gone, or gone altogether, but hunger and sexual desire remained, and were magnified. Hunger was the worst, by far.

They stopped at a drive-thru that had the sort of vegetarian options Cammy liked. It was against his policy to eat in one of his vehicles, but he made an exception this time. Food was the worst possible solution, but it was what he could acquire on short notice and would at least chip the tiniest chink off the hunger. Food was the least helpful, followed by water, the best being...what he resented most of all. In the meanwhile, food was not much, but better than nothing. Cammy nibbled on a vegetarian burrito while he wolfed down the five loaded ones he ordered for himself.

They took the edge off, but that was all. He drained the water he had purchased, and it helped a bit more.

"Why does the food taste so vile?" he grumbled as they drove away.

"What do you mean?" Cammy checked.

"Nearly all modern food tastes wrong," he said.

"I don't know. GMOs or something?" she suggested, then, in apparent curiosity, "All of it?"

"It's less vile at some of the high-class establishments," he clarified.

"Do you eat out much?"

He pulled up next to a trashcan, lowered his window, and tossed his burrito wrappers into it. She handed him hers as well, and that got tossed through the hail into the can. He had not eaten out very often since she had taken up residence at his manor. He never felt confident that she would not get up to mischief in his absence.

"Quite often," he said, which certainly *had* been true. "Not fast-food, though."

"So you have an active night life?" she asked, a little smile tugging at the corners of her mouth. He wondered if she were insinuating a double entendre. No doubt the idea of him going out at night was amusing her. He decided not to let this irritate him, and to assume she meant it rather innocently. His thoughts would play tricks on him now if he wasn't careful.

He took the freeway, but had to drive more slowly than usual, for the hail was hammering down. Out of curiosity, he tuned in to a local radio station to see what the newscasters were saying about the weather. A local DJ gave some useless commentary and admonished drivers to be careful, but nothing more.

Dracula's Death

Lightning crackled overhead, illuminating the road. He could see perfectly well in the dark, but he didn't want to be pulled over, so he drove with the headlights on. The hail collided with his windshield, the impacts creating a cacophony rendered semi-rhythmic by the wipers sweeping back and forth to clear the ice away.

"Do you think... is it possible the weather right now is supernatural?" Cammy wondered aloud.

"Very possibly."

"Really? There are thingies that can affect the weather?" she asked.

"Strigoii can affect the weather," Dracula told her. "If they bathe, they can cause rain to fall." Occasionally, a lord in Wallachia might order all his men to bathe if there hadn't been any rain, just in case one of them was a strigoi. He declined to share this information with her.

She looked askance at him.

"The ones with tails," he added.

She looked even more askance.

"I am not one of those kind," he explained. "This has nothing to do with me."

That mollified her somewhat, and she looked out the window. She seemed to think he had powers that explained everything he did, which was hardly true. As a matter of fact, he had next to nothing in the way of what she would consider "powers". Yes, he could see exceptionally well in the dark, and had enhanced strength—his current level of strength seemed to be a consequence of expectations perpetuated by movies, as he had only been endowed with it for a few decades—but all those stories of hypnotic powers and shape-changing were merely fantastic. Stoker had made up a character who was a mix of some sort of Irish ghost or bogey and a Satan-worshipping necromancer, with vague strigoi-esque aesthetic sprinkled artlessly on top, like a sprig of parsley dropped on a plate of shoe leather served up as a subpar steak. Stoker's bastard creation bore very little resemblance to what he was; instead, Stoker had imitated the lurid depictions of vampires popularized by such writers as Goethe, Dr. Polidori, and Le Fanu. It infuriated Dracula that his family name had been rendered synonymous with such crassness.

His phone rang.

"Hello?" he said into it.

"Hi! It's Lindsey. I was wondering if you were free tomorrow night? Hector won't be here again, and I don't want to dance with some of the creeps that show up."

"I apologize, but I have a project that will keep me busy for a few days. I doubt I will have the time," he answered.

"Oh." The disappointment in the young woman's voice was palpable. Lindsey didn't seem to realize how clearly she wore her heart on her sleeve. She also didn't seem to have realized she was infatuated with him. Not the first time that had happened, but it was awkward, given that Lindsey was one of Cammy's friends. He spotted Cammy watching him with hawk-like suspicion as he spoke. "Well, thanks anyway."

"I hope you are able to find a suitable dance partner. I will let you know if my schedule changes. Goodbye," he said, and hung up.

"Who was that?" Cammy asked.

"Your friend, Miss Lindsey, the one who likes dancing. Her regular partner is unavailable tomorrow evening and she was asking if I could step in. But I doubt I will solve this matter by then."

Lindsey was by far the most amiable of Cammy's friends. When Lindsey had discovered he knew how to dance, she had tentatively asked for his help, since there were several men in her dance classes who were "creeps" as she called them, and she couldn't always rely on more trustworthy partners to keep them at bay. He had accepted the chance to engage socially with a new group, and besides, his dancing skills had been growing rusty from lack of practice. She had asked him to partner with her a few times over the last few months for specific events, and he had accepted.

"Do you have to?" Cammy asked.

"To what?" he asked.

"You know, see her?" Cammy explained.

"I'm not 'seeing' her," he corrected. "I occasionally dance with her when she needs a skilled partner."

"Yeah, but I think she likes you."

"She does."

Cammy blinked at him.

"So could you stop encouraging her?" Cammy said. "I mean, that's my friend, you know."

"I know. I've told her where I stand. I'm also sleeping with her dance instructor."

She blinked harder to convey her shock and disapproval. "Are you kidding me?!"

"Why would I kid about that?" he asked, and took a right.

"Why are you sleeping with her dance instructor?" Cammy demanded.

"Because Belinda is a very attractive woman with no strings attached, and at an age I prefer." He found her discomfort amusing. It indicated she was unfamiliar with men. A rarity in the modern age.

"You're a pig," she told him.

"Forgive me, but I thought you wanted me *not* to engage with your friend?" he said. "Or would you rather I slept with Miss Lindsey instead?"

"That's it. I'm not having this conversation," Cammy said, and crossed her arms. "You're a pig. I can't believe you."

"Miss Lindsey is a very attractive woman," he told her. "If I were a pig, I'd have landed her a long time ago. Or perhaps the both of them at once."

"La la la!" Cammy stuck her fingers in her ears.

"When you think about it, I've passed most of the difficult hurdles. I've already had my hands all over her—"

"I don't want to hear this! La!"

He smirked in the dark while Cammy turned to the window.

"Why are you even dancing with her to begin with?" Cammy demanded. "I mean, suddenly you're friends with all my friends?"

"Not all. Officer Warren doesn't care for me. I frankly dislike your co-worker, Miss Quentin. And you may recall you were the one who introduced me to them. As for Miss Lindsey, it has been *decades* since I could go out dancing with anyone."

Cammy squinted at him suspiciously.

"So... what? You were lonely or something?"

Lonely? What a question. Could someone in his position be anything else? Who could he possibly call a companion? Lindsey, like Cammy, was a young woman by legal definition, but the both of them seemed much more like children than he recalled similarly aged women in the past.

They turned down a road that led away from the city, and Cammy pressed her forehead against the passenger window for a better view. Hail and broken branches and leaves lay strewn over the road. Just past a bend in the road a vehicle about the size and shape of a SWAT truck, bearing some sort of food logo, lay on its side, ripped wide open. About ten other vehicles were clustered around it, government plates visible in the headlights as they drew closer. Agents of Special Services stood in the hail, their collars up against the weather, marking off sections of the ground or holding strange devices. Maybe they were taking readings for ectoplasm or some such nonsense.

"Hoo boy, this looks bad," Cammy said.

"I knew it," Dracula grumbled.

"Knew what?"

"Knew they'd caused this." In truth, he hadn't *known*, but he'd had a suspicion that the department's agents had mishandled some situation. He pulled off behind one of the other vehicles and parked the car. "Did you bring a flashlight?" he asked Cammy. She fiddled with her phone and a bright light shone out of it.

"Never leave the bat cave without it," she said, and grinned. He frowned, trying to parse this phrase. It sounded like an allusion, possibly a reference to *the book*, though she knew he hated it. Additionally, she knew he had nothing to do with bats. He offered no comment, instead indicating the glove compartment. Cammy opened it to reveal a folding umbrella, one of his guns, and a pair of gloves.

"Thanks, I got one of those, too." She pulled the handle of a pocket umbrella out of her bag to show him.

"For me," he said.

She looked embarrassed and hastily passed his own to him. Freezing air rushed into the vehicle as he opened the door, hail pelting his knuckles, his head and shoulders. He opened the umbrella, indifferent to the temperature, but concerned for his suit. He saw Cammy shuddering from the cold. How curious and amusing that she carried an umbrella and flashlight—or at least a phone that served the same function—with her everywhere, but couldn't remember to dress for the weather.

She followed behind him. He assumed she had acquired the habit of using him as a shield in uncertain situations, a sign of intelligence, or at least prudence, for which he could be grateful. Small miracles. Hail pelted his umbrella, and wet grass clung to his shoes. He realized that Cammy might have some difficulty, so he slowed his pace in order not to leave her behind in the dark.

"You have got to be joking." Ah, the grating, gravelly voice of the man he detested most. A man in his late fifties or early sixties stepped into the beams of the headlights—though Dracula could see him without their illumination—scowling at Dracula and Cammy both from beneath the cover of his own umbrella. Director Roger Boese. Dracula adopted an expression of innocent bewilderment.

"You want to explain why you brought her along?" Boese demanded, pointing at Cammy.

"I couldn't hire a sitter in time," Dracula replied. Boese seethed, nearly snarling in rage. Dracula did not let his face smile, though he did inside his mind.

"Neil told me about your attitude this morning," Boese continued. He had a thin, drawn face, a series of scars cutting along one cheek to his ear, which was notched. Those scars had marred the man's face even when he was a young recruit for the department. Boese's head was shaved clean, as was his chin—no doubt a precaution against being hexed. Despite his age, Boese was a prime physical specimen, as were the other agents.

"Ah, Neil. That was his name," Dracula muttered. "I had it wrong."

"You think just because the Cold War's over I won't bury you again?" Boese growled. "Because I will. You give me grief and I'll have you back in your little box so fast it'll make your head come off. Literally." He poked Dracula in the chest. "You know what I'm talking about. See how well your little monster sanctuary does while you're on ice for a few years. Or decades. Now, *politely*, tell me what she is doing here."

DRACULA'S DEATH

"She wanted to come," Dracula explained innocently.

"And you brought her?"

"She's my guest, and she hadn't had anything to eat." Dracula maintained the affected, perfectly innocent tone, knowing it would grate on Boese's nerves.

"Can it. This doesn't happen again. Do I make myself clear?"

"Perfectly clear."

Boese squinted at him. "You're a damn liar."

"I am. But you have made yourself clear. I'm not disputing that fact."

"She doesn't come along anymore. Say it."

Dracula raised two fingers in salute. "Scout's honor," he said.

"That does it." Boese reached into his coat, pulled out a packet and broke it open. Dracula recognized it. The director liked to carry garlic to harass and chivy the vampires who reacted to the stuff. Once Dracula had realized Boese thought garlic affected him he had played along. In truth, he detested the smell and he could not eat the plant, but its mere presence was no deterrent. But to maintain the masquerade —one never knew when a feigned weakness could come in handy—he grunted and stepped backward before Boese could thrust the packet in his face. Cammy stepped between them.

Boese glared down at her. This was not their first confrontation, and it pleased Dracula to see that she had not lost any of her brash defiance. She did her best to puff herself up, comical as that looked, and not to blink at his pale blue eyes, nor give any ground.

"Camellia," Boese said, smiling like a snake. "We meet again. You and your bleeding heart, eh?"

"Well, yeah. I'm a vegetarian for a reason," she told him. "I don't like seeing animals tortured."

"That's not an animal." He pointed behind her, at Dracula. "That's a monster."

"So are you," she told him.

He scoffed. "You haven't seen how bad these things can be. Him? He's using you as a shield. Look at yourself. Look at what you're doing. How long have you known him? A year? I've known him for thirty. He's shifty. A manipulator, and a liar. No conscience at all, and no loyalty, no different from any run-of-the-mill psychopath. You haven't seen what he's really like, not like I have."

Dracula said nothing. He had defied the United States government over Russia's annexation of his homeland after World War II, and so earned himself a neat little prison sentence. Boese had spent most of those thirty years chopping his prisoner into varied bits to see what he could accomplish with science. It was hardly the first time he had been a prisoner, alas. Dracula had deceived the director as much as he was able, but he saw no reason to remark on this, nor attempt to defend himself. He did not think reticence could truly be interpreted as the actions of a deranged, evil maniac.

He tapped Cammy gently on the shoulder.

"As my guest, it's absolutely unthinkable for you to put yourself in danger to protect me from discomfort," Dracula told her. "Don't worry. He and I have a history and an understanding. Don't we?"

"You don't need your teeth to do your job," Boese said.

"You think you can take them?"

"You mean again? Of course I can," said Boese. "Now shut up and listen. This takes highest priority."

"I'm staying," Cammy insisted. Boese stuck a finger in her face.

"Shut up," he growled.

Dracula's Death

This time Dracula put an arm between the two of them, though he snarled silently when Boese waved the packet in his face. Appearances.

"Do not mistake the nature of this situation," he told Boese. "Cammy is my guest. I am an old-fashioned man at heart, and I am honor-bound to defend her."

"You so much as lay a hand on me and I'll have you put through a blender," Boese told him.

"Then I'll make sure to kill you if I lay a hand on you."

"We'll have you incinerated."

"You'll still be short a head."

"And all your little pets will be next," Boese told him. "We'll burn that whole place to the ground."

"Um, *excuse me,* but I thought there was something *important* going on?" Cammy cut in. Boese glared at her and then stalked towards the truck.

"We managed to get a hold of a pretty rare specimen," he explained. "Down near the border with Mexico. We were bringing it up here because we figured the climate here would conceal its presence. Who'd notice more rain in Seattle? However...." He waved at the demolished truck. Cammy peered through the gloom. The other vehicles were pointed more or less outward at the surroundings. Other agencies might want to shed light on the scene of the crime; this one wanted its eyes on the dark. One never knew what was lurking in the dark. Cammy flicked on her phone flashlight again and pointed it at the wreck.

Dracula had been studying the damage: rear tire torn literally to shreds, and there were obvious claw marks in the metal. The front was smashed by some incredible impact, but there was nothing on the road that could explain the crater in the grill. The truck's side was warped out, revealing two dead men in military gear, armed with guns. One was missing an arm and a leg, the other's head was in a corner. A few bullet dents dotted the torn edges of the metal, but only a few. Either the two men inside had been killed before they could get many shots off, or there were a lot of bullets that had walked off somewhere. Broken chains were fastened to the walls of the van, but no sign of what they might have restrained.

"Hang on a minute," Cammy said, noticing a blood stain on the warped metal. "Is that what I think it is?" She pointed.

Dracula put a hand up to the bloody paw print that had half-dissolved in the hail and intermittent rain. His hand and the print were about the same size.

"Tiger?" she wondered.

"That's my thinking," he agreed. "Curious. There seem to be a great deal more of them than we thought."

Cammy glanced at Boese. She had a natural, inborn cunning, but no experience hiding her intentions. If Boese did not already know about Emet, he could not possibly miss the hint she had just flashed at him.

"Would you mind?" Dracula asked her, gesturing at the truck.

She passed him her phone to hold while she pulled out the adder stone. She looked through it. Slowly, she made a pass over the truck, avoiding the two dead men and the bulk of the gore, then up at the sky.

"You were right. Something's causing all this hail," she said, and passed him the stone. "It's that funny glow again."

There was the glitter of magic hanging like a cloud inside the truck, and up in the sky he could see a faint haze as well. He handed the stone back, climbed into the truck, and looked over the carnage inside. This was doing nothing to assuage his hunger, alas. He inspected the wounds: the limbs had been ripped clean out of their sockets by something with incredible strength. Good to know. His own could also be torn free, and he did not intend to lose them in a fight. He'd had enough of that late last year when a *draugr* had ravaged the city. Hesitantly, since he knew Cammy would see, Dracula dipped a finger in the blood that pooled on the floor and tasted it. He could discern human blood not by taste, but by effect. Human blood tasted like life and carried with it a sensation that nothing else bestowed. The blood in the truck gave that effect, pure and unadulterated. If the guards had injured their assailant in the fight, it had left no blood behind as evidence, else it would have mingled with the rest by now. He informed the agents of the fact.

"What were you transporting?" he asked.

"A ccoa," Boese explained. "We have no idea what it was doing traveling north through Mexico. They're usually in Peru. Hell, we thought they were extinct, like centaurs and cyclopes."

"A ccoa?" Cammy asked.

Boese glared at her again. "Yeah, a sort of demon-god from Peru. It" —he nodded at the sky— "can cause weather like this."

"Why would you *want* this thing?" Cammy wondered. Dracula didn't wonder at all. Boese, and by extension the whole department, was fueled by a mixture of fear and suspicion and clinical curiosity. They wanted to study it, to see if it could be killed, then kill it. Boese must have some pull with his higher ups to get the thing transported this far north. There were other Special Services headquarters between the border of Mexico and here who would ordinarily have priority. Or perhaps they really had thought Seattle's climate would serve as camouflage for the creature's magical effect on the weather. While rain was common enough in Seattle, hail was not.

"Because you can bribe it with food, like all the rest of these ridiculous nature spirit-god-demons," Boese snapped, "and being able to control weather would be damned useful."

"What does it look like?" Dracula asked.

"About two feet long, if you don't include the tail. It's a gray cat with stripes."

"It's a kitty?" Cammy asked. "Sounds cute!"

"They sodomize and strangle women to death," Boese told her. Cammy shut her mouth. Dracula climbed out of the truck and handed her the adder stone back. Boese eyed the gesture with unveiled suspicion.

"Can it be killed?" Dracula asked.

"Sure. How else would they be going extinct?" Boese countered.

"Maybe they've moved elsewhere, like the Good People," Dracula offered. "Or they have been sapped of power because no one worships them anymore since the advent of Christianity and the subsequent taming and defeat of daemons and spirits, which everyone *used* to celebrate."

"Whatever. Look, we need this thing back, and we need to know how it already had connections. The van was attacked from the outside. Then we wipe those local threats out. Understand?"

"This seems perfectly straightforward," said Dracula. "I believe I asked for payment up front on this one. My encounter this morning took a lot of the fight out of me."

"Maybe if you weren't so distracted chasing your piece of tail all over the place, that wouldn't have happened," Boese told him.

"Um, *excuse me*," Cammy snapped. "I know no one believes me, but we're *not* a thing. Also, *wow*. You *sure* you've got the moral high ground?"

"I didn't say *you* were chasing *him*," Boese told her.

Dracula's Death

"Payment. Now," Dracula said.

"No, you can wait. Why don't you go make some friends in the Underground and get yourself something to eat? Or send one of your minions to fetch something," Boese suggested. "Then if you catch the ccoa and clear the weather up, we'll supply you what you need, right?"

They eyed each other. Dracula weighed the risks. Push his luck here, or wait, since time was on his side? He had always preferred acting from a position of strength; despite that, he had stupidly overreached himself in the past, to his own downfall. It was a flaw of some kind; his rage, or else his pride, or both. Push the tiny man? Or let the matter pass? He could wait for a better opportunity that would not put his tenants or Cammy at risk. His men and his country had paid the price when he'd overreached, and paid dearly. Not again. Not this time.

The hail was pelting Cammy's umbrella, and he saw how she shivered. Dracula walked past Boese to the car, and Cammy followed his lead. Ah, how the caged bird only sang at night indeed. She dropped down into the seat, knocking a few hailstones out of her hair as she closed the umbrella and set it on the floor.

He pulled out his phone and dialed. "Malcolm," he said, "I need a favor."

"You better not really," Malcolm grumbled in answer, "I have my whole evening planned."

"I need you to take Cammy back to the estate," Dracula told him.

"Hey, what? No, I'm going with," Cammy protested.

"Ugh. I can meet you at the donut shop near the exit to your place. Won't be a huge detour. You'll pay me?" Malcolm checked.

"Of course. I'll meet you there. Thank you." He hung up.

"Hello? I'm staying with you," Cammy said.

"By no means. Do you think I'm insane enough to drag you along on a quest after a god-demon that controls the weather and that rapes and kills women?"

"Err," said Cammy.

"Exactly."

Cammy refused to stay stumped. "But there will be more tiger thingies," she said.

"The last one almost took my head off. Where would that have left you?"

"Well, I—"

"What I'm saying is it almost went clean through me, and then it would have probably eaten you."

"I was right by the door," she countered. "I'd have escaped."

He scoffed audibly to show his derision. "You were going to make a run for it?" he asked, incredulous.

"Well, yeah. What else could I do if it took your head off?"

"Not shoot it, apparently."

"You gave me a gun!"

"Which you left in your purse with the safety on. You might as well have not had it at all. Since I know you don't take your own safety seriously, I can't take you with me on anything serious."

"That's not fair," she said.

"You want me not to treat you like a child, yet your only response is to say 'That's not fair?'" he asked. She made no sense at all.

The hail broke into small chunks on the windshield and was piling up on either side of the clear zone the wipers made while she chewed on her tongue and thought.

"So am I your pet or what?" she asked out of the clear blue.

"Are you my *pet*?" he repeated, deeply confused. The lights of the city turned the ice shards into little glittering stars on the windshield.

"What am I to you?"

"You're my guest," he answered. He had told her so a dozen times. Listening seemed impossible for her.

"But why? You could have kicked me to the curb. You could have let me deal with Heather all on my own. Like you did with Emet. Why didn't you?"

The wipers made obnoxious sounds as they swept away the hail clacking against the windshield. She could surely see his face in the dim glow as the streetlights passed overhead, if she was trying to read him, as she often did.

"Well?" she prompted. "I mean, since you say you didn't rescue me in the first place. Is Boese right? Are you're using me like some sort of chess piece against him?"

"Don't be ridiculous," he told her. "He'd put a bullet in you if he really thought you were in the way, and he'd do it at a time and place I would not be able to prevent. If anything, he is using you against me."

"Ok, so what's the answer?" she asked.

He had absolutely no intention of telling her that he had hoped to find some modern person to study as representative of the whole mass. He touched his mouth, tapping at it with his finger to think of an answer she might accept.

"*Food?*" she asked, horrified.

"Of course not," he snapped. "I have my own supply. Do you really think I would do that?"

"You tasted my blood!"

"Only because I thought I would never see you again and that was my only opportunity to ascertain whether you were still human."

"Can you answer my stupid question, please?" she grumbled.

He sighed.

"Because you came to find me," he said. "You came to find me, and you weren't trying to kill me or ask me to fight a war for you or want something from me. And you didn't open a dialogue by asking me how many people I'd killed."

"I wasn't sure whether you were real," she reminded him.

"Well, that's why," he told her. "You have your answer."

She watched him as the streetlights played over them both.

"You mean... because I wasn't afraid of you?"

"If you like."

She looked out the window. The hail continued its barrage. People on the street were covering their heads or huddling under umbrellas like frightened dogs. The ice piled against streetlights, beside the curbs, to the sides of buildings. So much for Boese's hopes of camouflaging the presence of a magical monster. Water ran down the streets, bits of crushed ice washing away with it.

"Boese says you're a liar." Perhaps Cammy was trying to dismantle his defense.

"He's not wrong," said Dracula.

"So you *are* a liar?"

"I've had a lot of practice."

"You're a liar and you just admit to it?"

"I don't lie to everyone," he said. "Just those who need to be lied to."

She squinted at him, then set her chin in her hand and watched the street pass by outside.

He pulled the car up beside the donut shop.

"I want to help," she insisted.

He reached across her and opened the car door. When she didn't move he made a shooing gesture at her.

"You're a jerk," she said, and scooched out of the car.

DRACULA'S DEATH

"Give my regards to Malcolm," he told her.
She slammed the door.

CHAPTER 6
UNDERGROUND

The internet told her more about the ccoa than Boese had, though it did provide some contradictory information, such as whether the cats were winged or whether they were usually female. The general consensus was that they were dangerous and powerful at least, and malevolent at worst. She watched the hail come down outside. The piles were inches high in some places.

She pulled out her earbuds when she saw a formerly beautifully polished cherry red car drive up. Under the shelter of her umbrella, she darted for the passenger side door and dropped down in the seat. The interior of his car was just as immaculate as any of Dracula's, but she doubted Malcolm had a team of household spirits to help him keep it clean.

"Hey, easy! I just had this detailed," Malcolm told her.

His cologne smell filled the whole car. This was going to be a fun ride.

"Hi," she said. "Thanks for coming to get me."

"Sure."

His eyes tracked her umbrella all the way to the floor as she settled it by her feet.

"Calm down, it's only water."

Dracula's Death

"I built this car with my own two hands," he told her. "My two little hands." He held up his decidedly *not* little hands to show her. He had the hands of a basketball player, though not the height.

"I get it. I'll be careful."

He turned his music back up, a synth pop track from his playlist.

"Doesn't all this chemical smell bother you?" she wondered as he took them back onto the road. So much driving back and forth today.

"It masks the other smells," he said. "It gets confusing in here otherwise."

Huh. Maybe having super keen werewolf senses wasn't all that great.

"How was your day?" she asked. Knee-jerk polite gestures were still ingrained in her, it seemed. *Thanks, mom,* she thought.

"Same old."

Not much of a conversationalist. Well, perhaps not much of a conversationalist if he wasn't interested in you. Considering how often he had dates, he must be charming when he wanted to be. She'd seen him turn it on and off before. No sooner had she thought that than his phone rang. He tapped his phone—he had an up to date one and could easily talk hands free.

"Hey, babe. Sorry, I have a little detour. I'll be by a little later," he said in a smooth, warm voice.

"Ooh, you're going to make me wait? What could possibly keep a naughty boy like you away?" a young, female voice responded. Cammy rolled her eyes.

"Just gotta run an errand. I'll make it up to you."

"What errand?" asked the woman on the phone. "Seeing your side girl?"

"Oh, bae, you know you're my one and only." Malcolm winked at Cammy. She leveled an expressionless, blank stare back. "See you soon, I promise."

"Bye, I'll be waiting."

He hung up, grinning that winning grin.

"Really?" Cammy snarked.

"Yeah, gotta keep busy," he said.

"What about the weather?" She pointed out the window. He glanced up at the sky through his windshield wipers and curled a lip at it.

"Sucks," he said. "But I'm not being paid to care."

"What if it damages your car?" she asked.

"It better not. Besides, she's got a garage. I can park in there."

"Apparently it's serious," Cammy said. "A ccoa."

"A what?" Malcolm laughed.

Wow. Even *he* didn't know everything. Maybe Boese having a whole squadron of goons made sense. There was too much for anyone to know. No wonder there were so many people hired by the department. Maybe no one had the full list.

"Some kind of cat from Peru," she explained. "And there are these tigers that can turn into people who are helping it."

Malcolm's smile evaporated and he scowled at the street.

"Were-tigers?" he checked. "From where?"

"South Asia, I think."

He fell silent and stared into the road ahead as the hail continued to *crunch* to pieces under the wipers.

"That's strange," he said. "Most of the were-tigers from that area aren't hostile unless they have to be."

"Well, these ones eat humans," Cammy told him.

"What, you saw one?"

"Three. One was dead at the start, though."

Dracula's Death

"Three? There are three of them here? In Seattle?" Malcolm checked.

"More than that. At least eight. Looks like more."

"That's damn weird," he said. "We've got a branch over there. I've got some cousins who are were-tigers, actually, a couple times removed, of course, but they don't have to be hostile. A lot of them live amongst humans without causing trouble."

"Really?" Cammy asked. Then the two Dracula had killed earlier had been telling the truth? But why did they have human flesh in their fridge? "Why would they keep killing and eating people, then?" she asked. He shrugged.

"No idea, honestly. Eight? Here? Strange. Maybe they're losing habitat back home. I suppose a lot of traffic from Asia comes through Seattle. That's how you guys ended up with that tanuki, or whatever it's called."

"Tanuki, yeah," Cammy confirmed. She tapped on the window. "Say, Malcolm—"

"No," he said, raising a hand. "To whatever it is, no. I'm not doing it. I have a date. Besides, I know you're broke."

"So what? You're always doing favors for Vlad."

"He pays me," Malcolm told her.

"Pays you what?"

"What do you think? Money, most of the time. Favors in return other times. I told you before, I don't work for peanuts."

"Well, this thing is big, like, really big. Boese came down himself."

"Uh huh." Malcolm turned the volume up a little.

"Hey!" She turned the knob down.

"Listen!" he snapped. "I know this is all fun and games and one big carnival ride for you. For me, it's not. It's work. It's hard work, and I don't like it very much, but unlike you, I don't get to choose my job, ok? Right now, I'm off the clock. I want to do nothing, think about nothing. I want to get drunk, I want to meet up with my date, and wake up tomorrow with a hangover that could kill a bear, all right?"

She sighed.

"Sure," she said.

"Thank you."

He turned the volume back up. The speaker vibrated next to her ankle and he bobbed his head to the beat.

"This is a big deal though," she cut in. He gritted his perfect teeth. "I mean, I know you're off the clock now, but it's possible you're going to get—"

"Cammy, if you jinx me, so help me I will find someone to put a hex on you. Mark my words," he said.

"Fine. Ok. Whatever."

Three tracks later his phone rang. He checked the number and started swearing like the most blasphemous sailor ever born. Carefully, he pulled over to the side of the road, seething so much he changed color. Then he turned off the music, answered the phone, and his tone was professional.

"Malcolm. Go ahead."

"We got a job. The department's paying half up front this time. You're up."

Malcolm glared at Cammy.

"What's the job?" he asked.

"They think there are were-tigers running in a group. They've stolen property from the department."

"Copy that," Malcolm said. "Send me the details. I'm on it." He hung up the phone and sat back in the chair. He punched the console, then slid his fingers gently across it, as though to check there was no damage or to soothe the car. Cammy noticed his knuckles were torn.

"Sorry," she said.

Dracula's Death

"I hate my life," he grumbled. "I really do."

Cammy hunched down and stared at her feet.

Sulkily, Malcolm texted the girl he'd been on the phone with earlier. His phone *pinged* and he opened the email that his higher ups at Ophois must have sent him. He read through it, scowling all the while.

"Just perfect," he growled. "*Perfect.*"

"Are you going to get someone to put a hex on me now?" Cammy asked. He slowly turned to look at her in disbelief. "Are you?" she wondered.

"How does he put up with you?" Malcolm grumbled. He put on his blinker, then pulled back onto the road.

"Well, since you're working now," Cammy said. "Maybe I could help?"

"Ha ha and ha," Malcolm snarked.

"I'm serious."

"I'm being paid to drive you back home safe and sound," he told her.

"Yeah, ok, so I'll come with you, and so long as I get back safe you'll get paid. It'll be like a detour."

Malcolm snorted and chuckled with disbelief.

"Are you certifiably insane?" he asked. "I'm serious. Certifiable. I'd bet good money on it."

"Don't be ridiculous," she snapped. She tapped on the window again. "You know, I could make it worth your while."

"*Gross,*" he said, wrinkling his nose. "No thanks."

"Ok, *wow*. I did *not* mean like that," she said.

"Then how did you mean it? You mean you'll pay me? With what? Your barista job wages? You still owe me for that whole package of fake documents for the elf kids."

"No, with information. You want to get this over with as fast as possible, right? Well, I know where to start. I already saw three of these things."

"Oh, *noooo*," Malcolm groaned. She pulled the adder stone out so he could see it.

"I bet this will make your job a whole lot easier. Perhaps go faster? Get you back to your date?"

Malcolm bared his teeth and gripped the steering wheel.

"I hate you. I hate you so much," he said, and turned the car around to head back into the city. She smiled.

She navigated him back to the apartment where Dracula had killed the two were-tigers, since she still had the address in her phone. Happy coincidence, and she was going to take it. They went back up to the fourth floor. The lights looked eerie at night, like going through a haunted hospital or something; it turned the floors and walls of dingy surfaces with the years of ground-in dirt into a feeling more than just the anti-aesthetic.

The door to the apartment was closed, but Malcolm walked up to it and opened it. She thought she heard a click like the lock turning, but she must have been mistaken, because the door popped open, no problem. Inside, everything looked perfectly normal. No blood, no nothing. The carpet looked clean, in fact, cleaner than it had before. The only thing amiss was that the easy chair Dracula had sat in earlier was gone. Maybe the department had decided getting rid of it was easier than trying to clean up the bloodstain he'd undoubtedly left behind.

Malcolm whistled.

"What is it?" she asked.

"Were-tigers, all right," he said. "*Phwoof*. Two of them? Must have been hybrids with something else." He walked into the apartment, his hands thrust deep into his pockets and looked the apartment over. She watched him walk to the walls, the corners, studying everything.

Dracula's Death

"Three," he announced when he came to the kitchen. He opened the fridge and crinkled his nose. "Oh wow. I see what you mean. Human. Gross."

"Is there still some left in there?" she gasped, horrified. "Also, three?"

"Parents and a child, if I had to guess," he said and leaned down to poke at the empty fridge. He pulled the meat drawer open and grimaced at the empty plastic. "Human meat stinks. You never forget that smell."

"You know this how?"

"What do you think my job is exactly?" he asked, closing the fridge.

She followed him at a distance as he moved into the back of the apartment. There were no personal effects of any kind. That meant the department had disappeared these tigers altogether.

"What's the deal with these were-tigers?" she asked.

"Depends. There are different kinds. These ones" —he pointed around the apartment— "were tigers that could turn into humans, not humans that turn into tigers. Something else blended in, though. I can't put my finger on it."

"They said they had interbred over the years," Cammy said. Malcolm nodded absently.

"Yeah. You do what you have to do." He wandered into the bathroom. "They did their butchering in here."

"Really?" Cammy gripped the strap of her bag, her stomach tightening.

"Yeah. Smells like it, plus there's the drain in the bathtub. Perfect place. Nothing too recent. A few days ago, maybe?" He checked the mirror, the medicine cabinet, down by the toilet. Satisfied, he backtracked to the bedroom.

"Huh, one bedroom," he observed. "Third one didn't live here, I guess."

"These guys were visiting each other. Maybe it was one of the others?"

"Maybe. But the third one was definitely related."

"The two Vlad killed looked like a middle-aged couple," Cammy volunteered.

"Well, you might wind up with a little revenge killing on your hands. Imagine if you come to visit dear old mom and dad and find someone's turned them into rugs, eh?"

Cammy thought about that while he opened drawers and leaned down to inspect them. She resented his insensitive gallows humor, though. He stood, shaking his head.

"I wish they hadn't used such strong cleaning chemicals. I'm missing something, can't tell what," he muttered. "Something else, or maybe two something elses that came by, not long enough to leave a lasting impression, but clearly different."

"Girl scouts?" Cammy volunteered.

"Har har. Something doesn't add up. Killing isn't how these sort of were-tigers usually behave. It's plain weird." He felt along the walls for a while, knocking periodically, but finding nothing. "This place is picked clean. I won't get much more out of it. What *is* that?" He pushed past her, drifting through the apartment.

"What is what?"

"Something sort of familiar, I think. I can't quite place it, there's too much chemical obscuring the scent." He walked to the walls again. "Incense and decontaminants. I'm never going to figure this out. It's going to drive me crazy."

"Incense?"

"They might have been Buddhist."

"They killed people," Cammy pointed out.

"I didn't say they were *good* Buddhists," he said, "I mean, they're tigers. Cut them some slack." He shook his head,

Dracula's Death

wiped his nose. "Ugh. This is impossible. I might as well—" He swung his head around. Ignoring Cammy's inquiring glance, he returned to the bedroom. Once there, he opened the closet that no longer had anything hanging in it and thrust his head in again.

"Did they have weapons?" he asked.

"Yeah, a sword," Cammy confirmed. "Almost took Vlad's head off."

"Albert," Malcolm said.

"Albert?" Cammy repeated.

"Yeah. I think they got it from him."

"You can tell? Also, who's Albert?"

"Or they might have gotten it from someone else who'd got it from Albert." He wiped his nose. "Albert is a dwarf who operates out of the Underground. Lots of the local monsters barter with him. There was more going on in here than just a happily married tiger couple and their visiting kid. What, I don't know. But I'll bet I'll find out more Underground, whether they bought a sword off him or not."

"Actually, why did were-tigers have weapons?" Cammy asked. "They have claws."

"If they get caught by local law enforcement defending themselves, it's much easier to explain when you had a sword or knife in hand, rather than a body that's been mauled by a tiger," Malcolm explained. "Even getting swept up by law enforcement would be preferable to being identified by Special Services, who would hit them with something harder than jail time."

"Ok, but why buy weapons in the first place?" Cammy asked. "Unless it was because of Emet?"

"Emet?"

"The guy who was killing these tigers."

Malcolm shrugged. "Yeah, maybe 'cuz of him."

He went for the door.

"Coming or what?" he asked her. Cammy trotted after him.

Malcolm explained that the Underground was more than just a place for supernaturals to hide. They had markets down there, hotels, even restaurants, all catering to the supernatural. If some monster needed blood or human flesh for food and didn't want to kill or was incapable of hunting, they could procure what they needed in the Underground. It made Cammy sick to think about that. She'd been dragged down there once—she still had the scars on her leg, though they were fading. Something, she didn't know what, had wanted to buy her. Maybe for... something like that. The Underground Malcolm was talking about wasn't the old, buried parts of Seattle that got toured, the parts of the city that had been built over in the early 1900s or whenever. Some of these sections lay under the cracked circles of old purple glass down near the ferry and Smith Tower. The supernatural sections had been painstakingly dug out over time. Malcolm explained there were rules: no matter what you saw down there, you didn't say anything or call any monster out on whatever it was doing. No fighting was tolerated, except to expel outsiders or miscreants who wouldn't behave.

"There's not a whole lot of ways for someone like me to get down there," Malcolm said. "I work for Ophois. We consider ourselves neutral, since we'll work for monsters and humans too, but we'll hunt monsters if the money's good, so there are things down there that don't like us. I don't go down there if I can avoid it, but I know a few ways. One that's pretty close to Albert, as a matter of fact."

"What are dwarves really like?" Cammy asked. "Are they like in movies?"

Dracula's Death

"Think more *Snow White* than *Lord of the Rings* and you'll have it," Malcolm told her. "They're miners and craftsmen, not fighters. They're very good at assessing the worth of anything fashioned from metal or stone. Albert's pretty old. I've pawned him some stuff over the years. He should talk to me."

"What kind of stuff have you pawned?"

Malcolm glared at her. He didn't do it often, but his glares were white hot, a combination of indignation and pure hate. Cammy turned to the window.

"Sorry," Malcolm said. "Sorry. I... I don't want to talk about that."

"It's ok," Cammy muttered, and traced shapes on the window.

Malcolm drove through the hail to a kitschy-looking little shop with a hand-painted sign that read "Mystic Portals" in beautiful, organic swirls. Vines climbed up the brickwork outside, obscuring the interior despite the big windows. Some electric candles were lit inside, but besides that the place was dark.

She and Malcolm hurried to the door. Before opening it, he paused and turned to Cammy.

"Ok, so this place is run by a witch."

"A...*witch* witch?"

"I think she uses the title because she's you know, modern and it's cool, but it's also more or less true. If you want to say sorceress, that would be more accurate. Anyway, I know her, she knows me, but she doesn't know you, so while you're in there, your name is..." He screwed his mouth to one side. "Rowan."

"Huh? Why?"

"First rule about running into folks who know magic: *don't* tell them your name."

"Why not?"

"Unless you like getting hexed," he added. "Just stay quiet and let me do the talking, ok? Don't touch anything, don't take anything, don't accept anything, don't leave any hair behind, nothing, got it?"

"Yeah, ok," Cammy agreed, dubiously.

He tried the handle, and Cammy heard the same *click* like a lock turning before he swung it open. She bumped into him while trying to rush inside out of the hail.

"Oh no, was that locked?" he asked.

"What?"

The electric glow surged, illuminating the little shop stuffed with herbs, crystals, New Age books, and other New Age-y paraphernalia, except Cammy spotted there was a dividing wall, and behind it she could see what looked like a stuffed alligator hanging from the ceiling, and a wall shelf covered with jars and vials and little statuettes and such, and several animal skulls and a horseshoe nailed up. That area remained dark.

A willowy woman with long, wild red hair streaked with gray and piercing eyes came hurrying from that dark area, glaring at Cammy and Malcolm.

"Whoa!" Malcolm put both his hands up. "Whoa, Phryne, sorry. I didn't realize it was locked. I apologize. Are you closed right now?"

Her piercing, pale blue eyes scrutinized him, then she turned her attention to Cammy. Malcolm laughed, maybe to try lightening the mood.

"Sorry, I'm babysitting. Look, I was hoping I could use your back door?"

Phryne studied Cammy some more.

"Babysitting for who?"

"Vlad."

Dracula's Death

Phryne straightened, and nodded to him.

"You, go on, she stays behind."

"Yeah, sure, yes, absolutely." He reached into his pocket and pulled his keys. He passed them to Cammy.

"Wait for me in the car. Don't even *breathe* too hard on the finish, clear?"

"Yeah, sure," Cammy took the keys. She rolled her eyes as soon as he turned away.

"I hope you're working on cleaning up this mess." Phryne waved a hand at the window. "And *knock* next time, will you? Also, you aren't the first Ophois to come through here tonight. How many of you are on this case?"

"Not the first?" Malcolm pulled up short, and Cammy hesitated at the door. "Who else has been by?"

"Not a local, that's for sure," Phryne told him, her hands on her hips. "Mexican, maybe. He was rude. I told him I'm a neutral party, always have been. Didn't take too well to that."

"Did he leave a name?" Malcolm asked.

"Ocelotl. Very creative," Phryne replied.

"Thanks," said Malcolm absently. He frowned at Cammy and waved her out. Cammy scooted for the car as fast as she could to get out of the hail.

*****

Once the door closed, Phryne nodded for Malcolm to come along with her. He checked over his shoulder to make sure Cammy was staying in his car before following. The front of her shop sold New Age and Wiccan stuff to normies. The back, which was usually hidden by a curtain that she must have drawn aside after closing, was for people or supernatural beings in the know. Ophois occasionally gave her shop patronage. Once they were in the little back room, Phryne walked to a side door labelled "Storage Closet."

"Here you are. I'll want some sort of payment for you breaking in here, you know."

"Sorry, sure," he apologized again.

He opened the door, to reveal a small closet with another door in the far wall, marked all over in signs written in chalk. He opened it.

"Thanks," he said, and Phryne nodded.

"Keep an eye out. Something odd's going on. This is much more in the open than I've ever seen," she said. "Even worse than last year."

"Yeah," he agreed, and descended the brick stairs lit by faint Christmas lights strung overhead. Better than needing to bring a torch or a candle, he supposed. Phryne shut the door behind him and locked it. At the bottom of the brick stairs was a thick, metal door. Malcolm knocked just so.

"Malcolm Marrock," he said to the door. "I'm with the Order of Ophois. I'm on official business."

The door swung open, and he stepped through into the darkness. A smell compounded of moisture, mildew, and way too many scents slapped him in the face. The tunnel was damp and dark. He'd never seen who or what opened the door. He wasn't supposed to, and he wasn't going to go poking his nose in where it wasn't wanted. He liked keeping his nose. He followed the tunnel, sidestepping scummy puddles. When the tunnel branched, he turned to the right. Past a few more turns dug into the dirt, partially shored up with beams of wood or even stones, he came to Albert's stall.

The hollow dug into the tunnel walls afforded a space to congregate, as well as room for Albert's series of tables on which some of his merchandise was displayed. He didn't show everything; those who knew him knew they could ask for all sort of things and he might just "have it in the back". Albert's shop was lit by candles and oil lamps placed here and there, interspersed with the merchandise. The tables were uneven; he had no doubt fished them out of dumpsters. Malcolm knew a lot of supernaturals went dumpster diving. Being above ground could be a risky business if Vlad, Ophois, Special Services, or some other group was out looking for them, but dumpsters were often overflowing with things people casually tossed away, especially at the end of term around the universities.

Two people were looking at a brass pot; they glanced up at the newcomer, their eyes glinting in the dark. A wolf nearly the size of a horse stood across from them, and it sniffed at Malcolm. One of the two human-looking customers wore a snakeskin suit, and the scent of *python* hit Malcolm square in the face. The man considered Malcolm, his eyes shining. The candlelight glowed on his dark skin.

"How much?" Scent of Python asked, turning back to Albert. The dwarf sat on a little barstool in the middle of all the tables, his white beard hanging way down past his knees. His beady eyes blinked at the unlit cigar in Python Man's hand and he asked for two thousand in cash. A regular cigar then, not a magical trade item. It sure smelled expensive to Malcolm's nose. Python Man passed a stack of notes over, then pulled a match from his coat and struck it against his thumb and lit up. He turned back to Malcolm, eying him hungrily.

"Good evening, Ophois," he said. He spoke with an accent.

Malcolm nodded. "Good evening."

"Miserable weather. Good hunting." Python Man and the woman wandered off into the dark, the glow of the cigar slowly fading with him.

Malcolm made a mental note to try to look up what *that* guy might have been. Might be trouble later—or maybe a client. He strode to Albert's tables. As he came near, he spotted another person standing behind the large wolf.

"Oh, no," he said for the second time that night.

"This is my home now, is it?" Dracula asked.

The wolf had hidden him from view, and Malcolm had been too preoccupied with the other weirdo. But he should have noticed the scent. He did *now*, but that wasn't much help.

"You've reached this place awfully quickly. You had time to drop Cammy off at my estate and come here?"

"Yeah. No traffic 'cuz of the weather," Malcolm laughed.

"I see. Thank you, Albert." Dracula dropped a couple of gold coins that *thunked* very solidly on the table. Albert picked one up and bit it. He smiled and touched the coin to his head in salute.

"Since we are both here, why don't we catch each other up on what we know," Dracula suggested. Malcolm nodded warily.

He followed Dracula through more mildewy brick tunnels to another open space with more tables salvaged from dumpsters. One had a creepy, off-putting black stain that dribbled sideways across the surface, almost bisecting it. There was a fireplace set into the bricks, though he didn't see where the smoke went. Rows of bottles lined the far wall, half covered in dust.

"Is this a bar?" he laughed. "I'm at a bar in the Underground?"

"You've never been here?" Dracula asked.

"I'm not usually welcome to hang out. *You* must play both sides against the middle pretty well if they let you in here. You work for the enemy, after all."

Without responding, Dracula gestured to the table next to the fireplace and walked towards the bartenderless bar.

Dracula's Death

"This place is dead," Malcolm observed. Probably for the best. The supernatural probably wouldn't like someone like him hanging out in one of their friendly meeting places. "The storm must have some of them spooked. Phryne thinks something is up."

"Who is Phryne?"

"Never mind, someone I know. You must have gotten in somewhere else." Malcolm sat at the table. The fire was warm and cozy, which was a relief. It wasn't all that cold down here, but it was moist. A cat lay curled up by the hearth. Smelled like cinders and cat to him. Probably not the cat everyone was looking for. Plus, it was too small. Dracula returned with two glasses.

"Beer?" Malcolm asked hopefully.

"Mead."

"*Mead?* You medieval philistines," Malcolm grumped. "Where do these guys get *mead* these days?"

"It's mine. I brew it. And sell some down here."

"No kidding?" Malcolm tried a taste. Not bad, just not beer.

"What do you know about ccoas or were-tigers?" Dracula asked, sitting across the table.

"Not a lot about the former, but the were-tigers you went after aren't usually vicious. Don't get me wrong, some tiger beasties from South Asia are extremely predatory, but not these guys." He took another sip. "Like a friggin' renaissance festival with too much time on its hands," he grumbled. "Hey, have you noticed we've seen a lot more exotics lately?"

"What do you mean?"

"Well, foreigners. Like your fuzzy Asian critters and the elves, and now we've got were-tigers and some other spooks crawling around. Seems like an influx, not just a concentration."

"Hmm," Dracula agreed. "Yes, it does seem odd. Do you think these were-tigers are cooperating with the ccoa? According to Albert, these tigers arrived only a few years ago and settled peacefully. However, about a week or two ago, some of them came to him to buy weapons."

"How many?"

"He guessed something like twelve in all."

Malcolm whistled. "Sounds like a lot." He shrugged and took another sip. "To be honest, I can't figure how they could have known about each other, or how they could have coordinated. Or *why*. Why would those tigers want something around that makes it hail or rain? We've got plenty of rain as it is."

Dracula folded his arms. "The timing is suspicious. *Sankt Walpurgisnacht* approaches."

"Absolutely agreed. But then, things in the supernatural like to happen together."

"Hmm." Dracula closed his eyes to think. "How did you know what sort of were-tigers these were?"

"I went to the apartment you guys visited earlier."

"Did you indeed?"

Malcolm chugged some mead so he could think of a good cover for not driving Cammy straight home. "Cammy told me where it was."

"I see."

"Anyway, I thought I smelled some really old weapon, or something just *silly* with scents from ages of use. So I figured maybe Albert. On that topic: something that wasn't a were-tiger had dropped by. I couldn't identify the scent. Your boss and his pals cleaned that place pretty well. Maybe more than one visitor, but at least one stranger, more than once, and pretty recent. But the weirdest thing I just found out: there's some Ophois chucklehead wandering around calling himself Oceloltl."

"Ocelotl?"

"Yeah, it means 'Jaguar' in Nahuatl. Basically, you've got someone in Ophois calling himself Jaguar. Like if I walked around everywhere calling myself Wolf. Laughs all around."

"You think this person is one of your were-creatures?"

"If the name is supposed to be meaningful, yeah. We have were-jaguars south of the border."

"The ccoa comes from Peru. Do you suppose your organization might have been transporting it and Special Services stole it, only to have it stolen away from them in turn? Possibly by Ophois?"

Malcolm sighed. "Not really our MO to punch holes in vans to get stuff back. We'd have negotiated, or used a hex. But I'll make a call once I get topside. Still, I don't buy that this Ocleotl character is one of ours."

"No?"

"The boys like me are kept on a tight leash," he explained. "One of us goes rogue, we don't live very long. If he's like me, he'd have to be on orders or he wouldn't be able to move. And I'd have been told to cooperate."

"Could your South or Central American branch have different orders?" Dracula asked.

"Hmm, maybe, but that means the branches are at cross purposes. That's... bad."

"So we have an additional unknown to consider. Hmm," Dracula mused again. "I find it more concerning that these tigers seem to have changed their behavior only recently. The timing troubles me." He tapped at his chin. "All the more so because they kept all their meat in bags. They didn't eat it, they were storing it. That has been bothering me all day."

"Yeah, that's weird, unless they were selling it down here."

"That's what I came to check. Albert hadn't heard of any deal to that effect."

Malcolm finished his mead. "So that's it? Did we just hit bottom?" he asked.

"All we need to do is locate the last few tigers," Dracula curtly pointed out. "They should be able to fill in the missing pieces."

"And you know where they are?" Malcolm asked.

"I have some idea, yes. Albert was quite cooperative. I suggest we team up so long as you're working. I could use your senses. I'll be the beater."

"Beater?" Malcolm queried.

"For hunting tigers, you need someone at the fore stirring up noise and trouble to drive them into the open. The Beater."

"Fine by me," said Malcolm.

"When we leave, you make the call to your superiors. I'll drive Cammy home."

Malcolm gulped. "I didn't—"

"Drive all the way to my estate, then to that apartment, then here just after I arrived," Dracula finished icily.

Malcolm sheepishly pushed the glass towards the edge of the table. Dracula stood, and Malcolm followed suit.

"Where is she? I assume she's somewhere safe and not wandering around down here *unescorted*."

"She's in my car."

Dracula glared at him. "Very well. Lead the way."

Once they had passed Albert's shop and were nearly at Phryne's, Dracula spoke again.

"As to the convocation of the 'exotics' you mentioned, I did find out where the next moot will be held."

"No kidding? Don't tell me Seattle drew the short straw."

Dracula's Death

"It did." Dracula nodded. "I don't yet have the date, but this city is confirmed."

Malcolm ran his hand through his hair and gritted his teeth. A meeting of the supernatural, here in Seattle. Things were going to heat up in a major way, which meant he could kiss his down time goodbye. But why here and not at Burning Man, or Machu Picchu? Malcolm knew Special Services kept an eye on Burning Man because certain monsters liked to attend, but really, the supernatural could have picked anywhere that afforded even minimal camouflage, like a FurryCon in SoCal. Well, a moot in Seattle was probably going to put money in his pocket. Better not to get too worried about what else it might put in his pocket—like trouble.

Malcolm led the way back upstairs to Phryne's. The woman eyed Dracula like an eagle when he came through her storage closet, but she didn't comment. She did follow behind as Malcolm made his way to the front door.

*****

Cammy watched Malcolm and, of all people, Dracula, stepping out of the shop into the precipitation that had turned into light sleet. Phryne shut the door behind them, then pulled down a rolling blind to emphasize that the shop was closed. The lights went out immediately afterwards. Cammy opened the car door.

"Hey, look, sorry about Cammy," Malcolm was saying. "I was going to drop her off after I—"

Dracula socked him hard in the stomach, knocking his wind out. Cammy gasped in horror. When Malcolm collapsed to the wet sidewalk, Dracula slapped him the rest of the way down.

"I know you have a particular weakness for women," Dracula growled down at him. "But I need a man, not a *dog*, if we are to succeed."

Malcolm glared up at him.

"Hey!" Cammy protested. Dracula turned his red eyes to her, and she gulped.

"You and I," he said, "are going to have a talk." He curled two fingers for her to come towards him. She felt cold, not just because of the sleet, but grabbed her umbrella and bag and made her way over.

"Are you ok?" she asked Malcolm.

"Mind your own business!" he growl-wheezed at her. She passed him his keys and he staggered to his car, shooting evil looks back at her and Dracula as he went.

"You didn't have to do that," Cammy told Dracula as Malcolm's car pulled away.

"He brought you within arm's reach of this place. That he walked away on his own feet just now shows that I must be growing soft with age."

"You called him a *dog*."

"If he's a man, he will demonstrate as much. If he *is* a dog, then he won't."

Cammy glared at him.

"And *you* need to stop talking him out of doing what I hire him to do. He isn't very disciplined, but I have no one else I can call on if I am unable to see to your safety. If you both demonstrate even once more that I cannot trust him, I will be forced to lock you in your chamber while I am gone in the future. Is that understood?"

She scowled and turned away, folding her arms.

He pulled a portable umbrella from his coat and held it open to cover both of their heads.

Dracula's Death

"Where are we? I need to find my vehicle to take you home."

That took a bit of doing. Cammy pulled her phone and, after checking some cross streets, Dracula was able to figure out he had parked a few blocks away. A miserable hike through slush later, and they were on their way to the mansion.

Apparently Dracula had said his piece, because he was silent all the way to his car, and all the way back to the mansion. All there was to hear was the sound of hail hitting the roof and the windshield.

"I have to go to work tomorrow," she said, when they were driving up the hill.

"I will lend you keys to one of the vehicles," Dracula told her. "I expect I will be busy for some time."

He parked the car near the steps to the back door. Cammy glared at the handle, but when she reached for it, he stopped her hand.

"A moment," he said.

She could barely see him in the light from the headlights reflecting off the hail.

"What?" she asked sullenly.

"You want to help people?" he asked.

"Well, yeah," she said. "There are people in danger."

"And you want to help me to track down this monster?"

"Yeah, I do."

"Very well. I doubt I will be able to keep you away from this for very long. You're like the dog that keeps following no matter how many rocks one throws at it."

"You throw rocks at dogs?" Cammy demanded. His eyes glinted.

"Attend to me: how can you protect others if you refuse to protect yourself?"

"What are you talking about? I protect myself."

"No, you don't. You refuse to do so."

"But you're there," she said.

"Cammy."

She looked down at her bag.

"You cannot rely on others for your protection. You must *never* put your life in the hands of others. Besides, you can only help others when you are in a position of strength."

"But you *do* protect me, right?" she asked. "Or are you just dragging me around for your amusement?"

He leaned back, obscuring his face.

"If that's how you feel, you may leave any time you wish," he said. "I'm not keeping you here against your will."

She tried to read his face, but it was invisible in the dark.

"Did I hurt your feelings?" she asked, genuinely curious. If so, that meant he had feelings to hurt, even though he'd punched Malcolm, and he might have impaled someone for making a shirt wrong, and he'd thrown her out onto the gravel once. He didn't make any *sense*.

"No, you uneducated peasant, you did not hurt my feelings. Don't think so highly of yourself."

Wow. Apparently not, then.

"If you want to help," he continued. "I suggest you take some time to look over my collection. Find something you are willing and able to use. Then, and *only* then, will I consider bringing you along."

"I want to help. I just don't want to hurt anybody," she said. She felt her hands shaking. This was bad. She couldn't see in the dark, but she knew he could.

"You didn't hurt Heather. She was already dead."

She shook her head. "What do you know?"

"About the pain of losing people you love?" he asked. "More than you."

Dracula's Death

Did he? Did he still feel anything about the girlfriend who'd committed suicide? Or his kids? He said he'd had some, right? They must be long dead by now. That had never occurred to her before.

"I have opened my home to you, offered you help, lent you a stone worth more than diamonds, and you still think me cold-blooded?" he asked. There was ice in his voice, just like the stones falling from the sky.

"But I don't know why you did any of it."

"I have explained to you."

"No, you haven't. Everyone says you're a monster, and you don't even deny it. What am I supposed to think?"

He remained silent. Frustrated, she yanked on the handle and stepped out into the rain and ice. She stood in the falling sleet, blinking to hide the tears that tried to form. He remained so still, it was hard to see him in the shadows, all in black. She wanted to tell him something, anything, but then his phone rang.

"Hello, Malcolm?" he said into the phone, then to her, "Think about what you're going to do."

She thought about slamming the car door, but saw what she thought was the reddish glow that came into his eyes sometimes, and closed it gently instead. The car pulled away and disappeared into the dark and the trees on the way back to the city.

Cammy wandered into the kitchen. She'd forgotten about the fridge, until she opened it to get milk for tea, then slammed it shut. It was going to be a project to clean it. Sure, the bags hadn't leaked, but the very idea of what had been in there made her sick.

He didn't have the right to get insulted for being called a monster. He didn't even bat an eye at a pile of chopped up dead people, or those men in the truck she had done her best not to see. What else would someone call a person like that?

He wasn't a person anyway; people didn't live hundreds of years.

The water in the old house took forever to heat, so she brushed her teeth after starting the water running for a bath, lit a vanilla-scented candle, checked her social media accounts, her favorite websites. Nothing cheered her up. She also decided to look into a little plan she'd hatched given that Dracula liked to call her "peasant" all the time. Something she'd found that would cost her, but she'd love to see the look on his face when she revealed what she'd done. She decided to splurge. Just the once. Plus, she wanted to have a win *somewhere*. However she could get it. Nothing cheered her up, though her splurge bolstered her spirits for a few minutes before present reality sank back in.

Her phone ran out power after only a few minutes in the bath. She pulled out her earbuds and tossed them to the counter of the sink. They hit the edge and clattered into the basin. Perfect. She ended the bath early and plugged in her phone. The feather bed remained comfy, like a big warm hug. It felt even warmer when she heard the hail and sleet pelting the window.

CHAPTER 7
MORE THAN ONE WAY TO SKIN A CAT

Cammy had permission to borrow Dracula's cheapest vehicle if she needed to get around when he couldn't drive her somewhere. It was black, of course. It was also a stick shift. She hadn't wanted lessons, but he'd insisted, so now she could get around well enough to work or school. Being able to drive herself was nice, though she didn't like having to pay for parking. The thing she still struggled with was the wipers. No two cars seemed to have the same system.

By morning the weather still hadn't made up its mind: freezing rain or sleet. The ccoa must still be on the loose.

Rather than borrow a gun from the weapons room, she'd deliberately left the mansion empty-handed. Also hungry. She wasn't going to set foot in that kitchen again until she was ready to scrub that fridge. She took Trausti and Fjola with her. There was a bus stop where she could drop them off, but it wasn't near the mansion and she didn't want them to have to walk several miles to get there, to say nothing of the current weather. Though she wondered how this compared to Iceland, where they came from.

"Oh, snap," she muttered when she was halfway down the hill. How were the cows going to get milked? The estate was part farm, and she wasn't sure who handled that responsibility. For some reason, she'd just assumed Dracula had. But that couldn't be right, could it?

She debated turning around. If she did, she'd be late. She kept going. Probably one of the other "tenants" would tend to it. One of them probably already did, she reasoned. She couldn't see Dracula milking a cow.

She dropped Trausti and Fjola off, then made her way towards the Mindful Bean. When she got there, she heard voices coming from the office in the back. She didn't try to eavesdrop, but Kenzie sounded annoyed and her voice was near-shouting.

"I don't *want* to reduce my hours, but my mom is *insisting* that I make sure my little sister gets home ok. I don't know, she's just worried. Some kids at the school ran away or something, so I guess all the parents are freaking out."

Luna's voice responded.

"I don't have anyone to cover you for those shifts, Kenzie."

"What do you want me to do? It's either that or I quit. This is my family I'm talking about."

"Fine, I'll try to make it work. But Cammy can't cover shifts the way she used to."

"Cammy can go to hell, for all I care," Kenzie snapped. She slammed open the door. Her hair was dyed in streaks of purple now, her lipstick black again. She noticed Cammy standing across from the office, where the lockers and the brooms and other cleaning supplies were. She glared at Cammy and stormed to the front.

Kenzie had been mad at Cammy for a while, but she'd never said why, not even when Cammy tried apologizing for whatever she might have done. All Kenzie had ever said was, "It's nothing." When Cammy asked her other friends why,

Dracula's Death

they said they didn't know. But she'd never heard Kenzie say anything like that about her before. That was a knife twisting in her back. It *hurt*. Kenzie was the first friend she'd made in college. Kenzie was the one who had introduced her to Andrew and Lindsey and Aslan.

She wiped angry tears from her eyes.

One absolutely miserable work shift later, she made her way to Capitol Hill. She parked near campus. Not many students were milling around; no doubt the weather discouraged everyone. It was a long, cold, wet walk to the building, and she was shivering by the time she reached the classroom.

Lindsey had decided to take a class with her, since their majors shared some requirements. Lindsey was going for a Business degree because her mother had insisted she take something "serious" which could "help her get a real job." Lindsey had wanted to major in Dance originally, but her mother would not pay for classes unless she picked something more "reasonable", so she was minoring in Dance. Cammy spotted Lindsey sitting by a window, her eyes glued to her phone. Why she preferred the window when she only ever had eyes for her phone was anyone's guess. Maybe she liked the light.

"Hey there," Cammy greeted her, and slipped into the seat next to her friend.

"Hi!" Lindsey responded, brushing an errant strand of her blonde hair from her eyes. "Can you believe this weather?"

"Yeah, it's real ... weird, huh?"

"It came out of nowhere. Do you think it will clear up by your birthday?"

"Yeah, maybe."

"I hope so. Lorelei was going to be at an open-air bar concert."

"Yeah," Cammy agreed absently.

Class started. Cammy took notes, while Lindsey texted every few minutes. It was hard to believe how quickly they'd be graduating. Cammy had transferred in with only two years' worth of classes left. She was coming up on a year. In all this time, she still hadn't found a new roommate, but it wasn't like she put much effort into looking for one. Given that there were monsters all over the place, she didn't feel safe striking out on her own. She felt pathetic. But what was she supposed to do if she ran into something out there? Attack them like Emet did? She didn't want to think about those two tigers lying dead on the carpet.

After class, she and Lindsey decided to head to a coffee shop to pass time until their next class. It was crowded. Cammy worried they wouldn't find a place to sit when a long, thin hand shot into the air from the back corner. Lindsey waved back at Aslan.

She and Cammy made their way over, and Lindsey dropped her bag on the table.

"Thanks!" she said. "I'm going to get a coffee. Want anything?"

"I'm good," he gestured at the half-full paper cup and a plate empty of all but crumbs in front of him.

Cammy and Lindsey returned to the table after placing their orders.

"I can't believe this weather," Aslan said. "I was going to go up to Andrew's place and snap photos."

"Yeah, it sucks," Cammy mumble-agreed. Of all her friends, only Andrew knew about the supernatural, but he didn't go to college with them. She'd have to let him know more about the weather later. His family ran a farm. She didn't know much about farming, but she guessed the sudden cold couldn't be good for the plants. She wondered if it would bother the chickens and ducks. Andrew's family sold lots of eggs and kept some more exotic birds, like quails and peacocks.

Lindsey was telling Aslan about her ideas for Cammy's birthday, but Cammy's mind kept drifting to the weather and how Dracula and Malcolm were getting along. And whether any more tigers were ending up as rugs. And how it all fit together. And trying not to think about what Kenzie had said. She'd been crying enough lately. She didn't need another reason.

"Hey, you ok?" Lindsey asked.

"Huh? Oh." Cammy sipped her cappuccino. "Yeah. Just thinking."

"Midterms? I'm pretty nervous myself. We can study together if you like."

"Study?" Cammy had about forgotten about all of that. "Oh, yeah, that's a good idea. Where?"

"I've never seen that mansion where you're living. Could I visit?"

"It is a mansion, right?" Aslan said. "If she goes, can I come? To take photos?"

Cammy shook her head. "He...doesn't like visitors."

"But how did you meet him? And he lets you stay up there," Lindsey pointed out.

"That...it's complicated," Cammy said. Lindsey fidgeted with her cup, and Cammy thought about the phone call she'd overheard. "Lindsey..." But she couldn't just *ask* if her friend had a crush on him, could she? And if Lindsey said yes, then what? What could Cammy tell her except that he was way too old for her?

"But if he's busy, it's just you up there, right?" Lindsey said.

"Lindsey..."

"What?"

"You... don't like him, do you?"

"Huh!" Lindsey nearly knocked her cup over. Aslan's eyes snapped to her, and he sat up a little in his seat. Lindsey's fingers twisted together. "No. *No way*! That would be so weird! He's like, *way* older than me."

You have no idea, Cammy thought. "So... you don't?"

Lindsey shook her head. "No! No, he's just... a good dancer. And he's really nice. Old-fashioned. Courteous. Like... a gentleman."

Aslan stared, but as his mouth dropped open to say something, Cammy cut in. "No, he's not. He's really rude. And surly. You don't know him."

"Huh? But he's always gentlemanly with me."

"He... you're right about him being old-fashioned, so I guess he acts polite. But you don't know how rude he can be. Just the other day, he answered the door naked!"

Lindsey turned scarlet and covered her mouth with her hands, while Aslan's eyes bugged.

"Wait, is he a pervert?" Aslan demanded. "Cammy, you can't stay up there with—"

"No, he was in the bathtub. I knocked on the bathroom door to talk to him."

Both her friends stared at her, and she realized she couldn't explain that she was just so freaked out about human flesh being in the fridge and being almost attacked by a satyr, so she had been majorly stressed out and mad and needed to talk to him *right then.*

"Cammy!" Lindsey scolded. "You can't just barge in on someone when they're—"

"I didn't barge in! I knocked. I was...I needed to talk."

"What was so important you couldn't wait until he was done?" Aslan asked.

Dracula's Death

Cammy balled her hands into fists on her lap. She couldn't tell them. They didn't know. Only Andrew knew.

"And he's a hypocrite, because he got angry at me for answering the door in PJs before."

"Yeah, but"—Aslan chuckled—"I mean, it wasn't like you had to go to the door in PJs. He was in the bathroom. It's totally different."

Cammy glared at her hands.

"I think I get why he was upset about the PJs thing," Aslan volunteered. "He's old-fashioned you said? Conservative. I get that. My parents are pretty conservative, and my grandparents even more so. They'd be pissed if someone, especially a"—he suddenly pursed his lips together apologetically—"young person was careless."

"Whatever," Cammy grumped. Aslan's eyes drifted to Lindsey again. Lindsey was playing with her phone and refused to look at anyone.

Way to make it awkward, idiot, she thought at herself. Was she just being protective of Lindsey? Or was she just tired of Dracula always acting like he was better than she was? Or him saying he was misunderstood by the world while being a monster anyway? Or was she upset about Heather? How long would she still be upset?

"Have you heard from Kenzie lately?" Lindsey asked.

"Kenzie?" Cammy made every effort to sound like she hadn't heard anything Kenzie had said today. "I don't see her much. She has to take time off to take care of her little sister after school."

"Yeah, she told me that some of the kids at her school have gone missing, so her mom is worried. But Kenzie hasn't really been herself. She... she doesn't talk about you anymore. Is everything ok? Are you still fighting?"

Cammy blinked angrily at the wall. *Don't cry*, she scolded herself. She was so done with crying.

"Look, there's that woman again," Aslan commented.

"Who?" Lindsey asked, and swiveled her head towards the window. Outside, the huldra who had moved to Seattle was walking by. Her long, wild hair hung in wet strands, her retro, bohemian clothes were soaked through. She seemed not to care, strolling along without any coat or umbrella, not even shivering. Her wet skirt was stained and tattered in some places, and it clung to her body. Cammy's heart suddenly leapt to her throat. Malcolm had told her that a huldra would murder anyone who mentioned her tail. If her skirt was clinging like that, did that mean...? And Aslan was watching her. If he saw...!

Cammy stood a little and leaned over Lindsey to watch Siri pass by. Yes, she could see the shape of the tail. Definitely something under the skirt.

"I... I have to talk to her," Cammy told her friends. "Sorry, I gotta run. We'll study tomorrow, ok?" she promised Lindsey.

"Uh?" Lindsey replied. "Everything ok?"

"Yeah, just...stay safe out there, you guys, ok?"

The last she saw of them as she went out the door was their worry and confusion.

She ran to catch up to Siri.

"What are you doing out here?" Cammy demanded. "People might see... your petticoat." Malcolm had taught her the polite way to warn a huldra that her tail was showing. If you called it a petticoat, she wouldn't murder you for mentioning it.

Siri turned to consider her, then looked down at the skirt. She twirled in it a little.

"Hmm, yes, they might," she agreed. "Vhat has happened to the veather? It rains here, but not like this."

"There's a ccoa. It's some sort of cat thing that messes with weather."

"Oh?"

"Yeah, and somehow were-tigers are involved."

"I see," Siri commented. "Is his Majesty seeing to it?"

"Yeah," Cammy grumped. "Don't you have anything else to wear? Where do you stay? You can't just wander around in weather like this."

"It is not so bad," Siri said, and cast her eyes up at the sky. "Merely stronger than it should be."

"You're not cold?"

"No."

Cammy remembered the huldra had come from Norway. Maybe she was accustomed to cold.

"We need to get you home," Cammy said.

"I have no home here," Siri told her. "I sleep under trees and bushes."

"Ok, that's no good. How about… let's get you new clothes, and then… you can hang out in my classes or something? At least you won't be so wet."

Siri considered her. The huldra had some half-baked plan to marry Dracula, and knew that Cammy lived in his mansion. Cammy suspected the only reason Siri was friendly with her was because she hoped it would help her chances. He'd given a pretty clear "No" to Siri's proposal, but last Cammy had checked, Siri hadn't given up.

"Very vell," Siri acquiesced.

Cammy led her to a trendy used-clothing store just off campus. The trouble would be finding a skirt the right length. Long skirts weren't exactly "in". Siri peered at the blouses and purses with interest, but she shied away from the jeans and short skirts.

"What about this?" Cammy held up a T-shirt dress that would be calf-length on Siri, who was pretty tall. It was a navy blue with white stripes across the chest.

"It is pretty," she agreed.

"Why don't you try it on? I'll see what else I can find."

Cammy left the huldra near the fitting rooms and went hunting for skirts. Of all things, she found a long denim skirt, and also a long, knit coat that *might* be enough to hide the tail. New clothes would help Siri to blend in a little better. Thinking that, she found some boots that looked like they would fit. Siri walked around in sandals most of the time, and Cammy had spotted her barefoot more than once. Even if she didn't mind the cold, people would look at her funny if she didn't dress for the weather. There was even a hoodie that looked big enough, and for the heck of it, Cammy found a hat. If Siri was going to be outside all the time, that big brim might help.

Siri emerged from the fitting room in the dress. It fell to just above her mid-calf, so Cammy asked her to turn around. The tail didn't peek out, though Cammy suspected it was close. She showed the other items, and Siri accepted them and tried them all on. The huldra was gone for quite a while before she emerged wearing the skirt and the long, knit coat. Cammy checked to see whether the tail was visible while viewing her from the front—perhaps between her legs, but she spotted nothing. Almost as if in answer, Siri said, "I tried wrapping my... petticoat around my vaist. Does it show?"

Cammy looked. She shook her head. Siri smiled with relief. She looked more like a normal person in all of these clothes. She'd draw way less attention now. Cammy wasn't sure she had enough to pay for everything, but Siri pulled soaking wet bills from her old clothes and they tallied it all up. There would still be money left over, so Cammy

Dracula's Death

suggested Siri find a purse she liked. The huldra's lightning eyes flashed with excitement, and she pawed at the collection hanging near the fitting rooms. She found a nice-looking leather one, which matched the boots fairly well, and looked big enough for a book or two. If she was going to be living on the streets, she ought to have something to carry things in. Cammy shot her a thumbs up, and Siri ran to the floor length mirror and admired herself in the reflection. She twirled a few times, taking in the boots and the jeans skirt and the coat, her eyes glittering.

"It is... it is as if I am one of you," she breathed.

"You are." Cammy patted her on the shoulder. For a moment, she wondered whether Siri had a hollow back—Malcolm had said some huldra did, or used to. She could't tell through the coat, and she wanted to be careful not to accidentally put her hand in there if it *was* hollow. The idea made her a little queasy.

The cashier tried not to make a face at the wet pile of bills that Siri proudly dropped on the counter. When the poor young man held out the change, Siri eyed the coins confusedly.

"Take it; you can put it in your purse," Cammy told her. Siri cheerily dropped them in, loose as they were.

The wet sleet had turned to hard, freezing rain, so Cammy walked with Siri to a nearby pharmacy where she knew there were little portable umbrellas sold for under ten dollars. She picked out a bright blue one.

"Here, now you don't have to get wet when it rains. Or sleets."

"Humans mind ven it is vet?" Siri checked. "I see them hide ven it is like this."

"Yeah. It's cold and miserable."

Siri accepted the umbrella and they went to the self-checkout. The screen could register Siri's fingers, but Cammy had to talk her through the whole process. The machine could not accept wet bills, so Cammy paid for the umbrella. Siri grinned like a child and opened it to get a better look.

"Thank you!" she gushed, and hugged Cammy tight around the neck. "I vill repay you for all your help, somehow I vill!"

"It's ok," Cammy assured her. "You just need to learn to blend in, is all." She thought about how Malcolm had gotten fake IDs so Trausti and Fjola could go to school. "You know," she said, lighting on an idea. "If you're trying to be human, you could get a job and an apartment, even. Then you wouldn't have to sleep under trees."

"Do you think so?" Siri asked. "Vhat sort of job?"

"Uh, well... I guess something simple," Cammy said. She actually had no idea.

"Vhat if I vorked vith you to make coffee?"

"Oh, uh... no. Well, actually, yeah. I think Luna needs someone to cover for Kenzie." Cammy didn't want to work with Siri, but someone *did* have to keep an eye on her, right? But even if Luna took Siri on, the huldra wouldn't be able to work enough shifts to pay rent. "And there are other coffee shops around, since you'll probably need two jobs. You're in Seattle, after all. But you'll need an ID and everything first."

"Oh," Siri's shoulders slumped a little.

"I'll call Malcolm, he'll know how to get that for you."

"Thank you!" Siri hugged her again.

"I've got to head to class. I can call you later once Malcolm gets back to me?"

"Call?" Siri played with a damp strand of her dark hair. "I don't have a phone."

"Right." Cammy felt stupid. "Well, I'll see you on campus, right? I'll let you know the next time I see you."

Dracula's Death

Siri agreed. They walked back to campus, and Siri held open her umbrella to protect them both. She seemed quite proud to do this. It was a good arrangement, since Cammy was much shorter than the huldra, who had to be nearly 5'10." Cammy hated being a runt.

She texted Malcolm the ID request, with an explanation of why she wanted it, when she went to class. On the way out, he texted back.

You already owe me for those Huldufolk kids. If she wants help, she better be able to pay

How much?

Ten grand is my going rate. I told you

Ah. Good old Malcolm. As mercenary as ever. Plus, he was probably in a bad mood after Dracula punched him and insulted him the other night. So now she had to hope she didn't run into Siri; she didn't know how to break the news to her.

She got to the parking spot where she'd left the car without spotting the huldra, and drove back. Her classes ended too late for her to pick up Trausti and Fjola at school. She hoped they got home safely. They could turn invisible, but she wasn't sure about intangible. Torrential downpours of sleet and hail might hurt them.

The mansion was silent as a graveyard, as usual. The thick walls muffled the sound of the hail pattering the stones outside unless you stood right next to one of the small windows.

"Hello?" she called out, just in case. No answer.

A quick pass of the rooms confirmed that Dracula wasn't home. She didn't really expect to see him anyway. More mobile games, more reading, more forgetting that there was no food in the fridge. Rather than drive back into town, she went to the chicken coop. There were new eggs, so she cooked those. The cows seemed all right. She bit her lip at the vineyard that sprawled around the back and side of the property. Were the vines going to survive this weather? They had to be used to cold and wet or they couldn't grow up here, but the grapes might not make it.

She went into the Study and did some of what you are supposed to do in such rooms, cramming for her midterms, then watched a movie on her tablet. After the sun went down, she stepped outside again to look at the blinking city lights below as hail pummeled her umbrella.

No sign of headlights coming up the road.

She turned to go inside and something bumped her ankle. Cammy screamed and kicked at the unseen object. It cracked and she felt wet chunks splatter over her shin. She ran to the door to open it and cast light on the pebble drive. The rectangle of light fell across a broken watermelon. Falling hail made the shards of rind dance, or perhaps the thing wasn't completely dead yet.

"Ugh!" she grumbled, and kicked the red, red juice off her shoe. "Stupidest things in the world." She slammed the door.

Brian called her the next morning.

"Can I pick you up?" he asked when she answered.

"Oh, yeah." she said. "Wait, I thought you said evening?"

"Melissa can't make it. And you're more of a morning person, right? I thought maybe this would be a better time."

"Um, yeah, actually," Cammy said. It would be bad enough going to the cemetery in daylight. Going in the dark, with sleet or hail pelting them, would be miserable.

She cooked some of the eggs she hadn't gotten to the previous night while she waited, and glanced out the window every so often.

Brian drove his sister's run-down, very used Honda when he needed to go any serious distance. The maroon Honda came up the driveway and stopped. Brian darted for the door when she opened it.

"It's like this is never going to let up," he grumbled, wiping his feet on the mat. As he came inside, he thumbed over his shoulder. "What's with the watermelon?"

"Huh? Oh, I dropped it," she said.

Brian was looking around the room. He'd never been inside the mansion before. "He's sure got money, huh?" he commented icily. "Must be nice being a bona fide European blue blood." He studied her closely. Suspiciously. So cop-like. Cammy looked away. She hated when he looked at her like that.

"Yeah," she mumbled.

"Who else lives here?"

"No one."

"No one?" Brian shook his head. "Lots of wasted space, then, isn't there? Does he throw house parties?"

"Not that I've seen."

"No one else drops by?"

She answered with a shake of her head.

"Well, let's go, ok?"

They ran to his car. Brian keyed the ignition, and an Indie track started playing.

"Who's this?" she asked.

"Lorelei," he explained, "Lindsey told me about her. I wasn't sure at first, but she's really grown on me."

"Huh. She's cool," Cammy said. The singer had a melodious, reed-like voice. The track was a mournful sort of threnody, with the same voice providing its own back up. There were instruments too, but it was the voice that was arresting. Somewhat like folk metal, but softer. Haunting.

They made their way back to the city.

"How you been?" Brian asked.

"Fine. You?"

He shrugged.

"Not liking this weather, that's for sure. Makes patrol unpleasant."

"Yeah, I bet," she said.

"Turns out those missing people were part of some sort of human trafficking ring," he said. "Feds jumped on it. Again. Can't seem to get rid of them since last year."

"Human traffickers?" Cammy wondered, aghast.

"No, Feds," Brian corrected. "Just figures there would be another high-level crime spree going on again."

"Oh," said Cammy.

"Just 'oh?' You seemed really interested last time I mentioned it," Brian pointed out. She heard the hostility in his voice.

"I was worried about you," she explained.

"Sorry." His voice softened.

She watched the hail come down. If her host was doing something, it seemed he hadn't made much difference.

"How's Melissa?" Cammy asked.

"Busy. You know, the usual ER stuff. This weather has caused more accidents."

"Oh," Cammy murmured. She fiddled with her bag.

They came to the cemetery. Heather's parents had been killed by the same vampire who had attacked Cammy and turned Heather. Dracula had somehow handled the funeral arrangements. Boese's people had taken Heather's body. Cammy had no idea what had become of it; so as far as she knew, Heather's grave was an empty plot Dracula had set up, but there was a headstone at least. It was a lot more than Cammy could have afforded, and while she would hate to admit it to him, the fact that there was a grave of any kind that she could visit was a blessing she could never have expected or asked for.

Dracula's Death

As Cammy gathered her bag, Brian ran around the side of the car and opened the door. He held up an umbrella for her.

"Thanks." She smiled at the sudden show of chivalry. He even offered to take her hand. She let him. She couldn't let Dracula be the *only* man she knew who occasionally acted that way. Brian's hand was warm.

They made their way through the plots, and Cammy wondered whether any of them secretly belonged to something other than human, or to persons who had been killed by monsters.

Heather's headstone was simple: her name, birthdate, death date, and some sort of Bible verse or prayer Dracula must have picked were engraved in the stone.

Brian had brought flowers. Cammy held a mug she had picked up at a secondhand store a few days earlier. They put the flowers in the mug and set it in front of the tombstone.

Cammy remembered seeing Heather's face half-obscured by blood and gore, the custodian lying on the floor. She'd tried to hide, but Heather had come after her. There was a broken, wooden broom handle that she'd grabbed; when Heather lunged for her, she'd impaled herself. Cammy had seen the look in Heather's eyes. It wasn't like a light going out. Her eyes had been dead to start with. Heather had just kept staring, unblinking, then went limp rag. That was it.

Brian put his arm around her. She was shivering. So very cold.

"You want to get out of here?" he asked. She nodded.

There was a little hot dog stand within walking distance. They both liked walking. She ate a tofu dog with hatch chiles, while Brian helped himself to a chili dog with extra onions and some hot sauce. They each ordered a hot chocolate. Food in hand, they hid under a leafy tree beside a brick building that blocked the worst of the weather. Leaves lay plastered all over the sidewalk and the building; it must have been much leafier before.

"I miss going out," Brian said, and wiped his mouth. "I mean, the guys and I get a beer, but it's not, you know, just hanging out. Melissa's always busy, and you're always off doing something with your *friend*."

"Not always," Cammy said. "I have classes. And my job."

"What do you see in that guy?" Brian asked.

"I'm not dating him," Cammy snapped. "We're not a thing."

He eyed her, then took another bite of his hot dog.

"He's more like, I don't know? Maybe like a dad. Like an old-fashioned one, the ones that are all tough love and survival skills."

"Like a *dad*?" Brian repeated doubtfully. But he sounded less hostile. He knew Cammy's parents; it would be pretty obvious that anything halfway decent would be preferable to them. Her dad hadn't been as obviously bad as her mother, but he hadn't stood up to the woman, and always backed his wife up whenever she did anything crazy.

"Yeah." Cammy picked at the paper wrapping the rest of her tofu dog. "Maybe he was just lonely or something. You saw how empty the house is. All that wasted space."

"You really think that? He's an eccentric shut in and he wanted company?" Brian finished his dog and sipped his hot chocolate, watching people hunched against the weather.

"I killed Heather," Cammy said, surprising herself. It just came out. It had been *wanting* to come out so badly. And it had slipped out somehow, despite her decision to keep it bottled up and never tell Brian.

Brian lowered his hot chocolate. She felt his eyes on her, but she dared not look at him. She couldn't bear to think of what he thought of her now.

"What?" he said.

"She... she'd killed the janitor," she explained in her tiniest voice. "She wasn't herself."

Brian's eyes burned. "Are you serious?" he asked.

Cammy nodded, wiped at the tears with her thumb.

"I didn't want to," she said. "I really didn't want to. I wanted her to be ok. I wanted her to be ok!" She sobbed into her hand. "I'm sorry. I wanted to tell you, but I just couldn't. I'm sorry. I'm so sorry."

She dropped the tofu dog and it fell onto the freezing, slick sidewalk. Hail pummeled it into mush.

Brian pulled her into a hug.

"I thought so," he said into her hair. "I knew something had gone wrong. Honestly. I'm sorry. I've treated you bad."

How else would you treat me? she wondered, *I killed our friend, and then lied to you about it.* She clutched Brian's jacket and buried her face against his shoulder. It was odd; the smell was comforting.

"You did the right thing," Brian told her. She pushed him away.

"What?" she demanded, and tried wiping the stupid water off her face.

"You did the right thing. It was hard, but you didn't have much of a choice."

"But it was *Heather*!" Cammy protested. "My best friend from school."

"I know. She must have *really* fallen off the proverbial wagon. She was on something strong, wasn't she? And it may have been laced with something worse. That happens, sometimes. Cammy, you did what you had to do."

"But, Heather—"

"Sometimes you have to do what you have to do. I mean, they taught us that at the academy. You don't want to pull the trigger, but sometimes you have to. You have to survive. No matter what."

"But you can choose not to," Cammy insisted. "You can find another way—"

"Sometimes you don't have the time to think of something clever. And sometimes it's not just your life on the line, and if you hesitate other people will get hurt, or die. Cammy, sometimes it's just you versus them, and then what? You can't just roll over. You have to fight back."

Cammy searched his blue eyes.

"I can't tell you how much it would have hurt me if you hadn't fought back," he said. "Heather wouldn't have wanted you to let her hurt you, either. You know that."

"But you don't—"

"Look, I don't know what she was on, or why all those government spooks showed up, but I know you. You wouldn't have done anything to hurt anybody unless you had to. I just wish you trusted me enough to tell me what's going on before. I just wish..." His jaw tightened. "I wish you would *talk* to me. Tell me what's going on."

Cammy bit her lip. Brian meant it, but he didn't really know what he was asking. Should she tell him? He was so earnest. She remembered seeing him raise his gun to shoot the *draugr*, then him lying on the ground, unconscious. He didn't remember how he'd almost died trying to stop a monster. If he found out monsters were real and there were more of them out there, wouldn't he go looking for them and get himself killed? But then, Vlad and Malcolm both seemed to think it was a good idea to tell him. Maybe she should? Like Dracula said, maybe it *would* be safer for Brian in the long run. To know. She took a deep breath.

A pair of feet came to a stop in front of them both. Cammy looked up to see a man in a raincoat holding a black umbrella. "Is this a bad time?" Boese asked. Her blood ran cold.

"Hello?" Brian greeted, confused. He looked to Cammy.

"Hi, there. You must be Brian Warren. I've heard so much about you." Boese extended a hand for Brian to take. Hesitantly, Brian reached out.

"I'm sorry, who—?"

Cammy grabbed his wrist and yanked his hand back.

"Are you kidding me?" she demanded, glaring at Boese. "What are you doing here?"

"It's so rare that I get to talk to you alone," Boese explained.

"I'm not alone," she snapped. "Go away."

"You know what I mean." Boese smiled coldly.

"I'm sorry, who is this?" Brian asked.

"I'm a friend of her father's," Boese told him, "I've been worried, you know, after what happened with her parents. Isn't that right, Cammy?"

"You son of a..." She stamped her foot, wishing her boots made her taller. "I'm here to visit my best. Friend's. Grave. *How dare you!*"

"I have something to tell you," Boese said, still smiling. "I'll be quick, I promise."

"Cammy, you want to get out of here?" Brian asked, standing.

"Do you?" Boese wondered.

She glared at his creepy, shaven head. He had never done this, never broken cover. How had he known where she was? Had he known Dracula had put her on a time-out, that she was alone instead of trailing him around like usual? How could he possibly know that? Her hands started to shake. He knew where to find her, and he knew when her supernatural friends weren't around. Worst of all, he'd shown up when she was with Brian. Was that why Boese had picked *now*? This was bad. Very bad.

"Fine. Be quick," she told him. Boese smiled harder, revealing more teeth. He raised his eyebrows, inclined his head towards Brian.

"Right here? Right now?" he checked.

"Fine. Brian, I'll be right back."

"Hang on, what?" Brian said, but she walked towards a tree about half a block away. She could see the cemetery over the low brick wall, the hail piled in tiny heaps against the tombstones. Traffic splashed crushed ice and water up onto the sidewalk every few seconds.

"What is it?" Cammy demanded.

"I want you to work for me," Boese said.

"This *again*?" Cammy exclaimed, throwing her hands up in disgust.

"You're very driven. And all your help taking down that *draugr*? Shows you've got some kind of good head on your shoulders. Word on the street is you go everywhere, no matter how dangerous. The enemy is getting used to your face."

The enemy.

"I haven't changed my mind. I will never work for you." She glared at him. "I've seen what you do. You kidnapped a baby uh... tanu..."

"Tanukitsune," he supplied. Why was it so *easy* for him?!

"You can't kidnap an animal."

"She can talk. She's just a kid. She's never hurt anyone."

Boese shook his head. "They all hurt people. They hurt people just by existing."

"Really? Because she hasn't hurt me at all in a whole year, same with her mother and her father. They haven't bothered anyone."

Dracula's Death

"Listen: you're late to this party. Not so long ago, humans were under these creatures' thumbs. You couldn't go into a forest without bringing some sort of offering or sacrifice for whatever spirit had decided that was its territory. They stole children, killed people. Do you have any idea how far science has come since we decided to fight back? If we let them run the place like they used to, we'd still be in the Dark Ages."

Cammy scoffed and crossed her arms.

"That little creature you saved? They have stories in Japan. Those things rob from people, they play pranks. *Dangerous* pranks. They trick people into committing suicide sometimes."

"No, they don't," Cammy said.

"They're not going to tell you so, obviously," said Boese. He thumbed at his chest. "I know. It's not like it's in the newspapers all the time over there, but it used to be. Hell, it used to be common knowledge. Same with all these creatures. Even the 'nice' ones. It's always been like that. It's Darwinian. We're competing for the same living space, same resources. In some cases, we *are* the resources. Some of them eat a diet exclusively of *human*. We're prey to them. We can't coexist with things like that."

"So you're saying what you're doing is self-defense?" Cammy checked.

"What would you call it?" Boese demanded.

Cammy glanced over her shoulder at Brian, standing next to the bench. He looked worried.

"They're not all like that. Vlad's not like that."

"Oh, did he tell you that?"

"He's never hurt me."

"Never?"

"No, never."

"You're a liar," said Boese.

"Only when he didn't know why I showed up at his house uninvited," she clarified. "Just that first time."

"Ah," said Boese. "Of course."

"He didn't know who I was! I just showed up out of the blue! He thought I was there to kill him!" she snapped. "He stopped the minute he realized I wasn't dangerous."

"Right. Because you were naïve and no threat and he could use you. He thinks that because you're a sweet kid I won't push him around anymore. He's wrong."

"What do you mean? Are you going to do something to him?"

"Are you going to work for me?" Boese countered.

"No. You haven't exactly made a compelling case."

Boese licked his lips. "You know your sugar daddy up there? You want to know what happens to stuff that he eats?"

"What are you talking about?"

"He eats things, right? Food, dirt, whatever. But he's not alive like you or me, so what happens to all of that?"

"I don't know," Cammy grumbled. *And I don't care.*

"It disappears," Boese told her, and snapped his fingers. "*Poof.* Like a bona fide magic trick. I've had cameras hooked up to monitor him. Hell, I've had cameras inside him! Whatever he eats disappears, and we've never seen how it happens. No matter how good the camera is. The food is there inside his gut one frame, gone the next. What do you think that means? Don't answer, I'll tell you: the Law of Conservation of Matter is getting violated, unless he's got the secret of teleportation in his stomach. That means, given enough time, and enough strigoi, they could literally eat this entire planet down to nothing. They don't ever stop eating, you know. They just stay hungry, and trust me: they'll eat anything. I got him to eat his own arm once. So how's that for a threat?"

DRACULA'S DEATH

"You... got him to eat his *arm?*" Cammy repeated, horrified.

"Sure did. Starve him long enough he turns into a rabid animal. Shows you what he's really like."

"So you just admitted to torturing him, so that's a great argument in your favor," Cammy pointed out sarcastically. "Even humans turn cannibal when they're starving, don't they?" You came across all sorts of strange stories online, especially if you had a friend who liked news of the weird, like Kenzie, or studied anthropology, like Aslan. "And as far as strigoi eating everything, that'll be millions of years in the future, even if you're right."

"Even knowing about these things is bad for people. It's why we work to stop people from bumping into the things that go bump in the night."

"Hasn't hurt me yet," said Cammy.

Boese drew in a breath, his cold eyes on her. He clenched his jaw, rubbed his mouth, and looked over her shoulder at Brian.

"Look, when I came back from college, my kid sister had gotten into all this spiritualism New Age folklore mumbo jumbo. You know, the Wiccan-hippie phase that girls seem to get into. I thought it was all stupid, but basically harmless. Then she found an entry in some book or other about some sort of magic cat from Japan that it said if you drink cat blood you can turn into one of these things. So one night, she did."

Cammy frowned.

"And wouldn't you know it? This stuff is real. It doesn't always work; you don't always turn into a vampire or an oni or a demon or a pennagal or whatever, but sometimes you do. Sometimes" —he looked at her— "like with Heather, things don't work out. Just knowing about this stuff is enough to make it real. The more people spend time with it, the greater effect it has on them."

"You made that up," Cammy said. He shook his head.

"My little sister tore our mother's throat out," he said. "I had to beat her with a baseball bat so she'd let go." He tapped at the scars reaching to his ear, one notch missing. "Just a little reminder I got from that night. I get to see that every day. It's not just that they can kill us, scare us. They can *make us them*. Like your friend does."

"Well, that's not how they all work."

"You heard what happened to Margaret?" Boese asked.

Whoa. The name from the inscription in that book by Lady Jane Wilde. *We were terribly sorry to hear about poor Margaret.* How did Boese know these things? She shivered.

"No."

"That was his last wife. The most recent one."

"He never told me her name. He just said she died."

"You should ask him how. See if you still think he's such a nice guy," Boese said. "If he tells you the truth." He pointed a finger in her face. "Just think about it. I could use someone like you. The human race could use someone like you. Fact is, there's something afoot, and I'm losing funding. Official story is the bigwigs on top think everything's handled, that we've won the war and all we're doing now is clean up." Boese leaned in close, she could smell his breath. He used mouthwash, but there was a bad smell underneath it. "They're wrong. You think we used to get were-tigers here? You think Seattle used to have vampires running around turning people like your friend whenever they felt like it? You think your sugar daddy used to give me lip? None of that used to happen. They're up to something. Something big. I don't know what it is, but I know they're planning something. And now my people are..." He frowned at the

Dracula's Death

ground. He shook his head a little, as if to knock a thought loose from his brain, or maybe something he intended to say. "Those monsters know we're not as strong as we used to be, and they're going to take advantage of that." He stared into her right eye, then her left. "You can either do the right thing, or you can get out of my way. *Capiche*?"

"Buddy, you can back right the Hell up," Brian interjected. He put a hand on Cammy's shoulder and stepped in front of her. "I don't know who you're supposed to be, but I don't like what I'm seeing here. I suggest you go on your way."

Boese held up both hands in surrender and stepped backwards.

"It was nice talking with you, Cammy," he said, and nodded to Brian. "And a pleasure to meet you, Brian."

"Can't say the same," Brian told him. Boese righted his umbrella and walked off into the hail. Brian watched him go.

Cammy felt frozen. Brian might do something stupid if he knew that Boese was practically stalking her. Boese wasn't a supernatural monster, but he didn't have any qualms about throwing people down in his dungeon-lab; she doubted he'd hesitate to toss Brian down there. Or he'd make trouble for Brian at work. She was on her own with Boese and would have to figure out how to deal with him.

Did that mean defend herself? Against a human? Boese was much creepier than a lot of the things she'd met. But that felt wrong. Besides, wouldn't the whole department come down on her and bury her somewhere? Or worse?

"You ok?" Brian asked.

"I don't know," she admitted. "I have to think about some things."

Brian clenched his jaw, trying not to say something. Whatever it was, he wrestled it into submission. Instead, he looked away. The hail still fell, relentless. That was the icing on this entire horrible cake.

"Want to keep walking?" Brian asked at last. He shook his umbrella. "Perfect weather for it."

She snorted, momentarily amused. They wandered through the ice and slush.

"Hey, April showers bring May flowers," Brian said, when they came to a puddle with hailstones bobbing in it. "How many flowers are we going to get out of this?"

"We'll be wading through them," Cammy mumbled. She couldn't muster a chuckle after what had just happened. Brian sighed.

"Should we head back?" he asked.

Cammy nodded. When they were halfway back to Brian's car, Cammy spotted a shop and remembered she needed food.

"Hang on, can we stop in there first?" she asked.

Brian agreed, so they crossed the street. Cammy hadn't been in this store before, but they had a decent organic and natural foods section. She also picked up a gallon of regular bleach. Having to purchase a bag to put her groceries in reminded her to rethink some of her finances for the future. This little splurge was all right, but she couldn't afford too many of them. *No more biohazards in the fridge, then*, she grumped to herself.

Brian stood by, no doubt trying not to keep track of what she bought—he knew she didn't earn as much as he did, and she guessed he was debating offering to pay. Cammy felt bad about not confiding in Brian. She'd been just about to, but Boese showing up out of nowhere had rattled her, and now she was right back to being unsure honesty was a good idea. If Brian got upset, she didn't know of any magical way to *un*tell him.

Dracula's Death

She and Brian dashed back to the car, and he opened the door so she could set the bag in the backseat rather than the trunk.

"Hey!" Cammy heard behind her, and turned. There was no one looking at her. She scanned the sidewalk, but no one stood out. As she reached hesitantly for the adder stone, Brian asked, "Everything ok?"

"Yeah, I just thought I heard something," she mumbled. She slid into the passenger seat. They listened to Lorelei on the way back to the mansion.

"You know, she's doing a gig here soon," Cammy said.

"Really? When?"

Cammy told him, and his face fell.

"I have to work that night. Wish I could go."

"I'm probably going with Lindsey and the others. If she has an album or something for sale, want me to pick it up for you? Maybe get it autographed?"

She saw the look on his face and smiled.

"Wow, maybe you've got a crush on her?" she teased. Brian shook his head.

"No, I just really like her sound."

"Ok, sure." She smiled. He looked strangely sheepish.

"Thanks for driving me," she said, getting out of the car. She got her shopping out of the backseat and hugged Brian when he came around to say goodbye. From the safety of the doorway, she watched him take the car down the gravel driveway and disappear. With a shiver, she shut the door, went to the kitchen, and opened the bag to put away her food.

"Please don't be alarmed. Goldie would like to talk to you." A yellow cat wearing a dishrag like a wig poked its head out of her shopping bag.

She screamed and jumped backwards, almost landing in the sink.

The cat jumped in surprise as well, toppling the shopping bag and sending food and cleaning supplies scattering across the table. It stood in the midst of the mess, its back arched and its short tail fluffed in wide-eyed alarm. It behaved like a cat, despite the talking and the dishrag.

"Sorry to startle you," said the cat in the sort of rough, high-pitched voice you'd expect a talking cat to have. It seemed to make an effort to settle itself and slowly sat down. "Goldie saw you today. You are the girl who follows *him* around."

"What are you?" Cammy demanded. "Why are you in my bag? You're trespassing here! If he finds out, you're going to be in serious trouble, buddy!"

"Please!" the cat sat up on its haunches and pressed its forepaws together in a sign of supplication that was positively adorable. YouTube, eat your heart out. "Please! Goldie only wants to speak with you! Goldie is sorry for startling you. It was too cold to walk any further. Goldie can't stand the cold and the wet." It hung its head and raised a paw as though washing its face. She realized it was performing a sort of face-palm. "Goldie couldn't approach earlier because you were being followed by the enemy. Please, Goldie hopes you can help stop the bad things from happening."

"Why should I trust you? What are you?" Cammy demanded.

"Goldie is a gotoku neko, a trivet cat," it replied.

"A what cat?"

"A trivet cat." The cat swept off the dishrag and squinted proudly. On its head was what looked like a little, flat iron crown, with three prongs. Was that a trivet?

"Goldie doesn't know if we dare trust *him,* and we do *not* trust Ophois. You are new; you might listen?"

Dracula's Death

The cat hadn't followed the supernatural formula: identify yourself and who you work for. That was suspicious.

"It's rude not to identify yourself," she told it, sliding her feet back to the floor so she could run if she needed to. Sure, it looked cute and cuddly, but apparently the ccoa did as well.

"Sorry, sorry," said the trivet cat, "Goldie only wanted to catch you before you disappeared again. This unworthy creature is called Goldie; Goldie's people are Katie Gibbs and her boyfriend Brett. Goldie doesn't remember his last name."

"Your people?" Cammy repeated, then realized, "You're a pet? People own you?"

The cat patted at a license dangling from a red and gold glittery collar she hadn't noticed and it squinted proudly again. Cammy pulled out the adder stone and looked through it at the cat. The animal stretched into a hideous, hunched creature that vaguely resembled a cat, with enormous, staring eyes, and little, creepy, people hands. Much less cute. Despite its repulsive appearance, she didn't see anything that looked dangerous, though she knew that didn't necessarily mean it wasn't. As she hid the stone again, the trivet cat's tail twitched.

"Thank you, miss," it said. "For not throwing Goldie out."

"All right, spill. What do you want?"

"We cats are in trouble," it said.

"Do you mean supernatural cats?"

"Yes, we gotoku neko and other kaibyō. Dangerous foreigners have come to the city. They are demanding that we join them in their cause."

"What cause?"

"To destroy the human world," said the cat.

Oh, no. It was just like Boese said. The creep had been right!

"Who are 'they?'" Cammy asked.

"Goldie didn't see. They came one night to the place Goldie sometimes visits to meet with the other trivet cats. There aren't many of us here." The cat let out a sound like a purr. "It is too cold here, and no one likes to light fireplaces."

"It's not good to throw so much smoke into the atmosphere," Cammy told it. The cat licked its nose in response. "Who are these foreigners? Where can I find them?"

"Goldie doesn't know," said the cat, looking sad, like a Scottish Fold cat with adorable, watery eyes. "But the others might know. Some of them want to join."

"Join? The 'kill all humans' movement?"

"Yes," said the cat. "Goldie does not want this to happen. If the humans go away, no one will feed Goldie and let Goldie sleep near the warm things. But if Goldie doesn't join, they will kill Goldie with the humans." The cat hung its head.

"Ok, so where can I find out who knows where these foreigners are?" Cammy asked.

"There is a place," said the trivet cat. "Goldie can take you there. Goldie's friends are always there. They will know."

"Other cats who like warm fireplaces and food?" Cammy checked. Could she trust this thing?

"Yes. And the other kaibyō. We like to talk there."

"Talk? What about? What's a kaibyō?"

"Kaibyō are supernatural cats. We talk about things secret to cats. Not for humans." Goldie's eyes opened, conveying that mysterious, inscrutable expression cats wear when they calmly contemplate whatever mysteries no one else can figure out. "Will you help? Goldie does not want the weather to get worse."

Cammy pulled out her phone. The cat placed a paw on her hand. It was warm and soft.

Dracula's Death

"Please, no. He might report us. He works for *them*. That's why Goldie came to you. *He* killed two tigers already. Won't he attack us also?"

Cammy bit her lip. If she could get information that could lead Dracula and Malcolm to whatever had caused this mess, then they wouldn't have to trudge all over the city doing things the hard way, and she could say "I told you so." That would be the *best*. She might have just gotten the key that would unlock the mystery.

Of course, she could be wrong, and this creature might be planning something horrifying. She hadn't seen a whole lot of supernaturals with the adder stone. She didn't know how well it would show her if something was dangerous. Until recently, she hadn't even seen what magic looked like through it. Still, this "trivet cat" didn't strike her as hostile at all. Basically a talking cat.

Should she take the risk?

I have to, she thought. *Otherwise Boese will do something big, and this whole mess will escalate even more. Maybe I can stop it before it gets much worse.* Like with the *draugr*. If she could stop it before things got *that* out of hand... She pushed the memory of Brian being hurled and landing unconscious on the ground to the back of her mind.

"Where are your friends?" Cammy asked.

"Goldie can show you," the cat said. "You drive. It is too cold to walk."

"Ok, but first, I need help." She couldn't afford to go out without some sort of backup. Especially not with murdering were-tigers and a misogynistic cat-demon on the loose.

She went outside, found Fjola and Ginko playing, and told them she'd be away investigating with Siri, in case Dracula came back before she did. The little elf girl promised to pass the information along.

Then Cammy drove to campus to look for Siri. She didn't know how much she could really trust the huldra, but she didn't have a lot of options for back up. She spotted Siri standing under the overhang of a building, people-watching. It seemed to be her favorite pastime. Cammy approached.

"Hi," she said. "I have a favor to ask, if you're not busy?"

"Vhat favor?" Siri asked, her lightning eyes flashing.

"You remember what I said about the weather and the ccoa? Well, I found a trivet cat who has information, but it might be too dangerous to go alone."

Siri's eyes pierced her, and then stared into the distance, calculating some decision in her mind. At last, she tossed her hair—damp from the weather—and elegantly folded her arms across each other.

"Let us be off," the huldra agreed. Well, that was easy.

So back they went to the car, where Cammy introduced Siri and Goldie to each other.

"It is nice to meet more friends," Goldie said, and squinted in a cat smile. Siri offered a finger for the trivet cat to sniff, and Goldie certainly made itself busy sniffing.

Cammy followed Goldie's directions, though they were confusing and ridiculous. Make a left turn, no, right. No, turn around. Pass this tree, that wall, there's an alleyway—no, the car can't fit. Around which building? After an hour of this, the cat climbed to the dash and scanned the street.

"There it is," it said, pointing with a soft paw.

This wasn't exactly a great part of the city to be. Rundown old buildings, some of them abandoned and derelict. Trash on the streets, and worse graffiti than in other parts of the city. There were tweakers standing on corners, and some women Cammy thought might be sex workers. Maybe this wasn't the best idea.

Dracula's Death

The cat was pointing at a tacky-looking neon sign in pink and green: "The Cat's Meow" that showed a bowl of noodles with a pair of floating chopsticks. The windows were darkened and two East Asian women lurked outside. Were they more tigers? One was dressed in a Japanese school girl sailor-fuku, the other wore a tacky pleather outfit with equally tacky boots that had heels like ice picks. They stood beneath the overhang above the noodle place, staying fairly dry, although hail was piling up against the wall.

Cammy found a place to park and used the adder stone to look at the two women. Rather than two tigers, Cammy saw one was a cat and the other was a fox, both standing on their hind legs.

"What the...?" she mumbled. The fox wasn't like the kitsune that lived on Dracula's estate, the one whose child she had rescued. It looked similar, but pale, not red-orange, like ordinary foxes, and not yellow like Aki. It had three tails. There was something alarming about its appearance. Its mouth was pulled way back in a super toothy, grotesque smile, exposing rows of sharp, pointy teeth, as if someone was pulling on the skin at the back of its head or neck, so even the eyes were slantier than normal. The cat in the schoolgirl outfit looked like a house cat, tabby stripes and everything, only impossibly posed, like the fox.

"Can you turn into a human?" Cammy asked the trivet cat.

"No. Why would Goldie want to?" it purred.

Cammy opened the door and the cat shivered. She watched it hunker down, curling its tail around its side. "Want me to carry you?" she asked. It sat up, squinting with pleasure.

She tucked the cat under her jacket, fetched her umbrella, and stepped out into the awful weather. Siri followed suit. The huldra had been studying the two women; Cammy wondered if she could tell what they were without an adder stone.

"They're a fox and a cat," she informed Siri.

"Ah." Siri nodded. "I vas looking for some sign to tell me vhat they vere."

As they approached the eatery, the two women studied them, the fox playing with the gum she chewed, stretching it out with her fingers. Schoolgirl Cat stepped forward, and at that moment the trivet cat poked its head out of Cammy's jacket. Schoolgirl Cat saw it and opened her mouth in an 'oh' of surprise.

"Hello. Goldie brought friends," said the trivet cat. "Please let us pass."

Schoolgirl Cat smiled behind one hand and waved them inside.

The interior resembled a ramen shop, with chairs, tables, and a small bar, but there were house cats all over the place. Most of them were curled contentedly around a fire pit. Several cats were wearing the same strange metal prongs on their heads as Goldie. So those were trivet cats. They seemed harmless enough; not like the fox outside. Against the wall a woman played a stringed instrument that Cammy guessed came out of Asia. It was long and thin, and only had three strings, which seemed an inadequate number to Cammy, but apparently three were enough. A huge, white house cat lounged on top of the counter that faced the door. It raised its head as they entered, staring through slit pupils at Cammy as she closed the door behind Siri. The lights were dim and tinted red. There were Egyptian statues of Bastet the cat goddess along one wall, interspersed with little paw-waving, plastic, good luck cats you saw for sale in Japanese restaurants and stores.

"Is this a restaurant?" Cammy asked.

Dracula's Death

"Certainly is, dear," said a woman leaning in a doorway that Cammy assumed led to a kitchen. Rather than a door, the opening was covered with a nearly bisected cloth decorated with the image of a cat gazing at a fishbowl in which three goldfish circled. Cammy opened her jacket and set Goldie down on the counter near the firepit. It trotted to the fire and settled itself down near the glowing coals, tucking in all its paws so it resembled a happy, fluffy bread loaf.

"Not often we get ladies in here," said the woman playing the instrument. She strummed some delicate notes, then gave her attention to Cammy and Siri. "Noodles?" she offered, smiling like a Cheshire cat. Cammy suspected she probably was a cat also, maybe like the one outside.

"Um," said Cammy, looking around. There were certainly a lot of cats. She wasn't sure where to begin. Goldie looked like it had gone to sleep. "I heard that you were having some trouble with foreigners?"

The huge white cat's tail curled and its eyes opened wide, its pupils dilating with hungry interest that made Cammy's blood run cold. The woman with the instrument smiled behind her hand.

If these creatures followed the normal custom, they'd want to know who she was and who she worked for. "I'm Cammy. I don't really work with anyone, but your friend Goldie asked me for help. Can I help?"

"Mmm," said the woman with the instrument, caressing its long neck. "Can you?"

"Well, maybe. I have some friends who want to put a stop to whatever's causing *that*." She pointed towards the door and the weather outside. "Will you tell me what's going on?"

"I don't think I should," said the woman with the instrument. "I doubt you can do anything. And if you did interfere, we will have trouble, won't we, my friends?"

The cats meowed in agreement. The white one continued to stare fixedly at her, its tail curling and uncurling.

"Has someone been bothering you?" Cammy persisted. "Someone from Ophois? Calling himself Ocelotl?"

All the cats turned to stare now. So there really was someone from the Order of Ophois interfering and making demands. She wished she knew what Malcolm or Vlad had found out. This was weirder than the *draugr* with his werewolf buddies, or the elves and Siri. The *draugr* and his friends had been a team with a simple purpose; the elves had come looking for sanctuary, and Siri was looking for a husband. These cats, who seemed to be from different countries, were gathering right out in the open, and now more monster cats were showing up: were-tigers and the ccoa and whatever Ocelotl was. Was this what Malcolm had tried to explain to her, that supernaturals tended to converge? Or was it a cat thing?

"I know someone in the Order. He can stop Ocelotl from harassing you." She hoped.

One of the cats, a lanky, tawny creature with eyes like golden coins, walked across the counter. "We would *never* work with him. He has lost himself."

Some of the other cats hissed at this. It sounded like there was some disagreement here.

"Lost himself?" Cammy asked.

"He took on the aspects of a jaguar. The jaguar consumed him, and he serves it, but he is human, not cat, and there is still that stink on him."

So there really was a were-jaguar in Seattle.

"There are foreigners—plural—bothering you guys? Not only this jaguar man?" Cammy checked. The trivet cat had said that, right?

DRACULA'S DEATH

The woman who had retreated to the kitchen emerged, carrying two lacquered bowls full of steaming ramen noodles. She set them on the counter, eying Cammy and Siri purposefully.

"Bothering?" asked the cook. "According to who?" She brought out another bowl for the woman with the instrument and set it down. That one contained a grilled fish.

Goldie lifted its head and blinked once at the cook. So the trivet cat wasn't asleep.

"You little sneak," said the cook. She leaned against the counter languidly and eyed Cammy. "Ocelotl and his minions have been going around, demanding that we join their holy cause."

"Are you going to?" Cammy asked. The cook smiled a little, knowing smile and touched her chin coquettishly.

"Why shouldn't we?" asked one of the cats on the counter, draping its forepaws over the edge and crossing them artfully. This one was a silvery tabby. "The jaguar man has a point. His Jaguar god is like our lioness goddess of Egypt. Sometimes destructive, as Sekhmet. Perhaps there should be a return to the old ways."

"Goldie likes how things are now," the trivet cat piped up.

The cook and the silver tabby cat crossing its paws both hissed at Goldie, who shrank from the reproach.

"Perhaps we can coexist peacefully?" Cammy suggested.

"Coexist?" repeated the cat-woman with the stringed instrument. She plucked at it and smiled at Cammy. "This is made from my father," she said.

"*What?*"

"My shamisen is made from the skin of my father," said the cat-woman, smiling. Her teeth resembled fangs. Cammy could only stare.

"Why do you—why are you playing it, then?"

"Shamisen don't have the correct sound unless they are made out of cat skin." The woman sighed. "It is a shame."

Siri lifted her bowl of noodles and sniffed at it.

"It sounds like this jaguar guy wants you to join his cult, but you're not all on board, right?"

"I don't like his methods," the cook sniffed. "He came in here and *ordered* us to join him."

"We do not like to be told what to do," added the woman with the shamisen.

"He is not alone," said the silver tabby with crossed paws. "He has yaoguai with him."

"Who is Yaoguai?" Cammy asked. At this, the cats in unison threw back their heads and laughed. Here, for the first time, Cammy understood that use of the word 'weird' the way it was meant, way back in older days. That sense that things were uncanny, disturbing, otherworldly. The cats' fangs stood out in the red light, their raspy little tongues curled in wide open mouths. The sound was no sound a cat should ever make, but nothing like a human could utter either. The room became colder, the lights dimmed.

"See here," said the huge, white cat, arching its back and standing on the counter. "You offer to help us, but you know so little? Silly child." It stalked across the counter, walking past the fire pit. The flame's red light lit the white fur, making it glow hellishly. Cammy scooted away from it. Siri held the bowl up and shook her head at Cammy. Something was wrong with the food?

"I do want to help you, but I can't if I don't understand what is going on, or who is bothering you. Giving me straight answers would be a great start to that whole process," she told the cats. "If not, then I guess I'll be on my way."

A cat stared at her, then batted the bowl with a paw. Was this one of those hospitality rules? Was she supposed to demonstrate trust by eating the food before the white cat would tell her more? But if Siri didn't trust it, maybe it was drugged? Poisoned? *Cursed*? Some of the cats were hostile, and some weren't. She had to figure out which ones were which. "Let's start at the beginning. I know that you're being harassed by this Ocelotl guy. Some of you are on his side, some aren't, right?"

The cook looked aloofly away, while the woman with the shamisen struck a thoughtful note.

"Ok. So who is this Yaoguai character?"

"Not who, what," said the silver tabby with crossed paws. "Creatures from China who have taught themselves the magic necessary to hide as humans."

"So the were-tigers?" Cammy checked.

"The were-tigers do not use the same magic. Yaoguai are changing creatures by nature. Like our huli jing outside."

"Hooley..?"

"The fox," the cook explained.

"So, like kitsune? The Japanese foxes?" Cammy asked.

"Hmm. A bit. Kitsune, however, are not vampiric."

Oh, snap. So the fox with extra tails was some kind of vampire. That couldn't be good news.

"So you guys have this jaguar guy trying to get you to join him, and some tiger yaoguai, and you don't like them playing rough," Cammy said. "Most of you would like things to stay as they are, with fireplaces and food and humans taking care of you, but some of you agree with the jaguar guy. Sound about right?"

"Just about," the cook agreed.

The door opened behind her and the Schoolgirl Cat woman entered, leading a man who glanced around nervously.

"Wow, lots of cats!" he said. He noticed Cammy and Siri and half-smiled. "Where are your guys' costumes? You don't match the aesthetic." He laughed.

Cammy took a few seconds to understand why he'd say that, then almost yelled at him when she realized what this "restaurant" was a front for. Oh. *Eww*. Schoolgirl Cat seated the man at the counter, avoiding the bowl of noodles that had been set out for Cammy.

Cammy wondered what to do. Was this man another person who was in on the supernatural? If so, he had his own reasons for coming in here. Cammy doubted it, though, from the way he had mistaken Siri and her for sex workers.

Some of these cats were vampires; Cammy couldn't leave this guy here. None of the cats had attacked her, but that might be because Goldie had invited her. Or else because of Siri. This guy probably had no such invitation or backup.

There was the other problem of whether she could continue her conversation with the cats. If this guy didn't know what was going on, that might pop his brain. Or the cats might simply refuse to speak so long as there was an outsider present.

So she had to buy time to either find an excuse to get this guy back outside, or wait until he left in case there was more information she could glean. Easy peasy.

She took the seat next to him, in front of the bowl of noodles the cook had brought out earlier. Siri's lightning eyes admonished her not to eat it. A quick exploration of the bowl didn't reveal any obvious pieces of meat; despite that, it smelled like maybe it had been made with beef or chicken broth.

"Does this have any meat products in it?" Cammy asked the cook, who had reemerged with a bowl for the man.

DRACULA'S DEATH

The cook only answered with a coy smirk. Cammy did *not* like that. Because this was looking pretty suspicious, she pulled out the adder stone. She turned to the man. "You may not want to eat that," she warned.

"Hey, what's going on here?" the man demanded. "I thought—"

"Don't worry about it," said the woman with the shamisen. "Everything is fine."

Hoping she had rattled him enough that he might exercise some caution, Cammy looked at the noodles through the adder stone. Instead of ramen, the bowl was full of blood, eyeballs, and what looked like human hair. The one the cook had served the man had severed fingers in it. Cammy jumped to her feet and reached for the man's wrist. She had to pull him out of here!

As she reached out, the woman with the shamisen jumped to her feet and pounced on the man, pinning him to the floor. He tried to shout something, but she buried her fangs in his throat. Cammy stumbled backwards towards the door. The cook barred her way.

"That wasn't polite," the cook scolded. "Everyone's got to eat, you know." She smiled, showing her fangs.

Cammy turned around, studying the room. There had to be an exit. Siri stood shoulder to shoulder with her, her electric eyes assessing each of the cats.

The white cat chuckle-purred in the most eerie-sounding way.

"The jaguar demands our service or else payment in human meat. But we resent that he takes a cut of what we earn for ourselves."

"You're monsters," Cammy gasped. The white cat's eyes flashed green, its pupils dilated. Its tongue looked red as blood in the tinted light.

"You might prove of use to us yet," it said. "Once I drain you, I shall take your form and your memories. Perhaps I shall be able to insinuate myself in with the enemy through your form. Yes."

"Goldie invited her! She's Goldie's guest!" the trivet cat protested.

"You do and Dracula will hunt you down!" Cammy shouted. "He'll kill you!" The white cat's lips peeled back into a combined grin and snarl, then it pounced on her.

It felt much heavier than it looked. The cat's claws pierced her jacket and its teeth pricked the skin of her neck. Siri ripped the cat off of Cammy and hurled it through the cloth divider to the kitchen, as though it weighed no more than a normal cat. The other cats arched their backs in terror. Siri's tail lashed as she glared at them.

"Do not touch her," Siri hissed.

The silver tabby and the woman with the shamisen hissed back. The cook still barred the door; Cammy couldn't see any other way out except through the kitchen, and she didn't know what else might be in there. But the cook was short and slender; Cammy realized she was actually bigger. That settled it: she'd go for the front door.

The cook made no effort to stop her, side-stepping instead. Cammy shoved the door open and tumbled out onto the slick, freezing sidewalk. Siri followed close behind and reached down to help her up. The fox woman still stood outside, pulling on her chewing gum and wrapping it around her finger. She glanced at Cammy and Siri, but returned her attention to the street. Cammy whirled around to see what might be pursuing them. Instead, she saw the woman with the shamisen rise, leaving the man she had killed on the floor. She went over to her bowl and retrieved the grilled fish. Only it wasn't a grilled fish. It was a severed human hand. The woman smiled and nibbled daintily on it.

Cammy screamed and ran. Her hands were shaking so badly that she scratched the car's finish getting the key into the lock, and she nearly stripped the gears trying to reverse back out into the street. Siri barely had time to hop into the seat. After swerving unsteadily on the road, Cammy pulled over, dry heaved for a while, then drove back to the mansion as fast as she could. She didn't care if every cop in Seattle pulled her over.

The mansion was cold and dark, and she slammed the door as soon as Siri had come in behind her. She leaned against the door and struggled to catch her breath. Boese was looking more and more right. Those *things* were *eating people!* Here, in Seattle, in the modern day! There were monsters eating people. And if it hadn't been for Siri, Cammy might…. She shivered, then began shaking uncontrollably. She could still feel those fangs on her throat. Her legs gave out and she slumped to the floor, her back to the door. Her lips tingled and her throat dried out as she hyperventilated.

The shaking finally stopped. She felt like she had been totally emptied out. Her body seemed heavy.

"Are you better?" Siri asked, kneeling beside.

"Yeah." Cammy swallowed. "Yeah, I'm fine. Give me a minute."

She stood and staggered to the kitchen and got a cup of water. After she'd chugged it down, she made a call.

"Hello?" Dracula answered.

"I have some information," she said into the phone, her voice harsh and guttural. It didn't sound right at all.

"What happened?" he asked. It sounded like urgency in his voice.

"I'll tell you later," she said.

"I'm on my way."

She glanced up, suddenly remembering that Siri was here. The huldra had taken up position in front of the fireplace and was putting some of the chopped wood Dracula always kept on hand onto the grate. Maybe she was cold? Her hair and clothes still looked damp.

"Siri is here."

"The huldra?"

"Yeah, I asked her to keep an eye out. She... saved me."

"I see. As long as she does not get up to any mischief, I have no objections to her remaining until I arrive."

"Thanks." Cammy hung up. "You ok?" she called to Siri. The huldra had gotten a fire started and was warming her hands.

"Yes, perfectly," Siri answered. "Are you?"

"Yeah, I just...." Cammy didn't want to talk about how, a year ago, she'd been grabbed by vampires. They had grabbed her and dragged her from a car. For a moment, with that cat pinning her down, its fangs on her throat, she'd been back there. Those grasping hands had her again....

"I have some changes of clothes, if you'd like," Cammy offered. "And a robe you can wear over all of it."

Siri considered her clothing, damp as it was.

"Thank you," she said.

Cammy led the way upstairs to her room. Siri was taller and bigger than Cammy, so she found a loose pajama shirt and a pair of old leggings that were stretched out. Siri eyed the leggings with concern, until Cammy offered the robe Dracula had bought her since the "pajama" incident. The robe wouldn't reach the floor if Siri wore it, but neither did Siri's tail, so that should be all right. Cammy sent her to a spare bedroom to change, and then told her there would be milk and other food in the fridge downstairs if she wanted to help herself. Cammy drew a bath, trying not to feel those

Dracula's Death

cold hands on her, but she couldn't. That man was still dead. The noodle-shop-brothel still stood. That man was still dead. Heather was still dead. She pressed her face against her knees.

After the bath, she wrapped herself up in the down blankets on the bed and poked pointlessly at her phone, her face to the lamp. It cast warm, yellow light around the room.

"Cammy."

She threw her phone at him. He caught it easily. He was standing near the foot of the bed.

"Why would you even give me a key if you can just come in whenever you want?!" she screamed.

"I apologize, but you sounded in a bad way on the phone," he said. "What happened? Are you all right?"

"I'm fine," she snapped, and hugged her ribs. "Siri didn't tell you?"

She grimaced at the floor while Dracula walked to the nightstand and carefully set her phone down on it. He retreated a bit, then just as carefully sat down on the bed beside her.

"I'd like to hear from you what happened," he said.

She shook her head. "I found out a little about this Ocelotl guy—"

"That can wait," he told her, and emphasized the dismissal with a wave of his hand. "What happened?"

"I went to a place I shouldn't have gone. There was this thing called a trivet cat. It said it had information, and that I'd be its guest, so I went. But they were all..."

"Monsters?" he supplied.

She balled a hand into a fist and pressed it against her knee.

"They killed this guy. I didn't know what to do. We can't exactly call the cops, can we? They'd get turned into hamburger. I tried to save him!"

"What happened to you?" he asked, sounding genuinely concerned. He gently touched the skin on her neck. She jumped, and felt her throat. There seemed to be some bumps on the skin. The white cat had bitten her!

"Oh, no!" She ran to the mirror in the bathroom. There were little swollen points all over her throat, but she couldn't really tell if the thing had broken the skin. It was a cat, not really the sort of thing you think of as a vampire, but she didn't know all the rules. It might be that this thing could turn you with a bite. Or drain you. What had it said it would do? She hurried back to the bedroom. "One of them, it tried to kill me," she explained, gasping, "I don't know what it was. Some of them were vampires, or they said they were. They were all cats, though, so I don't know what that means."

"One of them tried to kill you?" he repeated.

"It bit me. It said it would drain me and, and... take my form!" She held out one hand. "Am I ok? Please."

He had risen to his feet when she ran to the bathroom. He glanced down at her hand. He took it, then kissed her wrist. Well, not exactly kissed. He had disguised the first time he'd tested to see if she'd been turned as a kiss on the back of her hand, but she knew what he was doing this time. He briefly made contact, open-mouthed like a fish.

"You're fine," he told her. "But I can't do that too often. Once or twice is all right; more could prove dangerous."

"I'm so stupid," she said, gripping her hair. "I should have been more careful."

He said nothing, just watched her.

"What, no 'I told you so?'" she demanded.

"Do you want me to tell you that?"

"I'm an idiot," she grumbled. "I couldn't do anything."

He continued to look at her.

DRACULA'S DEATH

"Well, say something!" she shouted. "I mean, I messed up. I got someone else killed. I'm useless."

"You led this other person into danger knowingly?" he checked.

"No, he wandered in. I tried to figure out how to get him to leave. When I told him not to eat the"—she gagged—"they killed him. They eat people. Does everything eat people?" Boese was looking much, much saner, and that might be the worst part of this entire disaster.

"Not everything," Dracula told her.

Some irony there, she thought to herself.

"Precisely why do you say you got this person killed?"

"I didn't know whether he knew, or what I was supposed to do. Sometimes saying something is rude to the supernatural, sometimes it isn't, and I was scared if I said something they might attack, or refuse to tell me anything more. I guess I should have just tackled him and tried to push him out the door." She sniggered helplessly at the idea. He had been about half a foot taller than she was, and pretty heavy. She doubted she could have managed to move him an inch.

"What do you think you could have done?" Dracula asked.

"I could have tried telling him about the food. Maybe even if he thought I was crazy he might have left just to get away from me."

"I doubt you could have protected this person. It seems you barely escaped with your own life," he said. She rubbed her throat.

"I can't help anybody," she mumbled.

"It's a very daunting goal to hold," he told her. "An admirable one, but you have to be realistic or you'll only destroy yourself in the process."

"You talking from experience?" she wondered doubtfully.

"As a matter of fact," he said, "yes."

She squinted at him.

"You tried to help people?"

"You say that like you think it some sort of miracle on my part," he said, sounding unfriendly. She was beginning to realize that whenever she did hurt his feelings, he never sounded wounded, he sounded angry.

Cammy considered. He came to her rescue and protected her, but he'd impaled people. He just didn't make sense. Her mother was a toxic human being; Boese seemed unhinged; but Dracula? He was pretty subdued most of the time. If it wasn't for those occasional flashes into his past or the stupid things that got him angry, like pajamas, she'd think he was just an old-fashioned, stubborn, rich fogey. He could be blunt, sometimes *very* blunt, and not exactly "emotionally available", but he didn't seem like a bloodthirsty monster in the here and now. He had jerk tendencies, though. Like with Malcolm earlier. It confused her, and she didn't know how to feel about it. What should she trust? Common opinion or the man himself? Even the man himself presented different faces.

"What happened to Margaret?" she asked. Surprise slowly overtook his eyes, his shoulders slumped. He stuck his hands in his pockets and looked out the window at the hail.

"She died," he answered, which is what he usually said about people he had known, but then he went on. "It was my fault, however. And I have never married since."

"What happened?" Cammy asked.

"I told you that I briefly lived in London. It was the most appalling, squalid city I have ever seen. At the time, I explained to Margaret—my wife—that we should relocate to my home country, as we could no longer safely live in Ireland, which was her home, because someone had told

DRACULA'S DEATH

Catholic priests about me. I confess I was also concerned about the rumors I heard from my homeland and wished to return. But there was war: Russians and Turks fighting, and Romania joined with the Russians. Margaret wished to stay in Britain, and I decided to let her have her way. When you get to my age, you think that it might simply be easier to wait until someone grows old and dies than fight with them on every little thing. That was my plan. Then she contracted some ridiculous ailment of the lungs." He shrugged. "In that city, with all the smog and filth, it wasn't uncommon. I'd seen many other people, especially women and girls, come down with the same ailment. I had even told her it was one more reason to leave. In any case, I then expected my wait to be shorter, and I attended her and made her comfortable, as best I could."

He turned towards the door, then turned back.

"She asked me to 'save' her. To turn her into a strigoi. I refused, of course. I doubted I could even do any such thing. However, the terror of death drove her to ask me again and again, and over the weeks I began slowly to reconsider. I began to wonder whether, as I am some inexplicable freak even within the world of monsters, it might be possible to do as she asked. I even, to my shame, wondered if her request was not some consolation, some small comfort granted me by Providence. Perhaps..." He tapped his mouth. "So in a moment of weakness, I did as she asked."

"And?" Cammy asked.

"And my blood killed her," he said. "As I should have known it would. She came back, but as a strigoi, a mindless, ravenous, blood-drinking monster. I killed what she had become."

He met her eyes. "I should have let her die as a human with a soul. Did her death count against her as a suicide? I do not know. I would pray for her, but there is a barrier between me and God, and my prayers.... And I understood, with more certainty than at any moment save that first, terrible realization, that I am in Hell. This... hateful existence is the wages I earned for my failures. For my hubris. None of my family suffered the same fate, nor my political rivals, nor my enemies—not even the ones who exceeded me in cruelty—nor any friends."

"What failures?" Cammy asked.

"My legacy is failure," he told her. "I failed my country, when victory was in my hands." He held up one open, empty hand, to illustrate. "I let it slip through my fingers. Had I succeeded and proved the victor and my country made strong, as I hoped... Instead, well" —he put that hand into his pocket— "now the only thing anyone knows about it—well, the country with its current borders—is what an Irishman wrote. Apparently, it's full of vampires. Also, poverty, crime, so on. That is what, as you so aptly put it, 'everyone knows'."

His gaze turned to the hail that clattered against the window.

"What better sentence for such failure?" he muttered. "To take on the mantle of an illustrious order, come so close to salvation, only to fail?"

"Ok, I'm a little lost now," Cammy said. "But I think I get it. You're saying that you tried to protect your country, but you messed up?"

He guffawed. Actually guffawed. From never laughing to guffawing. The shock of it made her worry she'd broken him somehow.

"You have quite a way of summing up," he told her. "But I suppose that's the long and the short of it."

"You think you're cursed to wander the earth for all eternity because you messed up? Not because of the whole 'killing twenty-thousand people' thing?" she wondered.

Dracula's Death

"My contemporaries did exactly the same, and worse," he told her. "If that was the reason, they'd all be here."

"You're still not sorry about that?" Cammy asked.

He frowned. "Yes. I'm sorry it didn't work."

She fiddled with her hands. "What do you mean?" She'd always been too nervous to press too much. After that comment about him being *far crueler* last year. But she was never going to figure him out unless she got him to talk more...

"Because perhaps if it had worked I could have bought myself enough time to defend my country properly, lift it out of the poverty that had been inflicted on it by its enemies, fortify the borders against further attacks, and I might have spared my country hundreds of years of suffering, of being plundered and used by every country around it. So long as they painted me as a monster during my life, and after, I might as well have embraced it, if doing so could have prevented what happened."

She tapped her feet, bit her lip.

"I guess I get it," she said, though the idea still made her queasy. "I don't really have the context, though."

"You want context?" he asked.

"Yeah. I'm never going to understand unless I know what else was going on," she said.

He nodded. "Very well. Perhaps when we have the time, I will tell you more. But for now, you need to recover your strength. We have quite the enemy to defeat."

"Wait, you want me along?" Cammy checked.

"Don't you want to come along?"

"But, after what just happened..." She shook her head "I mean, I messed up. I almost got killed! I couldn't do anything!"

"Do you intend to remain helpless?" he asked. "Or do you intend to stand back up and try again?"

She cocked her head at him, incredulous.

"But," she said, "I mean, can I even learn how to stop failing?"

"The only way to learn is to move forward," he told her. "Failure is always a possibility, but that is no reason not to try. Not trying guarantees failure. So?" He stared straight into her eyes. "What will you do?"

CHAPTER 8
RAIN CHECK

The next morning, his guest slept in later than usual, but he let her be. He had talked with the huldra, who had confirmed Cammy's story, and he'd expressed his gratitude for her aid in protecting Cammy. The poor creature seemed unduly excited by this courtesy. He suspected she still held out hope he might marry her; but she was too strange for him. He let her stay the night so her clothes would have a chance to dry, then drove her to the restaurant that overlooked Snolqualmie Falls, and called a taxi to return her to the city. He sent her off with a basket of food and enough money to buy a better change of clothes in the future, ignoring her obvious disappointment.

Then he breakfasted at the restaurant since he had come out that way. He enjoyed the view, though the food was only a stopgap for his eternal hunger. He'd been up for three days and would need to rest very soon no matter what happened. Poor timing, very poor.

Back at the estate, he donned a pair of boots, selected an umbrella, and went out into the wooded part of his property, beyond the grapevines. He came to a den dug into the earth at the roots of a pine tree. "Good morning," he called out.

The fox, the tanuki, and their unusual child poked their heads out of the hole, noses twitching. "I will be calling a meeting," he told them. "Aki, gather the others, if you would. We will meet at the side door that is sheltered by the large oak tree." The fox yipped and darted away. Dracula had no interest in tracking down the invisible elves, and the fox seemed better suited for seeking them out, so he left the task to her. To the tanuki, he said, "I would like to review some expenses with you, so I must ask you to stay afterwards." The tanuki nodded.

Satisfied that he was understood, Dracula went to the glen where the satyrs usually cavorted when they weren't working. He found them huddled under trees for shelter.

"Good morning," he said to them. "I must call a meeting with you all. If you would come with me."

"It's been cold for days!" one complained.

"That is true," Dracula agreed. "Nevertheless, I am calling a meeting. I expect you all to be there."

He checked the grapevines on the way back. They had taken quite a beating from the hail and the cold. They would yield nothing this season. Worse, it looked doubtful they would even survive, for the satyrs had only covered a small portion of the vineyard. Many of the vines had been stripped completely bare by the relentless weather. He didn't relish the idea of having to start over, but by all appearances, he would have no other choice. He detested American grown wine, and lamented the loss of the vines he'd managed to acquire.

He smashed several of the vampire watermelons that were wobbling around in the shelter of the mansion's shadow while he waited for his tenants to gather. The melons were generally harmless, but when they broke free of their vines they sometimes harassed the cows.

DRACULA'S DEATH

Some of the satyrs appeared, shivering in the wet and cold. He knew better than to invite them inside; they were children of nature, and they preferred the wild at all costs. Besides, so long as Cammy was living here, he did not want them inside.

Rustlings amongst the trees alerted him that the rusalki had arrived. Nymphs peered around the trunks, avoiding the satyrs. A few of the elves who had taken up residence on his property appeared, and he assumed the others were attendant but remaining invisible.

"Good morning everyone," he addressed them. "I trust you have all been well since last I spoke with you. I know the weather has been appalling, so I will be brief. I wish to know how you have been progressing since last I spoke with you, and with regards to the vineyards—"

A satyr jumped to his feet—hooves, rather. Knowing an outburst was forthcoming regardless of what he might say, he gestured the creature speak.

"We have to do more work?"

"Yes. However—"

"All we do is work!" the satyr protested, and there was a grumbling consensus from the others. "We want to gambol and play!"

"I know." Dracula sighed. Being reduced to a small workforce of bizarrely childlike, but nevertheless rapacious, nature spirits was not ideal, but it was what he had. He wondered whether this was worse or better than the greedy, thieving councilors he'd had to deal with formerly. No, these were definitely better. They were less competent, but also less malicious. "I will grant you an extra stipend of wine today, the finest, if you cover the rest of the vines." He pointed at the damaged plants sprawling beyond them. The satyrs looked sheepish. "And I will set out another batch, a large one, if you do a good job grafting on new vines to replace the old, once the weather clears. I will have the domovoy or Aki bring these to you."

"Why can't we make our own wine all the time?" one satyr interrupted.

"We have discussed this. I will not have this conversation again. You have your allotment of vines for yourselves. Only you must do what is needful to protect the vineyards, otherwise you will have nothing. There will be no harvest."

The satyrs grumbled to each other. Unruly satyrs were not likely to be good for him, but he needed the stupid creatures to do the least which was possible for them. He would see how this played out. He turned next to the elves.

"What have you to report?"

"We need more materials," the elder, named Axel, answered.

"How much?"

"Seweral tons of stones or earth at the least," the elder replied. "And a great deal of wood."

"Draw up precisely how much you require, then I will see to it that you have the supplies. How are your crops?"

"All ruined," Axel answered sadly. Dracula had feared as much. This weather was setting them all off to a poor start.

"Why is it so important that they build that wall?" Aki inquired.

"I am not obliged to share all my plans with you," Dracula told her.

The fox bowed her head to the ground. "Forgive my impertinence."

The creature was demure and respectful, at least. He preferred her to the others for her obedience and deference. Perhaps she could teach the others how to conduct themselves.

Dracula's Death

"That is all," he said. "Thank you all for coming, and I thank you in advance for your hard work." Hard work was more than he could realistically hope for from the satyrs, but anything was better than nothing. His tenants departed, some grumbling about the weather or the work.

"You," he waved that the tanuki accompany him. No sooner had the little raccoon creature stepped forward than the elf girl, Fjola, appeared and hesitantly approached.

"Is something the matter?" he asked her. Fjola wrung her tiny hands.

"A satyr almost... he was going to hunt Cammy," the girl explained. Dracula waved the tanuki away and to wait some distance off. "How did this happen? When?"

"Ginko and I wanted to show her the lake," Fjola explained. The lake lay in the opposite direction from the vineyard. One of the satyrs must have decided to shirk his duties.

"Which one?"

Fjola's eyebrows knotted together. "I could show you," she offered.

"Do so."

She led him behind the group of satyrs and squinted at them as they dragged cloth from one of the sheds to cover the vines. Her bright eyes scanned their faces, until at last she pointed to one in particular.

"Him. The rusalki threw him into the lake."

Satyrs were not known for swimming prowess; the rusalki had tried to enact the justice he would have chosen. *But he did not drown.* He memorized the face.

"Thank you," he told Fjola. "I'll give you and your brother candied cherries, if you like those." Fjola nodded eagerly. Dracula returned to where he had left the tanuki and gestured that the animal should follow him. Upon entering the house, the tanuki changed itself into a pudgy, utterly mediocre-looking man. Dracula had no idea why it always chose to do this, but let it be. He wasn't very familiar with the creatures that came out of East Asia, so it might be some ritual the species liked to perform. He led the tanuki to the study where he kept his technology. There were several "old" computers, as Cammy liked to call them, as well as the laptop she'd advised him to buy.

"Let us resume where we left off," Dracula said, and turned on the laptop. The creature absolutely had a head for numbers, but it was not so familiar with modern technology.

Some hours later, Cammy appeared in the doorway. She took stock of the situation, eyebrows raised in interest, the corners of her mouth tight, trying not to smile.

"Still teaching him how to internet?" she asked.

He hesitated. Probably a modern phrase, better not to comment on it. "Yes," he agreed. "How are you?"

Cammy looked up at the corner of the doorjamb.

"Fine," she said. Then, "No, not fine. Bad, actually."

"We will continue this later," Dracula told the tanuki, who scooted out of the room as fast as he could. Cammy made way for him, then resumed hovering in the doorway.

He waited.

"What are we going to do?" she asked.

"About the monsters you discovered yesterday?" he checked. Cammy nodded, biting her lip. "What do you think we should do about them?" he asked her.

"Stop them," Cammy asserted.

"You understand what that will entail?" he checked. Cammy grimaced and covered her eyes with one slim hand. She just didn't have the constitution, it seemed, for what was necessary. He wasn't about to start another argument on the topic, however, so he said, "They will be dealt with, have no fear."

Dracula's Death

"I don't have fear about that," Cammy told him. "I have fear that I'm wrong, or I'm just not seeing this right. I don't want to hurt things, I want to help."

This tiresome diatribe. Under normal circumstances he'd have the patience to let her work her way through this, but time was of the essence if he was going to complete anything useful before tomorrow.

"I understand," he said, and was about to say more when he heard his domovoy creaking the wood near the front door. That meant someone was approaching from that direction, and only a very short list of people used that road. "*La naiba,*" he hissed.

"Sorry, what?" Cammy wondered.

"Someone's coming," he explained. "Someone we don't want to talk to right now."

Cammy followed him to the front door. He opened it to see a series of government vehicles parking on the gravel driveway outside. Several agents from Special Services emerged from the vehicles; last to do so was Boese himself.

What is going on?" Cammy asked.

"Boese is paranoid as a rule," Dracula explained. "And right now, he's terrified. So he'll rattle the cage, as it were. It makes him feel powerful."

Cammy frowned as Boese came to the front door. The director dumped his umbrella by the door and walked right in. Because of the gravel there was no mud to track in, only water, but he made certain to track as much of that as he could. His agents swarmed into the mansion behind him.

A pointless show of force. A sure sign Boese was scared.

"Good morning, Director," Dracula greeted him affecting a cheery tone. "You came all this way, in this weather? I'm positively flattered."

"You want to explain to me why *that*," the director pointed a finger out the open door at the puddles and the pattering hail, "is still happening? Why haven't you dealt with it?" Boese demanded.

"Why haven't *you?*"

Boese bared his teeth, but had no ready response. Instead, he said, "You realize you're only allowed out provisionally. If I say the word, we'll have you back in that box to stay."

"I fail to see how that will help your trouble with the weather," said Dracula, "but by all means, if you feel that's the only solution. I could do with a long holiday."

He did not grin when he saw the rage rippling under Boese's cold, pale face, though the sight did warm the deep, dark cockles of his heart.

"You think you're clever?" Boese snapped.

"Arrogance is a trap, Director. I know better. Surely a man in your position knows the same?" He pointed out the door. "Just as I'm certain a man in your position would't drive himself and the few people he still has at his disposal all the way out here without some pressing reason. With resources being so scarce and time being of the essence, after all." He pretended to be patiently but innocently waiting for the explanation he knew wasn't coming.

"I've got my eye on you," Boese growled, "I know you're up to something, and the same with all the other monsters out there. If you cross me—"

"Cross you? To ally with a cat? Please. As though I were so desperate for friends as that."

"You seem desperate enough to take on a total liability." Boese pointed at Cammy.

"Who the hey says I'm a liability?" Cammy demanded.

"Who says you're not? *You?*"

"Yeah, maybe," she said. Boese scoffed.

"*You're* the liability, my dude," she told him. "We were doing just fine solving this whole mess, but you have to keep interrupting, oh, and *stalking* me! I mean, there's a weather apocalypse going on and you think it's worth your time to harass me personally? Why'd you even come up here?"

That Boese was forced to contend with a small woman he could probably snap in half did cheer Dracula enormously.

"I came up here to make sure your sugar daddy is on task," Boese snapped. "He doesn't follow orders unless you take out a cattle prod."

"And you are a cattle prod, are you?" Dracula wondered.

"Do. Not. Push. Me," Boese growled.

He was using the strong mouthwash again. Dracula made a mental note to try to track down the brand; he could use something that long-lasting. He decided to end the confrontation; Boese was rattled, certainly, but pushing might force Boese to react rashly. It should now be clear to all parties how pointless this visit had been, and he didn't intend to give Boese a reason to tighten the leash again. He waited for Boese to say his piece and leave.

"I trust we understand each other?" Boese demanded.

"Perfectly," said Dracula.

"I want that solved," Boese insisted, waving at the open door. "If you haven't made progress by tomorrow, the gloves are coming off, you understand?"

"Absolutely."

Boese pointed one finger menacingly, and then led his minions out. Dracula waited until they had all piled into their vehicles and disappeared down the hill before swinging shut the door. Perhaps this had all been a show to impress his agents. To let them know that the director of Special Services in Seattle still had his famous monster under his thumb.

"What was the point of that?" Cammy wondered.

"Posturing."

"Oh, a dick measuring contest?"

The crassness of modern men—and women—never ceased to appall him, but he did not comment.

"Of a sort."

Cammy crossed her arms.

"What does he mean when he says he'll put you in a box again?" she asked. "Does he mean his lab?"

"Yes. That he'll have me incarcerated in some lab or other until he or his replacement decides to release me," Dracula answered.

"And you'd let him?"

"Not without a fight, and there would be consequences," Dracula told her, though he did not reveal the details. "It would hardly be the first time the department has done so. Special Services has locked me up twice before. I did cause some consternation at the end of the Second World War, earning a particularly long sentence. History was repeating itself. It seems to be some sort of curse."

"Curse?"

He didn't want to explain the Russian post war conquests and what had happened to his country. Given how rattled Boese was acting, he'd have to approach the ccoa problem more aggressively. That meant a change in plans.

"We'll deal with those cats tonight," he announced. "But I'm going to rest all day first." That should help a bit with the hunger. Not much, but a bit.

"Ok," she responded dubiously.

"While I'm resting, go ahead and think about what you wish to do." He dialed Malcolm.

"What the hell, man?" Malcolm said when he picked up.

"I need you to come to the estate at sundown. Find the huldra, she may be of help to us."

Dracula's Death

"Why do I have to drive all the way up there? And Siri, really? Why?" Malcolm demanded.

"Because you'll be paid," Dracula told him.

"Why do we need Malcolm and Siri up here?" Cammy asked when he hung up the phone.

"I need to speak with Malcolm about what he's found, then we need to find that restaurant."

Cammy bit her lip. "Yeah."

"Siri may remember where it is. And as you have discovered, she may also be helpful if those monsters should prove unfriendly again. Lastly, I like to rely on Malcolm's expertise in matters of monsters with which I am not familiar. In the meanwhile" —Dracula pointed to his armory — "Go. Find something. I'll check on you later."

Cammy trudged off to the weapons room. Once she was out of sight, he went the other way to one of the safe rooms he used for resting. He couldn't be entirely certain they hadn't been compromised by Boese or the department during his most recent incarceration, but the walls seemed intact. If they had found his hiding places they must have bricked the walls back up and plastered them flawlessly.

He took a side door out through the kitchen and made his way to the garage. There was a small enclave he had built behind a wall that he felt fairly confident Cammy had never discovered. It required him to move the tool chest to one side, which he did carefully so as to avoid scratching the finish of the silver Duesenberg. He slid the keyhole cover open and unlocked the door. The little trap door, made of concrete to blend in with the rest of the wall, swung open to reveal a small storage room, into which he lowered himself. With the door closed, the room was in total darkness, which was no problem for him at all. It locked from the inside, sealing him in the darkened space. So long as he would be utterly insensate for hours, he didn't like to take chances.

That had ended badly for him before. As secure as he could be, he slept as the dead do.

CHAPTER 9

WHEN IT RAINS, IT POURS

Her host vanished. He did that. It was incredibly annoying. Cammy spent the day trying to study. She didn't know how she was going to be able to pass midterms with all this insanity going on, but she figured she ought to at least try. Maybe doing something normal would take her mind off of... everything.

After several hours of mundanity, she went to the kitchen to look for snacks. At sundown a pair of headlights lit up the water droplets on the kitchen window. She hurried to the back door and let Malcolm and Siri in.

"Are we early?" Malcolm asked as he brushed bits of ice out of his hair. Siri's mood seemed as unaffected by the weather as ever.

"He's not around, so I guess so," Cammy told him. "Want something to drink?"

They waited in the kitchen while the world outside grew darker. Eventually her host reappeared.

"Are you helping yourself to my wine?" Dracula asked sourly when he came into the kitchen. Malcolm held up a glass as evidence and finished it in one gulp. Siri was drinking raw milk.

"Absolutely. You promised a bonus," Malcolm told him.

"Are all of you ready to go?"

"Go where?" Malcolm asked. "Last I heard was nothing much about some restaurant run by cats."

"The proprietors of that restaurant have been contacted by your compatriot in Ophois. I am hoping they will be able to point us in his direction."

"Are we certain this Ophois guy is related to the weather problem?" Cammy asked.

"Yes. I'll explain on the way. Did you select a weapon?"

Gingerly, Cammy reached into her bag and retrieved a nine-millimeter he'd shown her how to use despite her protests. Malcolm slow clapped at the sight.

"Shut up," she snapped.

"Why are you coming again?" Malcolm turned to Dracula. "Why is she coming again?"

"Because she wants to. Isn't that right?"

"Yeah," Cammy agreed, trying to sound confident.

"And that peashooter is all you're bringing?" Malcolm checked.

"I also have this." She retrieved her pepper spray from her bag and waggled it. Malcolm's eyebrows climbed an inch, then he let out a single, obviously fake "HA!"

"You've never been pepper sprayed, I take it?" Dracula asked him.

"What? No, of course not."

"Then how do you know it's ineffective?"

That stumped Malcolm; he rocked back in his chair and frowned at his empty glass. Cammy knew from experience it wouldn't work on Dracula, but he'd never said not to try it on anything else. It seemed logical that if her enemies were living creatures they wouldn't like the stuff very much. Maybe. The supernatural was weird.

Dracula's Death

"So is it silver bullets and wolfsbane for you?" she asked Malcolm.

He sneered and waved a hand. "Nah. That's Hollywood stuff. I'm old school," he said. "Honestly, I don't think Ophois will try for the 'newer' models. Being dependent on—or overwhelmed by—full moons is a pretty serious handicap."

"Being susceptible only to silver bullets would be a boon, though, no?" Dracula asked him. Malcolm shrugged.

"Yeah, sure," he said. "That might be nice. Maybe not if I'm ripped in half and still not dead, though."

"So what do we know about the jaguar guy?" Cammy asked.

"Malcolm made a call," Dracula explained. "It seems one of Ophois' South American branches went silent about four months ago. By all appearances they've been wiped out. Eviscerated, you said?"

"Most of them," Malcolm confirmed. "Flayed, beheaded. Someone had themselves a good ol' time. Anyway, they did have a were-jaguar working for them; his body never turned up. So odds are good he's gone rogue and he's the guy prowling around and harassing everyone."

"He took out an entire branch by himself?" Cammy asked, amazed. She didn't know a whole lot of the specifics about Ophois, but they were apparently nearly as powerful as the US government, and could use magic. For someone to take one whole section of it down alone was... alarming.

"Yeah, I was pretty impressed," Malcolm chuckled. "I mean, I dream about doing that all the time, but I know I could never manage it. And it seems he must have been in contact with someone in one of our Chinese branches, because two frontliners went missing, and one of them was found in South America. Dead. Not eviscerated, just heart exploded."

"Heart *exploded*?" Cammy repeated.

"Yeah. One of us frontliners goes rogue, someone up the chain has hair or blood or nails or teeth. Makes a *mumia*, kills us with it."

"A what?"

"You might know them as Voodoo dolls," Malcolm explained. "Magic users all around the world have been making those things for a long time."

"Oh," said Cammy. That explained why Malcolm hated his job so much. She realized that was a bit of an understatement.

"Anyway," Malcolm continued, "I'm guessing these guys had arranged to meet up. Maybe they were hoping to eliminate their respective branches. But this particular were-jaguar had done some jobs in Peru just before all this went down. Golly gee whiz, but wouldn't you know it, our little cat friend with the long tail and the annoying weather control is also from Peru. The Seattle department finds this ccoa hundreds of miles north of where it's supposed to be, captures it and brings it here. But before they can get it all quietly tucked away in some oubliette in a lab, our were-jaguar shows up to liberate him. And now he's leaning on every supernatural cat in the city to join his cause."

"And he wants to overthrow humans?"

"Sounds like," Malcolm shrugged.

"We're losing precious time," Dracula pointed out.

When they went for the door, he picked up a bag he must have left there in preparation and slung it over his shoulder.

"What's that?" Cammy asked.

"Always be prepared," he told her. "Especially when you expect a fight."

"What if you don't?" she asked.

"Be prepared anyway," he answered. He led the way to the garage. When he noticed halfway there that Siri was

Dracula's Death

following him, he pointed her towards Malcolm's car. Sullenly, Siri slunk the other way.

"I can't believe she still likes you," Cammy muttered as she took the passenger seat.

"She doesn't," Dracula informed her as he turned the key in the ignition. "She likes what she thinks I can give her."

Cammy gave that some thought, then changed the subject. "Did you find any more were-tigers?

"We found no more. They seem to have fled the city, presumably after discovering that their compatriots were all being slaughtered."

"So... what is the deal with the Order of Ophois?" Cammy asked. The sleet slapped the windshield, so she had to raise her voice.

"Members of Ophois like Malcolm are born and bred by the organization," Dracula explained. "They are the soldiers and vanguard, while the administration keeps to the shadows. However, as it would be dangerous to let one's war dogs off the leash, Ophois holds over them the threat of hexing them to death if they do not obey orders. They will kill any minion who steps out of line. Malcolm calls himself and the others like him 'cannon fodder' for the organization; I see them as soldier-slaves."

Cammy stared at him. He didn't look even a little disturbed at the fact that Malcolm had to work for an organization that would kill him if he didn't obey.

"We have to do something to help Malcolm!" Cammy asserted.

Dracula sighed.

"You do not know what you propose. To do so would require wiping out the entirety of the Seattle branch that Ophois has operating here, doing it swiftly, before they have a chance to use any of their hexes, *and* in such a way that their other branches could not find out afterwards who did it. That is no small undertaking."

"But you could do it, right?" Cammy suggested.

Dracula looked at her. "I have rarely encountered any members of Ophois, save Malcolm and a few of their other werewolves. The heads of the organization keep themselves very well-hidden. Even Malcolm doesn't know where they are located."

"Then we should find them."

"Cammy, these are very evil men. And I do not use that word lightly. These are men who will work for *anyone* for the right price, do *anything* for the right price, and have all—to the man—made deals with foul and unspeakable spirits for power."

"But—"

"Those who wish to hire Ophois hire them so they can attain riches, seduce the object of their desires, or kill their enemies in ways that will evade notice by the police. Even if Ophois offers to heal a loved one—and they do—it will be for a terrible price. These are people who will slather themselves with the fat of unbaptized children in order to gain the power of flight."

"They..." Cammy's skin went cold. "What are you talking about?"

"You know nothing of witchcraft," Dracula told her. "I have given the matter some thought myself, but I doubt that I have the ability to take on an organization such as that. Worse still, the US government works with Ophois on and off. They may decide that keeping the warlocks around is of more use than retaining me, if they should ever think they need to choose between us."

"Why would they work with people who murder..." She didn't want to finish the sentence. "Why would they do that?"

DRACULA'S DEATH

Dracula smirked in the dark. Apparently he found the question amusing.

"Ophois provides a marvelous way to accomplish your worst deeds. And it has become stylish for world governments to employ members of the organization to protect themselves from the hexes of other governments' warlocks. Almost all of whom are branches of Ophois as well."

"Become stylish since when?"

"Since people sought to hunt the supernatural personally, rather than leave it to itself and to the powers beyond Man, and since they have ceased to believe in God."

Cammy looked out the window. She hated everyone and everything. Why would anyone *do* such evil things? Side with people who would kill infants just so they can have more power? It made her sick. Even Dracula, who might have killed someone for making a shirt wrong, wouldn't work with any of them except Malcolm. *He's thought about it*, she mused. Meaning he had toyed with the idea of freeing Malcolm. That made him better than Boese or anyone else. Why did that keep happening? The guy who had impaled twenty-thousand people kept looking better than the people currently running things.

Then she thought about how Malcolm said he hated his job. No wonder. If people would kill you with magic if you didn't do what they ordered—and now she worried about what they *would* order, if they weren't opposed to the idea of murdering infants in exchange for some stupid powers. Flying would be cool, but *absolutely* not in exchange for... that.

Then she thought about Malcolm's threat to get her hexed by someone. That may have been no idle threat. She gripped her fingers together and bit her lip. Malcolm might not be the nicer of the two supernatural allies she'd made. Her stomach tightened.

"Wait," she realized something. "Ocelotl is working with another Ophois were-thingie? A were-tiger? Meaning not the local were-tigers from South Asia?"

"Yes."

"But Oceltol is also bugging the local were-tigers, and cats."

"That appears to be the case. If we can determine what he's after, then we may be able to locate the ccoa as well as any remaining were-tigers who slaughter humans, or at least discover for what reason they have changed their behavior. Special Services is aware of Oceltol. They were already investigating him when I brought up his name."

"Wait, really?"

"Apparently he's made a few appearances around Seattle, and kidnapped no fewer than forty people in the last few days. He is not shy about appearing on camera. He is working with individuals who appear to be East Asian. Given what Malcolm has told us, I think it is a fair assumption that at least one of them may be the Ophois were-tiger, while the others are the yaoguai you were told of."

"What is he kidnapping people for?" Cammy demanded.

"Perhaps the cats at the restaurant can tell us," Dracula said.

Cammy sure hoped so. The sooner this whole nightmare was resolved, the better. Maybe the local were-tigers didn't want to kill anyone, but they were being blackmailed. If she and Dracula could stop Ocelotl, the were-tigers could go back to living peaceably. Then Boese would be wrong.

The weather had hailed and sleeted and rained, sometimes all at once, and there were piles of ice against the corners of some buildings almost a foot high. She decided to

Dracula's Death

check her phone for news. The mayor had declared a state of emergency due to flooding. There were numerous alerts and warnings of streets to avoid, and general advice to remain indoors. There were *far* fewer cars on the road than she'd ever seen before.

"Is it safe for us to drive?" Cammy asked.

"Would you prefer to walk?" Dracula responded.

They passed a tow truck trying valiantly to load a hybrid car onto its bed in the pelting slush. The truck driver lost his footing and fell down into the freezing water dotted with bits of ice coursing down the street. The city couldn't take this weather much longer. People were getting hurt on the roads, and then there was the property damage. Trees were stripped of leaves, and she hadn't seen a bird or animal since the weather turned cold. How would they survive?

She did her best navigating Dracula to the restaurant, with Malcolm following behind. It was harder in the dark than she had expected, and she had expected it to be hard, but at last they found the street with the neon sign of chopsticks over a bowl.

They were able to find a parking space within eyesight of the restaurant. Cammy got her umbrella ready while Dracula hopped out of his vehicle—probably over a puddle Cammy couldn't see—and went to Malcolm's car, which pulled up beside them. There was a deep puddle just outside her door running along the curb, which Cammy stepped over, but even the sidewalk was partly submerged. She could feel the cold even through the soles of her boots, and the water trying to seep through. Walking carefully, she came up alongside to hear what they were saying.

"I suggest you stay with the vehicle, and leave it running," Dracula told Malcolm. "I'll call you and leave the phone on in my pocket. If you hear anything amiss, come in after us.

Otherwise, if we need to make a quick escape I will send Cammy to your vehicle."

Cammy pulled out the specialty earplugs Dracula had ordered for her. He had gotten them for her to practice firing guns—the lessons she had *not* wanted but he had insisted on. She didn't need more hearing loss if things got spicy, and she figured that, now that Vlad was here, things *would*.

Malcolm saluted a finger off his temple and turned off his lights. Siri stepped out of the passenger seat and adroitly leaped over the puddle to the sidewalk, then approached to take shelter under Cammy's umbrella. Was she trying to "be more human" now? Cammy obliged, holding it higher so Siri wouldn't have to hunker down so much to fit beneath it. Freezing clumps of slush pelted the plastic and slid off to the wet ground.

"Behind you?" Cammy asked Dracula, and he nodded. He wasn't using an umbrella, she supposed because the cold didn't bother him and he needed his hands free. She still wasn't sure she wanted to do this, but at the same time, if no one stopped these monster cats, they'd go on killing people.

No one else was on the street. Neither the fox woman nor Schoolgirl Cat stood outside, but the sign flashed and the sidewalk puddles reflected the lurid glow. When they came to the door, Dracula took hold of the handle and pulled. The door swung open. Some sort of flute played a few haunting notes, then fell silent as they entered. The interior flickered with dim light from several candles that had been set up in the alcoves near the statuettes of Bastet, and Cammy saw a fairly big, blocky silhouette in the middle of the room that had not been there last time, but she couldn't make out what the shape was. Her throat was dry, her fingers trembling. Things were about to happen; she decided to follow Dracula's "keep your hands free" example and put away her

DRACULA'S DEATH

umbrella. Doing so put her fingers against the handle of the gun in her bag, and she left her hand there.

The large, white cat crouched on the counter, its tail twitching slowly. Two other cats, the silver tabby and a black one, perched on the shelves near the alcoves with the Bastet statues. There didn't seem to be any trivet cats, nor the woman with the shamisen. The silhouette she couldn't make sense of before revealed itself to be an armchair. More than that, it was the same armchair that had gone missing from the were-tigers' apartment earlier. She could just see Dracula's bloodstain over the shoulder of the young man who sat in it now.

She noticed his eyes first, which seemed to gleam green in the faint candlelight. He wore a long coat with large, ponderous sleeves that seemed to end in mittens that dangled down over his hands, which were folded across his chest. His dark hair was long. In a way, he looked a lot like Malcolm: incredibly, stupidly handsome. Maybe that was the look Ophois liked to go for. He held a small, ceramic flute in his left hand. That must have been the sound Cammy'd heard when they'd entered.

"Ocelotl, I take it?" Dracula said by way of greeting. The young man smiled warmly.

"You're him, aren't you?" Ocelotl asked. He spoke with an accent that sounded Chicano-ish to Cammy. He stood and held out a hand. "In the flesh. I have heard much of you. But I never thought I would meet you."

Dracula took his hand and shook it. This was not what Cammy expected.

"Can I get you anything? Tea? Sake?" Ocelotl offered.

"Milk?" Siri asked hopefully.

"I haven't got any," Ocelotl told her, and looked her up and down. "And certainly not any that I think you'd like."

"Nothing for me, thank you," Dracula told him, then eyed the white cat. Its fur stood on end and its face deformed into a snarl. He looked to Cammy, and she nodded. He pulled out his Smith and Wesson and fired it. The flare blinded Cammy momentarily, and the blast stabbed her ears. She hated guns for that sound alone. The white cat flew off the counter, disappearing behind it, leaving a weeping bloodstain on the wall. The two other cats jumped down from their perches and scrabbled out through the kitchen in terror. Ocelotl stared, surprised.

"Excuse me," Dracula said. "That one tried to kill my companion earlier." He holstered the gun. "I believe you have something to say?"

The were-jaguar still looked stunned, slowly tearing his eyes away from Dracula to regard Cammy. He shook himself, adjusted his coat, and seated himself in the armchair again. Cammy realized the mittens weren't mittens, they were paws. He was wearing an animal skin; she had caught a glimpse of a head dangling behind his shoulders.

"That is fair," Ocelotl said. "My ally shouldn't have been so hasty." He studied Cammy silently, his eyes flashing as they turned back to Dracula, who remained unmoved.

"This current state of affairs is a travesty."

"I quite agree," said Dracula. Cammy studied his face, but she couldn't read his expression.

"I want to reestablish the natural order," said Ocelotl. "To destroy, in order that our world might be remade."

"Um, what?" Cammy asked.

"Humanity must be humbled," Ocelotl explained, coolly. "People have grown arrogant and careless. I wish to reestablish cycles of destruction and rebirth, that the world might be purified from the current decadence."

"Um," Cammy repeated, "*what?*"

DRACULA'S DEATH

Ocelotl squinted at her.

"To that end you acquired a ccoa?" Dracula asked.

"No." Ocelotl shook his head. "My former masters divined that there was one left, and sent me to fetch it from under the authority of a different branch of their organization so that they might take command of it. Some of my brothers in China divined that I shared a mind with them, and they reached out to me to offer their assistance. I have merely used the ccoa to mask my deeds. It is the will of the gods" — he spread his hands— "that we should succeed. Do you disagree?"

"I cannot speak for God," Dracula told him.

"God?" Ocelotl repeated, smirking. He reached under his jaguar coat to put away the flute—and pulled a silver crucifix out of one sleeve and turned it over between his fingers. "Really? You?"

"Why not?"

"I would have thought you would have abandoned any god that had abandoned you first," Ocelotl said. "You mean to tell me you're still carrying that tired torch after all these centuries?"

"Again, why not?"

Ocelotl snorted.

"Gods you worship should care for you in return, shouldn't they?" he asked.

"I do not worship God because He pays me in some way, but because He is God. There is no other standard one ought to use to measure what one should worship. In any case, you achieved this ccoa. But one storm demon can hardly matter in the greater scheme of rebuilding the world," Dracula said. "And it appears that since coming here you have been busy recruiting more allies to your cause."

Ocelotl's eyes flashed eerily at him, the crucifix sparkling as he rotated it between his fingers.

"It seems we will not be allies after all," Ocelotl murmured, almost to himself. "A shame. I thought you would have turned to the old ways after your God abandoned you."

"You would have me turn pagan?" Dracula asked. "Worship Zalmoxis, perhaps? Sacrifice gold and human life on mountaintops?"

Ocelotl grinned. His teeth were white, like Malcolm's, but filed to points set with bits of green jade.

"Oh, *yes!* Why not?" he asked. "Why not turn to the religion of one's ancestors? Especially now. Blood for the sun, blood for the moon. The moon is more a deity to you now, surely?" He pointed to the statuettes of Bastet. "These ones understand. The cat is a symbol for the moon or the night. Like the jaguar."

The cats earlier had told Cammy that this guy had been taken over by a jaguar, hadn't they?

"You mean like you?" she asked. Ocelotl gave his attention, his eyebrows knitted together over half-closed eyes of exaggerated disinterest.

"I mean, you think you're a jaguar now?" she checked.

"For many years I took on aspects of the jaguar," Ocelotl explained. "Now I am a vessel. I do the will of 'He By Whom We Live' as it is his strength that has been lent to me."

"He the who what now?" Cammy asked.

Ocelotl shook his head, then tapped the wing of the armchair with one finger tipped with an almost claw-like nail.

"I assume you recognize this?" he asked Dracula.

"Certainly."

"This is insurance. I am neither naïve nor trusting. And I take it you won't be working to help me?"

Dracula's Death

"I have no great love for the state of things," Dracula admitted, "but I fail to see how Armageddon will improve the situation."

"Oh ye of little faith," said Ocelotl, waggling a disapproving finger. "I said destroy *in order to rebuild*. Surely death and rebirth is a concept even a man of your faith can comprehend?"

"Nevertheless," said Dracula, "I'm not so far gone as to hope for the destruction of the whole of the human race."

Ocelotl pursed his lips, cast his flashing eyes down at the little crucifix in his hands.

"Do you know what I'm going to do with this?" he asked. He nodded his head to one side, as though indicating the armchair in which he sat.

Cammy was confused. Dracula had told her that crucifixes didn't bother him, but maybe Ocelotl didn't know that. She couldn't imagine why the armchair mattered.

"I think so, but I fail to see the point," said Dracula. Ocelotl's eyes flashed as he rose to his feet. Suddenly the ominous silence was shattered by a loud buzzing.

"What the...?" Cammy mumbled, as Ocelotl reached into his coat and answered a cell phone. Even supernatural werejaguars with god-complexes couldn't resist the sweet allure of modern tech, it seemed.

"*Ni hao*," he said into the phone. He *hmmed* a few times, then responded in whatever foreign language he'd answered in. He put his phone away and spread his hands. "I regret that it has come to this," he said, "I had hoped that I might find an ally in you."

"That you thought I would turn pagan to aid you in your evil schemes only shows that you don't know me at all."

"Pagan? You don't insult me by calling me such."

"It is only the truth, no insult," Dracula informed him. "Even if I called you a servant of the pit of hell it would only be the truth."

"Hell? Shall I send you to Xibalba?" Ocelotl answered with a small laugh and a maniacal grin that set Cammy's skin crawling for safety.

"If that is your term for hell, I fear I must disappoint your ambition," Dracula told him, "for I am already there."

Dracula drew his gun. Ocelotl pounced forward, moving inside Dracula's reach and raking his fingers across the back of his opponent's hand. The gun fell from Dracula's grip, Ocelotl ducked under the swing Dracula aimed at his head, rolled backwards as a black smear, and snatched up the gun. All in the blink of an eye. He raised the gun and aimed it at Cammy. She gripped her own weapon, but she heard the deafening *bang* and saw the flash before she could pull her gun out of her purse. Siri wrapped her arms around Cammy and pulled her towards the door. The magnum fired again and again and again, the flashes of light strobing and throwing shadows around the room. Dracula had taken the first shot and was chasing Ocelotl, who moved like a black shadow into the kitchen, leaving Cammy and Siri alone in the candlelit room.

No.

Siri released her and hurried for the kitchen. Cammy ignored her shaking knees and ran after the others. In the kitchen was a body that looked like the guy who had come in earlier. She purposefully ignored it and sprinted for the back door, which was swinging shut. As she started across the threshold, a hand shot out from the darkness and stopped her in her tracks.

"Call Malcolm. He shot my phone," Dracula told her. "Hurry, but stay behind me."

Dracula's Death

"Uh huh," she murmured breathlessly, reaching into her bag and pulling out her phone. She darted out into the rain, in pursuit. "Malcolm! He escaped out the back! Come around, we're on foot!" she shouted into her phone. She realized she had the gun in her other hand. She probably looked like a crazy person. Ocelotl was nowhere to be seen in the pelting sleet, but she guessed Dracula or Siri still had an eye on the shadowy enemy. Siri was way ahead, but Cammy could still see her in the dark because of the paleness of her clothing. Cammy did her best to keep up, but her stupid short legs let her down and she was losing ground when a set of headlights threw her shadow long in front of her. Malcolm's car scrunched to a stop beside her and she yanked hard on the door.

"Where did he go?" Malcolm demanded.

"That way." She pointed.

With a cresting wave of ice water sent up by the muscle car tires, Malcolm drove up alongside Dracula, who also jumped inside. He had retrieved his gun and was reloading it as Malcolm peeled out onto a throughway white with ice. He almost sideswiped another car in the process.

"He is very fast," Dracula said. "Faster than I am by far. I wouldn't recommend getting too close."

"Ok, but where is he?" Malcolm growled.

"And where is Siri?" Cammy asked.

"He climbed a building, and she followed," Dracula explained.

"Damn it!" Malcolm rolled down a window and slowed the car. He yanked hard on the wheel and turned down a street, sometimes speeding, sometimes slowing. Cars honked at them, and they passed a fender bender with the two drivers bickering at each other in the heavy, freezing rain. One flipped Malcolm off as he passed too close for anyone's comfort.

"Is it safe for us to drive like this?" Cammy asked, looking at the rivulets of water running down the sides of the street and choking the storm drains. Malcolm gripped the steering wheel like it would fly away if he loosened his grip.

"Do you want to walk?" Dracula repeated to her.

"*I* do," Malcolm grumbled.

"Why are you driving with your head out the window?"

"Scent," Dracula answered for Malcolm. "Though it might seem strange, wet weather can help."

"Me to catch pneumonia," Malcolm finished, grumbling.

A black shadow darted into the street and narrowly avoided Malcolm's car, spinning backwards and then around behind.

"That's him!" Dracula shouted. Cammy swiveled her head around and saw Siri dart through the droplets, now red from Malcolm's taillights, chasing the shadow. The car spun haphazardly and then collided hard, parallel with the curb. Malcolm let out a whimper of horror at the impact.

Dracula was already out of the car and running after Siri. Cammy opened the door and stared through the freezing rain, trying to track Dracula in the dark and the flashes of passing headlights. Malcolm got out and ran to check on his car, whimpering the entire time. He moaned at the damage.

Cammy spotted Dracula going into a diner they had just passed. She sprinted after him. Then she realized she still had the gun in hand and threw on the safety and dropped it into her purse. She didn't want to show up in a diner armed.

She peered through the window. Ocelotl was standing by the wall farthest from the door, flanked by two guys who looked East Asian. One of them had a tall walking stick. On second glance, Cammy saw it was a spear with a ball just under the blade. She opened the door, which jangled. It was a relief to get out of the stupid weather. Siri stood a little into the entryway, with Dracula behind her, so Cammy almost bumped into him.

Diners sitting at their little booths along the wall stared at the newcomers, wide-eyed with apprehension. Someone near the back wall stood up, until the Asian man with the weird spear pointed it at him, and he sank back immediately. He looked familiar; Cammy blinked in surprise when she recognized him. It was Emet. He was sitting across from a young girl who had golden skin and Asian features similar to those two were-tigers Vlad had killed.

Given what she'd learned about Ocelotl, she assumed his two friends were the *yaogaui* she'd been warned about, or maybe one was the Ophois were-tiger.

"And now you are interrupting a little transaction my friends are conducting here," Ocelotl said, addressing Dracula. "You care about *her* safety; what of the safety of other people?"

Dracula raised his magnum.

Ocelotl smirked. "Let's call your bluff," he said.

The tiger with the spear thrust it at Emet, but the girl sitting across from him jumped onto the table, turning into a tiger as she did so and knocking the spear point aside. Some of the patrons screamed. The other tiger guy pulled what Cammy thought was a submachine gun from his coat and aimed at Dracula, but he fired the magnum, causing the tiger guy to dodge.

The diner erupted in screams.

To Cammy, everyone seemed to be moving in slow-motion. Siri ducked aside as the AK aimed for her and Dracula. The tiger girl swung a paw at the man with the spear. Shots rang out. Dracula pivoted as he fired his magnum again. "Run!" he told her, pushing her out of the diner and shielding her with his body. She staggered back onto the slick sidewalk and heard glass shatter beside her.

One of the front windows had been shot, and shards of glass were spraying all over the sidewalk. Siri jumped out through the opening.

"Go! Get to Malcolm and stay out of this!" Dracula barked at her. "And get your weapon!" Suddenly he pushed her head down so she was ducking almost down to her knees. More shots roared through the pelting rain.

Dracula let her up. She pulled out the gun, though she hated the weight of it in her hand, and splashed her way towards Malcolm's car, running into Malcolm halfway.

"What's going on?!"

"He's got tiger friends and they have guns!" Cammy shouted. Malcolm swore.

"Come on." He turned around. "This way."

"Wait, we have to make sure Emet is ok," she protested.

"WHO??" Malcolm demanded. Cammy looked behind her and saw Emet crawling out the broken window. The tiger girl was not with him. Cammy ran back and grabbed his hand.

"Come on!" she told him. Emet's eyes widened on recognizing her, but he came along just the same.

"Ma...!" he mumbled, turning his head towards the diner. "Where's Masayu?"

"Who's Masayu?"

"The... one of the were-tigers," he answered.

"Stop talking and let's *go!*" Malcolm shouted, grabbing Cammy by the arm. He checked the traffic and then darted across the street, dragging Cammy and Emet along behind him.

"What about your car?" Cammy asked.

"Never mind about my car!" Malcolm snapped. He ducked when another shot rang out. Cammy and Emet did their best to imitate him. Cammy nearly fell forward onto her face. Malcolm grabbed her by the wrist and pulled her up.

DRACULA'S DEATH

"You gotta get out of here," he told her. "Get to cover somewhere."

"Where?!" Cammy demanded.

"ANYWHERE!" Malcolm bellowed.

More shots, and they all ducked. They'd gone partway back up the street, when a shot smacked into the brick wall behind them, spitting shards all over them. Malcolm forced Cammy down to the ground, and swore the entire time as he spun around and aimed his own gun back the way they'd come. He fired twice.

This was bad. Tiger thingies and guns firing everywhere. And Emet in the midst of it all, for some reason in the company of one of the were-tigers he'd been hunting. Where was she supposed to go? What was she supposed to do? Cammy spotted a sidewalk advertisement pillar, about twelve feet ahead and under a tree. She darted for it, dragging Emet with her. Once she had them both sheltered behind it, she peered back towards the diner. She spotted the flash of a muzzle flare, then the dark silhouette of a car blocked her view. The car swerved towards her into oncoming traffic and crashed right in the middle of the road. Tires squealed, and three more cars rear-ended others trying to avoid the accident. Horns blared, the droplets of freezing water flashed gold in the headlights before dropping into darkness. Malcolm grabbed Cammy around the shoulder to lead her further away, then drew up short with another string of curses.

There was a large food truck parked on the other side of the street about ten feet ahead. A man had just exited the cab, carrying another shotgun of some sort. From behind them, Oceoltl's voice roared over the car horns, the shouting, and the falling rain, booming something in that other language he spoke. Cammy turned to see him standing just outside the diner, pointing her out specifically.

The truck driver aimed his weapon. Malcolm took a shot at him, but the man ducked aside, and Cammy realized he had *dodged the bullet*. She tugged Malcolm back around the other way. With cars between Malcolm and her and Ocelotl, he shouldn't be able to shoot them as easily, whereas the newcomer guy had a clear shot at them.

Apparently, Malcolm and Emet agreed with her, because they ran with her around the corner. They nearly bumped into Dracula coming from the other direction, having gone around the crashed vehicles. He came around behind Cammy, she guessed to protect her from any bullets.

Once at the corner, he took up position at the edge and peered around.

"How many have you seen?" he asked.

"There's at least three besides our jaguar buddy," Malcolm answered. He changed magazines in his nine-millimeter. "I don't have enough ammo for this sort of thing. Do bullets even hurt these guys?"

"They bleed, if that's what you're asking," Dracula told him.

Beside her, Emet gasped for air, his hands shaking so hard his fingers blurred together. Cammy tried taking his hand and squeezing it to reassure him. He stared wildly into her eyes.

A slim, petite young woman popped up beside them. Malcolm swore and aimed his gun.

"No! Masayu!" Emet shouted, and reached for her. Cammy pushed Malcolm's hand down.

"Who is this?" Malcolm demanded.

"This is Masayu," Emet explained.

"Is she with us or with them, young man?" Dracula prompted him.

"You," Masayu answered.

Dracula's Death

Dracula addressed her. "You can become a tiger?"

She nodded.

"Then help me to pin some of these villains down. They are too fast for me."

Masayu moved forward, ignoring Emet's protest. Dracula leaned around the side of the building and fired, then ran out beyond the corner to confront the guy at the truck. Masayu followed.

Malcolm started heading the other way, so Cammy grabbed Emet's wrist and dragged him along, though he murmured Masayu's name again. They hadn't gotten far when a shadow jumped over the nearest crashed vehicle and blocked their path. Malcolm raised his gun. The passenger in the crashed vehicle, who had opened the door to step out, screamed and slammed the door shut. Ocelotl ignored her; his eyes, blazing like a predatory cat's in the dark, were fixed on Cammy. She spotted movement from the corner of her eye. Someone else was leaping over the crashed vehicle directly to their right.

"Malcolm! Watch out! To the right!" she warned. By instinct, she raised her gun and fired at the figure hanging in the air, descending towards them.

The muzzle flash lit up one of the East Asian accomplices. His shoulder jerked backwards and he fell, landing on his hands and knees. He let out a guttural growl of pain, and his grimace changed into a snarl. Then he turned into a tiger. Malcolm fired into the tiger's face, and the enemy collapsed, a dead man on the street. Cammy felt ill. *Not again.* The werewolves who had attacked people at the Fremont Troll had been like this. And they all turned human when they died. She heard Emet speaking some other language, rapid and strained. It sounded like praying. She'd shot someone. She'd *shot* somebody! Her fingers were cold, and not just because of the icy rain running down the back of her neck and her spine.

Ocelotl had vanished. Malcolm swore again and looked up. Cammy squinted up into the sleeting rain and spotted movement up the side of the building. Malcolm pulled her further down the street, away from the diner and the truck.

"He *is* fast," Malcolm grumbled. He scanned for more enemies, but kept moving. All Cammy could see was the man she'd shot, illumined by the muzzle flash, leaping for her. More movement drew her eye. Siri was jumping over the two cars separating them from the diner. The man with the spear was running behind her. Cammy tugged on Malcolm's shoulder and pointed. He raised his weapon and aimed. The enemy with the spear saw the motion and ducked down between the vehicles, out of sight. Siri leaped down beside them, glancing back to see where her purser was.

Some people were getting out of their cars and running. Cammy couldn't blame them. All they knew was that crazy people were firing guns all over the place. She felt ill, and so very, very cold. Emet was still praying beside her. She tightened her grip on his hand.

More movement. She spotted two black shadows darting through the headlights, coming from the street with the truck, making their way towards the diner. A tiger was loping behind.

Vlad and Masayu, Cammy realized.

A shot rang out and the tiger ducked down, Dracula could not as easily cross the pile up of crashed vehicles, which the tiger easily cleared with one leap, then Cammy lost sight of it. Siri stood on her tiptoes to see better. Cammy tried to make sense of where that shot had come from, and after seeing no one on the street, cast her eyes up again into the

DRACULA'S DEATH

freezing rain. She saw the slightest movement on the roof of the building beside the diner.

"Vlad! Masayu! Look out! There's someone up high!" she shouted as loud as she could. There were still honking horns and people screaming and the hard patter of hail amidst the rain coming down. She had no idea if they had heard her. Siri leaped onto the hood of the nearest car and then hopped to the next and the next to cross back towards the diner.

Malcolm ushered them into an alley between the corner building and its neighbor and peered out at the street. Cammy stood a little further in, craning her neck to get a look at what was happening. Dracula rejoined them and took up position as before, apparently as a meat shield for her.

Another shot, this one high. Cammy looked up to see some sort of movement atop the buildings across the street. Malcolm trained his eyes on it, but he didn't do anything.

"What is happening?" Emet whispered behind her.

"Siri is trying to avoid the enemy tiger. The tiger woman is there but can't pin him down," Vlad supplied. He could see *really* well in the dark, evidently.

"We have to help her!" Cammy said. Vlad let out a long breath, raised his magnum, and took aim.

BANG!

He grumbled, aimed again.

BANG!

A smear tumbled off the building, and crashed onto the roof of a parked car below. Emet gasped in horror. Malcolm stepped out into the weather in a daze and stared at the destruction.

"Are. You. *Kidding me??*" he demanded. Cammy stepped timidly out onto the street to take a look at what had happened.

Malcolm stared at his ruined car, both hands on his head in horror. A dead tiger lay sprawled across the hood and roof; its weight had caved in the hood and damaged the engine. The windshield and side windows had exploded out. Something pale moved on the roof of the building above; Cammy could just make out Siri's form at the edge, leaning down to see what had transpired.

Malcolm's horror transformed into pure rage. He bared his teeth in a totally inhuman expression of savage fury, his eyes no longer looked human. Somehow he'd gotten taller and bigger—a sure sign he'd just gone berserk. Cammy gasped and stepped backwards. Not now, there were all these people around. She scanned the street. People were running to get away from the chaos, but there were still a few huddled in their cars, and she felt queasily certain that Malcolm could run down those who were fleeing.

Instead, he pounced on Dracula, seized him by the lapels of his coat, lifted him straight into the air, and slammed him down onto one of the crashed cars. Then did it again. And again.

"Malcolm!" she called. Maybe she could talk him down. He whirled on her. Malcolm's eyes blazed clean through her, his white teeth gleaming with spittle. They'd morphed into those weird, long canines Cammy had spotted that time when Malcolm had turned into a wolf. He snarled, glaring first at her, then Emet, and she realized he didn't recognize either of them.

Dracula grabbed one of Malcolm's wrists and pried the hand free of his lapel. Malcolm snarled like a dog and head-butted him. This might get bad. Cammy felt pretty sure that Malcolm couldn't actually kill Dracula, but Dracula could absolutely bleed, and his blood was dangerous. And Malcolm wasn't going to stop attacking him.

Cammy didn't know how to stop Malcolm from berserking. In the past, he'd just run until he was out of steam. If she didn't figure out how to switch him back, things would go badly for him, and he wouldn't even realize it. Dracula's hand, she saw, was already bleeding from his fight with Ocelotl. It would only be a matter of time before Malcolm got that blood on his own hands.

Cammy dropped the gun and reached into her purse. The movement drew Malcolm's attention, and he swung around, teeth bared and one hand raised to strike her. She pepper sprayed him point blank. Malcolm howled with pain and reeled backwards, covering his face with his hands. He bounced off a car and fell to the wet ground, rolling over and over in agony, howling like a wolf sometimes, but sounding more human with every breath.

Good to know that, like guns, pepper spray worked on some of the supernatural.

Cammy collapsed on the sidewalk and let out a shuddering gasp that *hurt*. All her insides spasmed at once. She threw up, right there on the sidewalk.

Malcolm continued to scream and kick his feet. Emet lowered the knife he had drawn from his jacket, staring uncomprehending at what was unfolding around him.

"Are you all all right?"

Cammy jumped and whirled. Dracula stood over her. The girl-tiger stood beside him in her human form. Siri knelt beside Malcolm and offered a corner of her knit coat to wipe his face with.

"Yeah," Cammy mumbled. Dracula nodded, then looked to Malcolm and the others.

"Will he be all right?" the girl-tiger asked.

Cammy shook her head. She had no idea.

"I'm just peachy, thanks," Malcolm growled. Cammy's insides burned white hot. Him *snarking* after all of that!

"Well, I'm sorry, but what did you want me to do?" Cammy demanded. "You weren't going to stop!"

Malcolm squinted at her, blinking against the pepper spray.

"Sorry," he said.

"Sorry?!" Cammy repeated. "Sorry you attacked Vlad?!"

Malcolm flinched.

"Thank you for your swift and clever response," Dracula told her.

"Excuse me?!" Cammy demanded, then realized he'd complimented her. Praised her, even, though his face soured at her knee-jerk harsh response. She felt numb.

"Sorry," she said. "It's just... you're not usually that nice."

"I give praise when it is due, and it is due," he said. "You did well."

I did well? Cammy thought. *I did well!* She'd... she'd actually helped! Euphoria erupted in her chest.

A distant police siren drew all of their attention.

"If a call has gone out, everyone will either need to get their stories straight, or else we should leave immediately," Dracula advised. "I can't do anything about the corpses, however." He walked back out into the night and squinted in the direction the sirens were coming from. Ordinarily, his "all business all the time" attitude would have irked her. But not now. She'd done *well* and *helped*. What a pleasant change.

"We were attacked by them," Emet said, wiping at the cold water dripping down his face. "I met with Masayu near the diner. They showed up and told her she had to join them, or she would meet the same fate as her family and friends." At this, Cammy thought he looked very uncomfortable. "She said no. Then they started asking everyone strange questions about what they believed, whether they had *faith*. They took a few people outside, I don't know where. Then you showed up."

Dracula's Death

"Telling the police that a gang of tiger-monsters attacked you is *not* going to fly," Malcolm grumbled. He cleared his throat. "Just say you and your girlfriend were leaving and these crazy bikers tried to mug you."

"What about the guns, and the dead tigers?" Emet asked. "The police will have to investigate!"

"No, they won't. They'll say you're crazy, search high and low for the slimmest of 'rational' explanations and latch onto it like a drowning rat. The higher-ups will say something about a gang that was trafficking rare animals illegally and disappear the whole thing, because the cops would *much* rather have that story than a bunch of fairytales running around," Malcolm informed him.

Emet tried to form words, but nothing came out.

"So what story are we telling? We went for a drive in this weather?" Cammy asked pointedly.

"Yup."

"And then I pepper sprayed you?" she said.

"Sure. It was dark and there were people shooting at everything. Anyone can make that mistake."

"Like you wanting to kill Vlad?"

Malcolm wiped at his eyes sullenly.

"My car is *wrecked*," he grumbled.

"So you went *berserk*."

"I *built* that car!" Malcolm seethed. "It took me almost ten years! And *yes*, I went berserk! That's how berserking *works!*"

"We are going to tell the police that your friend is a berserker?" Emet cut in.

"No. I guess we say we were out getting supplies or something," Cammy said. "I ran out of food, and needed to pick some up."

"Do you all have your stories straight?" Dracula asked. Then, "I need to borrow someone's phone. Someone who doesn't mind me using it to call Boese."

Emet had volunteered his by holding it up, but Cammy shook her head at him. Dracula went to Malcolm.

"I'm not talking to you," Malcolm growled.

"You don't have to talk to me, just lend me your phone."

Malcolm sulked, but passed it over. Dracula drew a stylus out of his breast pocket and pressed the sequence for Boese. He seemed to have all of his phone numbers memorized. Cammy wondered if his old flip phone even *had* a contact list. Since he wasn't running now, she was able to see that his clothing was riddled with bullet holes. For the first time, she could see he was wearing a bulletproof vest under his coat, and it had holes blown in it as well. Why he felt the need for a vest when bullets weren't a problem for him she couldn't guess—until she remembered his warnings about his blood. He quickly explained the situation to Boese, hung up, and passed the phone back to Malcolm.

"I have to take care of something," he told Cammy. "Stay with Malcolm and Siri."

"Like *he's* going to protect me," Cammy mumbled.

"Better than what's out there. I'll be back as soon as I can."

"What about you? What is the story we're telling about you?" Emet asked him.

"I don't intend to talk to law enforcement," Dracula told him. "And I would recommend your best plan would be to do likewise. Have your stories only if you can't get away in time."

"Then how are we going to get back in touch with you?" Cammy asked. "You don't have a phone or a car."

He held out a hand, and she passed her phone to him.

Dracula's Death

"Does anyone have a working vehicle?" He looked at Emet and the girl-tiger as he asked this. "That would be our best option at the moment."

"I have a car," Emet volunteered quietly.

"Everyone get into his vehicle. Cammy, direct him back to the restaurant where we first met Ocelotl, if you would."

"Ok," Cammy agreed, dully.

Satisfied, Dracula disappeared. Emet led the way, and Siri helped Malcolm along, leading him by the hand as he continued to wipe pepper spray off his face. Cammy had thought the rain would clear it out, but when she asked he barked, "It keeps washing it into my eyes!"

Emet had a cute little Yaris. They piled in and cranked the heater before nosing towards the restaurant. Emet pulled over and let the approaching police cars and the SWAT vehicle race past them. Cammy gripped her hands together and tried not to think about Brian being in any of those. Siri did the directing, and after a few minutes, they came to the restaurant and parked beside Dracula's vehicle.

"Where's..." Emet licked his lips, "the other one?"

"He'll show up. Just wait," Malcolm told him, wiping at his eyes.

"How do you all know each other?" the girl-tiger, Masayu, asked. She was soft-voiced and spoke with an accent.

"We, that is, Vlad and I, met Emet a few days ago," Cammy explained. "We were trying to figure out what was happening to all the were-tigers."

"His name is Vlad?" Emet asked. Cammy realized Dracula had never introduced himself. Probably he didn't want to have the usual "Wait, that's your real name?" conversation again.

"Yeah," Cammy said, then, very hesitantly, because she knew the girl was another were-tiger, "How did you meet Emet?"

"I was looking for whoever was hunting us," she explained. "I thought they were working for the man who calls himself Ocelotl."

"How'd that lead you to Emet?"

"I had the killer's scent from the first of us to die, but I hadn't found the culprit. I retraced my steps, and it occurred to me that Ocelotl and his yaoguai might not have had anything to do with it, since the first killings preceded their arrival." She turned to look over her shoulder at Cammy and Malcolm. "So I assumed that we had been found out and we were being eliminated by professionals."

"We weren't—" Cammy weakly began.

"When I retraced my steps, I happened to meet Emet," Masayu said. Emet tapped the steering wheel. Malcolm wiped at his eyes and sniffled.

"Are you being funny?" Cammy hissed at him.

"You try getting pepper sprayed and then *you* tell me how funny it is," he snapped.

"So...you worked it out?" Cammy asked the girl-tiger. "I mean, you weren't mad?"

"I felt anger and sorrow, but I understand he didn't know what to think. Besides, my father's cousin *did* kill his friend's girlfriend. I choose to think of it as karma. I wish I could have done something before monster hunters killed my parents, though."

Cammy felt ice run down her spine. She looked to Malcolm. He had his eyes covered.

"Oh," Cammy said. She didn't know what else to say.

Someone tapped the window, and they all jumped. When she saw it was Dracula, Cammy opened the door. He had taken off his coat and the bullet-proof vest. She saw at least two bullet holes in his shirt as well.

Dracula's Death

They got out of the car into the freezing shower again and hurried inside the restaurant-brothel. Cammy avoided the armchair with the bloodstain on it. Emet eyed it, clearly baffled. Siri, seeming as unaffected by the weather as ever; sat next to Malcolm on the stools in front of the counter as he grabbed a handful of napkins and scrubbed his face with them. Dracula slicked his hair out of his eyes and shut the door.

"First order of business," Dracula said to Masayu, "who are you?"

"My name is Masayu," said the girl-tiger. "Who are you?"

"My name is Vladislav Dracula. You may have heard of me. I'm with the enemy."

He and Masayu eyed each other.

"Your name is *what?*" Emet asked.

"You work for them?" Masayu asked.

"After a fashion."

"So you kill monsters? You are a hypocrite?" she asked.

"I kill the ones who kill humans," he replied. "I don't bother about the others."

Masayu glared at him. Tears welled up in her eyes, and she turned to the window.

"I understand," she said.

They all caught each other up on what they knew. Emet asked how Cammy's group knew what was going on, and what should be done about Ocelotl's threat as well as Boese and his people.

"I warned you about them. Though now you remind me: the director will be heading to my estate soon. He wants to know how this" —he pointed at the bloody chair— "came to be here, and how Ocelotl knew about it. To that end, I and my companions should be off."

"This Boese person, he gave the order to kill my parents?" Masayu asked. Dracula nodded. Her eyes glittered with tears and she bit her lip.

"I would like to see him."

"Suit yourself," Dracula told her. "I won't stop you if you follow me." He then went into the kitchen. Cammy heard him rummaging around; he came back out a moment later opening a small container of lighter fluid. He poured the liquid onto the chair, then extracted a lighter from his pocket and held the flame to the seat. It ignited in a sudden rush of flames and dancing light. He made a gathering gesture to Cammy and Siri and Malcolm, and headed for the door.

"Wait!" Emet called out. "We will go with you."

CHAPTER 10
RAINING CATS AND DOGS

Cammy shivered in the passenger seat until the heater warmed up. She noticed Dracula periodically scanning out the windows, but didn't comment on it. The highway was nearly empty of traffic, but the there was so much ice and slush on the roads that they had to drive slowly, especially up the final hill of the estate. Cammy hoped Emet's car had good tires.

Everyone hurried out of the freezing rain into Dracula's mansion. As usual, it was dark and cold inside, so Cammy went to the fireplace to light the wood that was laid there. Malcolm flicked on the electric lights and hurried to a downstairs bathroom. Siri made for the kitchen to get a glass of milk. Emet and Masayu looked around, clearly awed.

"How long until Boese gets here?" Cammy asked.

Dracula shrugged.

"That will depend on how he wishes to handle the trouble with that chair. It could be any minute, or tomorrow morning."

Cammy considered Emet and Masayu. It wouldn't be good for either of them to be found here when Boese arrived, but for whatever reason, Masayu wanted to meet him.

"What about them?" Cammy asked.

Dracula eyed them both. "What do you intend to do, young man?" he asked Emet.

Emet looked helpless and chewed his thumbnail a moment.

"He is the one you said would try to recruit me to fight monsters?"

"He is."

Emet visibly gulped.

"I don't think I want to meet him."

"The mansion is large," Dracula told him. "I'd suggest you find some place to wait. But don't touch anything or make a mess, if you please."

Emet hugged himself, and looked around the group helplessly.

"I'm going to change clothes. You can wait in my room after, if you want," Cammy offered. "If you're hungry, we have some food."

"Thank you. Do you have anything vegetarian?" he asked. Cammy smiled. At last, a fellow plant-eater. Neither Dracula nor Malcolm liked her diet very much. She showed Emet the options and left him in the kitchen while she headed up to her room to get changed.

Malcolm had come back from the bathroom and was wiping his face with a towel. He glared at Dracula and demanded, "Hey, can I have a change of clothes here? I'm soaked."

"Can you have one of my thousand-plus-dollar suits?" Dracula retorted. "No. Absolutely not. And they wouldn't fit you anyway."

"You wrecked my car," Malcolm growled.

"I believe it was gravity that wrecked your car," Dracula informed him. Malcolm glared. That white hot glare he usually kept hidden away.

Dracula's Death

"Hey, Masayu, I don't really have a lot of clothes, but do you want a sweater or something?" Cammy called down. She was out of anything she could loan to Siri that would hide her tail, so she didn't offer. Besides, Siri didn't seem to mind the weather.

"No, thank you. I'm all right," Masayu replied.

Cammy switched out of her shirt and leggings for a sweater and jeans, and retrieved her raincoat. Then she went back downstairs, got Emet, and showed him where her room was. On the way up, she thought of something. She reached for her phone, to discover it gone. Then she remembered she had lent it to Dracula.

"Is it ok if I borrow your phone?" she asked. Emet looked confused.

"I need to look up some stuff and I don't have mine," she explained. "You'll need some help against Boese."

Emet fingered his phone.

"I don't know who you people are," he said. "You work for this man?"

"I don't," Cammy told him. "I just fell into this whole mess, like you did."

"Really?"

"Yeah." Cammy fiddled with her bag.

"But you don't have to worry about this Boese person?" Emet wondered.

That wasn't exactly true. Boese had stalked her pretty efficiently. She was starting to wonder if Dracula really had enough pull to keep Boese off her back.

"Sort of," she said. "Stay here." She hurried back downstairs. She found Malcolm in the kitchen arguing with her host.

"Look, I *am* a guest, right? I don't live here, and you invited me in," Malcolm said. He had the bottle of *țuica*

Dracula kept for special occasions in one hand and a mug in the other.

"If you drink all that you'll kill yourself or pass out on my kitchen floor. I'm not cleaning up after you," Dracula told him, and snatched the bottle away. Malcolm threw up his empty hand in frustration.

"My car is dead and we have no leads, let me have this!" he insisted, raising the mug. Dracula slapped a hand over it.

"*No*. You've made a mess of yourself once already tonight. I need you to pay attention. I've been compromised, so you're going to have find your manhood and do your job." He snatched the mug out of Malcolm's hand, then downed the contents in one gulp before Malcolm could reach for it. He then carefully set the mug in the sink, purposefully eying Malcolm.

"Compromised?" Cammy asked.

"The chair," Dracula explained, "had my blood on it. Our enemy can use it to hex me. I don't know what he can do to me, but I assume he wouldn't have bothered to take it unless he knew a spell he thought would work. I burned the rest of it, since the department couldn't do something as simple as keeping it out of the hands of other maniacs, but the damage is no doubt done."

"What sort of hex?" Cammy asked.

"Anything. Sorcerers and witches can use things which belonged to you or bits of your hair or fingernails to hex you," Malcolm explained, sulkily. "Or your name," he added.

Yikes.

Dracula eyed Malcolm, put the *țuica* away in the fridge, and came towards her. Malcolm sulked harder. Cammy racked her brain.

"But can someone *kill* you with a hex?" she asked Dracula. "I mean, aren't you, you know, already dead?"

Dracula's Death

"That remains to be seen," he said.

Cammy swallowed. That didn't bode well. Ophois was looking scarier all the time.

"So now we wait?" Cammy asked. Her host nodded, clearly frustrated. Masayu seated herself on the divan in front of the fireplace and Malcolm made himself some tea.

Cammy decided to look up "He By Whom We Live" on Emet's phone while they waited.

"Hey, you guys, you're not going to like what I found out," she said.

"You think you found something that's going to make our night *worse*?" Malcolm grumped from the kitchen as he nursed his tea. Siri was sitting across from him, eating a slice of cheese on butter on bread from the pantry.

"Yeah, so Ocelotl mentioned something about 'He By Whom We Live'. I just looked that up. It's an Aztec deity associated with jaguars. Apparently this is one of the big guys."

"Yup," said Malcolm and he gulped down his tea as though it was booze and slammed the mug down on the table. "That makes my night worse."

"Is this god associated with human sacrifice?" Dracula asked.

"Yeah. Oh, and to make matters worse, his month is May, and we're coming up on May first," said Cammy. She scrolled through the article she had found, then looked to her host. "Are gods real?" she asked.

He shrugged. "I believe so."

"You're a Christian, I thought?" Cammy reminded him.

"Exactly. All the others are demons," he said.

Her mouth dropped open.

"You can't just say everyone else's gods are *demons*," she snapped.

"I absolutely can, and I believe I just did."

"What if someone said that to *you*? And what about the whole 'do unto others' thing?"

"If they called God a demon, they'd be guilty of blasphemy, and that maxim does not trump telling the truth."

As ever, he liked to prove there were reasons people thought he was a psychopath, historically or otherwise. Apparently the man just had the *weirdest* ideas. So maybe he still *was* a psychopath, but less Hannibal and more... Sherlock Holmes? All coldly logical.

"Do you know more about this deity?" Dracula asked Masayu. She adamantly shook her head.

"No. I am Buddhist," she said. "My family and friends came here to practice our religion more freely." She looked into the fire. "Then we allowed someone to intimidate us into doing the opposite."

Holy cow. Malcolm had called it. A Buddhist bunch of were-tigers who had killed people. That had to be a bad joke.

"What else have you found?" Dracula asked Cammy. She scrolled through the article.

"He causes change through conflict," she said. "That lines up with what Ocelotl was saying."

"Oh, I see what happened," Malcolm mumbled to himself. When he had everyone's attention, he explained, "Some of the guys in Ophois are kind of like shamans, right? But they channel an animal spirit specifically. I kind of do the same thing. I'll bet our buddy was doing some sort of channeling things and went too deep, if you get my meaning. He lost control, and it took over."

"What *do* you mean?" Cammy asked.

"Well, you know, stare into the abyss, the abyss stares back, like Nietzsche said," Malcolm explained. "There's a lot of *things* just outside the realm you know as reality. I don't

Dracula's Death

poke at it myself, but some of the others do. And sometimes you open doors to stuff you shouldn't." He poured himself another cup of tea. "Poor bastard."

"So he really poked an Aztec god?" Cammy asked, horrified.

Malcolm shook his head. "Maybe. Maybe not. Could be something posing as a god. He wouldn't know the difference if he let it get *inside him*, you know. Could be a ghost or a spirit or a demon or a friggin' pooka." He blew on the tea. "Or a god. Hard to know for sure."

"So there *are* gods?" Cammy asked, still horrified. Malcolm shrugged.

"Beats me. I've never talked to one. Don't plan to if I can avoid it."

"Is there anything that you've found that can help us?" Dracula asked.

She shook her head helplessly. "Not really. Just creation myths and symbolism. It doesn't look like he has any weaknesses."

"You're wondering if a god has weaknesses?" Malcolm chuckled.

"Anything that seems relevant, at least?" Dracula asked.

"Well, he's got some ties to storms or rain, so that may be why this ccoa is working with him," Cammy said. "Besides that? Stuff about duality of the Mesoamerican deities, whatever that means.... Oh, this god was supposed to have created the world, and he can recreate it. Blah blah blah, human sacrifice, he's got a lot of different titles. It seems pretty complicated." A thought occurred to her, and she asked Dracula, "Did Cortez happen after you? You were alive back then, right? Don't you know more about this?"

"That was after my death, and I wasn't very interested in what Spain was doing," he explained. "I was occupied with my own matters while the Spaniards were mucking about in the New World."

"Was there a century you *weren't* busy?" Cammy griped. Whether he planned to answer or not, he turned to face the door as headlights shone through the front windows. His eyes briefly seemed to glow, but it was impossible to be certain in the firelight. Cammy set the phone on the stairs and returned to her spot near the foyer with her arms crossed.

Dracula opened the door and waved Boese in.

"Do you know who your leak is?" Dracula asked him as Boese closed his umbrella. Boese chewed on his thumb and nodded.

"I think so."

"Who?"

Boese eyed him suspiciously.

"I don't think you have a right to know."

"Since it's led to my being compromised, I think I do," Dracula countered.

"Well, you don't."

"Are you aware that the rogue Ophois agent believes he is either serving for or acting as the vessel of a god?" Dracula asked then.

Boese spotted Masayu and stared at her.

"You better have a damned good explanation for that," he growled, pointing at the girl-tiger. Masayu's face remained unmoved.

"She's helping me solve *your* mess," Dracula explained. "If she goes, then my investigation does too. Your choice." Boese raised a finger to point at him, but Dracula mirrored the gesture and added, "And since I might be hexed, you don't want to push me right now. No telling *what* I might do."

Dracula's Death

Boese shut his mouth. He glared at Masayu.

"You wish to kill me?" she asked him.

"Shut up, monster. Soon as you're out of here I'll put a notice out on you."

"What have I done to you that you hate me so much?" Masayu asked.

"You exist," Boese told her, then noticed Malcolm.

"Ophois, you find out anything yet, or are you milking this job for all you can?"

"Get off my back, asshole, I've had a bad night," Malcolm groused. "And for your information, the freaking civilian seems to be the only one with any real information." Malcolm jerked a thumb at Cammy. This put Cammy under Boese's sudden scrutiny. She glowered at Malcolm, who sipped his tea, pinky extended mockingly.

"You know something?" Boese demanded doubtfully.

"Well, sort of," she said. "I think that guy from Ophois is connected to an Aztec god. Maybe."

Boese pursed his lips and nodded absently to a wall. He turned in a small circle, thinking.

"Shit," he said at last.

"That's what *I'm* saying!" Malcolm added.

"I don't think any of us know much about the Aztecs and I don't want to make assumptions," Cammy added. "So that's basically it."

"Which one?" Boese asked.

"Um," Cammy tried to remember the name. "Tezcat..."

"Great," Boese grumbled. "I know that one. *Perfect*."

"Does that information tell you anything that might help *us* to locate the ccoa or him?" Dracula asked.

"He's a creation god," Boese explained. "He represents strife and chaos and a whole bunch of other garbage. He has associations with jaguars. He creates chaos and strife to rebuild afterwards." Boese must have noticed the look that came over Cammy's face. "What?" he demanded.

"That's what Ocelotl was talking about. He wants to rebuild the world," Cammy said. Boese frowned at her, then turned his attention to Dracula.

"You *talked* to this joker, and he's still out there somewhere?" he demanded.

"He's very fast," Dracula told him. "And *very* good at climbing and jumping."

"Why didn't you do the one thing you're good at and shoot him?" Boese seethed.

"The one thing?" Dracula asked, obviously pretending to be wounded. "Surely I have more to recommend me than that. Otherwise I imagine you'd be better off sending one of your men instead."

"Ocelotl *is* really fast," Cammy put in.

"Oh, and you brought her along?" Boese asked. "Is this some sort of joke to you?"

Dracula eyed Boese and began closing the distance between the two of them.

"No, Director. I think *you're* a joke," he said.

"You push me, I'll—" Boese reached into his coat. Before anyone could react, Dracula pounced on him and pinned both his hands.

"You'll do what?" Dracula asked softly, practically touching noses with Boese. The director did his best not to blink, but Cammy saw him try to hide a nervous swallow when he realized that he couldn't wrestle his wrists free. Dracula continued, even and unemotionally, "Now, of those present I think you are the only one not taking this situation seriously. If you have anything you'd like to say, then say it. If not, then get off my property. I was hoping for an exchange of information in both directions, but it seems you have nothing to offer. Not even the name of the traitor in your ranks."

"You can't order me around," Boese insisted.

"No?"

For a moment Cammy wondered what was going on, because it looked like they were locked in a staring contest until she saw Boese trying not to grimace and realized Dracula was increasing the pressure of his grip. She worried he would crush Boese's hands like eggshells.

"Well?" Dracula prompted.

Boese turned red, then yanked hard on his wrists. Dracula released him, maintaining his disturbing, unblinking eye contact the whole time. Slowly, Boese took his hand out of his coat. It was empty.

"My guess," Boese said, slowly, "is that Ocelotl has got to feed this ccoa. It needs a lot of power to do what he's been having it do." He pointed out the window at the rain. "So wherever it is has to be safe, but not too far away. Tezcatlipoca had a mountain-related form. Might be there's a hillside just outside of town where he has it hidden. It had occurred to me it might even be here, but I ruled out that possibility on my previous visit."

"That is marvelously unhelpful," Dracula commented. "Is that all?"

"Well, if he really intends to recreate the world, he's going to need to kill a lot of people. The Mesoamerican gods needed blood for fuel. He'll need effectively a river of blood. Of course, there should also a lot of ritual involved, so if he's really doing something like that you'd think we'd have stumbled across evidence of it."

"What sort of rituals?" Masayu wondered.

"Why? You have some connection to him?"

"He threatened to turn us over to you, so my parents forgot why they came here in the first place and did things they should never have done," Masayu replied. "I told them not to, but they were more afraid of you than of abandoning their beliefs."

"So you say," Boese sneered.

"Now we know why he wanted us to kill humans for him," Masayu said. Boese glared at her.

"Doubtful." He shook his head. "Sacrifice was a ritual thing. I have no idea why he wanted you to do that. Not that he probably needed to twist your arms that much, right?"

Cammy noticed Dracula had a finger pressed to his mouth in thought.

"Now," Boese said to him, "I need to debrief you so I can deal with that horror show you caused with the cops. Make it short and to the point."

"I told you all the important information over the phone earlier," Dracula told him. "Now you're in the way. Get out." He opened the door.

"If you think I'm going to forget your attitude once this is all said and done—"

"Yes, thank you, Director." Dracula swept his hand towards the door. Boese stood like a statue, clearly considering how to react. He narrowed his eyes. Cammy was preparing some sort of insult to get the guy to leave when Dracula drew his magnum and pointed it out the open door at the rain. He fired it, sending Masayu jumping clean over the back of the divan in surprise and Malcolm knocking the mug over in a scramble to see what was going on, though Siri beat him out of the kitchen. The magnum roared four more times and Dracula reached to swing the door shut—then his head went sailing back to the far wall, his right arm hit the nearest wall, and his chest exploded.

Malcolm skidded to a stop at the puddle of gore and pulled out a gun of his own. Cammy stared, horrified into silence, as Dracula's heart tore itself free from his chest, blood dripping down invisible paws, and then it disappeared out the door.

"What the...?!" Cammy gaped.

"*Move!*" Malcolm shouted at her, and he leaped clean over Dracula's body and out the door. Cammy scooted aside. She noticed, for a moment, Boese's look of dread, and that there was blood splattered on his pale face.

She dove out into the dark and the rain. Boese had left his car running, and the headlights formed a glowing road.

"You drive!" Malcolm shouted at her, and took the passenger seat.

"What?!" Cammy shouted.

"Drive, damn it!" Malcolm repeated. She ran around the headlights, threw open the door and dropped into the seat. Boese had longer legs than she did and she had to slide the seat forward, which gave Masayu and Siri a chance to jump into the backseat.

"What about Emet?" Cammy asked.

"Forget about that. Dive!" Malcolm shouted, and pointed towards the trees.

"No, there," Masayu pointed just a little to the left.

Boese's car was an automatic. Cammy put it in gear and stepped on the gas. The tires spun in place, spitting gravel high into the air before the whole car wobbled side to side and finally lurched forward.

"What are we doing?!" Cammy demanded.

"We gotta follow that! But I can barely see, thanks to you," Malcolm snarled.

"There!" Masayu pointed to another direction. They crossed the tree line and Cammy felt the tires sliding over the wet grass. She narrowly swerved to avoid a tree.

"If I kill you all, I'm real sorry," Cammy told them, yanking the steering wheel back under control and aiming towards where Masayu pointed.

"Did anyone see what it was?" Malcolm asked.

"Nothing," Cammy said. "It was invisible." Instinctively, she reached for the gearshift to change gears before realizing she couldn't do that in this car, then winced as she barely corrected in time to avoid another two trees.

"That's one *helluva* hex!" Malcolm said. Cammy tried not to think of his earlier threat to hex her as the car jumped over a root, bouncing her up off the seat and slamming back down, her face almost colliding with the steering wheel.

"We are too slow," Masayu said. She opened the sunroof, drenching Cammy with water.

"What are you doing?"

"I'll chase it," Masayu explained.

"Hang on, do you have a phone? Can you call us?" Cammy asked.

"Hurry," Masayu pulled her phone out of a jacket pocket. Malcolm grabbed it, entered his number into it, and handed it back. After she had returned the device, Masayu pulled herself up out through the sunroof and leaped forward and slightly to the side, hitting the ground running as a tiger. With that momentary distraction, Cammy plowed the car straight into a tree.

Dazed by the impact with the air bag, she blinked at the blurry rain falling in front of the windshield as Malcolm nudged her.

"You still alive?" he asked.

"Yeah." She rubbed her eyes. The rain had run all over her face, down her neck and the front of her sweater as well as the back. She felt like she was sitting in a bucket of cold water. Why had she even bothered changing clothes?

Dracula's Death

In the dark and wet, she fumbled for the handle and let herself out. Malcolm stood on the other side of the car squinting into the growing dark that fell at the edge of the headlights—headlight. The other had been obliterated in the crash. Siri was staring into the dark.

"This way," Malcolm said at last.

"You sure?" Cammy asked, climbing over a root and crossing around the light towards him.

"No. I can't smell all that well right now," he grumbled.

She and Siri followed him as they hiked through the woods in the dark, using a flashlight they'd found in Boese's car to avoid roots and sudden dips in the ground. Periodically, Malcolm would come to a stop and cock his head to listen or sniff, but all Cammy could hear was the roar of rain coursing down through the trees and leaves. Malcolm walked with his gun in hand, held low, one finger aside the trigger, like a police officer or some other professional. Cammy wasn't certain that a gun would work on an invisible monster that could explode your chest and steal your heart, though. She had no idea what could kill Dracula, but she figured decapitation, chest explosion, and heart stealing ought to be a pretty good way.

She decided not to ask. She couldn't deal with that answer right now, so she held out the flashlight and scanned for pitfalls in the downpour. They were heading downhill, away from the mansion towards the road. Presumably, once Ocelotl, or whatever he'd sent, had crossed the property line, something ought to have attacked him. The fact that he'd gotten through meant that none of Dracula's tenants could stop whatever it had been, or maybe they couldn't see it either. Troubling thought, that.

They came to the road, sliding in the mud of the verge, and darted across. "What are we going to do if we find them?" Cammy panted.

"Shoot anything that moves is my motto," Malcolm said.

"Of course," she grumbled. "Just try not to hit Masayu, ok?"

The trees grew just as thick on the other side of the road. Malcolm paused a moment in the sucking mud, closed his eyes, and seemed to be listening.

"There," he said, more definitely, and pointed. Cammy and Siri followed him in the dark. Malcolm advised Cammy to turn off the flashlight to avoid alerting the enemy they were coming.

Oh snap, what about the invisible chest-exploder? she wondered. Sure, you needed hair or blood or fingernails or whatever to hex someone, but suppose it was a summoned *demon* or something? Dracula had been able to see it, but no one else had. Maybe he could because he was the one who was hexed, but that meant it would be invisible all of the time to the rest of them. She fingered the adder stone. What had Malcolm said earlier? That she was certifiable? Average college-student living below the poverty line decides to fight an Aztec god and an invisible demon that snatches hearts out of chests. Probably the worst idea she'd ever had.

She followed Malcolm's shadowy figure through the dark. Siri walked a distance away. She didn't seem to have any trouble in the dark, and Cammy wondered whether the huldra had some other means to navigate, or if she simply wanted to avoid being near the others in case of an attack. Out here, no streetlights penetrated the foliage. This must be a bit like how forests were back in the Dark Ages when these monsters roamed freely. Everything was a shadow cast by more shadows, the faint silhouettes of trees barely visible in the black. And the black was everywhere. Branches cracked and tumbled to the earth periodically under the weather's assault, and damp leaves turned the forest floor into a slippery adventure she didn't need.

Malcolm led them up a mild incline and all of a sudden drew up so quickly she walked into his back. He put up both his hands.

"Whoa, buddy," he nervously chuckled, and she peered around him to see a shadowy figure she couldn't make out. "Whoa, there," Malcolm repeated. "We're all friends here, right? I'm Ophois too, just like your boss. No need for that."

One of their enemies then.

"Nice AK you've got," Malcolm said, probably to explain to her why he had surrendered. Cammy considered the situation. This enemy had the drop on Malcolm, as the saying went. But it might not know Cammy was there. She might be able to shoot at it from under Malcolm's armpit without it seeing her. But the enemy was probably one of those yaogaui tiger things. It could probably see just fine in the dark. Cammy glanced to the side, but Siri was gone. That was something. The *yaoguai* didn't shoot. Take the risk, or no? She raised the gun under Malcolm's arm, but he slapped his hand down over it.

"Hey, now, no need to get carried away," he said, still chuckling nervously, and held up a hand to show he held no ill will to the yaoguai.

"Shoot everything that moves?" Cammy whispered to him.

"New plan," Malcolm muttered back. "He knows where we need to go."

Cammy supposed that was true. Maybe Malcom figured that since the yaoguai trusted Ocelotl he might trust him, too. He certainly hadn't shot them yet.

The shadow stepped forward, and the silhouette of a hand thrust out towards them. Malcolm passed over his gun, then took hold of Cammy's. She shook her head and tightened her grip instead, so Malcolm said to the yaoguai, "You speak English, right?" The yaoguai did not answer.

"You've got your secret weapon?" Malcolm whispered to her.

In the end, it all came down to pepper spray. She wanted to laugh and cry at the same time.

"Yeah," she murmured, and hesitantly relinquished her gun to Malcolm, and he gave it to the yaoguai. The shadow waggled its gun at them, and they went before it into the dark. They stumbled—Cammy actually did most of the stumbling and slipping—up the embankment to the top.

There was some sort of natural cave opening into the earth, and a fire inside that looked absolutely magnificent in all the cold. Ocelotl stood behind the fire, a bloody heart in his hand. Cammy stared at it. The blood running down his fingers and his wrist, disappearing into his sleeve. Dracula was absolutely paranoid about people touching his blood. He'd practically shouted at her to avoid it. Their enemy was half-drenched in it. Blood dripped down his chin, and she realized he'd been *eating* the heart in the meanwhile. *Eating. Dracula's. Heart.*

Breakfast, lunch, and dinner all did their best to come up at once, even though she'd lost them earlier. Cammy managed to stop them—or their ghosts—but her stomach was not happy.

"You again? Really?" Ocelotl observed, and wiped his mouth. She could clearly see now that he'd gotten about a third of the way through the organ. Ocelotl eyed them curiously. Cammy glanced around. No Masayu, no Siri, and she didn't see any other yaoguai. It seemed to be just the two of them, Ocelotl and the yaoguai with the AK. Ocelotl's glinting eyes watched them approach and he helped himself to another bite of the heart. Cammy's stomach tried regurgitating the day's meals all over again.

"That's really not a good idea," Malcolm told him.

"Why, because it'll kill me?" Ocelotl asked.

"Well, yeah," Malcolm said. Ocelotl shrugged.

"Or it might kill him and give me his power," he said around his mouthful of heart. "So you survived." He swallowed and turned his full attention on Cammy. "So who are you that you convince a famously treacherous undead to shoot a fellow vampire for daring to threaten you? I can't imagine you're a witch, or your stuffy Christian friend would be foaming at the mouth."

"I work for Ophois," Malcolm pointed out to him. "I don't think he cares about other peoples' spiritual affiliations."

"Will you join me? I can kill your handlers for you," Ocelotl offered.

"That would be great, thanks," Malcolm told him, and Cammy suddenly realized that Malcolm had all the motive in the world to want to join the crazy Aztec god guy if it got him out from under Ophois' thumb.

"Really?" Ocelotl took another bite of the heart. Even if they got it back now, would it help? Getting his heart half-eaten wasn't the same as getting staked, she supposed, but she didn't know that it was any better.

"Absolutely. I mean, what has the world ever done for me, right?" Malcolm laughed, and spread his hands. Ocelotl chewed thoughtfully.

"I don't believe you," he said. "Your stubborn friend drags you around. My new friends saw you working together."

"It's not like we're *married* or anything," Malcolm snapped. "Uncle Sam likes using him, I tend to be the first one my branch sends on missions. It's not hard math. Of course we work together. Doesn't mean we're going to the bar on weekends or exchanging friendship bracelets. He killed a lot of my relatives, you know, during World War II."

Cammy had not heard that, and now she wondered how Malcolm actually felt about Dracula.

"A lot of mine, too," Ocelotl remarked off-handedly. "One managed to get to Argentina, or I wouldn't be here. But you expect me to believe that you'd turn on your friend over that? It wasn't anything personal; your friend was 'just following orders', wasn't he? Hunting down and killing off occultists who worked for the Reich? After all, we're cannon fodder. None of us matter."

"*Not. Friends*," Malcolm corrected, grimly.

Cannon fodder, Cammy repeated to herself. *None of us matter*.

"You." Ocelotl turned to Cammy. "Why are you here? Why did you come to the restaurant earlier?"

"I was trying to figure out what was going on," she answered. She shivered in the rain. Ocelotl had not invited them to come into the cave, and she knew the *yaoguai* stood behind her with an AK-47 drawn and ready. She had no idea how she was going to get close enough to Ocelotl to pepper spray him without getting shot first.

"But who *are* you?" he repeated.

"I'm a guest," she explained.

"A *guest?*" the were-jaguar repeated dubiously, obviously confused.

Yeah, me too, she thought. "Apparently."

"How... unexpected," Ocelotl murmured.

"Why don't you guys matter?" Cammy asked. Maybe that would get him to talk to her, instead of taking another bite of Dracula's heart. Besides, she really wanted to know. Ocelotl squinted, seemingly insulted by the stupidity of the question.

Dracula's Death

"Because we don't," he replied. "Ophois handlers breed us to do the jobs we can do. Sacrifice the ones that need to be sacrificed for the powers they want. But they don't use that blood magic for the frontlines, oh no. They keep that in reserve for the heads of the Order. Not us. We're... expendable."

Sacrifice and blood magic. So it wasn't like Ocelotl latched onto human sacrifice out of the clear blue.

"What do you mean?" she asked.

Ocelotl stared at her, and his mouth pulled into a smile of genuine amusement. His sharp teeth studded with bits of green jade gleamed red with blood. He looked horrifying. Like those laughing cats in the restaurant earlier. Orange and red light glowing and dancing on his brown skin, his black hair, his glinting eyes. Strange how a flickering light made a man who looked as handsome as Malcolm seem so menacing.

"The extra children that won't mature into useful cannon fodder get sacrificed," he explained. "Blood for fuel for dark rites. Ophois is a cult of the damned."

"Sacrifice...?" Cammy repeated. She saw the look on Malcolm's face. "Y-You..." she said, feeling sick. "You're all... everyone's a monster!"

"Precisely," said Ocelotl, and licked the blood off his lips. Boese was a monster. Ophois were monsters. Ocelotl wanted to end the world. Dracula? What did *he* want? She had no idea.

Actually, in a lot of ways Ocelotl made perfect sense. He'd been born into a death cult that used him, profited off his work, and didn't care what happened to him. If he stepped out of line, they'd explode his heart with some sort of hex. Malcolm, too. *The boys like us*, he'd said. *Unlike you, I don't get to choose my job.* Compared to that, an Aztec god that promised to unmake the world in order to make it better seemed like the perfect out. She'd be tempted to take it.

"Suppose we help you?" Cammy offered, and both members of Ophois eyed her in surprise. "Help you get away from the Order of Ophois. You can have the life you want."

Ocelotl smiled the ingratiating smile you put on when talking to an idiot but you were on the clock and had to pretend you cared. Only he had sharp, jade-studded teeth and glinting cat eyes, with blood all across his mouth, teeth, and chin, so the effect made her skin crawl.

"I mean it," Cammy told him. "I mean, Vlad has a sort of monster sanctuary up there. He says that any of them who ask for asylum get it, so long as they don't make trouble. You could do that. The branch of Ophois that had your hair or whatever are all dead now, right? No one can hex you. You could get away and never have to worry about them ever again."

"And leave the world in this sorry state?" Ocelotl challenged. "The supernatural pressed so hard it'll either pop or die altogether, and leave the world sorrier for its loss? Let humans chatter at each other through social media, forming little echo chambers and whipping themselves into delusional frenzies over issues they used to be able to talk to each other face to face about? Let them keep dumping plastic into the ocean, nuclear waste, whatever the hot topic of the day happens to be? Despite all their claims that they understand nature and the universe now, let them still blunder forward with their untested theories doing more and more damage as their reach becomes greater? They ignore their gods, except to lay claim to virtue for themselves to salve their own meaningless existence. As a pageant for others to show how inclusive and open-minded they are. No, there is no balance anymore. There is no fear. There is no awe. There is no faith. Leaving things as they are, something's going to tip right off the scales. "

"We can work to help the supernatural," Cammy asserted. "That's sort of what Vlad's already doing. And yeah, things are kinda bad now, but a lot of people are trying to fix things. Humanity's gotten by somehow even though we used to have a whole lot of worse stuff."

Ocelotl shook his head.

"We were supposed to renew the cycle already. Now the cycle and proper order of this world are out of alignment. Don't you see? Things are only going to degenerate. Better to let the forest burn than try to save it, only for the decades' worth of debris to go all at once and burn the whole west coast of your country down, killing an ancient ecosystem that would have been fine if not for human meddling. Fire is part of the cycle. No long, slow, quiet rot, but a quick, painless rebirth. If you thwart the natural cycle of death and rebirth, if you do not allow suffering to clear the way for new growth, then you condemn the world to decay with no hope of renewal. Surely you can see the evil in that? Sekhmet must be brought back to her father; order must be restored."

"Well, maybe that's what your god says," Cammy conceded, "but there are other gods that say other things, right? Maybe we could shop around, see if someone else has a better idea?"

"Like what? What *your* god says?"

"I don't really follow any god," Cammy told him, and Ocelotl snorted.

"Oh, you're from the department then," he said. "They're all godless."

"Huh? No! I don't want to have anything to do with those creeps."

Ocelotl's eyes glinted. He took another bite. He nodded towards the yaogaui.

"He's a Uighyr. His wife and son and brother were taken to a prison camp in China. If they reveal what they are, the Chinese government will do far worse to them than what they currently suffer, though I imagine eventually they will have no other option—and as bad as you think the US government is to their unwanted supernatural inhabitants, other governments are far less kind. Ask *him* how he likes the state of things."

"I know you're angry about what happened to you," Cammy asserted. She knew what it was like to have someone trying to control every single second and aspect of your life, making you a piece of them. You wanted to scream every single moment, but you had to shut up and smile when people asked you how you were. You wanted to lash out at everything. Maybe she still *did* feel all of that, deep down. How much worse would it be if there was someone who could kill you at any moment with magic, who had killed your siblings already, and who wouldn't think twice about killing you, too? She was grateful her mother didn't have access to magic. She couldn't imagine how much worse that would be. Rather, she didn't want to imagine it. "I understand that. It kills you inside. But you got rid of those people already, right? We can help you, help Malcolm, and the other guys like you in Ophois. You can all have your own life."

"I am not angry," Ocelotl told her, his glinting eyes speaking nothing but the serenity of truth. More than that, peace. She stared, but it was so. There wasn't the slightest shadow of rage, or frustration. "I am at peace now," the were-jaguar explained. "I had to kill them so I could fulfill the purpose I have been given by He Whose Slaves We Are, but I didn't hate them. Not then. They were simply lost, pathetic souls bereft of virtue and respect for the gods,

Dracula's Death

consumed by greed and lies. They were merely an obstacle. How could I possibly be angry when it has been given to me to help the whole world?"

Cammy felt her blood freeze.

"Hey, um," Malcolm said, grinning his winning grin. "This is all fascinating, but maybe we could talk less and get rid of my branch more, huh?"

Ocelotl looked at him with glinting eyes.

"What would you do if I did?" Ocelotl wondered.

"Piss on their corpses for a start," Malcolm said. Ocelotl nodded absently.

"As I thought. Faithless. I can't set you free. You, either," Ocelotl said this to Cammy. "You are both purposeless. Find yourselves first, if you wish for me to recruit you. To think the Christian would have been a better ally. He understood better than either of you."

"Who?" Cammy could not believe Ocelotl was talking about the very person whose heart he was eating. It was getting close to half gone now. Not much left to save if she was going to do anything. Ocelotl seemed to read her mind and waggled the remains of the heart in answer.

"Why are you doing that, then?" she asked him.

"Hearts have power," Ocelotl answered. "And he has more than either of you."

"You're going to die," Malcolm told him.

"Soon, surely," Ocelotl replied casually. "I can feel it. This tastes like death. It hurts my soul. It burns, it freezes, it tries to eat my soul in turn. Curious, isn't it? He is consuming me as I consume him. It's perfect. But I don't need to live much longer; I won't survive the renewal any more than anyone else will. You can't do things over unless you wipe away everything that came before. I give my life to that willingly. I am glad to do so." He fished something out of his coat and held it up for them to see. It was a black box of some sort, with long, claw-like appendages so it resembled a robotic spider. Ocelotl waggled it a bit in the firelight, then pressed down on the top of it. The claw-legs tightened, and a small, sharp shape popped out between them. He held it out so the firelight could illuminate it.

"What is that?" Cammy asked.

"Isn't it obvious?" Oceolotl replied. "It's a remote-controlled stake, set to spring into action when triggered." He held up the heart—what remained of it—and put it to the boxy spider. Even though some of the bloody organ was missing, Cammy could see how neatly it would have once settled into the claw-legs, and if it had, the little stake would have gone right through it when it popped. Cammy frowned. Boese was always threatening Dracula. Had he installed that device in him at some point when he had him captive? Was that the reason he let Dracula walk around? Was he always reaching into his coat for the button to spring the little stake and kill him?

That made Boese no different than the leaders of Ophois who threatened to kill Ocelotl and Malcolm if they stepped out of line. Maybe that was why Dracula was such a miserable jerk all the time.

It was all suddenly too much. Maybe it would be better to let the monsters do what they wanted. Sure, the vampire cats had been eating people, but that was probably because that was just what they ate, like people eating cows and chickens and sheep. They didn't take control of people and threaten to blow up their hearts or stake them to death if they stepped out of line.

"I'm with the enemy." That's what Dracula had said, again and again. Cammy turned that over in her mind. Maybe Dracula had been telling the monsters he met that he didn't like Boese, he didn't want to work with the

department, but he had to. It was a code: "They'll kill me if I don't." That's why Masayu had forgiven him. She had figured out what he meant.

"If I'd known about this earlier, I might have tried to get it out before I decided to steal his heart," Ocelotl said, seemingly to himself. "I had the impression he didn't really want to fight me. I think he also hated the state of things." He tossed the device over his shoulder.

"You know you're talking crazy," Malcolm told him. "You mentioned Sekhmet there. You throwing Egyptian theology on your Aztec cake?"

"Sekhmet is another vehicle to restore order, *Ma'at*," Ocelotl responded.

"Yeah, from a totally different pantheon. And Sekhmet needs to be placated, but you're talking about... what, blood sacrifices? Look, remember when she was so bloodthirsty she had to be tricked into drinking beer she *thought* was blood, so she'd pass out and wake up all nice again? How about offering a river of booze instead of blood? Now that's something I think we can all get behind!"

"Blood is necessary for the gods."

"Maybe the *Aztec* ones," Malcolm retorted. Ocelotl pointed to the sky.

"I brought water for Sekhmet. The earth was destroyed before by a flood."

"In the Bible. You're Christian too, on top of all of that?" Cammy asked. Well, if elves and Dracula could be, why not some weird were-jaguar?

"Of course not," Ocelotl snapped, sounding deeply offended. "The second sun. The destruction of the world and mankind by the gods. But it is true that mankind is lost. Man used to understand that we must worship and participate in the rituals which perpetuate the world and keep chaos or death at bay. Now no one knows. And look at the state of the world, its people. So, I work to restore balance.."

"Maybe," Cammy said. "But maybe there are more constructive ways to help the world? When I clean my room I don't burn everything and start over; I keep the good stuff and take care of it. If you give the heart back we can ask Dracula if you can stay with him. He doesn't like the state of the world either. Maybe the two of you can come up with a better plan."

Ocelotl shook his head.

"You offer a possibility in exchange for a certainty, one that I am so close to reaching. I can't take that risk. To die by sacrifice or in battle is how one reaches the best heaven. Do you test me? We are all tested, and everyone gets only one chance." He pulled out a glittery red and gold collar. The little golden license shone red in the firelight. Cammy couldn't read the name, but she knew who it belonged to.

Cammy gasped and covered her mouth. "Did you kill Goldie?"

"I did not kill him," Ocelotl said. "That would have been a waste of power. I used his life, as I am using your friend." He held up the heart for a moment again. "I would never waste a life if I could put it to use."

Ocelotl studied them both, a different sort of calculation glinting in his eyes. Cammy felt like he was measuring her for a dress. Her stomach sank inside her, tightening at the very idea of him sizing her up like that. *Never waste a life I could put to use.*

She reached for her purse. It didn't matter if she wasn't fast enough. Ocelotl was going to kill her and Malcolm both.

"None of that, please," Ocelotl admonished, pulling a gun from his jaguar coat and aiming at her. "I don't want to kill you just now."

DRACULA'S DEATH

"If you shoot me now, then you will," she pointed out.

"I'm going to shoot you in the knee," he informed her. "Or the shoulder. I'm a better shot than you, and I can pull the trigger faster than you can get whatever you're reaching for."

His blazing eyes shifted to the side, and he stared, wide- and somehow vacant-eyed. Cammy followed his gaze and spotted Siri. Despite the weather, she seemed illumined by faint moonlight, her silhouette clear even in the dark. She stood, one hand beckoning invitingly, the other playing with the water and the air. Cammy had a sense the huldra was smiling, her lightning eyes fixed on Ocelotl. He was transfixed by Siri, almost bewildered. The hand holding the heart dropped slowly, almost slumping against his leg. Cammy checked Malcolm, but he'd also spotted Siri and stood equally mesmerized. Siri beckoned to Ocelotl.

A tremendous *bang* and flash of light broke the spell. The yaogaui had fired his gun at Siri. Before the light briefly blinded her, Cammy spotted Siri ducking. The yaogaui stepped into the darkness and fired again. Cammy caught a glimpse of Siri's pale clothing retreating. Then she realized she should have used her secret weapon on Ocelotl while he was distracted. She turned back, hoping he still was.

But Ocelotl had recovered, his gold eyes scanning the darkness. Then he aimed the gun at Malcolm. "Give me a reason to do the same to you, and I will."

"Go ahead and shoot, then," Malcolm told him. "I'm going down swinging if I'm going down." Malcolm sucked in a ragged breath as though he'd been running for the last ten minutes, and he hunched strangely. Cammy reached for the pepper spray, expecting any second for the AK-toting *yaoguai* or Ocelotl to kill her. A roar sounded from behind her as Malcolm pounced forward with a snarl. Ocelotl fired his gun, stuck the heart between his teeth to hold it, and spun effortlessly out of Malcolm's way.

Cammy didn't give herself a second to think. She couldn't afford to. She ran for Ocelotl, holding out the pepper spray. The were-jaguar heard her coming and turned, though he kept the gun pointed at Malcolm, who snarled his inhuman snarl from earlier in the night, his perfect white teeth now long and gleaming in the firelight, his eyes as yellow as the flames. Cammy sprayed Ocelotl in the face.

The were-jaguar let out a scream of surprise and pain, and dropped the heart. In the same moment Malcolm pounced on him, knocking him to the ground and trying to tear out his throat with his teeth. Ocelotl hooked his arm under Malcolm's throat blindly to keep him at bay, and they wrestled on the ground. The heart bounced off a rock and disappeared into a shadowy depression hidden by grass.

Cammy turned, hoping the pepper spray would work on the yaoguai. Instead, she saw him spinning slowly, eying the dark, his gun set to his shoulder in readiness.

Masayu, Cammy realized. The were-tiger must have attacked from the darkness, then retreated. Cammy didn't see any pale shape in the dark that looked like Siri. She hoped Siri hadn't been shot. She couldn't let Masayu get shot, either. She reasoned the heart probably wasn't going to get up and walk away, so she tried to sneak up on the yaoguai while his eyes were on the trees. Behind her, she heard snarling and growling, nothing that sounded human.

She had barely taken three steps down the incline towards the yaoguai when he turned. His dark eyes took her in, considering how he felt about her as a threat. The firelight cast faint, orange light, illuminating the trees. He aimed the gun at her.

Oh no, she thought.

The gun flared brilliant white, like a bolt of lightning, but a great shadow obscured the muzzle flashes. She felt her torso. No bullet holes. She looked down. A tiger lay at her feet. The yaoguai aimed once more. Unthinking, she threw the can of pepper spray at his face. The yaoguai ducked his head to one side to avoid it, and the barrel of his gun waggled just a little to one side. Cammy jumped down the incline, throwing her weight on the gun, trying to drag the barrel down to the ground. Like he needed the gun to kill her.

The yaoguai relinquished his hold on the gun and Cammy dropped onto it, face first into the long, wet grass. She felt something on her shoulder, powerful, pinning her down in the grass and mud and crushing the life out of her. Then there was a roar and the pressure was gone.

She coughed out grass and rainwater, rolled over, waving the gun like some hysterical horror movie victim. Two tigers stood to one side, roaring at each other, their tawny fur standing up despite the rain trickling down their sides and their snarling faces. Their breath steamed hot in the rain and the firelight, a faint cloud of it hanging on their bodies. They hurled themselves at each other, biting and clawing. She looked up the embankment. An enormous wolf, too big to be the real thing, faced off against a black jaguar. The jaguar bared its teeth, its eyes pressed shut.

She could shoot him right now. She should. She raised the gun.

The two tigers roared like thunder, and she saw one fall back against the embankment, its golden eyes wide with fear, its pupils great black circles drowning out the yellow. Red ran downs its sides and flank, its white stomach turned pink. Now Cammy could see it was smaller than the other one, more than a hundred pounds smaller.

She fired the AK at the bigger tiger. Points of red exploded from its shoulder and the great cat roared in pain, rolling over in the dark and the wet, then ran off into the trees. Cammy stood up, swinging the gun around to fire at

Ocelotl. But the jaguar was disappearing into the brush. The wolf bounded after it, its yellow eyes murderous and hungry.

"Great."

Cammy climbed the embankment and stared into the dark. It was no good. The rain ran into her eyes and she wiped them. She felt the cold coming back. In the distance—the distance! That was fast!—she heard a wolf howling.

She slid down the embankment, accidentally firing off four rapid shots before she realized what happened. Thankfully, they had gone wild, not hitting Masayu. Cammy crawled over to the fallen tiger, hearing her labored breathing, teeth bared against the pain, ears flat against the wet head. She looked even smaller than before.

Cammy tried to take stock of the wounds. Some looked like the skin had been torn by claws, long, deep gashes. Others were bullet holes.

Cammy looked down at the AK. Masayu shook her head. With a deep, inhuman gasp of pain, she shrank and became her golden-skinned human form. The wounds were easier to see now. Torn flesh around her throat, shoulders, and chest. Bullet holes down one leg.

"I can call an ambulance…" Cammy realized she didn't have her phone.

"Get the heart," Masayu told her. "I can call."

"What? I can't leave you here!" Cammy protested.

"Get it," Masayu repeated. "Who else is going to stop Ocelotol in his mission to end the world?"

"But you…" Cammy wasn't a doctor, but she didn't have to be to know this was bad.

"Get it," Masayu repeated hoarsely. "Do not worry about me. I will be all right."

"I can help you to the road—"

Dracula's Death

"Go!" Masayu told her, her black eyes flashing gold, and she fell back against the embankment, a grimace twisting her features into a despairing snarl.

Cammy climbed the embankment. Which clump of grass had it been? Worse than that, how was she going to pick it up? Cammy felt her heart beating against her ribs.

No, think. Calm down. Panic later.

She went to the fire inside the cave and carefully pulled out a long piece of wood burning at the far end. It was a slit log, not wet forest wood; Ocelotl must have brought the firewood on purpose. She went back out into the rain. Her torch sputtered under the falling drops as she thrust it down towards the clumps of grass. At last, she saw something glistening and black, half-covered by blades of grass, the center of the clump bowed down, forming a little hole. Cammy stared at it. How to pick it up? Should she risk picking it up directly?

Malcolm said it was going to kill Ocelotl, she thought to herself. Ok, better not to touch it. What then? She looked at her purse.

"Even greater," she grumbled. She picked out her wallet and stuffed it into her back pocket—these jeans only had back pockets. Thank you, women's clothing manufacturers—and her keychain, which she stuffed in the other pocket. Remembering she had gotten a little keychain flashlight as a giveaway at some movie premier or other, she took it back out and tested the light. It wasn't much, but it was better than nothing. She would have to rely on that to find her way back. Then she turned the bag over and dumped out everything else. Carefully, she lowered the mouth of the bag over the clump of grass and felt through the bottom of it until something squished a little against the weave.

She felt her stomach flip, but tightened her fingers around the disgusting object and lifted it up. A little awkwardly, she turned her hand, now wearing the purse inside out like a glove, towards the fire. Sure enough, there was the heart, almost half-eaten, looking like the grossest thing in the world. She retched at the sight, but pulled the straps over it, turning the purse right-side out and ensconcing the heart inside. It didn't weigh very much, but she felt the lump inside wobbling the purse around as she moved.

She held it away from her body—better not to take a risk the blood would soak through the weave and her sweater—and returned to Masayu. The young woman had resumed her tiger form and lay panting against the embankment.

Cammy was going to say something to her, but the tiger nodded for her to go. She wanted to stay, but turned to leave, biting her lip. She heard a low growl behind her. When she turned back she saw Masayu nodding at the AK. Cammy shook her head, but the golden eyes stared into hers, cool and calm. "I need my flashlight to see," Cammy protested. Masayu chuffed and growled, and nodded at the gun again. Cammy went and picked up the gun. "I'll be back to help you," she promised.

She figured the best way to go would be to carry the purse over her left wrist, the gun in her left hand, the teeny flashlight in her right. If she needed to fire, she'd put her keychain in her mouth and pull the trigger with her right hand. She wasn't so certain she could run with the keychain-flashlight in her mouth and her finger on the trigger. If nothing else, she might trip and accidentally fire the thing again. She headed down the embankment, since they had come up it, but did not know where to go after that. All the trees looked the same in the rain and the dark. No sign of Siri. She hoped once again that the huldra hadn't been shot.

Dracula's Death

The cold air burned in her lungs as she jogged back the way she thought they had come. Her fingers felt numb, and she slipped more than once on a leaf-coated root or slick puddle of mud, to fall sprawling in the freezing muck. She reached the road. No cars, so she darted across, skidded in the mud, her arms pinwheeling to keep her balance, pulling her feet high up out of the muck to keep it from swallowing her shoes.

So far so good. Now all she had to do was climb the incline; the mansion lay somewhere up there. In the midst of who knew how many square miles of trees. She could wander around until dawn in the pouring rain and the cold and die of hypothermia while Masayu bled out and Malcom did whatever he was going to do, which, now that she thought about it, might be *kill Masayu* when he came back.

Great.

She couldn't jog through the trees and up the slippery incline, but she did her best to climb quickly. Maybe she'd see the single headlight of Boese's car piercing the rain and the gloom. If she saw that, she could use it as a beacon.

She paused a moment to squint through the rain, lowering the flashlight so she could see if a beam of light shone through the darkness. Nope, just the patter of water dripping off pine needles and splattering against branches on the way down. Cammy raised the flashlight to resume her hopeless journey. She screamed as the light illuminated a white shape directly in front of her. She fumbled with the gun and the flashlight, sticking the light between her teeth and aiming her weapon, then she saw what the shape was.

A girl, maybe eleven or twelve, wearing a white night gown or plain, shapeless dress stood in the rain. She wore a crown of woven leaves and green shoots over her green hair. Cammy stared at this stranger, who stared back with heavy-lidded, watery eyes. Water glistened off her unnaturally pale skin, and her hair seemed to float slowly in a wind that didn't blow.

The girl beckoned to Cammy, then turned and stepped through the trees, moving like someone had slowed down the film in a movie, almost floating as though she weighed as much as a soap bubble. The girl came to a stop at the edge of the beam of light, then turned and beckoned again. Her green hair glowed in the faint light, undulating like a living thing. Cammy racked her brain. This girl was something supernatural, that was for sure, and she was on Dracula's property again.

"Are you a rusalka?" Cammy asked. She wasn't one of the nymphs, Cammy had seen those. The girl crossed her arms across her stomach as though she wished to pin an invisible shawl in place in the crooks of her elbows, and watched Cammy. If she was on Dracula's property, then whoever or whatever this girl was, she had to be friendly, right? Hesitantly, Cammy lowered the gun and reached for the adder stone. She held it up to her eye.

The girl was a bloated corpse, purple and blue. A drowned girl, wearing what looked like a girl scout uniform, but old-fashioned. Cammy lowered the stone and saw the girl had covered her face and turned away.

"Oh, I'm sorry," Cammy said. The girl shook her head, turning away to hide her face more. She beckoned that Cammy follow anyway, but no longer looked at her.

Hesitantly, Cammy followed. Dracula had told her rusalki were sometimes the spirits of drowned women or girls, though not always. This one was a child. Just a kid. Maybe she'd been murdered, for all Cammy knew. She'd sought shelter here. Boese wanted to wipe this girl's ghost out of existence. So did Ocelotl, just in a different way. "I'm sorry," Cammy said again, but got no response.

Dracula's Death

She followed the pale figure, which kept to the edge of her light, climbing up through the darkness. Soon enough, Cammy spotted a beam of light illuminating the sparkling points of rain dropping from the sky. Shortly after, she came up to Boese's car. It was still running. Cammy shivered, felt the purse swinging on her wrist. This night couldn't end soon enough.

Siri appeared beside her out of nowhere. Cammy screamed.

"You scared me to death! Where were you? Are you all right?"

"They did not hit me," Siri said. "Do you have his heart?"

Cammy showed the purse, and Siri seemed satisfied.

"What about the others?" Cammy demanded.

"I led the tiger on a little chase," Siri said. "He is veak and losing blood, but he might be following still."

"What did you do to Ocelotl back there?"

"Do?" Siri repeated. "Vhy, nothing. Only vhat ve do. Men cannot resist us if ve set our eyes on them."

Ah. What a weird power. Cammy wondered why she hadn't used it on Dracula.

The ghostly rusalka led them to the road and all the way up to the mansion, then stood to one side to let Cammy pass her on the way to the door, which was still open. A single pillar of light shone out across the pebbles.

"Thank you," Cammy told the rusalka. The drowned girl stepped backward, drifting through the air, her hair obscuring her face, and disappeared into the dark. Cammy took a deep breath and staggered towards the door. She slipped on the stone floor as she entered. The air was warmer and drier in here, at least, and she heard the water running in the sink.

"I'm back!" she shouted raggedly, wanting to collapse on the floor.

She looked down at Dracula's body. His arm hadn't gone far, lying against the wall, but his head was all the way across the room. She could see the sprayed trail of blood that pointed to it, the drying, blackish, crusty trails which had frozen in their dripping journey to the floor. Normally he breathed, but he didn't breathe now. There was the rib cage ripped open, the bones standing up. She ran to the door to shut it and tried not to throw up. How did doctors and nurses manage? She retched helplessly, trying to catch her breath, steel her nerves. She couldn't chicken out here, they needed Dracula up and on his feet again. Now that they had Ocelotl on the run, and Dracula didn't have to fear Boese killing him, he could do what he really wanted to do.

And what is that? Cammy wondered. He'd never said. What had he done after World War II that the department thought they should keep him "in a box" until the nineties?

"Where is my car?"

Cammy turned. Boese was standing in the sticky puddle of blood, looking tired and pale. He was rubbing his hands with a towel from the kitchen, scrubbing his skin with maniac energy though his eyes looked listless. His collar and part of the front of his shirt was wet. Maybe he'd been washing his face, too, and his clothes.

"I'll tell you later," Cammy said. She tiptoed towards the body on the floor, trying not to look at it while also avoiding the drying puddles of blood. Boese watched her silently. Siri had fetched the torn arm and placed it beside the body and was going for the head.

"What about your friends?" the director asked.

"They're coming," Cammy answered. She held out the purse and shook it. The heart seemed stuck to the inside, so she steeled herself and went to the fireplace. She got one of the pokers, the one with the hook on the end, and returned to the body. Boese was scrubbing his face with the towel.

Cammy tipped the purse out, shook it, and was about to stick the poker up in there to dislodge the heart when it tumbled out. Once again her stomach flipped. The heart landed on the body's shoulder and flopped to the floor past the torn stump of a neck. She focused her eyes with all her might on the end of the poker and hooked the hooky bit into the gaping hole where Ocelotl had chewed through. *Don't think about it. Don't think about it*, she told herself, carefully balancing the organ and moving it into place.

"What are you doing?" Boese asked, then, "Wait, where's the kill switch?"

"Gone," Cammy answered, lowering the heart into the little space between the lungs. *Don't think about it. Don't think about it.*

"Waitaminute! Where's the rest of it?!" Boese shouted and dropped the towel. "Stop what you're doing!"

Cammy let the heart drop off the hook as Boese jumped forward to snatch the fireplace poker from her hand.

"What did you just do?!" Boese demanded, his face white. Before Cammy could answer, he shoved her backwards. She lost her balance and sprawled against the wall.

"What is wrong with you?!" she demanded.

Boese pulled out a little device with a button in the center, then hurled it angrily at the divan. He cast his eyes around the foyer and the stairs. He leaped over the body and went to the fancy little coffee table that sat before the fireplace and kicked at the legs. The table jerked back across the polished floor, unharmed.

"Shit!" Boese shouted, and lifted the table with sudden energy. He threw it against a wall, and a leg splintered free. The director climbed over the divan to get it. Cammy noticed movement at the top of the stairs and spotted Emet crouching behind the banister, watching what was going on below with wide eyes. Siri had the head in hand and watched the director while she walked slowly across the room to place it near the body as well. A strange sound drew Cammy's attention, a sort of wet gurgle, and she turned back. Dracula's chest had closed up, and blood was bubbling out of the stump of the neck. She realized the torso was trying to breathe, sucking the blood into and out of the lungs. She retched again.

The arm was back in place, the sleeve fallen down to the elbow. Apparently having half his heart eaten didn't kill Dracula. Kill him more than he was already killed, anyway. Good to know.

Boese came around, the piece of table leg in one hand. He stood over the body, raising the chair leg over his head to thrust it down into the chest.

"Stop!" Cammy screamed. She jumped to her feet and tackled him. Well, she tried. Boese bumped into the wall, still clutching the makeshift stake in his hand.

"Get off me, you idiot!" Boese shouted, and elbowed her right in the face.

White hot pain shot across her cheek under her eye and she let go, staggering back. She held up her hands to shield her face against him hitting her again, her vision blurred with tears of pain. She saw Boese's hazy outline, as well as Siri's backing slowly away as a third form suddenly rose from the floor beside Boese. Hurriedly, she wiped away the tears so she could see.

Boese turned in time to see Dracula standing there, as whole as ever, though his clothes were torn and his neck was ringed with coagulating blood. His eyes were red as blood. Not metaphorically, literally. His face was white, almost

DRACULA'S DEATH

blue-gray, like a corpse, his pupils glowing red as molten metal in the center of the bloodshot rest.

"Shit!" Boese tried to thrust the table leg into Dracula's chest. Dracula caught his wrist and pinned him against the wall, snarling without an ounce of recognition in his eyes. He leaned in, ready to kill Boese, and hesitated. The red eyes drifted over Boese's face and chest, revealing no understanding, but he dropped the director all the same, an evil hiss escaping his bared teeth.

Cammy stood there, frozen, trying to make sense of the situation.

"What are you doing? Run!" Boese told her.

"Why? What's going on?" Cammy quavered. At her voice, the red eyes flicked over to her, settling on her as though the very act could pin her in place. She felt sudden and immediate dread. He'd never looked at her like that, not even when he was threatening to kill her. There was absolutely no human intelligence behind the burning points of red, no light of recognition for the guest towards whom he had shown some chivalric reflex. Boese put himself between Dracula and Cammy.

"Are you stupid or something?" Boese shouted over his shoulder. "You only put half his heart back, and left the kill switch somewhere. He's going to murder everything in his path."

Ah. It'd be nice if people told her things before she could go and make everything worse. She went for the door, wondering why Dracula didn't attack Boese if that was true. As she turned the knob the door jumped open, hitting her in the face, shooting pain through her bruised cheek and into her brain.

"Sorry," came Malcolm's voice, and he stepped inside, carrying Masayu in her human form in his arms. "I lost him, and—oh shit!"

Something knocked Cammy aside. She hit the wall and her head hurt worse. She blinked past the pain, saw Dracula tear Masayu out of Malcolm's arms and latch his teeth into her bleeding throat. Masayu screamed and beat at his chest, helpless to dislodge him. She changed into a tiger, but he held her close, her hind legs scraping helplessly on the polished floor, her forelegs unable to pull him off.

"Masayu!" Cammy shouted. Masayu roared, wriggled, but could not get free. Malcolm pulled out a silver chain from his back pocket and held up a teeny, tiny crucifix.

"Get the hell off her!" he shouted.

Rather than do anything of the kind, Dracula retreated from the entranceway, carrying the flailing tiger as he went. Cammy could see Masayu's struggles losing strength, her tail dragging limply on the floor, one leg half-kicking and the other dragging. Dracula carried the tiger, one arm wrapped around her chest, holding her up, the other cradling the back of her head. The gesture almost looked tender, except that it was a man holding a struggling tiger with his face buried in the animal's throat.

Malcolm came forward with the little crucifix, which did not seem to help much. Cammy had no idea what to do. Shoot him? She knew guns didn't work. Boese stood against the wall and watched Malcolm still holding out the crucifix, all while Dracula retreated, but did not drop his prey. Siri stood against the back wall, horrified.

Emet came charging down the stairs, shouting Masayu's name. This drew Dracula's attention. Malcolm took advantage of the distraction to approach and thrust the crucifix up against one red eye. Dracula dropped the tiger with a silent hiss of pure hate, and he swept like a shadow towards the stairs.

DRACULA'S DEATH

"No!" Cammy ran for Emet, who hesitated, realizing he was next on the list. Dracula beat her by a mile and grabbed Emet by the ankle as the young man tried to run back up the stairs. He fell face first onto the stairs as Dracula pulled his foot out from under him effortlessly and dragged him down to the floor.

"Cammy, what did you *do*?!" Malcolm shouted as he ran towards the stairs. Emet screamed and flailed his arms, kicked his legs, but Dracula threw himself down on the young man, almost hiding him from view. Emet screamed and clutched at the torn sleeve, then grabbed a handful of Dracula's hair, tearing it from its roots, but he remained pinned.

"What do we do?" Cammy shouted as Malcolm thrust the crucifix once more at the corner of one red eye. This did nothing more but begin the cycle of Dracula retreating from it, dragging his prey along while Emet screamed and sobbed in terror.

"He needs blood to put himself back together," Malcolm growled, running with the crucifix. "He's going to keep attacking people until he gets enough. Let *go*, dammit!" Malcolm grabbed Emet's leg and pressed the crucifix into Dracula's temple. Dracula hissed and practically threw himself backwards to get away from the silver object, his eyes still red and hollow, windows to nothing resembling human intelligence. So much for crucifixes not bothering him. Apparently he'd lied about that. If so, then what else had he lied about? Or... had something changed?

Malcolm pulled Emet away, and the young man scrambled to hide behind him. Cammy spotted Boese standing in the foyer, watching the scene unfold with an expression of pure, distilled hatred and disgust. A thought occurred to her. She ran forward, drawing Dracula's attention, and she saw the shadowy blur from the corner of her eye. A hand caught her by the wrist and by the back of her neck, drawing her up so fast her legs kicked up in front of her. The room tipped backwards and she raised her free hand to her throat to protect it.

He bit your knuckles before, she thought helplessly. *What's your hand going to do?*

Dracula dropped her to the floor as Malcolm chased him with the crucifix again, hissing and retreating towards the fireplace. She wanted to cry.

No. Later, she told herself, and sat up, feeling her stomach wobbling inside her. She ran to Boese. This time Malcolm anticipated the predatory lunge and threw himself and the crucifix between Dracula and Cammy.

"You have garlic, right?" Cammy demanded of Boese. He looked down at her like a sleepwalker, reached into his coat, and pulled out little plastic packets. Cammy cracked one open and wrinkled her nose at the stink. She squeezed the whitish paste inside out onto her fingers and slathered the contents on her throat. Seeing that seemed to galvanize Boese to some sort of action, because he produced more packets.

Cammy walked slowly behind Malcolm. Boese came up behind her, heading towards the back wall. As Cammy cracked open another packet of garlic, Dracula lunged for Masayu, who lay on the floor panting heavily. Malcolm had anticipated the move and jumped forward to put himself between her and Dracula. Apparently, despite his condition, Dracula could still plan, because he seized Malcolm's wrist with a hiss and knocked the crucifix free.

"Shitshitshit—!" Malcolm gasped as Dracula pinned his arms.

"Get that!" Cammy shouted, pointing at the little glint of silver that lay nearly in the kitchen. Boese ran for it while she

Dracula's Death

and Emet scrambled after him, and Malcolm shouted out curses and tried to get free. Boese snatched up the crucifix. When Emet reached him, Boese offered a packet of garlic and told him to wipe the stuff all over his skin. Cammy waved her packet of garlic in front of her as she advanced on Dracula and Malcolm. Dracula had pinned Malcolm in nearly the same way he had pinned Emet earlier, and Malcolm was just as helpless to get free.

"Get him off me!" Malcolm screamed. She waved the packet by Dracula's face and got absolutely no response.

"Hey what?" she said, and thrust it closer, once more to no effect. She tried to smush the garlic against his mouth, but he jerked his head sideways and it landed in his ear. His white hand closed around her wrist and the glowing red eyes looked up at her.

"I knew he was faking it," Boese said from the foyer, watching the scene unfold. "I *knew* it. Lying, sneaky bastard."

Cammy tried to twist her wrist free, but the white fingers held her fast, just like those grasping hands pulling her from a car. Her heart thrummed and screamed. Apparently the smell didn't matter, but he had mentioned before he couldn't eat the stuff. She took the packet with her other hand as he yanked her towards him, making to bite the exposed flesh of her arm. She squeezed the packet on her skin, and Dracula hesitated. He flung her aside, nearly wrenching her arm out of its socket as he did. Her shoulder and elbow throbbed and ached, but she pushed herself back to her feet.

Boese came forward with the crucifix to drive Dracula off his latest prize.

This was getting them nowhere. They were going to play hot potato with him until they messed up or they came up with something better. Still, Boese had managed to get

Malcolm free, and he crawled across the floor towards Cammy while Boese guarded his retreat.

"I'm going to kill him!" Malcolm growled hoarsely to himself. "Chop him up and put him through a wood chipper and barbecue him!"

"How much blood does he need?" Cammy interrupted. Malcolm looked up at her, half indignant and half resigned to the fact that she wasn't going to leave him alone until she got an answer.

"How should I know?" he snapped.

"Here." Cammy knelt down and handed him the open packet of garlic. "He really can't eat it. I have an idea."

"Oh, goody," Malcolm grumped, pushing himself up off the floor and taking the packet to smear on his exposed skin. "I hate this stuff," he growled to himself, wrinkling his nose.

Cammy darted into the kitchen and opened a cabinet. She retrieved one of the cooking pans, then opened a drawer and found a knife. Dracula liked to keep them razor sharp. She held a hand over the pan and sliced her palm. The blade was so sharp it only itched, didn't even hurt. She felt the warm liquid dripping off the side of her palm before she saw it. Red spattered into the pan.

She heard a female scream. Cammy picked up the pan and held it below her hand as she came back towards the others. Dracula had grabbed Siri and was retreating from Boese, who was far less enthusiastic about saving the huldra than Emet or Malcolm. Emet snatched the crucifix from him and hurried towards Dracula, who had Siri by the waist and the throat. She punched his head, and though she could not dislodge him, Cammy could tell there was considerable strength to those blows. When Emet got close, Dracula grabbed the wrist holding the crucifix and held it out as far as he could. Siri wriggled, now that only the hand around her

DRACULA'S DEATH

waist held her. Malcolm swore and tried to peel them all apart, but he lacked the strength. All he earned was a second or two of Dracula's attention—enough to headbutt him. Malcolm collapsed on the floor, hands over his face. Dracula ignored him. Emet sobbed and tried to kick himself free, while Siri clawed at him.

"Hey!" Cammy held up the pan. She got no response, so she stepped closer, trying not to wobble on her unsteady legs. "Hey!" she shouted again. Still nothing. She had to come almost within arm's reach before the red eyes suddenly settled on the pan. There wasn't really a lot in it, but she hoped just the sight of a bunch of available blood would work. Dracula did not release Siri or Emet, so she set the pan on the ground and reached for the crucifix. Emet released his grip on it instantly and she shoved it against Dracula's forehead. He dropped Emet, and she tried to catch him as he fell. Siri managed to wriggle free and leaped backwards over the divan to safety. Dracula moved shadow-like around the room, circling them, then going for the pan. At least that worked.

Dracula tipped the pan up to drink its contents. Cammy turned around, holding out the crucifix. Dracula dropped the pan, now empty, his red eyes fixed on the crucifix. She saw him glaring at it, then eying the blood that dripped down her fingers. The only two things in the world that mattered to him were the silver obstacle and his target.

"What now?" she heard Emet ask from behind her.

"Don't move," she told him. "Nobody move." Slowly, she backed towards the kitchen, careful to give Masayu a wide berth. She didn't want Dracula to remember there was still another target he could go for. She held out her bleeding hand, and it seemed to arrest his attention, and his red eyes bounced back and forth between her two hands. She went a little faster for the kitchen door.

She kicked it open, stepping back out into the rain, feeling its iciness on her skin, running down her face and her neck.

Washing away the garlic, she realized. Great. This had better work. She walked backwards through the dark, hoping against all hope she didn't trip over something, like one of those stupid vampire watermelons—

She tripped over a vampire watermelon, and sprawled backwards into the blackness. No sooner had she hit the earth than she scrambled backwards, holding up the crucifix with a trembling hand. Dracula had lunged for her, but pulled up short when he saw the tiny piece of silver. He snatched up the rolling watermelon and broke it open, scooping out handfuls of red, red flesh. He'd told her the watermelons sometimes bled. Apparently he meant literally.

She took the opportunity to get to her feet and waited until she had his attention again and led him to the shed where the cows were sheltered.

Vegetarian, she thought to herself, *I'm such a joke*. She led him into the darkened shed, her heart in her throat when she noticed how *dark* it was inside. Once he came in the doorway, she'd lose sight of him if he hid in the shadows. His silhouette slipped inside and disappeared instantly. She ran for the doorway in a blind panic, seized it, and slammed it shut behind her. She pressed herself against the wood, trembling all over. Shivering? It *was* cold out. She sank to her knees, pressing the crucifix to the wood. Behind the door, she heard the cows bellowing and stomping around, passing by the door, following the wall.

The bellowing continued for minutes, maybe a half hour. Then she realized she hadn't heard a sound for a while. She snapped to attention. The door would stop the cows, not

Dracula's Death

him. She threw open the door, holding the crucifix before her in case he was still in there and jumped her.

She couldn't see that well, but her eyes had adjusted to the dark. By her feet she saw hooves and a tail, unmoving on the hay. With a little effort, she could discern motionless forms all around the shed. A black shape next to one of the dead animals shifted a little, and she caught the faint gleam of red. Her breath caught in her throat. It made no move towards her.

"Don't look at me," she heard him say. His voice was hoarse and strained.

Hesitantly, she stepped forward. He had said something, hadn't moved to attack her.

"Get out," he growled.

"Are you ok now?"

Suddenly he was standing over her, his face still white and dead, his eyes still red, the glow only a little dimmer than it had been. He seized her wrists, and she realized she had stupidly let the crucifix down, thinking she was safe. She whimpered, squeezed her eyes shut, expecting any second for him to drag her into the shed, into the black, and kill her. Only he didn't. She opened her eyes, terrified and trembling.

He was staring at her bleeding hand, frozen. She tried to think what she should do. Say something? Break the silence? Her throat felt like a lump of ice, it wouldn't work when she tried to speak. The tiny croak she managed drew his attention, and his red eyes fell to meet hers. His face contorted into a grimace, revealing teeth stained red, and he shoved her out of the shed. She heard the door slam shut as she hit the mud.

She felt light-headed, the world swimming around her. She couldn't sit up, didn't know where up was. Someone tapped her shoulder.

"Hey," Malcolm said. His face was covered in blood, but the rain was washing some of it away. It looked like it was all coming from a wound on his forehead.

"He's in there," she told him, and felt a sob come up out of her. Malcolm helped her to sit up and she saw he had a stake in one hand.

"You were going to kill him?" she asked.

"Yeah, sure," Malcolm mumbled, then wiped blood out of his eye. "Sorry I was gone so long. I figured you had a plan. Got this out of one of his cars." Malcolm eyed the shed.

"He's almost fine, I think. Maybe the chickens—"

"Human's better," Malcolm interrupted, and he reached across her, held up her hand. It was still bleeding. "Don't know how much you've lost, but maybe a little more. Will he stay in there?"

"I think so," she said, trying to steady her voice.

"Good, 'cuz I have no way to keep him in there anyway."

Malcolm helped her to her feet and walked with her to the kitchen. He let her down gently into a chair and went to get the pan. She held her hand over it and tried to stop sobbing. Malcolm dragged Emet into the kitchen by his elbow. Emet protested, but Malcolm slapped a knife into his hand.

"We need more," Malcolm told him.

"More?" Emet wondered, horrified. "How much more?"

"Dunno," Malcolm said.

"What about you?" Emet asked him.

"I'm your best line of defense. That means I'm not a donor. I've got problems with my own leak anyway." He pointed at his face, blood still dripping down it onto his shirt and the floor. He grabbed a towel hanging by the sink and pressed it to his head, wincing and almost whimpering for a moment.

DRACULA'S DEATH

"Masayu..." Emet murmured, looking at her prone form on the floor in the other room. She still panted, but had not moved from where she lay.

"You help fill this thing, and he'll get her fixed up," Malcolm told him, poking him in the hand. Emet's eyebrows met each other in confusion. "He's a doctor."

"A doctor?" Emet repeated, stupefied.

"Cut your stupid hand and stop pestering me," Malcolm told him, and went to the other room. Emet looked at the knife in his hand, then at Masayu, then at Cammy. She tried to wipe the tears and the snot from her face. Her cheek throbbed like there was a hammer beating a nail into it, and her shoulder and her arm. Hesitantly, Emet winced and cut his hand.

"Fine! Whatever!" she heard Malcolm shout from the other room, and he came striding back into the kitchen.

"What is it?" she asked, her voice cracking.

"We're not getting any of Boese's blood," Malcolm growled. "Woulda helped, but them's the breaks."

"What a jerk," Cammy growled. Malcolm glared down into the pan, the knuckles of one hand pressed to the table, supporting him, while the other pressed the towel to his head.

"This has been the worst night of my life," Malcolm grumbled.

"Same," Cammy agreed. Emet looked at Masayu, and Cammy felt a pang of guilt.

"You really think he can help her?" she asked Malcolm.

"You wanna call a vet instead?" he snapped.

"But..." Cammy looked at the prone tiger, panting laboriously. "I mean, won't he...I mean, she's hurt."

"I don't know," Malcolm said, "but I don't know anyone else who can."

"What about a hospital?" Cammy asked timidly. Malcolm made a face at her.

"You want to drive a tiger to the ER?"

"But she can look human."

"Sure, let's wake her up and ask her to change back," Malcolm snarked, and nodded over his shoulder. "See the problem?"

She sure did. Malcolm looked at her hand, then left the room again. He was gone for a few minutes until he returned with some tissues and bandages. He pulled the bottle of *țuica* out of the fridge and unscrewed the lid.

"This is probably going to sting," he warned.

It did.

After he had bandaged up her hand and frowned at the contents of the pan, Malcolm bandaged Emet's hand.

"Hope this'll be enough," he mumbled to himself.

"The watermelons have blood in them," she told him. Emet's eyes bugged.

"The watermelons!" he repeated.

"Got it," Malcolm said, and went out the door with the pan. He was gone for a few minutes, then let himself in, grabbed a teacup, and poured himself some *țuica*. He gulped it down, bared his teeth, then grumbled, "I hate my job."

He placed the cup on the table, then poured himself another. Cammy noticed his hand shaking. Fear, or strain? She couldn't tell. He raised it to his mouth, hesitated, looked up at the ceiling.

"Wow, that really *is* strong," he said, grinning, and started to laugh. He set the teacup down hard on the table, spilling some of the clear liquid, and hit the table with his fist. "That stuff is *strong!* His best batch yet!" He laughed all the harder, rocking forward in his chair.

Dracula's Death

The door swung open, and Cammy almost jumped at the sound. Malcolm spun in his chair, holding up the crucifix he had retrieved from Cammy. His arm shook a little. Emet fell backwards out of his chair and pressed himself up against the wall.

Dracula stood in the doorway, soaked from the rain, his hair falling down over his eyes, which still showed red, face still white, but he didn't look quite so terrifying. His shirt was hanging open, revealing an intact, hairy chest. All the coagulated blood seemed to have washed off in the rain, which was a plus. He hesitantly slicked his hair back, glanced around at them, and stepped inside. He slowly closed the door behind him.

"How are you?" Malcolm asked flatly.

"Is everyone all right?" Dracula asked, almost whispering.

"No one's dead yet," Malcolm answered. "Not for lack of trying, though."

Dracula nodded. He noticed the *țuica* but said nothing. His red eyes did not meet Cammy's even when she tried to read him. He seemed only willing to look Malcolm in the eye.

"You up for some surgery?" Malcolm asked him. Dracula stood, unmoving, for what felt like a solid minute, then glanced over Malcolm's shoulder at Masayu.

"Perhaps," he answered, then gestured at the kitchen table. Cammy got up and moved into the other room, bringing Emet with her. A little while later, Dracula and Malcolm stepped out of the kitchen and approached Masayu. Malcolm grabbed her forepaws to lift her up. Dracula stood over her, frozen once again.

"Can you do it or can't you?" Malcolm snapped. "We don't have all night." He looked up at Emet. "Give me a hand, willya?"

Emet chewed his fingernails, eyed Dracula, then slunk timidly forward. He placed his hands under the tiger's neck and the three of them lifted her, though Malcolm and Emet struggled mightily with their half. They bore her into the kitchen. Emet reemerged, chewing his fingernails, and went down one of the halls to a side room.

"Where are you going?" Cammy asked him.

"Supplies," Emet answered weakly, and disappeared. Boese stepped forward, into the firelight.

"Thanks for your help," Cammy mumbled. And added sarcastically, "For all your talk about protecting people, you sure did a stand-up job back there."

Boese said nothing, just walked past her like a sleepwalker, not seeing her. He went to the kitchen to peer inside, silent. Emet returned with an old-fashioned doctor's leather case, hesitated when he saw Boese lurking like a vulture in the doorway, then pressed past him. Cammy wanted to get up and slap the man, but she also wanted to pass out on the divan and never get back up. She shook all over, dry heaving for a full minute.

She covered her face and tried not to picture anything. *This isn't healthy,* she told herself, *You're going to go crazy. Normal people can't handle this sort of stuff. You're going to go crazy like Boese.*

She felt a hand on her shoulder and jumped, swinging her fist at whoever it was. Emet stumbled backwards, raising his hands defensively.

"I'm sorry! I didn't mean to wake you!" he said.

"Wake me?" Cammy wondered, then looked around the room. It was all gray. All the blood had dried black and crusty, the table lay against the wall, one leg missing. The pile of ash in the fireplace smoldered, a thin wisp of smoke twisting up the chimney.

"What time is it?" Cammy asked. Her throat was so dry it felt like jerky.

Dracula's Death

"Seven, I think," Emet answered.

"Where is everyone?" Cammy looked around.

"Masayu is in one of the bedrooms, resting," Emet answered. "I don't know where that man, Boese, is. He wandered off while we were trying to help Masayu. The other woman disappeared at some point. Your friend, the one who complains all the time, he's passed out drunk."

"What about…?" Cammy felt her throat tighten.

"He's resting too," Emet answered quietly. "At least, that's what he said he was going to do."

"How are you?" she asked. Emet began to tremble all over. She watched him shaking like a leaf, then stood up and put her hands on his shoulders. He practically collapsed onto the divan. "Sorry, whoa. Have you been up all night?"

"Y-yes," he said.

"Coffee," Cammy mumbled, then remembered that there wouldn't be a single bean in the entire mansion. She stumbled to the kitchen. There was blood on the table, on the floor, bloody handprints on the empty bottle of *țuica*. She told her eyes they didn't see anything and went to the fridge. There was nothing inside, so she closed it, then went to the pantry. Empty too. She started noticing crumbs here and there. The place was a wreck. It was strange, he usually kept such a tidy ship, as it were. The domovoy was probably going to pitch a fit.

"He ate everything," Emet said, coming up behind her. He hugged himself with one arm and chewed the fingernails of the other hand. Cammy drifted out the kitchen door to the chicken coop. When she peered inside they were all dead. She went back to the mansion. There was no milk, either.

"Everything." She nodded. "Got it."

"I didn't know…" Emet said, and cleared his throat, "that they eat food too?"

"Mostly it's just him," Cammy told him. "Apparently that's what they were all like, but we've told different stories over the years and now they're different, too."

"So he's really..." Emet made meaningless gestures with his hand.

"Yeah."

Emet nodded vigorously to himself, but said nothing.

"Will you show me where Masayu is?" she asked him.

Emet led her to a downstairs bedroom. It was dark inside, the curtains drawn, but she could hear the tiger's breathing the moment they entered. Emet led Cammy to the bed, which was sagging in the middle and puffed up all around the sleeping tiger. There were bandages wrapped around her throat, her leg, and the wounds down her side. The tiger was breathing heavily, her chest rising and falling rapidly.

"She's going to be ok?" Cammy asked Emet.

"She drank a lot of water last night," he replied hesitantly. "He... he said that was a good sign." Cammy didn't have to ask who "he" was.

She followed him to another guest bedroom, where she found Malcolm face down, half on and half off the feather bed, one shoe kicked off while the other's laces dangled undone and forgotten. With Emet's help, she rolled Malcolm fully onto the mattress. He snorted, opened his eyes and squinted.

"Oh, my *head*!" he groaned. "What time is it?"

"It's morning," Cammy answered, then, with a little smile, "You said you wanted to wake up with a hangover that could kill a bear, right?"

"That was days ago," he snarled, and pressed the palms of his hands to his eyes. There was a goose egg swollen on his forehead. Probably from that savage headbutt from last night. "Augh, I want to die."

Dracula's Death

"I guess I have to go get us all something to eat," she said. "What would you like?"

"Aspirin. Coffee," Malcolm answered, squinting at her from behind his fingers. "A bullet."

"I can get the first two," she said. She turned to the window, noticing how bright it seemed.

"Wait, if you're serious, get me lots of Gatorade and bone broth and some *meat*," Malcolm told her. "Transforming wipes me out. I didn't do it for too long last night, but I berserked, too."

"Ok," she agreed absently, going for the window. She drew open the curtains, flooding the room with morning light. Malcolm barked obscenities at her, and she shut them.

"What is the matter with you?!" Malcolm growled.

"It's not raining anymore."

Emet lowered his hand from his mouth, came to the window, and peeked out of the curtains. "I hadn't even noticed," he said.

"Hooray," Malcolm grumped, and buried his face under one of the downy pillows. "Maybe that cat's dead. I can get paid. Go home. Throw an end of the world party. Hookers and blackjack."

Cammy doubted their luck could have turned like that. Ocelotl wanted to remake the world and had come up here from Mexico to get that ccoa back. He'd had tigers and vampire cats chopping up humans to feed it in the meanwhile. So what had happened? Had it just run out of power?

She had no idea, and neither did Malcolm when she asked him. She left him there and heard him snoring the moment she stopped talking to him.

Nervously, she opened the door to Dracula's study just a crack, and there was Boese sitting in the big, leather armchair. She threw open the door. Boese looked up at her, bags under his eyes, five o'clock shadow on his jaw. The beard hair was gray. There was an open and empty bottle of wine on the table next to a glass tumbler, and his gun on the desk in front of him.

"What are you doing in here?" Cammy demanded.

"Go away," Boese told her.

"Whatever. Creep." She shut the door. She decided not to look for Dracula; he tended to hide. Instead, she went to the kitchen where he stored some of his spending cash—he had told her she could use it if need be and that she ought never to fear running out of food—fetched some, and then got one of his sets of car keys.

"Where are you going?" Emet asked.

"Food run," she said. "Want to come along?"

"Sorry to involve you in all this," Cammy told him as she made her way down into the city. Emet looked at her with hollow, fearful eyes. "This got way out of hand."

"So it isn't always like this?" Emet wondered. "Is there always fighting?"

"This is a first for me," Cammy told him. "Especially this much. I think it's a first for everybody. Malcolm seems pretty out of his element, and Boese, and Vlad. We all got surprised."

"Oh," said Emet, and he stared out the windshield.

"How did you end up meeting Masayu?"

"She sought me out. She"—he nibbled on his thumbnail—"she wasn't angry, she just wanted to know why I did what I did. I..." his eyes fell to his lap. "I didn't know... that they were... basically people. I thought they were monsters. I'm a murderer."

Cammy was going to tell him he wasn't, but... he sort of was.

Dracula's Death

"Why did I do it?" he asked himself. "I should have known better than to harm another like that. I thought they were undead, or rakshasas. I didn't know. I abandoned what I was taught. What is wrong with me? How could I have been so blind?"

"You were scared," Cammy told him. "You didn't know what else to do. There were tiger monsters."

"I should have asked him," Emet said, miserably.

"You thought they were killing people. Heck, they *were* killing people," Cammy pointed out.

"I shouldn't have been so hasty." Emet covered his face.

"You didn't kill her parents, you know," Cammy told him, and he looked at her helplessly. "Um, Vlad did that. They attacked him, but they were scared." She fingered the steering wheel. "I think he only killed them because... he was worried they were going to kill me. I'm not really sure he would have cared if they attacked him, if it was just him there."

"Really?" Emet wondered, doubtfully.

The previous night he had pushed her away once he had the faculty to reason. He could have killed her. But he'd pushed her away. When she had called after being attacked by the vampire cat, he had come to see that she was all right. It had to be that he cared about her wellbeing, even if it was only because she was his guest.

"Yeah," she said. Emet chewed his thumbnail. She watched the trees pass by, the mud on either side of the road. "I had to kill my best friend, you know."

Emet stared at her.

"My friend was... not herself. She was going to kill me, but I killed her first. I didn't know what to do, either. I panicked. I didn't want to kill her."

Emet kept looking at her. He didn't say a word.

"I guess I'm trying to say that... I get where you're coming from. No one knows about this stuff, the rules, what everything is, what's going to kill and eat you, what's just trying to get by. And Masayu forgives you."

"I know," he said, ashamed. "I think that makes it worse."

Cammy watched the road. She had to agree. That did make it worse.

She drove to the nearest grocery store, loaded up a cart with food, picking up a coffee maker that she saw on sale, some beans, filters, and a grinder. Then they made their way back to the mansion. Dried blood still caked the foyer, and she made sure to step carefully over it on her way to the kitchen. She pulled on her dishwashing gloves and wiped down the kitchen. It was all Masayu's blood, she reasoned, not Dracula's. He'd been more or less intact in this room. Now she was grateful she'd gone and splurged on bleach earlier.

She cooked eggs and toast for herself, Emet, and Malcolm. For Masayu, she had purchased a whole rotisserie chicken, as well as cans of chicken noodle soup, not really sure what to buy for an injured tiger. There had been a butcher's nearby, and she'd picked up some pig's blood, doing her level best not to think about it or look at it, and put that in the back of the fridge. She ground up some coffee beans to make herself a decent cup of coffee. While that was brewing, she took the chicken to Masayu, whose golden eye slowly slid open when they entered. The tiger raised her weary head to watch them approach.

"I brought you breakfast," Cammy said, and held up the chicken on the china plate, carried on a silver platter. "Breakfast in bed."

DRACULA'S DEATH

The tiger chuffed and sighed, so Cammy set the tray on the down comforter beside her.

"Can I get you anything else?"

The tiger answered with a weary, almost imperceptible shake of her head. Emet seated himself on the bed.

"Do you need any help?" he asked her. Masayu opened one golden eye to study him. Emet's leg twitched nervously, and the golden eye was drawn to the movement. Masayu closed her eye and offered a small nod.

"I'm going to check on Malcolm," Cammy let them know, and left them there while Emet went to work stripping meat off the bones for his bedridden patient.

Cammy brought coffee, toast, and aspirin, and found Malcolm buried under the covers with all the pillows piled on his head.

"Breakfast," she announced loudly, earning a gravelly, prolonged groan of pain. "This is just a little bit. You want more, you're going to have to crawl out of there and eat at the table like people," she told him.

"You're a wonder," Malcolm snarled at her, raising his head enough to peek at the coffee and the rest. Even with dark circles under his eyes, that swollen goose egg, scruffy, unshaven chin, and his hair in a total disarray, he managed to look like it was a style. He'd make a fortune in Hollywood, if Ophois ever let him, which she doubted they would. Maybe she could let them know they'd make *way* more money off of Malcolm's looks than off of monster hunting. That was an idea. Slowly, he pushed himself up and snatched the bottle of aspirin, knocking some uncertain but alarming number of pills into his palm, slapping them into his mouth and downing some of the coffee.

"Where's my bullet?" he asked hoarsely.

"Ask Boese. He's sitting in the study with his gun like a psycho."

Malcolm squinted up at her with one eye.

"Guess he got it worse than I thought," Malcolm said, and sipped more of the coffee.

"What do you mean?"

"He got hit in the face and the hands," Malcolm said. "I saw it. I wasn't sure it was enough, but I guess it was."

"What are you talking about?" Cammy asked, growing angrier.

"The blood, idiot. Vlad's blood. He's infected now, if that's the word for it. The blood won't kill him right away, but it'll get him. Maybe a year from now, or ten years from now. He's going to die, and he's going to come back."

Cammy frowned.

"You mean he's going to come back as a strigoi?"

"Of course I do, what else would I mean?" Malcolm snapped. She snatched the mug out of his hands and set it on the tray.

"Hey!"

"Manners, dude. I made you coffee and everything."

"Fine, sorry," Malcolm said. "You touch vampire blood, and some of the time you turn into a vampire. Not with the modern ones, but old school ones? Bad idea."

Cammy thought about Boese's pale face and his listless eyes.

"Why didn't Vlad attack him?" she asked.

"That's the other thing." Malcolm pulled the mug from the tray again and slurped the coffee. "You can use vampire blood—I mean the old school ones—as a charm to protect yourself from them. You'll still turn into a vampire, but they can't attack you in the meanwhile."

Cammy chewed her lip.

"That's no good," she said, and Malcolm squinted up at her again. "That'll mean Ocelotl is protected, too."

Dracula's Death

Malcolm let out a long, dramatic sigh.

"This job never *eeeeends*," he groaned, and set the empty mug on the tray. "Tell me you got some bacon."

"No. I got some avocados and toast—"

"You *philistine*," Malcolm hissed, covering his eyes against the dim light that filtered through the curtains.

"—*and* some bacon, and a steak and eggs. And tomato juice and so forth. Come to the kitchen when you feel up to it."

Malcolm sighed with palpable relief. "Sure."

"Do you know where Vlad went?"

"In the walls or something." Malcolm waved a hand at the nearest wall as if to illustrate. "Least, that's what it looked like. He's not going to be up until the sun goes down, I'd say."

"The walls?" Cammy repeated.

"Yeah, I'd do that, if I was him," Malcolm said. "Might as well have a safe place all bricked up so no one can accidentally stumble on me and put a stake through my heart while they're at it."

Cammy considered how her host disappeared when he rested. A hole in the wall would explain it. But which wall? *Not the study, I hope*, she thought to herself.

"Can we trust him?" she asked Malcolm. He glared up at her with bloodshot eyes.

"What do you mean?"

"Well, was he only on good behavior because of Boese's little kill switch, and he's actually the psychopath that everyone says he was back in the fourteen hundreds or whenever?"

"I don't know," Malcolm snapped. "I imagine he's had that thing in since before I was born. But I know he's had friends before—human friends, I mean. And he's worked with the Vatican on and off. That probably counts for something."

"The Vatican?" Cammy asked doubtfully.

"Yeah. I mean, don't get your hopes up too high, Ophois has worked with them on occasion too, so I don't know that it's really a great letter of recommendation, but"—Malcolm drew in a breath and forced a painful looking smile—"I can say for a fact he wasn't a Nazi."

Cammy punched him playfully in the shoulder, then apologized when he winced. He followed her back towards the kitchen, blinking blearily at the mess in the foyer.

"How do you know?" Cammy asked him as he let himself down with a groan into a chair.

"Know what?" he asked.

"That he wasn't a Nazi?"

"Because my grandfather, great grandfather, great uncle and so forth, worked for the Reich, and he killed most of *them*, so it stands to reason," Malcolm explained. Cammy turned to eye him.

"Your grandfather was a Nazi?" she asked.

"No. Worked for them. With them. Whatever. You know how good ol' Adolf was obsessed with the Occult. Well, the Occult is real, so..."

"Oh," she said. "Did they agree with him, or...?"

"It's all money to Ophois," Malcolm said. "I don't think they ever cared about ideology, to be honest. Maybe once, a long time ago, but that all died down out of love for that sweet, sweet dolla." He shut his eyes and leaned back in the chair. A moment later he was snoring. She fried up bacon and the steak to go with a cheesy omelet. He started, squeezing his eyes shut against the hangover, when she set the plate down hard in front of him.

"How did you lose Ocelotl?" she asked him.

Dracula's Death

"What?" He wiped at an eye, looking at nothing with the other.

"How did you lose Ocelotl? Weren't you chasing him?"

"He got in a car," Malcolm answered absently, searching the table for utensils. "I can't run that fast."

"A car?" Cammy handed him a fork and knife.

"Yeah. He didn't hike all the way up here." Malcolm savaged the steak with the knife and severed a huge chunk of meat, practically inhaling it. "Overdone, but ok," he told her. "I like it medium rare. *Juicy*."

Cammy ignored the comment. "How could he drive? I pepper sprayed him."

"Someone else was driving." Malcolm grabbed the bottle of tomato juice that sat on the table, opened, it and drank straight out of it.

"Hey," she pulled the bottle out of his hand, spilling some of the red liquid on his shirt, near the blood stains.

"Oh, come on!" he groused.

"Didn't your mother ever tell you to drink out of a glass? Honestly." Cammy got him a tall glass from one of the cabinets and set it and the bottle down in front of him.

"Not even once. But thank you for asking," Malcolm grumped, and poured the juice. He raised the glass mockingly, as though toasting her. "Thanks for setting me straight, *mother*."

Cammy almost said something snide, but she remembered what Ocelotl had said last night. He, and the other Ophois frontliners, were cannon fodder. The others were killed. Did Malcolm even have a mother?

Well, of course he has a mother, she thought angrily to herself, *But maybe he didn't know her.* She decided not to ask, since he got snarly about personal questions, and left him there to eat in sullen peace.

She took a cup of coffee to the study and opened it. Boese had not moved.

"Coffee," she informed him, and set it down on the desk. "I'm making breakfast if you want something."

Boese eyed her, but still didn't move. She went back out, closing the door behind her.

Emet was sitting beside Masayu, who seemed to be sleeping again; the plate was empty, save for bones. Cammy wondered if were-tigers healed faster than humans; most supernaturals seemed to. She crept forward and offered Emet coffee.

"Cream and sugar?" he whispered hopefully. She took the tray and got him some. He dumped six lumps of sugar and almost half the cream decanter into his mug before he was satisfied.

Back in her own room at last, she drew a bath. While she waited for the water to warm up, she started a load of laundry so she'd have *something* to wear later, and even got everything hung up or in the dryer before pulling out the scented candle she kept in a drawer for when she needed a little extra relaxing time. She spotted the shards of the dog print mug still sitting under the window. While the water filled, she glued them back together as best she could and left the mug to set. Then she bathed, and fell asleep the minute her head hit the pillow.

CHAPTER II
EYE OF THE STORM

She woke up somewhere around 5 pm, feeling her shoulder aching, and her cheekbone, and her ankle, which she must have twisted without realizing it, and her hips from falling so much. Now she understood how Malcolm felt.

One bullet for me, too, she thought. Stiffly, she got up and got dressed in her last set of clean leggings. She had one long-sleeved shirt left. Everything else was muddy and covered in grass or worse, blood from an unknown source. Just perfect.

Her mouth was so dry her head pounded. She staggered down the stairs to the kitchen, drank two glasses of water, then poured herself a glass of organic orange juice.

Coffee, she thought. After she had drunk three glasses of juice, she brewed fresh coffee and made herself a sandwich using avocado, mayonnaise and cucumber slices with a sprinkling of dill, and went in search of everyone else. The foyer looked clean; she wondered whether the domovoy or the brownies had tended to it, or maybe Malcolm or Emet. She couldn't imagine Boese doing anything of the sort. Given how much damage had been done, and that the brownies could only clean during night hours, they must have had their hands full. The broken table was gone, leaving an uncanny empty space, but the divan still faced the fireplace. Cozy. Then she noticed two sets of bloody handprints on it.

She ran outside to scream so she wouldn't wake anyone. There weren't any chickens walking around, nor the sounds of cows mooing in the shed. The estate was eerily quiet. Even though the rain had stopped, she didn't hear the satyrs and nymphs bothering each other in the distance, the way they usually did when the weather was good. *I hope he didn't kill them, too*, she thought, but she didn't dare go check.

Even Komamaki, Aki, and Ginko wouldn't be safe in their little den if he'd tried to get them. Thinking that, Cammy ran to the tree that sheltered their den and called their names. Little eyes and twitching noses came poking up out of the ground to greet her. She slumped to the ground, relieved.

"What happened?" Aki asked, coming out of the den and sitting in front of her.

"The worst night ever. Are you guys ok?"

"We are fine, but the master..." Aki fell silent, her yellow, cat-slit fox eye darting to the cowshed for a moment before she remembered herself and snapped her attention back.

"He's better now. Did he hurt any of the others?"

The three of them shook their heads.

"Ok, good," Cammy said.

"The weather has cleared up," Komamaki observed, sitting on his fat haunches, and eying her sandwich hungrily. Cammy broke off a piece and offered it to him. His wife snapped her jaws in disapproval, and Komamaki hung his raccoonish head, ashamed. Cammy smiled at his embarrassment. It was impossible to stay angry at the pudgy, little raccoon dog.

"I'm not that hungry," she lied, and set the sandwich on the ground for them.

Dracula's Death

"Thank you," Aki said, bowing her head respectfully. She picked up the sandwich in her mouth before the tanuki could snap the whole thing up, and lifted it out of his reach. Once he had sat down, the fox tore the sandwich into three pieces and the family shared it.

Cammy walked back to the mansion. There were absolutely no watermelons. Even the ones that were normal —or at least, didn't roll around so they probably weren't vampires—were gone. Only some battered vines remained. For a moment she wondered if he kept them around *just in case* things ever got as bad as last night. Some sort of emergency rations. The thought made her laugh, and she stumbled back inside. There were still a few hours until sunset, so she went in search of wherever her phone might be. She found it helpfully plugged in on one of the kitchen counters, and she looked through her social media for news.

Everything was about the weather. Big surprise. Andrew had texted, asking when the weather would get better—sent yesterday—and another text this morning thanking her and Dracula for solving the weather mess. She didn't have the heart to correct him, so just replied "Sure."

She scrolled through more news. Apparently the National Guard had been called. Parts of the city had been badly damaged or completely destroyed by the flooding. Flooding! She wondered if the Underground had been affected; maybe the monsters had cleared out. There was an announcement that the President would be coming to visit to give condolences and promises and show camaraderie.

The President? Cammy stared. The President was coming because the weather had cleared, and the National Guard was here, and the hail had been declared an emergency. People were blaming climate change or aliens or government projects, but the President was coming.

That couldn't have been Ocelotl's plan, could it? But then, why would he care? He just wanted to end the world, right?

She hurried down the stairs to the study. Boese wasn't there, but she heard rustling in the kitchen and found him staring into the fridge.

"Hey, any reason an Aztec god would care about the President of the United States?" she asked him. Boese shut the fridge and frowned at her.

"What?" he demanded.

"You heard me. Any reason that might be the case?"

"Why?"

She showed him her phone. He scrolled through the news, his frown deepening.

"*Perfect*," he hissed, and pulled his phone out of his pocket.

"We need to get everyone mobilized," Boese said into the phone. "Don't ask me. I'm fine. Do you have those files I asked you for? No, send one up. Yes, I'm still here. It's *wrecked*, that's why. Bring supplies for Subject D. Because *I said so*. Shut up and do what I tell you." He hung up.

"So you're a jerk to your own people, too," Cammy observed.

"Shut up," he told her, pointing a finger at her face.

"Sorry you got... um, infected," Cammy said. Boese glowered at her. "I mean, that's gotta suck."

"Shut up," Boese snarled, and he pushed past her.

"That's the jerk I know," she mumbled to herself.

About an hour later some government vehicles made their way up the drive. Boese glanced out the window, then turned to Cammy.

"You don't work for me, fine, but I'm guessing you'd like to go on living, right?"

Cammy didn't so much as blink at him.

Dracula's Death

"When he wakes up, you tell him what's happening, *capiche*?" Boese told her, pointing a pale finger at her. "Do it."

"Sure, boss man," she told him, and mock-saluted. He glared at her, opened the door, and stepped out. As he got into one of the vehicles, he waved for one of his men to do something. One of them got out, opened the trunk of his car, and lifted out two coolers which he stacked one on top of another. He carried them to the door. Cammy wanted nothing to do with any of that, and stepped back. The agent dropped the coolers outside the door, then left. The government cars pulled away.

Malcolm came wandering out of somewhere about twenty minutes later, looking a bit better. Washed, at least. He still had that big goose egg on his forehead, though, as well as a scabbed over cut. He was dressed in the biker gear she'd seen him in when he came to rescue her from the elves, and carried the shotgun and axe she'd seen him bring to the Fremont Troll to rescue her last year. He set them down by the fireplace.

"Remind me not to let him suck my blood again," Malcolm told her, running his hands through his glossy hair with a weary sigh. He still looked like he needed a few more days of sleep. "I feel terrible."

"I'll do that," she said. "By the way, the President's coming."

"Why?" Malcolm demanded acidly.

"Because of the weather," she explained. "Boese and I think your cousin's going to try to... do something."

"What does the President have to do with anything? Some sort of symbolic revenge about Mexico or something?" Malcolm asked, flopping into an armchair and sliding halfway down it.

"Well, apparently kings need to make sacrifices," Cammy said. "I read that last night while looking up Tez...the Aztec god. Maybe a President is the closest thing here to a king."

"Ah," said Malcolm, drumming on the armchair with one hand. "Ocelotl should have flown to Europe. Wait, maybe that's why he went for Vlad?"

"Huh?"

"Well, I mean, he was a prince or something, right?"

Cammy hadn't thought of that.

"Well, kings don't have to get sacrificed like your average person," Cammy explained. "They just have to give blood."

Emet emerged from the bedroom and approached.

"Where is the soup?"

Cammy told him where, and then warned him there was no microwave and he'd have to warm it on the stove. Which she then realized hadn't been lit since that morning and would take at least a half hour to come up to temperature.

"Well, cold is better than nothing," Emet said, and went to the kitchen anyway.

The sky was tinted orange and silver. Malcolm glanced out a window, stood, and went out the front door. He returned with one of the coolers, which he took to the study.

"Boese left?" he asked, as he walked back to the door and disappeared through it.

"Yeah," Cammy told him when he came back in with the other cooler. Emet emerged from the kitchen with a pot of the cold soup and spotted the coolers.

"All that?" he asked, his voice cracking.

"I don't know if we need all of this," Malcolm said, "but better safe than sorry, right? Boese might have actually helped for once."

Dracula's Death

No one commented on that. Emet passed by, and headed to Masayu's room with the pot of soup. The room darkened as the sun set. Malcolm began to pace in front of the study.

"Hello, Malcolm."

Malcolm whirled around with a girlish shriek and waved a fist in Dracula's face. Cammy hadn't seen him enter, and apparently Malcolm had missed his entrance as well.

Dracula still looked pale, thin, and corpselike. His eyes were still bloodshot, and he still wore the torn clothes of the previous night. He looked like a wino who'd been dead in the gutter for a day, complete with five o'clock shadow. She'd seen him shaving before, but she couldn't get her head around the concept of a walking dead man growing a beard.

"In there," Malcolm pointed angrily at the study. Without a word, Dracula passed by him and disappeared into the study, shutting the door behind him.

Malcolm returned to the armchair and sank into it.

"I hate this job," he grumbled.

Half an hour later Dracula emerged, looking even worse. His face was disgusting and red, every vein in his forehead popping out like worms swollen under his skin.

Eww, Cammy thought. *Like a mosquito. Gross.*

"You look *great*," Malcolm told him, shooting him a pair of mock-enthusiastic thumbs-ups.

Dracula said nothing, but shut the study door behind him. He ascended the stairs. Malcolm spent his time twiddling his thumbs and flicking through his phone messages while they waited. Cammy did her best to settle her nerves.

"Did you catch our enemy, at least?" Dracula asked as he returned down the stairs, looking more like his impeccable self—immaculately pressed black suit, clean-shaven, hair combed. His face and hands were still puffy and red, though.

He crossed the room and looked out a window. "It's cleared up, I see."

"We've got some bad news," Cammy said. Dracula reluctantly met her eye, then looked away again. She explained the situation, and finished by describing Boese's departure.

"He went back to that den of vipers," Dracula mumbled to himself.

"Did you know he got your blood on him?"

"I suspected so," he answered. He added nothing else. Whether the news made him happy, angry, or indifferent, he gave no sign.

"Ocelotl ate some of your heart," Cammy said. "Sorry. He was already chewing on it when we got there."

"I know," Dracula said.

Cammy squinted at him.

"How?" she asked.

"It houses my soul," he explained, tapping at his chest. "So yes, I know."

"Is that why the stake thing kills you?" Cammy asked him. He looked at her with an expression she couldn't make out past all the gross red color. He was really hard to look at, and she did her best not to. "Well, at least the kill switch isn't there anymore," she said. "So no matter what Boese does now, I guess you're free."

Dracula snorted in response.

"Do we know where the ccoa is?" he asked.

"No," Cammy said.

"Well, the night's not getting any younger," he said. "We should get to work."

"Yippee," Malcolm grumbled.

"Where is the tiger?" Dracula asked. Cammy showed him Masayu's room. They found her leaning over the bed licking

Dracula's Death

up the cold soup from the pot on the floor while Emet sat in the chair watching her. Emet screamed when they entered, and Masayu looked up, her golden eyes staring warily.

"I apologize for my actions yesterday," Dracula told them. "How are you?"

Masayu stared, soup dripping from her chin. She chuffed. For a moment Cammy wondered why she didn't change shape, but then she realized the bandages might all come off if she did.

"I'm afraid I must go out and deal with the matter at hand," Dracula said, "but you are both welcome to stay here in the meanwhile. Though I must warn you, please, not to wander the grounds in my absence. I will be certain to bring anything you require. Young man."

Emet flinched in his chair.

"Is there anything I can offer you?"

Emet shook his head silently.

"Masayu?"

The tiger shook her head also.

"I see," said Dracula. "In that case, I offer my sincere apologies once more. Please stay, if you wish, only do not wander about."

Neither of the guests said or did anything, so he retreated and shut the door.

"What's the plan?" Malcolm demanded.

"The same as before: find the ccoa, retrieve it," Dracula told him. "Only I propose now that we also work to stop Armageddon along the way."

"Why, I've always wanted to stop Armageddon," Malcolm said with a fake, toothy grin. "What are we waiting for?"

"A plan," Dracula told him. "We have been careless." He did not look at Cammy when he said so. He noticed her avoiding his gaze as well. That was only fair, after what had happened.

"A plan?" Malcolm repeated, slouching in an armchair Dracula had purchased at the turn of the previous century. Malcolm slid down in it like a pouting child. "Like what?"

"We still lack information. If we had been prepared, last night's disaster could have been avoided," Dracula told him. He looked at the empty space where the neat little coffee table he'd received as a gift in the 1930s had once stood. Such a small thing, but it reminded him of his greatest shame—going off half-cocked. He knew better, he always knew better, but he still blindly walked into traps every so often. It was absolutely unforgivable, unconscionable. *Lazy*, he told himself reproachfully. That was the heart of the matter. Complacency. Sinking into meaningless ennui. After the Second World War, after everything else... he hadn't had much reason to care about anything. He knew it; getting up in the evenings to do whatever work the department had for him, while giving his donations, while building up the estate for the future, he knew he didn't really care if it all burned down around his ears. Burning down around his ears might be a welcome respite. It might do him in, at long last; put an end to the long, bleak nights and days that were never going to stop coming unless someone stopped them for him. For a while he had hoped Boese would, but it had become clear that despite all the director's paranoia, despite his loathing, he had no intention of killing his prize test subject. Boese knew that ridiculous little kill switch was a near-worthless shock collar only, yet had still relied on it.

And all this complacency, this foggy, aimless wandering had just about nearly killed Cammy and Malcolm both.

Unacceptable.

Worse still, it was inexcusable.

"Information?" Malcolm wondered, drawling like a drunk. He probably was drunk.

Dracula's Death

"We did not have the opportunity to learn much about our enemy," Dracula pointed out. "That's bad tactics. We still don't know why he needed human flesh, for example."

"I thought that was for the ccoa," Cammy pointed out.

"I did a bit of research on my own," Dracula told her. "One can feed it fruit or meat as offerings; it does not require human flesh. If Ocelotl meant these deaths to be sacrifices for his pagan god, then why did he force cats and tigers to kill people in their bathtubs and kitchens? That is not the way of sacrifice, to my understanding."

"But why else would he ask them to do it?" Cammy wondered.

"Exactly the trouble: we don't know. We are missing something. We have his goal, some of his methods, but they do not come together. There is a piece or two of this puzzle missing. Until we have it, we will be chasing phantoms and accomplishing nothing."

"Well, the President is coming," Cammy pointed out.

"Very good," he said, uncaring.

"Maybe Ocelotl wants to sacrifice him or something," Cammy pursued.

"Why?" Dracula wondered.

"Well, because kings...?" Cammy proposed.

"You Americans," Dracula grumbled to himself, then to her, "What is your President? I'll tell you what: a glorified mayor. A peasant elected to rule over other peasants. They're so meaningless that none of you remember the names of the spares. You can't even name most of them, I'd wager. Your Presidents, I mean, not the spares."

Cammy frowned, insulted.

"Well, it's *fair*," she said. "Letting the people decide..."

"Which is precisely why they don't matter," Dracula told her. "Not since your first President has a single one been a man I would call worthy of being a king, as *he* could have been, but he walked away from the title."

Cammy pouted at him, then averted her eyes. He had a sense she was not voicing something that she felt smug about, but he did not ask what silly idea she entertained. There were far more important things than the childish imaginings that went on in her head.

"It is not impossible that he wishes to kill your President," Dracula said to mollify her, "but I do not see that such could have been his plan from the start. No. I believe that to be a coincidence. Your Presidents make appearances at every natural disaster of any size, do they not?"

"We should still look into it," Cammy asserted. "Just to be certain."

"Boese is looking into it. He'll be of great use to us by not hounding me and interfering with my methods every waking moment. Besides, I imagine his department is better suited to look into the safety of individual politicians than that of the common citizen. No, I propose we search for information."

"Yeah, well, the Underground is all cleared out," Malcolm told him. "I checked today and no one's home. Seems they all read the writing on the wall and decided to bug out." He sighed. "So where do we start?"

"Our only real lead is that cat restaurant that Cammy discovered," said Dracula, "so I propose we start by returning there."

To placate Malcolm, he handed off the keys to his customized jeep. The werewolf grinned toothily and swung the keyring around his finger in a manner Dracula supposed was meant to make him anxious about the state his vehicle would be in once all was said and done. He deliberately ignored the gesture and went in search of Aki.

DRACULA'S DEATH

"Yes, my lord?" the fox said, when he called down into her den.

"You know something of the supernatural in Japan and China, I presume?" he checked.

"Japan, yes," said the fox, "less of China. I did not live there."

"Will you come with me? I have need of your expertise."

Aki agreed and bid her family goodbye. She changed herself into an attractive, modestly dressed woman with her straight, black hair tied at the nape of her thin neck. Her dark eyes seemed brighter and more angular than the few Japanese women Dracula had seen before. She stepped gracefully over the roots, and followed him back to the vehicle.

Malcolm had pulled the jeep out into the drive, his grin visible even from this distance as he fingered the steering wheel. Cammy stood by the door, watching him approach.

"Do you wish to come along?" Dracula asked her. Cammy looked at him.

"Are you all right?" she asked him.

The question stopped him dead. He heard Aki's light footsteps come to a stop just a few paces behind him, became aware of Malcolm's eyes on him, saw Cammy's look of concern. No, this would not do. This would not do at all.

"Are you armed?" he asked.

"No," said Cammy.

"If you wish to come, go and get something," he told her. "We will wait for you."

Cammy's eyes narrowed almost imperceptibly. She went inside.

He waited in the passenger seat while Malcolm tapped eagerly on the wheel and ran his hands over the dash and fiddled with the radio, searching for a station he liked. Aki sat silently in the back. Several minutes later, Cammy came out the front door and seated herself behind him. He felt her eyes on the back of his head.

"I checked on Emet and Masayu. I think they're all right for now," she informed them. "I got their numbers, too, so we can keep in touch."

"Good," he said. Malcolm dialed the volume up until the speakers shook to the beat of some inane noise he had found, but it seemed like silence when Cammy did not have a response for him.

"Turn that garbage down," he told Malcolm.

"I'm driving," Malcolm insisted.

"It's my car, turn it down."

Malcolm obeyed, grumbling, and pulled the vehicle off the driveway, taking them into the city.

Traffic was unbearable, as there were emergency vehicles clearing away fallen tree branches and other debris, so they did not reach the restaurant until after ten. The nearest street they could park on was a pond three inches deep. He had worn boots, of course, but Malcolm had not thought to wear water-proof footwear. Cammy had learned that lesson, however, and waded through the water to the sidewalk. Aki leaped to dry pavement with the agility of a gymnast and the grace of a bird.

Yellow crime scene tape crisscrossed the door, and the interior was darker than it had been the previous night.

"The police came by?" Cammy asked, pointing at the tape.

"I set fire to the chair inside," Dracula pointed out. "I imagine the fire department was notified, and once they came, they found the bodies in the kitchen and so notified the police."

DRACULA'S DEATH

She shuddered, and he noticed she didn't carry her purse. She had found a satchel of his, he supposed from one of the spare bedrooms or a chest or some other location, and wore that instead. Her purse was probably soaked with his blood. He gritted his teeth at the idea.

He walked past her to the door, spotting the trouble before he tore down the tape.

"Hey, that's a crime scene!" Cammy protested.

"Was," he corrected, and opened the door. Inside, the candles were dark and cold, and the ashes of the ruined armchair sat in the middle of the room. The ceiling was blackened and had partly collapsed in the middle, exposing the space above. One wall was also scorched. The agent inside the restaurant whirled when the door opened, drawing his gun.

"Don't," Dracula told him, pulling his own magnum. "I'm in no mood."

"What's going on?" Cammy asked, and Dracula pictured her on her tiptoes trying to peer over his shoulder.

"Just a moment," he told her, keeping his eyes fixed on Neil. "Lower your gun," he told the man.

"What are you doing here?" Agent Neil demanded.

"I could ask you the same thing, and I am. You answer first."

In the dark, Neil could not make out who had come to confront him, as Dracula could easily see the man struggling to recognize his face, and to make out who had come behind. Neil was one of the department's *dhampirs*, however, which meant the man would know instantly that whoever had come to confront him would and could not be stopped by a gun. *Dhamphirs* were born vampire-hunters, the offspring of a *strigoi* father and a human mother. The agent grimaced, and held up his hands. Dracula entered the restaurant, relieved him of his weapon, and made a quick search for more.

"Can I come in?" Cammy asked, poking her head inside.

"Yes. But be careful. Let Aki in first, then Malcolm, if you please."

He kept his weapon trained on Neil while the others came inside.

"Oh, wow," Malcolm said, stifling a cough. "Oh wow, lots of smells in here, boy. Who you got over there?"

"One of Boese's pets," Dracula answered. "Aki, Malcolm, if you would, take a look around. See if there is anything the police and the department have overlooked." He eyed Neil, and waved him to the stools in front of the bar. Stiffly, Neil shuffled towards them and took a seat.

"What are you doing here?" Cammy asked him, flicking her phone flashlight into his face. He frowned and averted his eyes from the sudden light. It amused Dracula to think that she was trying to intimidate a man who could probably break every bone in her body in a physical fight. Women. "Making sure it's clear?"

"No," Dracula told her. "This time he was snooping. Isn't that right?"

Neil swallowed the lump in his throat, his hands beginning to tremble.

"Snooping?" Cammy repeated, sounding amazed at the very concept.

"Hey, how did I miss these last time?" Malcolm said, pulled down one of the Bastet statues set in the little alcoves that ringed the room. "Oh, right, I was wiping pepper spray out of my eyes." He shot Cammy a look.

"Sorry. Are they important?" Cammy asked.

"Bast," Malcolm mumbled to himself, rolling the little statue back and forth between his fingers. "What sort of cats did you see?"

Dracula's Death

"There was the big white one," Cammy answered. "I think it was a vampire." She looked to Dracula to confirm, and he nodded. "A black one, an Abyssinian, this grey tabby—"

"An Egyptian Mau?" Malcolm checked.

"I don't know. Maybe?" Cammy said. Malcolm pulled out his phone, searched for an image, and showed it to Cammy. She nodded.

"Yes, just like that," she agreed. "Actually, that one said something about Egypt. I guess I didn't think about it. Is it important?"

"Maybe," said Malcolm, "Bast, in the later periods, was an aspect of Sekhmet, the lioness goddess. The one who," he looked at Dracula, then Cammy, "to bring *Ma'at*—that is, balance or justice—has to bring the waters of the Nile in the form of a flood to rejuvenate Egypt. Our buddy Ocelotl also mentioned Sekhmet. I thought he was being crazy, but maybe he's focused on the blood aspect of both gods. The Aztecs believed the sun needed blood just to run, and Sekhmet drank blood... maybe that's the angle he's connecting them with. I mean, that's just the first thing I can come up with. But the flooding might also help invoke Sekhmet."

"Is there anything else we ought to tell you?" Cammy asked.

"How should I know unless you tell me?" Malcolm snapped.

Cammy glared at him, and closed her eyes to think.

"He was saying at first he'd send Vlad to... I guess Aztec hell, but then he turned around and said that dying in battle or sacrifice was better."

"Xibalba was the word he used," Dracula added.

"Then he's definitely mixing his pantheons. Xibalba is Mayan. If he'd been sticking to Aztec one hundred percent he'd have said Mictlan. Not that either of those are really hell the way most Americans mean it. Just the underworld."

"Ocelotl would know this, I assume?" Dracula asked.

"I mean, he *ought* to. And Egyptology is something we all get. That was what Ophois was founded on back in the day," Malcolm explained. "We specialize from there to local stuff. So maybe that's all he's doing: taking some local research and folding it into the Egyptology. As far as the cats, Maus are a breed of cat often associated with Egypt, so I don't think it was here by accident."

"Keep looking," Dracula told him. Aki had gone into the kitchen without a sound and had not emerged.

"What about him?" Cammy asked, waving her light at Neil.

"That is what we will discover. Do you have anything you wish to confess?"

Neil clenched his teeth, struggling to keep his eyes from showing fear. He failed.

"I know there is a leak in the department," Dracula said, "and that someone brought that chair to Ocelotl instead of destroying it. Given that you are here, shall I assume that the leak is you?"

"It's not as though he could have killed you with it," Neil protested, grimly. For a moment, Dracula felt rage, white hot, burning, and he almost lost control of himself and broke the man's skull with one hand, but he restrained himself, kept his gun level.

"So it was you. Why?" he asked. Neil stared at the gun.

"You wouldn't kill me," he asserted.

"No?"

Neil's eyes rose to meet his.

"You wouldn't."

DRACULA'S DEATH

"I've killed better men than you," Dracula told him. "You presume too much."

"But..." Neil said, losing confidence. "But I'm..." Once again, the man tried to reach out, groping for some paternal recognition. Dracula had always denied him that connection, that acknowledgement, in the past. Strange that he still reached for it.

"One of Boese's pets," Dracula finished. "Is that not true?"

Neil's hazel brown eyes searched his, looking for compassion, mercy, or some other floating piece of salvation he could latch onto. He sagged, realizing there was nothing of the sort.

"Now speak," Dracula told him. "Why?"

"My wife," Neil answered, defeated.

"What about her?"

"She..." Neil shook his head. "She's dead. Or, maybe she's not dead. I don't know."

"What happened?" Dracula asked flatly.

"It was a couple weeks ago," Neil explained. "I got home late, we had only just heard that there might be a human killer on the loose. We didn't know it was those tigers yet. I got home late, but I guess it wasn't late enough. I got home in time to see it."

"See what?"

"This big, white cat. Vampire cat." Neil glanced at Cammy, who wore an expression of absolute horror. "Biggest house cat I've ever seen. It had her. By the throat." Neil gasped, wiped at tears. "Had her, and it saw me, and I couldn't move, and it dragged her off somewhere, I don't know where. Then she came back. But it wasn't her. It was that *cat*." He covered his face. "It talks like her, looks like her, remembers our first date, remembers my birthday. It's her, but it's that cat, too."

Cammy's eyes were wide. She clutched at the satchel strap across her chest, her mouth hanging just a little open, her breath shallow.

"What did you do?" Dracula asked him.

"I didn't do anything!" Neil shouted. "Not a damn thing! What am I supposed to do? It's her, but it's not her! I can feel her—it—*her* sucking out my life, but I can't" —he looked up at Dracula, his eyes red with tears, with exhaustion— "I can't hurt her. I can't stop her. I love her, I hate her, I can't kill her. It would be easy. I *know* it would be easy. I should. But I can't."

"Did you report this?" Dracula asked, knowing the man had done nothing of the sort.

"*Report it?*" Neil demanded, his hands closing into fists. "Report it? So they can take her down into that lab with all the others? Torture her for years? Like his *sister*? The one that screams and begs to be let out, but he doesn't *care*?"

"Boese's *sister* is down there?" Cammy gasped, her eyes wide with still more horror.

Dracula wondered how she knew about the sister, but didn't want to get led astray just yet.

"It's not your wife. You know it's not," Dracula told Neil. "Your wife is dead. You know this *thing* is wearing her like a mask to feed on you."

"I *know*," Neil agreed, miserably, his head falling forward into his hands. "I know it is. But I can't get free. I can't. I want to, but I don't want to. I can't, I can't..."

"What does this have to do with Ocelotl and the chair?" Dracula interrupted. "Where does he fit in?"

"He approached me a few days after it happened," Neil replied. "He told me that Boese was responsible for what happened to my wife."

Dracula's Death

"For turning your wife into a *vampire?*" Dracula asked, almost laughing at the absurdity of such an accusation. "And you believed him?"

"Why not?" Neil demanded. "It's the same type of cat as his sister. Maybe he let her out. Or maybe he wants some other kind of science experiment. See what happens when you take a *dhampir* and a... whatever she is. Put them together. He knows I couldn't say no."

Dracula thought about it. Boese had few qualms authorizing and overseeing all sorts of experiments—Dracula could personally attest to that, having been subject to quite a few himself over the decades, including the ones that resulted in the department's *dhampirs*. But breeding a *dhampir* and some sort of vampire cat together? That seemed like the sort of thing the director would only do in the lab where he could keep a close eye on the results. The man did not like uncontrolled variables.

"Did Ocelotl *say* Boese was responsible, or did you conjecture it?" Dracula asked. Neil's eyes stared into his, wildly, uncomprehending.

"What?"

"Precisely what I said. Not now," he told Malcolm when the werewolf emerged from the kitchen. "Neil, did you mention Boese first, or did Ocelotl?"

"What?" Neil repeated, stupidly.

"I have to know if he knew about Boese's sister, or whether you mentioned her and he latched onto it. I have to know if he had access to that information before he spoke to you." *One leak, or more?*

Neil blinked, wiped at his eyes. "I don't remember. It's—it's all like a nightmare. I'm so tired all the time. I can't think. She won't leave me alone, but I don't want her to."

"What is it, Malcolm?"

"Just found this," Malcolm said, holding up a larger stone statue. "Sekhmet, kinda like I feared. Some of the usual offerings in front of it. I also found some Egyptian black magic curses written in hieroglyphics. I think this place was peddling in hexes on the side, maybe that's how it was able to operate up here instead of Underground. I don't see how it could have gotten away with so much killing out in the open unless there was something else going on. One thing I will say is this: a *ton*, and I mean that literally, a *ton* of cats have been through here. This wasn't just a little club, this was something big. I can't keep them all straight, it's like a convention in here. More than that, there were a lot of monsters. Bad ones. I can smell just the shadows because there's too much to sort through, but there were *things* here."

"Perhaps the vampire cats?" Dracula proposed.

"More than one type. Ocelotl, obviously, and I think his yaoguai buddies, but more. A lot more. I think this is a much bigger operation than we originally thought. Much, *much* bigger."

"Cats can't drive cars," Cammy pointed out, and Dracula turned to her. She had her eyes on Neil, who looked down at the floor. "Did you help him get away last night?"

"The vehicle didn't have government plates," Malcolm said, "but that doesn't mean anything. Is this guy the leak?"

"Yes. We are simply trying to determine how far his involvement goes."

"Yay," said Malcolm, setting the stone figurine on the countertop and retreating to the kitchen once more. "Let me know what you find out."

"Did you?" Dracula asked. Neil nodded.

"Why?"

DRACULA'S DEATH

"Because he's got a point," Neil snapped. "We're losing the war, and it wouldn't matter even if we won. We're not exactly as white as the driven snow. I'm proof of that. But it doesn't matter, we're drowning anyway. Every time we think we are on top of the situation the monsters change. Even if we wiped them all out, they'd just *poof* exist again. Same with the *oni* and ogres and the others. We're wasting our time. And"—he swallowed—"I can't take it anymore." He stared at Dracula. "You don't—you *can't* know what it's like. When you can see all the things that walk around all the time. They're *everywhere*. Running shops, buying milk, working in hospitals, everywhere. I can't take it. Everyone else can go to work, clock in, clock out, but not me. It's twenty-four hours a day. Before, I could go home, brush my teeth, watch TV, sit with my wife, but at any time some extra-dimensional daemon could go crawling across the screen or come out of the mirror or across the bedroom ceiling."

"It's worse now than when I was alive," Dracula admitted. "There are more vampires here than I ever saw in my home country, or over the previous several hundred years. However, the West has a certain love affair with them, so the numbers hardly surprise me. But you have better sight than any dhampir I've heard tell of. A little something extra Boese did to you, no doubt."

"You see what I mean?" Neil demanded. "We've got to take this whole system down. I can't do it myself. Ocelotl's going to put a stop this whole circus. What do you want me to do? Shelly—" His words caught in his throat, and he fell silent. "I can't stand it anymore. I can't. I'm going insane. Now she's killing me, and I guess I can't get away because I want her to. Or she made me want her to do it. I can't tell, my head's so messed up." He pressed the heels of his palms to his temples.

Aki came to the doorway to the kitchen. "Have you found something?" Dracula asked her, and she nodded.

"Would you please follow me?" she asked.

"Keep an eye on him," Dracula told Malcolm, who shrugged and came around the counter to take a seat next to Neil. Dracula went around the counter to Aki's side, and she retreated, leading him through the kitchen and out the back door. Cammy came shuffling behind him, hesitating to look over her shoulder at Neil before exiting into the clear night air.

"That's awful," she murmured. Dracula said nothing. Aki led them down the street to an alleyway where a woman sat in a pile of newspapers and trash, her long black hair ragged and clinging to her shoulders and her cheap-looking pleather outfit. She looked up, one eye socket empty, bloody, and swollen, and her right hand missing from just above her wrist, hastily wrapped in rags.

"The huli jing—the fox woman," Cammy gasped. "What happened?"

"You again?" the huli jing asked, summoning a seductive smile, turning her face to hide the missing eye. "You're bad luck for us."

"What happened?" Cammy asked again.

"The man who thinks he is a jaguar does not like disloyalty," said the fox, and fixed her sultry eye on Dracula. He felt inexplicably drawn to her, despite the raw wound in her face. That was doubtless how she managed to feed. He'd heard of huli jing from a Chinese immigrant who had worked for him in the early part of the 20th century.

"What do you mean, 'disloyalty?'" Cammy asked.

Dracula was grateful she had said something; for a moment, he had forgotten why he had come here in the first place. Apparently huli jing were quite formidable succubae, though she seemed less harmful than most. If he could trust his judgement.

"He wanted us all to join his holy war," said the huli jing. "After you came, Maat demanded those who were loyal to make the pilgrimage. Those who were not, were punished," she smiled coquettishly, flashing her single eye at Dracula, covering the empty socket with her only hand. "They had me captured, but I escaped. I have sharp teeth." She slid her tongue over her beautiful, pearly teeth, still smiling.

Dracula could see there was a ragged wound in her tongue, it seemed to have been sliced in the middle, forming a bleeding hole.

"Maat?" Cammy asked. "That's the Sekhmet cat?"

"Maat is the Mau. You must have seen her when you went inside. Her owners called her that, and I think she likes the name. She took to the jaguar man immediately when he first came. She and the nekomatas and the others."

"What is a nekomata?" Cammy asked.

"It's a cat that has grown so old that its tail has split in two," Aki explained. "They can command corpses to rise if they jump over them."

"These cats can create living corpses if they leap over them?" Dracula checked. Aki nodded. "That is curious. The Magyar tradition holds that if a cat leaps over a corpse it becomes a vampire. Does this creature raise vampires also?"

"Yes," Aki answered, "and they have command of them after."

"But if he has these nekomata working for him too, then why haven't we seen any vampires?" Cammy wondered. "We've only seen those yaoguai."

An excellent question. An army of vampires under his command would doubtless be at least as effective as the handful of tiger demons who went with him. With his firepower, he could have gone into any store, gunned down all the customers inside, and commanded his nekomata to leap over them before any law enforcement or the department could mobilize to stop him. He could surely use such reinforcements now that he had lost two of his tiger minions.

"What can you tell us of these vampire cats?" Dracula asked the fox woman. Her eye flashed at him and he felt the fire in him burning for her, even as she was, sitting in an alley in a pile of trash with one eye and one bleeding stump of an arm. He did not need this, not so soon after losing control yesternight. He had never been so hungry, not since Boese had starved him to see what would happen, had not been so incapable of commanding himself since those times. "*Stop*," he told the *huli jing*. She looked insulted.

"As though I want you," she sniffed. "I'll bet you don't have very much yang to spare anyway, being dead."

"Huh?" Cammy wondered, confused.

Dracula did not understand her reference to yang. He'd learned some from the Chinese immigrant he had befriended when he had made his home in San Francisco, before he'd crossed the department for the first time, the end result of which saw him shipped up to this rainy city. The man had talked about yin and yang, but Dracula did not understand the concept very well. He supposed that was the Chinese name for the life energy the huli jing needed.

"Tell me more about these cats."

The huli jing shrugged. "They appeared about a year ago, one after the other. There were four, but one was killed shortly after they arrived; I suppose your boss must have done her in. They aren't as friendly as the trivet cats. And they look down on the others."

"Did they take to Ocelotl's holy war?"

Dracula's Death

"They liked the idea of preying on the whole human race, but they resented him, because he gives orders and makes demands. Tsuki, Yui and Chou disliked his manners too, but they joined him even so. I think they followed Maat more than him."

"Who are Tsuki, Yui and Chou?"

"The other cats who worked here. The bakeneko yūjo."

Dracula had no idea what those were.

"Were they the lady with the schoolgirl outfit, the one playing the instrument, and the cook?" Cammy asked. The huli jing nodded. "So they joined, but you didn't," Cammy noted. The huli jing sat up, unable to hide her wince of pain.

"I worked here for the money, for the yang," she said, "I'm not old enough to do more on my own. They liked having me around because I could bring in *any* clientele they wished." She smiled. "Some of the *enemy*, for example."

"If you'd killed any of the department's agents they would have swarmed the place," Dracula said flatly.

"Not to kill, to take yang," said the huli jing, stretching her body, arching her back in a way that drew his eyes inexorably to the movement. "They knew what I was, but they can't resist me once they see me. Besides, I don't hurt them; I don't hurt anyone. They let the others keep running the business because they liked coming here; they kept coming back to spend time with me or Tsuki or Yui. So I had a home, food, money, yang. What more could a girl ask for?"

"You said the others went with Maat," Dracula said, forcing himself to keep his focus. "Where?"

"To the place of sacrifice," replied the huli jing. "I don't know where it is, they never told me. At some point I think they decided it was for cats only." She smiled sadly. "They are proud creatures. It is said they fell from the noses of lions and won the hearts of pharaohs. They did not weep when the

Buddha died. They do as they please, and why not follow a jaguar?"

"Do you know anything else which might help us find them?" Dracula asked her.

"They said something about a pyramid," said the fox woman. "But I don't know what they meant."

A pyramid? If Egyptology was something all Ophois frontliners were taught, then perhaps Malcolm could weigh in on that.

There was a throughline here, of blood, of sacrifice, and of felines, but what did it point to? In his soul, he knew that Ocelotl was the only member of Ophois who was a man of faith. Pagan faith, but faith nonetheless. He meant what he said, and he was willing to give his life to it with no thought whatever of profit. Blood. Was that the key to this conundrum? The Aztecs worshiped gods who demanded blood, Sekhmet was a blood drinker. But weren't pyramids for entombing pharaohs?

"Which agents came to visit you?" he asked the fox-woman. She casually listed names. Neil was not one of them. The other leaks, perhaps. He committed the names to memory.

"Can we call an ambulance for you?" Cammy asked the huli jing.

She giggled.

"An ambulance? What for?"

"For your hand," Cammy said. "Your eye."

"If the world ends, I don't see how they will be of much use to me," said the huli jing with a sly, amused grin. "I'll wait here. Perhaps Tsuki or her sisters will return. They will realize that revenge for how their kind have been treated won't help any of us. We can start up the business again. If not..." She smiled sadly. "Well. It won't matter then, will it?"

DRACULA'S DEATH

"But you're hurt," Cammy insisted.

"You keep such silly companions," said the *huli jing* to Dracula, laughing. "She doesn't understand anything, does she?"

"Please speak politely to and about my guest," he advised her. "Can you tell us anything more?"

The huli jing shook her head sadly. "No, I'm sorry. I think you might be able to stop them, but I know nothing more. If you should find them, will you please spare Tsuki and the others?"

"That will depend very much on how I find them," Dracula told her, though he wasn't entirely sure who they were. Apparently the other shape-changers Cammy had seen at the restaurant before. "You know my reputation."

She flashed that sad smile and nodded, resigned.

"You could claim asylum," Cammy told her, kneeling. "We can keep you safe."

"*Cammy*," Dracula snapped. "You are a guest. You can extend no such invitation."

Cammy glared at him, and the image of her terrified eyes from the previous night flashed through his mind. He averted his gaze momentarily before he steeled his nerve and stared her down. As expected, she did not retreat. That trait made her frustrating and impossible to deal with, but he could not find it in him to hate her for it. He *liked* fighters, though the modern folk all fought for no reason. Yet he suspected they would crumple like paper dolls if real pressure was applied to them. For all his bluster, Cammy's demure suitor, Brian, refused to come for her or whisk her to safety. Very little pressure was needed to keep him down.

"I don't think so," said the fox woman, drawing her knees up to her chin. "I don't think so. Leave me be. Save them, if you can. Stop them if you cannot."

"Thank you for your help," he said. "Aki, is there anything else that you have found?"

"Not yet. Shall I search inside now?"

"Please." He nodded to the huli jing, who smiled that alluring smile at him, and for a moment he considered sending the other two on ahead so he could screw this strange creature right here in the alley on a pile of trash in front of God or any homeless junkie that happened by.

He did *not* want her on his property, or anywhere near him, ever again.

Aki changed into her fox form in the kitchen and sniffed at the floor and the corners, while he and Cammy returned to the dining room. Neil sat on his stool, his head in his hands. Malcolm sat beside him with an open bottle of sake and a small cup of the liquid in his hand.

"Anything useful?" Malcolm asked, and he drained the cup.

"Did Ocelotl mention pyramids?" Dracula asked him.

"Pyramids?" Malcolm repeated, screwing up his eyes and lifting the cup he had already refilled to knock it back also. "He talked about Sekhmet, but he wouldn't need any pyramids for her. The Mayans also built pyramids. If he's conflating a bunch of stuff together, maybe he's referencing them? If he wants the help of the Aztec Jaguar god Tezcatlipoca, he needs blood. Human blood. Lots of it."

"Ocelotl can raise vampires, it seems," said Dracula.

"Vampires? You serious?" Malcolm poured another glass, knocked it back, and made a face. "There's a wild card. Where are they?"

"Precisely," said Dracula. "We are still missing something. Perhaps Aki can discover more. Neil."

Neil flinched.

"What became of the dead man who was in here?"

DRACULA'S DEATH

"Police took him down to evidence, we pulled our weight, got him removed."

"Has he gotten back up since then?" Dracula asked. Neil, Malcolm, and Cammy looked at him.

"You think the people they killed here were being raised as vampires?" Cammy wondered.

"I don't know. That is why I am asking."

Neil shook his head helplessly.

"I don't know. The director has us all scrambling right now. He thinks there's a national threat."

"I must ask you two more questions," Dracula said. "You must answer me honestly, and completely. Your life depends on your answers." He held up his magnum, letting the dim light from the slits in the doors glint off its surface.

"What are you doing?" Cammy demanded. Neil's forehead beaded with sweat, but his tears were drying on his face.

"Did you deliver that chair to Ocelotl?" Dracula asked him. He had inferred it earlier, but he wanted to be completely certain.

"No," Neil said. "I heard about it, though. Boese was asking everyone afterwards."

"Very well. What is your home address?"

Neil's eyes widened, and he shook his head.

"No, you can't."

"Your home address. Tell me, or I will go to Boese and tell him—"

"You *can't!*" Neil protested, "You can't! He'll turn her into a lab rat! He'll keep her in a cage! No!"

"Your address, or the lab. Your choice," Dracula told him. "But those are your only choices."

"You can't!" Neil whimpered. Dracula turned to Malcolm.

"His wallet," he ordered the werewolf.

Neil shouted and made to escape, but Malcolm grabbed him by the wrist and tripped him to the floor. He dropped his knee onto Neil's wrist, pinning him down as Neil screamed in agony, and fished the man's wallet out of his back pocket. He pulled out the ID.

"Got it," he said, dropping the wallet.

"You *can't!*" Neil wailed, sobbing.

"Tie his wrists and ankles," Dracula told him, and Malcolm made a face. "I have an idea. Perhaps it will pay off. But we can't have him running on ahead to warn her that we're coming, or tell our enemy our movements."

"I assume you have some sort of rope in your vehicle?" Malcolm asked.

"I do."

Malcolm got up. Dracula grabbed Neil's shoulder as he jumped up to follow Malcolm, and hurled him easily into a wall, stunning him. Cammy stared at the action, her eyes judging him. *You're a monster.* He'd seen the look often enough, heard her say as much.

"My lord," said Aki. He gave his attention, placing himself at the door so Neil could not try to escape. Aki stood on the counter in her fox form.

"What is it?" he asked her.

"The nekomata. They were here. I can smell them."

"Do you know if they raised any vampires here?" he asked her.

"I do not know."

"Well done," he told her. "I will arrange a better reward for you when this is all over."

The fox bowed deeply, pressing her whole body down in deference. Much better than all these modern peasants and their ignorant disrespect.

Dracula's Death

Malcolm returned with the rope, and they worked together to restrain Neil, who sobbed and protested so much Dracula at last used his handkerchief to gag the man.

"What now? Leave him here?" Malcolm asked.

"No. He's coming with us."

Malcolm turned the radio up as they made their way to Neil's house. Dracula decided he preferred the noise to Neil's muffled sobbing in the back. He felt Cammy's eyes on the back of his head the whole time, and he purposefully ignored her, answered none of the questions she wasn't brave enough or willing to voice. He didn't feel inclined to reward timidity.

Neil lived in a modest little place in Beacon Hill. No lawn, part of a small suburb snuggled just close enough to the Industrial District that he would not have to commute far should he be called to the lab. Dracula supposed other agents might live in this neighborhood as well, though it would be bad tactics to put too many all in one place. Malcolm pulled the jeep up to a mailbox lovingly painted with white flowers with an earnest but untrained hand. Dracula looked over his shoulder at Aki.

"Keep him in here. Malcolm."

Malcolm spun the keyring around his finger deftly and slipped it into his pocket as he stepped out of the driver's seat.

"Wait," said Cammy. Dracula turned to her.

"Listen to him."

"I am. I am going to set him free."

Cammy looked at the man sobbing beside her, his wrists bound, gagged so he almost choked.

"Do you want to come?" he asked her. She looked at him, hollow-eyed, conflicted. After all this time, she still didn't understand. "Stay in the car," he told her, and stepped out into the clear night.

Malcolm snuck to the door, took hold of the handle, and turned. The lock popped open. That little bit of enchantment that Ophois put on their frontliners was quite useful. No locked door would ever stop them, though there was a cost attached—as ever—to that little convenience. Malcolm slipped inside, hesitating at the fork to the living room and the hallway to the garage and laundry room.

"You're home," a sultry, siren-like voice called from within, as Dracula crossed the threshold. He heard light footfalls on the hardwood coming towards the door, eagerly. So eagerly.

"I've missed you," said the voice, like honey, like wine, like the voice of every lover he'd ever known. This one, he realized, might be worse than the huli jing. He pulled his magnum, Malcolm drew a nine-millimeter.

A pretty woman with curling brown hair came into the living room, dressed in a short silk robe scarcely drawn about her body. She was not as slender as the huli jing; her curves were more inviting, soft-looking flesh. The woman peered into the entryway, confused that she neither heard nor saw the man she expected. Even to his sensibilities, she seemed utterly human. There was no hint to her true nature. Had he passed her in the street, he would have thought nothing of her. These creatures were incredibly dangerous, and not to be taken lightly. Small wonder Boese kept his own sample of this species under lock and key.

The cat wearing the woman's form saw them both standing in the entryway, and her eyes widened for a moment in surprise. Then she smiled, so very invitingly.

"Oh, dear," she said, biting her finger playfully. "Did he blab at last?"

Malcolm raised his handgun, and she looked straight into his eyes. His arm lost its strength, and he fell against the

DRACULA'S DEATH

wall, then to the floor. Dracula raised his own gun. She stared into his eyes, and he felt the most confusing sensation. It took him a moment to remember that it was the sensation of utter exhaustion, the kind that made your eyelids so heavy, your head droop, sleep impossible to fight off.

But he was dead. He didn't sleep. Not truly. He rested. He didn't even remember what sleeping felt like.

He fired the gun and her chest exploded, her shoulder splitting from her torso, the weight of her arm pulling the wound open. Her eyes stared, wild, surprised, and she collapsed on the floor. The woman's shape melted away, her form and memories released, revealing a large, white house cat, one foreleg lying apart from the body, attached only by tendon and skin.

He went to Malcolm and roused him.

"Holy crap!" Malcolm said, starting awake. "Holy crap! That's some powerful mesmerism! Am I alive?"

"Indeed you are. She's dead. I don't think she could tell what other creatures are at a glance."

Malcolm peered into the living room at the dead cat.

"Wow, they make them different across the Pacific, huh? I'm glad I don't work over there."

"Yes. Let's go talk to Neil again. He might be in his right mind now."

They returned to the vehicle. Neil had ceased sobbing, and he sat very still, resigned. They removed the gag.

"She's dead. Are you yourself again?" Dracula asked him.

"She *is* dead," Neil repeated, and hung his head. "She was always dead."

"Did you tell Ocelotl about Boese, or did he say the name first?" Dracula asked him.

"I did," he said. "I think."

"He told you what he plans to do. Did he tell you the specifics?"

Neil looked up, defeated, wasted, spent.

"He needs humans to sacrifice, but you know that," Neil said. "He wants willing victims, though. He said those who volunteer are better liked by the gods."

"What did you tell him? What were you to give him?"

"He wanted to know what the department was doing. He wanted me to tell him when they were moving the ccoa. He" —Neil looked Dracula in the eye— "he wanted to know about you. He'd heard you were here. He wanted to recruit you."

Dracula considered that. A sacrifice to feed an Aztec god, one who would willingly give up his heart. Perhaps Ocelotl had hoped to find someone so weary of the state of things, the never-ending tedium, so alienated by the modern world, that he would long for a return to old ways. Someone who wished he had died and stayed that way hundreds of years ago, and could not achieve that faded dream without help. One who might die if his heart was destroyed.

"Turn pagan indeed," he grumbled to himself. Give up his heart to some bloodthirsty demon-possessed madman who wished to unmake and remake the world? No. The ennui had been on him, like one of those self-absorbed, so-called "romantics" of the 18th and 19th Centuries; but to give himself up to such a vile dream? Never. Not now that his plans were coming close to fruition. Patience. He had grown complacent in the waiting, bored, restless, careless, but to throw away everything and undo all his work? No. To die, yes; even to die pointlessly, though atonement, even without accomplishing his goals, would be better than this tedium; but to unmake everything? Never while he drew breath.

"What else? Where does he plan to perform these sacrifices?"

"He'd need some suitable structure for the ritual, as much like a pyramid as possible. I thought he'd go back down to

Dracula's Death

Mexico, use one of the Mayan pyramids that are still intact. I think that was what he was planning when we captured the ccoa," Neil said. "Bringing it up here caused him to come north after it."

"There has been no hail in Mexico that I have heard of," Dracula pointed out. "That cannot be all of it."

Neil furrowed his brow. "If an ordinary hill would work, and if he knew where you lived, I'd say he'd have his eye on your place. But the director already checked. No sign of him there."

Dracula saw that Cammy had started fiddling with her satchel. "Hey, um, I have a terrible, horrible, gross question," she said. They all gave their attention. "Well, remember how we couldn't figure out why Ocelotl was asking the tigers and the cats to kill people and chop them up and store them? They were using bags and stuff to transport it all, right? Well, do the bodies that these nekomata jump over have to be... you know, in one piece?"

"Aw, crap," Malcolm groaned. "How many people are missing?"

Neil licked his dry lips. "It's hard to know when homeless people go missing, but we track reports of missing persons. Close to sixty of those in the last few days; that's why the sense of urgency at the department."

"He might have *sixty* vampires?" Malcolm demanded.

"Not necessarily," Dracula said. "Do we know for a fact that they have *all* been killed?"

"Wait, you mean, that he only killed a few, chopped them up, vampirised them, and then... kidnapped the rest?"

"If there is to be a ritual," Dracula said, "He will need living sacrifices for a river of blood."

"But why the hail and rain?" Cammy asked.

"It would make abducting people easier for him," Dracula mused. "There are more accidents on the road, more injuries. You have said there was flooding. What of the homeless? Would they remain on the streets or begin to find shelter? As you said, no one would notice if they went missing. Law enforcement and emergency services have been overwhelmed, and the department was wasting all its energy trying to recover the ccoa, rather than look into the missing people. I myself got called off that first investigation to find this creature."

"Wait a minute, you're saying that he might have grabbed, like, *hundreds* of people and we never even noticed?" Cammy said. "Because we were too busy looking at other stuff?"

"It is possible. If that's the case, then the weather has stopped because he now has what he needs."

Cammy blanched. "What do we do?"

"We must locate him, as quickly as possible. If he does have what he needs, then he is going to withdraw to his place of sacrifice. Unfortunately, we don't know where that is."

"You mean, if we don't figure out where he's doing what he's doing, then by tomorrow the world might *end?*" Cammy said.

"I doubt he truly has the power to do that literally," he told her. "But I imagine he can do enormous damage with his demon gods. If he has what he needs, then he will either be making preparations or have already started his sacrifices." Dracula felt that was true, which meant Ocelotl would not likely appear to them again. That he had tried to make use of the heart of a famous strigoi had merely been curiosity on his part, or an attempt to reach out to a like-minded ally, or to find someone who would willingly give up their heart to bloodthirsty gods in order to be quit of this world. They had taken a small step towards discovering their enemy's plans, but scarcely come any closer to stopping him.

DRACULA'S DEATH

"Damn," Malcolm grumbled. "I wanted to arrange a *ménage a trois* before the world ended."

CHAPTER 12
STORM BREAK

"Hi, B," Cammy said to Brian's answering machine. "Um, it's me. I hope you're doing ok." Her mind blanked. What was she going to say on a voicemail? *Hi, by this time tomorrow the world might have stopped existing to be remade by a jaguar god?* What good would that do? Brian didn't know about the supernatural; it would take an hour or more to bring him up to speed, only to tell him it didn't matter anyway. "I.... Bye," she said at last, and hung up. She texted her friends, trying to say without saying that she loved them. None of them knew what was really going on, except for Andrew. He knew, but she couldn't bring herself to tell him about Ocelotl. Tell him that he and his family and all their friends might be dead tomorrow? She couldn't do it.

They were all back in the car. Cammy untied Neil; there was nothing else she could think to do. Dracula didn't tell her not to, though he clearly saw what she was doing. Neil rubbed his wrists.

"What now?" Cammy asked.

"We need to figure out where Ocelotl might be," Dracula told her, "so now is the time to put our heads together."

Silence. Cammy played with her thumbs.

DRACULA'S DEATH

"What we know is that he has been moving people, whole or in pieces, and needs to perform a ritual sacrifice of humans."

"Or cats," Cammy mumbled, thinking of Goldie.

"Cats?"

"Ocelotl killed a trivet cat named Goldie. The trivet cat that led me to the restaurant in the first place," Cammy explained. "He was one of the cats who didn't want Ocelotl to succeed, so he contacted me because he didn't know whether he could trust you."

"Trivet cats are a kind of *henge* creature from my homeland," Aki supplied. "Harmless, but they used to frighten people and light the hearths and waste fuel to keep warm."

"That was where Ocelotl got that collar, right?" Malcolm checked. "Do you think it will help us to find more of these critters?"

"Maybe," Cammy said. "There *were* other trivet cats at the restaurant. Most of them just wanted to stay warm."

"Would you recognize these other trivet cats if you saw them?" Dracula asked.

"I don't know," Cammy confessed. "But do we have time to drive all over the city looking for them?"

"Do you know anything else about Goldie?" he asked.

"I know he was a pet. He told me"—she almost gasped—"he told me the names of his owners! Oh, um!" She slapped her forehead. It was a long shot, but what if they had another trivet cat? Maybe, if they did, that one would know where to go... She pulled her phone. *Come on, brain, don't fail me now. Some girl and her boyfriend. Come on. Cathy? No...* "Katie Gibbs," she said. "I think. She has a boyfriend, but Goldie didn't know his name."

She looked up Katie Gibbs. It took a bit of digging, but she found profiles on social media. Katie was a plump girl with glasses, holding Goldie up for a selfie and smiling. She probably had no idea what had happened to Goldie. She would be anxious, wondering...the same way Cammy had been desperately anxious when Heather had gone missing. Cammy felt her throat constrict and her hands start to shake. She slapped her leg. *Not now*, she told herself.

Katie owned two cats. They looked nearly identical. A look at a few posts revealed that they were siblings. The other one was named Sunny.

"Goldie has a brother," Cammy said. "He's gotta be another trivet cat. He might know something."

"Can you get an address?" Dracula asked.

"Let me try..."

"What is her name? If you can't find it, perhaps Special Services can provide it to me."

She told him, and he dialed. He argued with whoever it was on the other end of the line that it was serious, he did need to find this girl, and that no, she wasn't a were-tiger or some other creature, nor did she know about the supernatural world. Cammy kept running into sites that wanted her to pay to see past them, so Dracula beat her to the answer. He gave the address to Malcolm, who put it in his phone, then started the car and pulled away from Neil's house. Neil watched it disappear behind them.

"I'm sorry," Cammy said to him. He ignored her.

Emergency crews and vehicles still clogged the streets, dragging the journey out as they made their way to the apartment complex where Katie lived. Cammy wondered whether Katie would have any information. Had Goldie revealed himself to her, or was she another unknowing member of the general public? It wasn't much of a lead, she thought, but there wasn't much else to go on.

Dracula's Death

Neil's phone vibrated in his pocket, and he jumped in his seat. He pulled it out and opened the link that had been sent to him. He stared at the screen, then closed the link.

"Who was that?" Cammy asked.

"The target just posted to every major social media platform," he explained. "You can see for yourself." He opened the link again to show her a video. Ocelotl had posted an actual video to the internet. What a crazy world it was.

"People of the world," the were-jaguar announced, staring directly out of the screen into her eyes. His own glinted like flint every so often, and he had painted his face in yellow and black stripes. There was nothing remarkable in the background of the video, nothing she could see that would tell her where he was. Firelight and stone; she guessed it was night and he was outside. "Rejoice, repent, think on your sins, and atone for your transgressions. For by tomorrow, you will either be in heaven or the underworld. My advice is this: do your best to die a violent death, for those are best. But whatever you do, make your peace with whatever deity you worship. One way or the other, the world shall be scourged, shall be purged, and it will be better after. I am Ocelotl, I serve He Whose Slaves We Are, and I look forward to seeing some of you in the afterlife." He smiled serenely, his face pulled back from the camera, and a flicker of shadow fell over his face. Suddenly it was the face of a black jaguar, its yellow eyes looking out of the screen, calm yet eager, and the video ended.

"He posted that in Spanish and Mandarin, too," said Neil.

"What's it posted under?" Cammy asked, reading the name of the video. It was titled "Repent, Atone." She searched for it. No hits anywhere, no useful hashtags for anyone to search for. He understood phones, but he didn't understand trends and clickbait. Cammy debated forwarding it to her friends, but realized they weren't going to understand it without her explaining the context.

"He just posted that?" Malcolm asked.

"Just now."

Malcolm fingered the steering wheel uncomfortably.

"I think he's going to try tomorrow, then."

"Tomorrow, why?" Neil asked him.

"If he's trying Aztec or Mayan or whatever, he would probably need the sun rising. Can Boese's people trace where that came from?"

"We're working on it," Neil said, flatly.

They made their way through the bad traffic, having to detour periodically around a street blocked off because of a downed tree or flooding.

Cammy's phone pinged.

Happy birthday! Lindsey had sent. *I know we're going to the show after midterms, but I wanted to say it today! Best of luck on those tests!*

Cammy stared at the message. It was like getting a text from a decade ago. Her birthday? She checked the date. That *was* today. And midterms? Oh, right. They were going on right now. School felt unreal, like something she'd dealt with a million years ago. She was trying to stop some guy from ending the world, and today she was turning twenty-two.

They got to Katie's apartment eventually. Katie lived on the second floor. Cammy realized the poor woman was going to have a heart attack trying to figure out why a whole crowd of people were heading up to her apartment in the middle of the night. Dracula led the way and had nearly knocked on the door when Neil stepped in front and knocked for him. Dracula eyed him, then stood to one side and waited. There was no answer, so Neil knocked louder and longer.

Dracula's Death

"What?" came a muffled voice from the other side of the door.

"Ma'am, I'm Agent Donovan Neil with the FBI. I need you to open the door."

"FBI? What are you talking about?"

Neil held up a badge to the peep hole. It was probably fake, like Dracula's.

"Ma'am, you can see my badge. We need to search your apartment. We have reason to believe someone broke in and left dangerous materials inside."

The lock clicked and the door swung hesitantly open. Katie was only a little taller than Cammy, and she was dressed in a T-shirt and pajama pants. She studied the crowd outside her door.

"I don't understand. The FBI is—"

"Thank you." Neil pushed past her, also opening the door all the way.

"Hey, wait a minute!" Katie protested. "What are you doing?!"

Neil stepped inside and scanned the apartment, with Malcolm and Dracula coming behind and Cammy at the rear. Aki stood at the door and watched the hall. The apartment living room was a mess, with papers scattered here and there, and a pile of clothes on the worn-out sofa. A well-worn cat tree, fuzzy from fibers scratched out, stood behind the couch near the window. A yellow cat was lying on the very top level, its eyes wide, taking in all the intruders.

Malcolm pointed it out.

"Hey, there, Sunny!" he said. "We've got some questions for you!"

The cat bolted, and Malcolm dove partway over the couch after it. He came back up holding a wriggling, angry cat.

"What are you doing?!" Katie demanded. "Put him down!"

"This is important business, ma'am," Neil told her, and flashed the badge again. He stood in her way. "I need you to back up while we conduct our investigation."

"You can't just come in here and attack my cat!" Katie protested. "You can't do that!"

"Sorry, your cat knows the location of some place and we need to ask it where," Cammy tried to explain. Neil glared at her.

"W-what?!" Katie stammered, staring at them all. "You people are crazy!"

"Sunny," Cammy said, addressing the cat directly, "Ocelotl killed Goldie, and we have to know where he might be!"

"*Who* killed Goldie? Someone killed him? Someone killed my cat?" Katie's voice rose to a panicked wail.

"Ma'am, please calm down," Neil told her. She tried to push past him to get to Sunny. The cat took that opportunity to scratch Malcolm's wrist and he shouted in pain and dropped the cat. Sunny darted past everyone's legs and shot out the front door.

"Get that cat!" Neil shouted, and they all crammed into each other on the way out the door. Neil slammed it shut when Katie tried to follow them. Aki wasn't outside, but everyone else was off and running, so Cammy just followed them. They made their way down the hall, then down the stairs, and out beyond some bushes onto the grass, when Cammy heard behind her: "Sunny!"

She turned, to see Katie running off in the opposite direction. That was strange. Had they missed the cat?

"You try that trick again and I'll skin you alive," Malcolm growled at someone. Cammy trotted over to peer around his back. Aki held the cat in her arms, and Malcolm was looming over him. Sunny's ears were pinned back with fear.

Dracula's Death

"Sunny did not want to speak in front of Katie," he replied in a raspy little voice like Goldie's.

"Where did Katie go?" Cammy asked.

"I made an illusion of Sunny running the other way for her to chase," Aki supplied. Cammy hadn't seen the fox-woman cast illusions before, unless her transformations were illusions.

"What do you know about Ocelotl?" Dracula asked the cat. "Where might he be?"

"He said he was improvising a place of sacrifice," Sunny answered, twitching his short tail and staring in fear at them all. "Sunny told Goldie not to go."

"He didn't go," Cammy told the cat. "Goldie asked for my help. He took me to the restaurant to try to talk the other cats out of it. Ocelotl got to him somehow." She wiped her eyes. "I'm sorry, I think he's dead because he talked to me."

Sunny buried his little face in his paws.

"Sunny warned him," the cat moaned. "He shouldn't have said anything!"

"Where might Ocelotl be?" Dracula repeated.

"He said a place of sacrifice. He needed a hill or a pyramid or a mound," Sunny replied. "He's been taking people there for a while. The cats have gone. It's a long journey. Those that go never come back. He said it would be a few hours in the truck."

"Wait a minute," Neil said. "Was he talking about Pyramid Mountain?"

Everyone else looked to him.

"Pyramid Mountain is a hiking location," Neil explained. "A couple hours out of Seattle by car. Between here and Forks. It's a pretty tough hike, and the trail's been washed out for a while. I can't imagine all this rain has helped. But..."

"Hey, yeah," Malcolm agreed. "It's not exact, but it sort of fits the bill. If nothing else, it has the name. Plus, if it's hard to get up there, then there's less chance of him being discovered. So how have your boys missed this? You don't have satellite footage of unusual traffic over there?"

"The cloud cover's been blocking our visuals," Neil retorted.

Cammy felt uncomfortable knowing that Boese could potentially spy on her from *space*.

"Has the cloud cover shrouded this mountain?" Dracula asked.

"Checking," Neil murmured. He dialed his phone and said a code of some sort into it, then asked about the cloud cover the last couple of days.

"I'm sorry," Cammy told Sunny. "I didn't want anything to happen to Goldie."

The trivet cat heaved a sigh that was two sizes too large for such a little creature.

"Sunny is sorry too," he said, and buried his face in Aki's elbow.

"Cloud cover's been over that area, but not as far as Forks," Neil told them. "Looks like it covers just the mountain, the route there to here, and Seattle. Sounds like that's our location."

"Great, I can almost get paid," Malcolm said.

"We need to prepare," Dracula told him. "If it's several hours to the location, we haven't any time to waste."

*****

Brian wasn't able to press as much weight as before the… whatever it was that had happened. Something involving a giant dead wrestler, Dracula, and a werewolf. His shoulder and his wrist weren't quite what they had been. The shoulder especially twinged horrendously if he moved just the wrong way. "Eye of the Tiger" was blaring stereotypically into his

Dracula's Death

ear. He liked the classic stuff, his uncle had raised him on 80s music, so his playlist for working out included the Scorpions, AC/DC, and others. It felt more powerful than modern stuff—not that he hated modern stuff. Just not while working out. The weather had him indoors and waiting for a clear day to go vampire hunting.

He used the gym at the precinct. It was cheaper than paying for membership elsewhere. And he could clear his head a little while lifting weights, or while on the treadmill. He had considered getting out his skateboard again. It felt like forever since he last skated. In some sense, it was. A lifetime ago, at least.

No sign of obvious vampire lady from months ago, the redhead with the strange perfume. He sort of wanted her to show up again so he could test his vampire-killing stuff on her. If he showed up at Dr. Acula's mansion with the wrong set of tools, he doubted he'd make it out of there alive. Or even make it out just regular dead.

He set a small number of weights on the bar. He wasn't trying to gain, he just wanted to maintain where he was. Also, he didn't want to risk re-injuring himself. That two-month recovery had eaten all of his PTO, sick days, vacation days, and then some. He had to pay off the credit card debt he'd accumulated while he had no income. He hadn't wanted to make Melissa pay extra for him.

He lay down under the bar. Mostly, his shoulder didn't scream at him anymore, but every so often...

One.

His shoulder had nothing to say. Good start. Now, if he could only be sure about methods vampire hunting. Turns out there were a *lot* of legends and myths, and some of them obviously didn't apply to this guy. The whole "only comes out at night" thing, for one.

Two.

He knew garlic worked. Or at least, made Dr. Acula sick. If he ate some.

Three.

Stoker's book had focused on the garlic flowers. Would those help? No need to eat those.

Four.

Running water? Stoker insisted on it as a way of stopping vampires. But the guy lived in Seattle. Running water everywhere. Probably made up, or somehow didn't apply to Dr. FBI.

Five.

Beheading. That would be hard. But he had one of Dr. Acula's swords from when the creep's car was impounded. Maybe he could use that. Imagine, using a sword in the modern day...

Six.

Crucifixes. Not all legends agreed on that one, but Brian had ordered one from online. He wore it all the time. There were at least two vampires in town, plus the Wolf Man and who knew what else. He hoped crucifixes worked.

Seven.

Creep also had wooden crosses in his vehicle. Brian couldn't imagine why, but this was all super-secret monster stuff. Maybe it didn't have to make sense.

Eight.

Silver was harder. Not cheap, and no one sold silver weapons or bullets. He'd found a partial set of silverware with forks and knives for sale online and bought them. They were plated, but he couldn't afford sterling. The trouble was, the business end of the knives were obviously steel. Well, at least the forks had pointy, jabby ends that were silvered.

Nine.

Dracula's Death

There was that vampire hunting kit down in Ye Olde Curiosity Shop over by the gum wall and Pike Place, but that wasn't for sale. There were loads of vampire hunting kits to find online, but they were all really pricey. Still, he had decided, so long as he was going into debt, to buy one. It didn't seem super authentic to him, but it claimed it contained actual holy water in one of the vials. He wasn't sure how else to get a hold of any of *that,* short of stealing some from a church. If holy water worked, then he figured he needed God on his side, and probably stealing from a church wasn't a good first step. He hoped the kit was real and that he hadn't been cheated.

Ten.

Most of the other stuff he'd found online seemed to apply to non-western, or at least, non-European vampires. Dr. Acula wasn't shy about his European roots. Romania or Russia or wherever. So probably Brian was safe sticking to Europe. Although some looking at the man's history revealed he had been to Turkey at least. Brian had no idea if that mattered as far as the vampire stuff.

That was probably about as much as he wanted to risk using his shoulder, so he hung the bar back up and sat up, massaging the joint. No pain. That was good.

"Hey, look at that. The rain finally stopped," someone commented. A round of cheers and applause made its way through the gym room. Brian glanced out the small window. Sure enough, he could see out into the parking lot. No rain, no hail.

He walked past the treadmills to look out into the darkness. There was still cloud cover.

He had been going back and forth with himself about when to go up the hill. He was better now, but not 100%. But maybe he'd never be 100% ever again. Meaning if he was going to go, the only thing he was waiting on was certainty. If there was such a thing. The right way to kill the most famous vampire ever. Right.

Akerman hadn't gotten back to him. Brian couldn't tell anymore if Akerman had chosen to brush him off or if he was still "thinking" or "planning" or whatever the excuse had been. He decided to bother Kenzie instead. Just one more time. Brian had asked her questions a couple of times, masking his interest as curiosity about the horror movies she and Cammy liked to watch.

"Hello," Kenzie answered acidly. "More vampire questions?"

"Yeah, hey, sorry," Brian said. "I was just... wondering... for European ones, is there a sure-fire kill method?"

Kenzie didn't answer. That seemed weird. She'd always been forthcoming before.

"Why?" she asked.

"I... well, just... curious."

"Curious maybe about the guy we know with the garlic allergy?"

Brian stared out at the darkness. Was he that obvious? If she knew, then maybe Dr. Acula knew. And if *he* knew, then Brian's element of surprise was probably gone.

"You know he is, right?" Kenzie followed up. "Because that was you who did the garlic thing, wasn't it? You've suspected for a while."

"Yeah," Brian admitted. "Yeah. Plus some other details I can't really share."

"You're a cop, right? I bet you see all kinds of stuff. Like last year. All the tourist spots getting hit."

So Kenzie knew. And a lot more than just about Cammy's host.

"Yeah, all that."

Dracula's Death

Kenzie made no comment, but he waited. He didn't know her that well, but it was obvious there were *some* people out there who knew about this stuff. Akerman had said so. Obviously, some other cops at the precinct knew. After that mess with the undead wrestler, dug up from his grave and rampaging around Seattle. Some videos had been posted online, then yanked. And anyone who suspected vampires probably had questions about Councilman Wright's death. No one had been charged for that murder, and the *exsanguination* part wasn't being referenced in articles anymore, if the murder was mentioned at all.

"Stakes through the heart *always* work," Kenzie said at last. "Always."

"Thanks," Brian said, and hung up.

"Hey."

Brian turned just enough to acknowledge Akerman's greeting, but said nothing.

"I thought I'd check in."

"Thanks," Brian told him, curtly.

Akerman walked up beside him. He was in uniform, must have just gotten off duty.

"Are you serious about what you were saying the other day?" Akerman asked.

"What do you think?"

Akerman gazed out into the parking lot.

"If you're really going..." He turned towards Brian and held out a hand. Brian considered the gesture. He accepted the offer.

"Thanks, man," Brian said. "Weather's clear."

"Best time to go fishing," Akerman commented, and sighed. "Right now?"

Brian thought about it. He'd been wondering what time was the best to go. Clearly Dr. Acula could be out in the day, and often was. Cammy would be asleep at night. Hunting a vampire at night seemed like a bad idea, but he wasn't sure Dr. Acula would even be home unless Cammy was there. It probably had to be night. Just like in Stoker's novel, then.

"I guess now."

"All right. Let me drive. But I gotta swing by my place and change, all right?"

"Sure."

Akerman was quick at changing into a jacket, T-shirt, and jeans, so it wasn't much of a detour—especially since he didn't live that far from the precinct. Next, he drove to Brian's and Melissa's apartment.

"Hey there," Melissa greeted Brian when he unlocked the door. "I've got some Thai food in the fridge and—oh, hey, babe."

"Hi," Akerman said, as he let himself inside behind Brian. Melissa got up from the couch and wrapped her arms around his neck. Brian made himself scarce. The vampire-hunting stuff he'd gotten from Dracula's car was stored under his bed. He pulled it out. A trip to a thrift store had gotten him the duffel bag to carry it all—except the sword. That would have to be carried or worn. Brian felt a little silly strapping a sword to his side, so he just carried it in its scabbard. Melissa and Akerman were still wrapped around each other when he closed the door of his bedroom behind him.

The usual "get a room" line was not what he wanted to tell his sister and best friend to do, so instead he cleared his throat.

"Oh, sorry, BB." Melissa chuckled and straightened her shirt when she turned around. "What's with the bags?"

"We're... going fishing," Brian said.

"At night?"

Dracula's Death

"Some of the best fish can be caught at night," Akerman explained.

"Oh." Melissa smiled quizzically at the sword.

"Oh, I...borrowed this. From someone I know. I need to return it."

"A sword?"

"Yeah. Just... researching," Brian muttered.

"Researching what?"

"I'll tell you later. We've got to get going, it's a long drive."

"Yeah. I'll call you tomorrow, ok?" Akerman promised.

"Sure thing," Melissa replied. "We still on for next week?"

"Wouldn't miss it."

Melissa kissed him again. Brian walked towards the door and shoved the duffel bag into Akerman's chest.

"We ready?" he asked. Akerman nodded. He smiled at Melissa before letting himself out. Brian just caught a glimpse of Melissa smiling back. He didn't want to think about it.

The duffel bag went in the trunk, while the sword ended up on the backseat. Akerman loaded up a playlist of some weird sounding folk music Brian didn't recognize.

"Is this the stuff you're into?" he laughed.

"I'm in the mood for it. I feel homesick," Akerman explained.

"What language is that?"

"Swedish."

"Swedish? Wait, you're Swedish? I thought you were Jewish."

"Who said I was Jewish?"

"Suze said Akerman was a Jewish name. You don't have an accent. When did you get here?"

"Many years ago," Akerman said. "Under better circumstances."

"We are not listening to some weird folk music if we're going 'fishing,'" Brian asserted, and unplugged Akerman's phone out so he could plug his in. He loaded up his workout music. "Dirty Deeds" was up first.

"We have to be in the right mood," Brian explained.

"Sure, sure," Akerman agreed, and cranked the volume. He pulled a sticky note from his pocket and held it out for Brian to see. It read,

You have your phone on you, right? Don't answer, just nod or shake your head.

Brian frowned at the note, then at him. Of course he had his phone with him; he'd just plugged it in. But wait, this note was pre-written. *Oh.* Akerman nodded to the note. Brian answered with his own nod. Akerman pulled another note.

When we get there, leave it in the car.

What was all this, all of a sudden? Akerman pulled out of the parking lot. Brian studied his face in the flash and darkness of streetlights passing overhead. Was Akerman worried about being spied on? But why? And by whom? There shouldn't be a long list of agencies or people who could do that.

Brian had suspected Dracula might also be a foreign spy for a while, or that Homeland Security or something was involved. But then, Akerman knew more than he was letting on. Akerman had talked to those people who had left the phone number. Whoever they were. No matter what had happened or who those people Akerman had called to get Dracula out of being arrested were, those individuals had the power to get him released. Chief Deble had just let it happen. So they either had power, or money, or, as Melissa theorized, both.

Dracula's Death

Dracula had money. Loads of money. He had a multi-million-dollar car, at the least. And an estate purchased by actual royalty. And he had a werewolf working for him.

Maybe none of this had to do with spies or governments. Maybe there was some secret cabal of vampires running the show. That could be why no one had been charged with Wright's murder. If so, then maybe whoever Akerman had called was in on it.

Was that too paranoid? Even if all that was true, Akerman wouldn't... betray him, right? Wouldn't trick him into leaving his phone behind so if things went south he wouldn't be able to call anyone?

No. He shook his head. That couldn't be it. Absolutely couldn't. No way his best friend would do that to him. His best friend who was dating his sister. But something in the back of his brain refused to let that go.

It would be more than hour-long drive up to that estate—worse now because of the weather. A long time to think. So he settled in to do just that.

*****

Though he'd said they had no time to waste, everyone else was ready to go long before Dracula. While waiting, Cammy went to check on Emet and Masayu.

The tiger was sleeping in the bed. Emet sat beside her, one leg jumping up and down. There were bags under his eyes, wispy stubble dotting his chin and upper lip. It looked like he hadn't brushed his hair in days. His face looked even paler than when she'd met him, and drawn. He'd aged ten years.

"We think we know where Ocelotl is," Cammy told him. The young man's eyebrows drew towards one another. She explained what she and the others had learned.

"What are you going to do?" Emet asked.

Cammy hadn't even really thought about that. The plan was to stop Ocelotl, but precisely *how* she didn't know. She assumed it would be *kill a lot of vampires, and maybe even cats*, but not the details. "I don't know," she confessed.

"Oh," Emet replied, and chewed his thumbnail.

"I'll be back," she assured him. She didn't want to talk about what was going to happen, she wanted to stop Ocelotl somehow and never have anything this bad happen ever again. She wanted life to go back to the way it had been. But it couldn't. Not now that she knew there were people who wanted to end the world and who might *be able to*.

Cammy found Siri in the great room. "Where have you been?" Cammy asked.

Siri played with her fingers. "I vas...thinking," she answered.

"Thinking?"

"Of many things. Things his majesty told me. About himself, and about love."

Oh, not right now, Cammy thought. "We have to stop Ocelotl. He wants to end the world."

Siri's electric eyes looked up at her. "I vill help. It vould be bad if that man vere to succeed."

"Thanks," Cammy said. Siri nodded absently and played more with her fingers.

Cammy tried doors to rooms. No sign of her host until she came to an upper bedroom in a wing neither she nor her host often visited, and discovered Dracula inside, kneeling in a full suit of armor.

"What are you doing?" she asked, bewildered at the sight.

"I was praying," he answered, and rose.

"I thought you said we had no time to waste," she pointed out.

Dracula's Death

"Time is not wasted on prayer. We are about to fight a spiritual battle."

"I'm pretty sure we're going to be fighting a regular battle," Cammy asserted.

Dracula glared at her. "We are fighting a man who is possessed by a pagan god, and who wishes to summon at least one other god. This is a spiritual battle, which must also be fought in the world. But without help, we are lost."

Cammy considered his attire, and noticed something like religious pictures on the wall he had been facing.

"I thought you said crucifixes didn't bother you."

"I did say that."

"...But... they do, apparently."

"I lied."

Cammy mulled on that.

"Why?"

"Do you suppose I would tell you that they did? So that you would use them against me?"

"I wouldn't have," Cammy mumble-protested. "So crucifixes work on all vampires, then?"

"It has more to do with belief, and the intention of the wielder. A crucifix is not a talisman."

"So... it only works on you... because *you* believe it does?" Why would he *let* that be the case? "Also, I thought you said your prayers didn't do anyone any good anymore."

"I am not going to stand here and be interrogated by a peasant and an atheist about matters of the spirit," he growled. "But it is clear to me that none of the rest of you are going to do as much, so it falls to me. We are at war with spirits and gods and demons, and you lot would go in alone and without defense."

"Well, what *else* can we do?"

"What *I* have been doing!"

Oh. But if that required faith, she knew she didn't qualify. That was that, then.

"Where'd you get the armor?"

"The elves made it for me, on my request. I did not ask how they made it."

He was really wearing a suit of armor like from movies or books. With two cloaks, one in red and one in green. She'd never seen any of that in real life. It was impressive, actually, to see all those bits of metal fit together so well. Like *being* in a movie. She almost giggled helplessly, remembering how last year she'd thought that tracking him to his mansion was like being a character in a film answering her call to action. She had hoped for the "magical school" adventure, though; nothing like this, not killing and stuff.

Now that she thought about it, didn't almost all stories eventually go to "save the world" mode? She had hoped for more time. And that... it would be more fun. No Heather being dead, no Brian getting hurt. No other people—or trivet cats—getting killed.

"We should head out," Dracula said. "If we wish to reach that mountain by dawn."

"I..." Cammy's mouth felt dry. "What are we going to do?"

"We? Meaning you wish to come as well?" Dracula asked.

Cammy didn't. Not at all. She wanted everyone to be safe and for none of this to be happening. But someone had to do something. She clutched her stomach. "I want to help."

His eyes bored into hers.

"I do."

"And you understand what that means?" he checked. "You are asking to go into a battle. There will be death and bloodshed."

The image of that Chinese were-tiger from Ophois, white from the muzzle flare, him dropping dead on the ground

DRACULA'S DEATH

flashed before Cammy's eyes. She grimaced, and her eyes watered.

"Yes," she answered in a small voice. "Yes, I understand."

He studied her, his eyes searching for any hidden lie.

"Very well," he said at last. "But I must warn you: if we are overrun, I cannot guarantee your safety, nor will I guarantee that I will be able to come to your aid. Our adversary must be stopped first, and your safety secured secondarily. Do you understand that?"

That had never been true before. Dracula had *always* come to rescue her. Even if he complained about it or lectured her about it. She gulped.

He pushed past her and went out the door.

"If you do, you know where the armory is," he called back to her.

She was alone in the bedroom. Just her and those religious pictures of people she didn't recognize. He had kept his distance, but she could walk right up to them. She didn't want to. She closed the door behind her.

Downstairs, Dracula was in the armory packing a backpack with weapons. Emet had heard the commotion and come to see what was happening.

"There is plenty for you to choose from, if you wish to choose something," Dracula informed him. Emet glanced around the room.

"What are you going to do?"

"We are going to fight, and God willing, we shall stop this madman before he completes his heinous ritual. There may be a number of vampires or undead assisting him, as well as other monsters."

Emet gulped. "How do you fight them?"

"With faith, and with courage, and with skill."

Wow, thanks a lot, Cammy thought.

"Faith?" Emet murmured. "Yes. With good deeds and thoughts and speech. That is the way to ensure that goodness thrives in the world."

"You are the first person I've spoken to tonight who understands any of that," Dracula said.

"I haven't... taken my faith seriously," Emet confessed. "I... should begin."

"What is your faith?"

"I am a Parsi—you might know us as Zoroastrians."

Nope, I don't know that, Cammy thought.

"A Zarathustran?" Dracula checked.

Don't know that, either.

"Oh. Errm, yes," Emet agreed. Dracula shrugged.

"I've never heard of any of those," Cammy said.

"Freddy Mercury was a Zoroastrian," Emet mumbled. "But, perhaps like me, he didn't take his faith to heart." He fingered the necklace she'd seen earlier. "I'm wearing this silly thing I bought to show off my faith, rather than what I am actually to wear. I'm only vegetarian because I was dating a Hindu girl and got into the habit." He covered his eyes.

"Huh?"

"Hey! We ready to go or what? Coffee only gets me so far here," Malcolm griped, poking his head through the door. "It's a long drive, too. We got a vehicle? Or several?"

"Yes, I have one in mind," Dracula said.

"When did you get *armor?*" Malcolm demanded.

"Recently."

"Where's mine?"

"I'll have some made for you, if you prove worthy of armor," Dracula told him.

Malcolm grinned. "Sick." He ducked back out.

Dracula's Death

"We could use anyone willing to defend against a man with such evil designs," Dracula told Emet. The young man met his eyes.

"I don't know how to use any weapon, though. The knife... I... it was what I had."

Dracula fetched a sword and held it up for Emet to see. The young man blanched.

"A hatchet is easier to use," Dracula told him, offering one of those next.

"I..." Emet began to shake. Dracula observed it, and put the axe away. He walked past Emet without a word. Cammy touched the young man's shoulder, but he shied away from her.

"I... I don't think I can," he whispered.

"It's all right," Cammy told him.

He shook his head and miserably answered, "No, it's not." A tear rolled down his cheek, and he hugged himself.

Cammy walked out to join the others.

Dracula was waiting in the main room. When Cammy came over, he asked,

"May I borrow your phone?"

"My phone?"

"Yes, I need to make a call."

She passed him her phone.

"Who are you calling?"

"Allies who will, God willing, be of immense help to us."

*****

Brian mulled over what he was planning to do. He didn't know if the creep ever slept. Working together, maybe he and Akerman could pin him down. Or one of them distract him and the other stake him.

Then what? Say "Happy birthday" to Cammy? "Happy birthday, I just saved you from Dracula"?

Maybe. If Dracula was using hypo-mind powers on her, then she'd be fine afterwards. In which case, saying that would be the most epic thing any man had ever said to any woman.

That bolstered his spirits.

"Turn off your headlights," Brian told Akerman as they came up the driveway. Akerman glanced at him, but obeyed and switched them off. They rolled up beside the garage, and Akerman put the car in park. Brian reached for his phone, but Akerman grabbed his wrist and shook his head.

This.

Whatever *this* was.

Nothing good. But Akerman left his own phone on the dash before he stepped out of the car. So Brian did the same, his playlist still going. As soon as he shut the door, Akerman leaned over the top and spoke to him quietly.

"Ok, Warren, let me start by saying that I'm sorry we're having to do it this way—"

"Do what? Who's 'we'?"

"We is you and me. About Dracula," Akerman pointed at the mansion. "You have no idea what the deal actually is."

"And you do?" Brian asked flatly. He was still hoping he wasn't about to be betrayed.

Akerman pressed his hands together in front of his face and drew in a deep breath.

"Ok, so here's the deal: there's a government agency that works to keep monsters and such hidden and out of sight. Like in movies."

"The weirdoes in the sunglasses who visited me in the hospital and left their card with the number?" Brian checked. Akerman nodded.

"Yeah. These people are not very nice. And Dracula"—Akerman pointed at the mansion—"was captured by them something like a century ago. They have him working for them."

Brian tried plugging this all in. Fake FBI badge, the phone call that handed him a Get Out of Jail Free card. So far, that didn't trip anything up. There was more to this, though. Akerman had left his phone in the car.

"You work for them," Brian realized.

"Sort of, yes," Akerman said. "I work for them the same way he"—he pointed at the mansion—"does."

Brian chewed on that.

"So...you're what? A vampire too?" Dracula could go out in daylight and eat food and all that. Akerman had been with the department for ten years and still looked like a high schooler. That plugged in.

But Akerman shook his head. "I'm a nicker."

"You're a what?" Brian wasn't sure what his ears had just heard, because for a moment he thought....

"It's complicated, but I came with you so I could bring you up to speed, and because I actually want to ask him"—Akerman pointed at the mansion again—"for a favor."

Brian blinked coldly at him.

"You want to ask *Dracula* for a favor?"

"Yeah."

"Dracula."

"Yes."

Brian squinted at him.

"Why?"

"Because my brother is in prison—"

"Wait a minute, you have a brother? You never mentioned—"

"Not while we've got phones spying on us, obviously!" Akerman hissed, and pointed at the car.

Ah. That was why he wanted those left behind. Brian digested all of this. A shadowy government agency would explain a lot of it, certainly. He had no idea what a "nicker" was, but Akerman seemed normal, except for how young he looked. But that last bit, the part about Akerman wanting a *favor*. That bit he couldn't digest. From inside the car, he could just hear the playlist switch to "Back in Black". He was about to ask about what sort of favor Akerman thought Dracula could do for him when, to Brian's horror, the back door of the mansion swung open. The vampire-hunting gear was all in the trunk. That would take too long; he'd have to ask Akerman to pop it open. He opened the door to the backseat as quick as he could and grabbed the sword. That was all he had.

He stared, absolutely bewildered by what he saw coming out of the mansion. There was Dracula in a full suit of armor, like he had just time-warped from the past. Behind him were Cammy, the werewolf guy, the weird woman with the long hair and flashing eyes who had told him how to find Cammy when she was kidnapped, and some other man Brian didn't recognize. While he tried to figure out how he was supposed to fight Dracula in armor, Akerman stepped forward.

"Your Majesty, please forgive us for trespassing. I had hoped to—"

"Is that Officer Warren and..." Dracula considered Akerman.

"Felix Akerman. At your service."

"Mr. Akerman." Dracula glanced at the sword in Brian's hand.

The element of surprise was gone, but the whole plan was blown anyway. Brian had no idea what to do.

"Brian?" Cammy asked. "What are you doing here?"

"Akerman? The nicker we've got working for us? Subject B1?" said the unknown man.

"Oh, *skit också*," Akerman murmured.

Dracula's Death

"What's a nicker?" Cammy asked.

"It's a kind of sea monster," the werewolf guy explained. Brian side-eyed Akerman. He didn't look very sea monster-ish.

"If we could all remain focused," Dracula cut in. He considered Brian and Akerman. "You have been sent to us by Providence. As it happens, I have a need of able-bodied and brave men who are willing to fight to defend this city and perhaps even the world from a terrible threat." Dracula nodded at the sword. "Officer Warren, is that mine?"

"Yeah," Brian mumbled.

"Do you have the rest of my effects?"

"... Yeah," Brian admitted, defeated. Dracula grinned.

"Marvelous. Then you are just in time to help us to stop a madman from summoning ancient pagan gods to end the world."

"Wha...?"

"Hey, they're not cleared to know any of that," said the extra guy.

"I'm clearing it. We haven't the time to bother about secrecy at the moment. As is so often the case, time is of the essence. And I assume it is no trouble if one extra man and some monster or other knows about all of this?"

"We haven't cleared B1 for any of this! His job is to keep us appraised of what happens at the precinct we've assigned him to."

"Another police officer? Even better. He ought to know his way around weapons. You both" —Dracula waved at Brian and Akerman— "follow us. We have a long drive ahead of us. Use your phones and we will brief you on the way."

Dracula marched to the garage and opened the door, apparently confident there would be no more questions. Dimly, Brian heard his playlist inside Akerman's car start up "Danger Zone".

*****

Dracula had a hummer, and so he, Cammy, Malcolm, Siri and Neil could all fit in. Dracula told Brian and his friend to follow behind. Cammy had Brian on speaker so Dracula could bring him up to speed.

So that was that. Brian knew everything. He seemed to be taking it pretty well, all things considered. But he'd never be safe again. The next time some sort of supernatural threat came by, he'd want to do something about it. Cammy felt sick.

"So, let me get this straight: you're... *helping* to save the world from some Aztec god?" Brian asked dubiously, over the phone.

"Yes," Dracula replied.

Several moments of silence followed. Then Brian asked, "Cammy, you...you've known about all of this?"

That was the thing that hurt. Right there. She heard it in his voice. She had known.

"Yes," she confessed. She could barely hear herself.

"Since last year?"

"Yes," Cammy said. She felt ill. "He... he was helping me to find Heather."

There was no way Brian didn't remember getting invited along to do that, however briefly.

"So was he the one who actually killed her?"

"No, that was me. He rescued me from the guy who had killed Heather. I went to go stop him, but..."

Brian had no response.

"She saved your life, Officer Warren," Dracula said, filling in the silence. Cammy jumped. Why would he say that? Why would he say so right now? "Last year, when you tried to come to her rescue. Mr. Thorirsson—the *draugr* who

DRACULA'S DEATH

terrorized the city—threw you with considerable violence. Had Cammy not taken you away from the scene, I imagine you would be dead today."

Still no response. Cammy hugged herself. She'd known Brian would be mad if she didn't tell him, but she couldn't have told him. He just would have gotten himself killed.

"And you came to get her, at long last. Well done," Dracula added.

"Mind your own business," Brian grumped. Dracula smirked in the dark.

"Anything else I need to know?"

"If you are a man of faith, I would tell you to take this time to pray."

"Not me. I think Mom had us both baptized; we went to Mass once for Christmas with my uncle, but that was it."

Dracula said nothing.

"I'm sorry," Cammy said. "I'm sorry I didn't tell you. I... I was worried you'd go try to stop every monster out there, and you'd get hurt, or worse—"

"It's ok," Brian sighed. "It's all right. I know you. Don't worry about it. I guess... I'm just glad to be in the loop, finally."

Neil stewed in the backseat. Cammy hoped he wouldn't go running to Boese and have Brian arrested and thrown in that cell down in the lab. Like Boese had done to her. Her mouth felt so dry.

"All right, I guess we've only a few more hours," Brian said. "We'll call when we need to get gas."

"That is well. Do your best to prepare yourself," Dracula admonished him.

"Yeah, *thanks*." Brian hung up. Cammy fingered her phone.

"Something the matter?" Dracula asked. They were skirting the city as best they could to avoid traffic, so there wasn't much to look at out there but downed trees and crushed plants. Cammy ran her thumb over the giraffe on her phone cover.

"I'm scared."

"That shows you have learned to be careful."

"Not for me, for Brian."

"For Officer Warren?"

"He might get killed."

"He certainly might."

Cammy glared at Dracula in the dark.

"I guess you don't care."

He let out an angry-sounding sigh. A growl-sigh. He tapped the steering wheel angrily.

"You asked to come, and—based solely on the fact that I thought you understood what that meant, and because I imagine this fight will be difficult enough that I require all the help I can get—I let you come."

"But what if Brian—"

"*Listen*," he cut her off. "You said you wanted to help people, and that you would do what was necessary if I brought you along. Worrying about him is *not* how you do that."

"How can I just not care about him?" Cammy demanded.

"I didn't say don't care. I said do something." She detected annoyance in his voice.

"But—"

"*Listen*," he snapped again. "Here are the choices before you: I can stop the car and let you out to weep if you want while the rest of us press on, or you can stop weeping and you can be of some help. I don't have all night; which is it going to be?"

Dracula's Death

"You're a heartless monster," she told him. "Nothing phases you, huh? Anyone can die or you can just kill whoever and it's just no big deal, right?"

She saw that red glow in his eyes and he wiped at his mouth. He took a deep breath and let it out between his teeth.

"No. I don't," he said. "Do you want to know why?"

"Wha—?"

"When I was seven, my father took my oldest brother and me with him and raided a Christian town. We got to watch."

Cammy frowned.

"Why would he do—"

"Because if my father did *not* raid that village, the Turks were going to, and if *they* did, anyone they did not kill would be taken as slaves. Whereas if my father conducted the raid, anyone he captured he could set free and send back home."

"Why not just *not* attack them?" Cammy demanded.

"Because my father had to do his best placating the Turks and the rest of Europe. Neither side particularly cared about him or his country, and either would have killed or deposed him in a heartbeat if they thought he was not loyal to them and placed someone else on the throne as their chosen puppet. That is what happened to his predecessor. So he told Mircea and me why we were attacking our own people. Later, he wrote how pleased he was and grateful that if he had accomplished nothing else, that he had managed to save those ten thousand or so poor souls."

"So he wasn't friends with anyone?" Cammy asked.

"He did what he could," Dracula told her. "He even put my life and my youngest brother's life at risk to support the Christians later, in a failed campaign against the Sultan. For all the good it did him or us."

Cammy tried to read his eyes, but they were on the road. The glow had subsided.

"So that's why you don't care?" she asked.

"Life is the easiest thing in the world to snuff out," he told her. "I spent most of my childhood understanding that simple truth. Anything you value can disappear at any moment." He snapped his fingers to illustrate. "Your eyes. Your family. Your own life. Anything. If you want to weep about it, you'll accomplish nothing, or die. I told you: if you were afraid of death, you shouldn't have come."

"You let me come!" she shouted.

"Because I thought you finally understood. Until I saw you come out of the weapons room empty-handed, again. And I realized that you still didn't understand," he told her. "Do you understand now?"

Cammy glared at him.

"Even if I don't care about myself dying," she said, "I can't not care about Brian."

"Of course you can. I said 'if you were afraid of death.' That means others' deaths as well your own. Once you don't fear death, you can do anything."

What a stupidly morbid inspirational speech. Well, that sure explained why he was such an unfeeling killjoy.

"So your father rescued those people. That was nice," Cammy mumbled.

"The Sultan eventually demanded that he turn them all over to him. As slaves. To ensure his loyalty." Dracula tapped the steering wheel again. "I don't think my father ever fully recovered from that."

Cammy checked his eyes. No red glow. So... maybe that was why he'd been so ruthless back when. He'd seen someone try to be nice, only for it all to not matter. She felt ill. What if they tried to help now and it all ended up not mattering? Her stomach hurt.

Dracula's Death

"You modern people have convinced yourselves that death is far afield," Dracula told her. "Everyone knew, once, that they would die. Men knew they might die in war, women knew they might die in childbirth. They might take a chill and never recover. They might die from a snake bite, or an infected wound. The only thing they could possibly do about it was decide what their death was *for*."

"Is that why you were so ready to just... impale twenty thousand people?" Cammy asked.

Dracula grumpily sighed. "No. That was—"

"That was a war crime, you know," Cammy told him. The red glow came back.

"War crimes are a modern concept. Once, that was simply *war*," Dracula told her. "Such as when the Moslem Ottomans took so many Christian Georgians as slaves that humans sold at market for less than animals. They were marched en masse from their ruined home to the slave markets; infants who were dropped were trampled underfoot."

"What?! When did that—"

"That is the history of this wretched world," Dracula told her.

"Look, if we're all wrapped up, I'm going to take a quick nap," Malcolm announced. "Too much berserking and getting my blood drunk lately. I'm wiped; only so much Gatorade and bone broth and coffee can do. Next time we get gas though, wake me or get me a Monster. Maybe three."

"Is there nothing more you can tell us about what Ocelotl might be doing when we arrive?" Dracula asked. Malcolm sighed.

"Well, at the end of the day, he's going to have to wing any sacrifices or rituals he's trying to do. He's on some kind of normal mountain, not a temple complex. He doesn't have a lot of priests, even if he views himself as one. So on and so forth. And given that's he's willing to mix and match his gods and such, I'm guessing he's making some kind of soup out of all of that, plus magic from what he's learned from Ophois. Meaning we're going to run into something vaguely like the real thing, but largely something he's cobbled together. I mean, Tezcatlipoca's month is mostly in our modern month of May, so maybe he timed it all so he'd start on May first, I dunno."

"Will that still count?" Cammy asked.

"It should. There's a few ways to do ritual and worship and all of that. Obviously, there's the actual ritual part, but there's also intent. You can participate in the ritual without intent and still worship the deity or power the ritual or whatever. Or you can have mostly intent. Both will work."

"Wait a minute! You're saying that people can participate in this stuff *without even meaning to?*" Cammy demanded.

"Yeah. Ophois gets people to do that all the time. Stuff like, 'Hey! You know what would be a cool tattoo?' or 'Here's this esoteric statue you can use to decorate. Just a parting gift' or 'You don't have to believe it, but for the magic to work, it helps if you bow' kind of stuff. Or for the more influential clients, they might ask them to include something in a concert or a social media post."

So even if people don't agree with Ocelotl, if they go along with him, then...? What a terrifying thought.

"He said he wanted willing sacrifices," she said.

"Yeah, well, he's going to have to hunt high and low for that. Can't imagine there are a ton of people who want their hearts cut out."

"Hmm. Anything more you can tell us about the gods he's mentioned?" Dracula asked.

"Well, Tezcatlipoca was the most powerful of the Aztec gods, if memory serves. Which is weird, because he's a trickster. Those tend to be underdogs. Like, if you manage to catch him and grab his heart, he'll promise you anything if you let him go, but he's also a liar and a cheat so there's no guarantee that he'll actually do as he said. In any case, he's the god who tricked mankind into warfare, since they didn't want to do it—because the sun or the gods or the actual universe itself or whatever needs blood. I don't know if that was ritualized warfare or the real deal. It might not matter to him, but the Aztecs had a dedicated war god: Huitzipochtli, and I don't know how much overlap there was. Tezcatlipoca also caused the downfall of the Tolmecs because he didn't like them. He tricked their king and the people into dancing to their deaths or engaging in other activities that ended up killing them in droves. He's nice like that. Sacrifices to him were usually some guy who was supposed to be his incarnation or manifestation or avatar on earth. Guy lived like that for a year, then got sacrificed. Usually along with four other people."

"How delightful," Dracula commented.

"Sekhmet is a totally different animal. She's the daughter of Ra, and usually protects him as the uraeus on his forehead. In that position, she can spit fire to protect him or judge evildoers. She can command demons—one of those cases of 'calling on a terrifying god to protect you from terrors' sort of deals. Apotropaic. She can also cause plagues and disasters—a pretty spooky goddess if she's unhappy. Her being a lioness had worse connotations, since lions eat people. The Egyptians thought you needed your body to be whole in order to be resurrected."

"What, like a mummy?" Cammy asked.

"No, legit resurrection. They believed that everyone would be eventually."

"Hmm," Dracula murmured.

"Anyway, there was a yearly ritual the Egyptians had to perform because Sekhmet would leave her father and travel upriver. If she was placated and reconciled to Ra, then she would bring life-giving water of *Nu* with her. The Egyptians viewed water as a sort of medium of chaos from which life could spring."

"Hmm."

"She did have connections with the sun, or at least its burning rays and heat and all that. That was viewed as her more angry manifestation. There was that other myth when Sekhmet became so bloodthirsty that Ra had to dye an entire harvest's worth of beer red, so that it looked like blood. She drank it all, became drunk, passed out, and woke up back to normal. Fact is, she *loves* blood. So there's a very violent aspect to her. But Sekhmet was also a warrior goddess and a protector of Order, and we know he's trying to lean into a judgment aspect. So there is definitely enough glue there, depending on how he's trying to play this."

"I see," said Dracula.

"What about the cats? Maybe he's also using... what's that goddess' name, Bastet?" Cammy asked.

"Bastet is a demure goddess," Malcolm replied, "so I doubt it. But you can do some black magic with cats if you're Egyptian. Or... in general."

"The Egyptians would use cats for magic?" Cammy asked, confused. "I thought cats were sacred?"

"I said *black* magic," Malcolm told her.

Cammy's phone rang. She didn't recognize the number.

"Who is that?" Dracula asked.

"Dunno."

He glanced at the number. "Will you answer it? Just unlock it for me. I know who they are."

They? The mysterious people he had called earlier, then. She did as he asked and passed him the phone.

DRACULA'S DEATH

He greeted whoever it was, and listened to what was being said, growing increasingly angry with every passing moment. She could see that red glow coming back with a serious vengeance. He answered in some language Cammy didn't know, then passed her the phone.

"I need you to dial Boese."

Cammy's stomach tightened even more. Boese? Why?

"Mmm, Latin," Malcolm commented. "Some Catholic friends of yours?"

Dracula ignored him.

"You can use my phone," Neil volunteered. He dialed and passed the phone to Dracula.

"Director, did you interfere to *prevent* the Order of Saint Michael from joining us?" He listened to whatever Boese was saying, and the red glow remained. It was as intense as Cammy had ever seen it. "Director, let me clear: this *is* a spiritual matter. You know that I work with them—it is of no consequence to me that you have no faith, man. *I* am telling you that at the very minimum—I am *telling you* that they are necessary... *Superstition?!* You ignorant, pompous, paranoid *imbecile*"—he pronounced it "ahmbehseell" so Cammy wasn't sure what he'd actually said at first—"On your head then, you ape! Devil take you!"

He threw the phone over his shoulder back at Neil.

"What was that?" Cammy asked.

"Director Boese found that I contacted one of the Orders with which I work, and has actually taken the time to intercept them and stop them from coming to aid us."

"Oh, those Saint Michael guys?" Malcolm said. "That's a shame. They're pretty hardcore. What was Boese's excuse?"

"That he has to mobilize his own people and secure the area and he doesn't want a bunch of 'throwbacks to the Dark Ages' getting underfoot," Dracula seethed. He cursed in whatever language again. "To think that only *pagans* understand the way of things in this day and age!"

"Who are we talking about?" Cammy asked.

"One of the Catholic Church's old-timey Orders from way back," Malcolm told her. "They predate Ophois by centuries. These guys were formed to fight monsters back when the whole idea to fight this stuff got off the ground. There are only a few of them left, so they don't field a lot of people anymore."

"And they work with Ophois?"

Malcolm guffawed. "No way do they work with a bunch of Occultists who sacrifice babies, no! We don't get along, and never have."

Cammy wondered if it was for the best for Malcolm that they not come, if that was the case. The thought of what Ophois did made her ill, though. Her head hurt. Her stomach hurt. She hid her face in the crook of her elbow and rested against the door of the car.

"Hey, watch it!" Neil groused from the backseat.

"Shut up, Junior. I've got to get some rest back here or I'm gonna be useless. And her lap is a *lot* nicer than yours."

Cammy peeked back to see Malcolm had done his best to lie down with his head on Siri's lap and his feet on Neil's. He was too tall to straighten out, but that was the best he could do to get comfortable—be scrunched up into a ball. She buried her face once again.

Cammy heard another phone call come through at some point. Neil answered, then Dracula growled responses into it. Neil must have passed him the phone again. She didn't pay attention. She was tired; she felt sick. She didn't want to be doing any of this, and she didn't want Brian along.

Happy birthday to me, she thought. At least her mother wasn't in the mix. She might have to joke with Brian

Dracula's Death

afterwards that this birthday was still better than last year's because her mother wasn't along. They stopped for gas some time in the early morning, and though Cammy wanted to stay in the car, she figured she ought to use the bathroom—gas station bathroom, ugh!—before they went up a mountain. It would be embarrassing if she had to go while on the way to saving the world.

They all piled out, and Brian and his friend pulled in behind.

"We really need gas?" Brian called out.

"I think it best if everyone takes a moment to collect themselves, before we go up the mountain," Dracula told him. "And while we're at it, refuel. We don't know what we may encounter."

Brian shrugged. He spotted Cammy, and she played with her fingers self-consciously. He came towards her.

"You ok?" he asked.

"Yeah." She nodded while looking at the concrete beneath her shoes.

"We should get a coffee," Brian suggested.

"Where are we?" Cammy asked.

"Port Angeles. We're pretty close."

Cammy hadn't ever been outside of Seattle, except once when she was little. Her mother had wanted to say she'd traveled internationally, so they'd flown up to Vancouver. She didn't remember the trip very well. Her mother had a few pictures of their trip on the walls, framed and hung beautifully. She would comment on them on the rare occasions anyone came to visit. Grandma Constance had come twice, before Cammy's mother decided there wouldn't be any more visits from her, though Cammy had never heard the *why*.

The bathroom wasn't as gross as she'd worried it would be, and when she came back out she found Malcolm with two cans of energy drinks and three Gatorades in his hand at the register. Brian was lurking by the cold drinks.

"All they have is the big chain which must not be named," he told her, and forced a little chuckle. Cammy grinned in spite of herself. He'd learned to hate the famous Starbucks because of her disdain for it, picked up from working in a coffee shop.

"You sure you're ok?"

"Yeah." She nodded again.

"I...I guess I'm not," he confessed. She looked up at him. "I mean, up until a few hours ago I was planning on killing him. I thought he was, you know, the embodiment of evil. Now it turns out my best friend is some kind of sea monster, the US government is hiding all this, and there's some crazy Aztec warlock who wants to end the world. It's...it's a lot."

She took his hand and squeezed it. He squeezed hers back.

"I guess you already went through all of this, huh?"

"Yeah."

Brian glanced over all the bottles of sugary coffee.

"I'm sorry I wasn't there to help you with that."

"It's ok," she told him.

He bought her two bottles of coffee, not that she really wanted them, but it was probably a good idea. Plus a bottle of water and trail mix.

"It's a serious hike," he told her. "I looked it up while we were driving."

"Maybe we should get more snacks, then," she mused.

So they grabbed more trail mix and some Gatorades as well, and left the gas station still hand in hand. As much as she didn't want Brian along, she felt better to have someone who was like her in this whole mess. Even though Andrew knew, she didn't think he could have handled any of this. He'd have reacted like Emet, probably.

When they got to the base of the mountain, Neil received a call and coordinated where they should go and where they should end up.

"We've got some eyes on the ground," he explained. "Looks like he's got a lot of friends up there."

Cammy felt ill.

"The hike is several hours long," Neil warned. Cammy didn't know if she could do a several hour hike, actually. She'd never hiked before, unless she counted her wandering around Dracula's estate trying to get back into the mansion with his heart. It was already early in the morning. How much time would they need?

"This vehicle can handle difficult terrain," Dracula replied. "I will get us as far up the mountain as we can."

"I've got coordinates," Neil told him. "I'll navigate."

"Brian's car can't make it up there," Cammy pointed out.

"Aww, man, it's going to get way crowded in here," Malcolm grumbled.

"Some of you are going to have to double up," Dracula told him. "I'd suggest the women sit on someone."

Malcolm whistled. "I volunteer as tribute!" he quipped.

Dracula shook his head.

Once the gear from the other vehicle was packed into the back with the supplies Dracula had already brought—Cammy discovered Aki the fox was also quietly resting in the trunk, though no one had said she was coming—they set out for the last leg of their journey. Cammy ended up on Brian's lap. Not that she wanted to, but better Brian than anyone else. Siri was on Malcolm. The guy named Akerman was sandwiched between Malcolm and Neil, looking pale and like he'd just discovered he was claustrophobic.

"So, um, what is the plan when we get up there?" Brian asked. Dracula switched off his headlights and started the engine. The vehicle's tires spun for traction, but he eventually got it moving.

"We are heading into a very dangerous situation where demons and devils may lie in our path," Dracula replied. "Hence why I asked about your faith. In any case, I will drive the vehicle as close as I am able, and entrust you and you"—he nodded to Brian, then to Malcolm—"with spare keys, should you need to retreat. Given the variety of enemies we will be facing, I recommend as wide a variety of weapons as you can manage. Officer Warren, you already have a sword of mine. That was blessed, and therefore should be of some use, even if you have no faith of your own. You also have your gun with you?"

"Yeah."

"That is probably the best armament you can manage at this point. I suggest you and Cammy and Officer Akerman stay together. He knows more about the supernatural than either of you. Is that right?"

"Yeah," Akerman agreed, dully.

"And do you have any abilities which might be of help in a fight?"

"Not really. I could maybe carry some people out, if we needed to run."

"You have super strength?" Cammy asked.

"No. I" —he cleared his throat— "I can be a horse."

"You're telling me you're a *horse?*" Brian demanded. "You're a *horse??* And you're dating my *sister??*"

"He's dating Melissa?" Cammy asked.

"You didn't know that nickers vere vater horses?" Siri asked.

Dracula's Death

"I *still* don't know what a nicker *is!*" Brian retorted. "Except apparently it's a sea horse that's dating my sister!"

"*Gentlemen,*" Dracula cut in. "Now is not the time. Malcolm, what will you do?"

"Not go berserk if I can avoid it. I've got a gun and an axe."

"Siri?"

"I shall see vhat ve encounter. If they are men, I think I should be able to overcome them."

"Then keep an eye on Malcolm. Aki, you will use illusions to help cover the rest of us?"

"I shall, my lord."

"I am not certain whether I will be able to harm Ocelotl after... what happened," Dracula explained. "So I will make it my priority to slay his yaogaui and the nekomata. If there are other, unexpected monsters of strength I will do what I can to intercept them. One of the rest of you, or all together, should try to prevent or stop Ocelotl's ritual. Let Boese's men deal with the horde of vampires or undead. That is what they are trained for."

"Piece of cake," Malcolm said.

"We are riding into the pit of Gehenna," Dracula told him.

"Well, if that's where we're going, this is an awfully hummer-sized hand-basket. And if we *are* going there, I want a rocking playlist," Malcolm retorted. "Given Freddy Mercury got brought up, let's put on some Queen."

"What?" Brain demanded, but Malcolm just set his phone on the center console and loaded up some music.

"None of you understand what we are dealing with," Dracula growled, "to want to play such trash!"

"Vlad, if I'm going to die, let me listen to some killer music on the way," Malcolm groused.

"God help us," Dracula said.

CHAPTER 13

BLOOD RED SKY IN MOURNING

The hummer couldn't make it all the way up the side of Pyramid Mountain. The soil was soggy and slippery from all the precipitation. They got most of the way, however. According to Neil, they had maybe sixty minutes left to hike. Cammy felt rocks and mud under her feet when she stepped out of the vehicle, sliding just a little wherever she stepped. Hiking in the dark was going to be really hard.

Dracula handed her a sizable dagger and told her to stick with the others, and repeated that he would not be able to come to her rescue as a first priority. She gulped. But there wasn't any turning back now. They couldn't bring all of the gear from the trunk, so Dracula let everyone pick what they thought best, then turned to Akerman.

"How much can you carry?"

Akerman let out a long sigh. "Depends on how well you balance the load."

"Let's see what we can do."

Akerman sighed again.

"Worst idea I've ever had," he mumbled to himself, and looked to Brian. Then he turned into a big, white horse reared up on its hind legs. Its fore-hooves crashed down to the earth. No slow transformation, just *boom*, horse. Brian grumble-swore at the sight.

"Ha, *that's* what I smelled," Malcolm commented. "At the bar! Now I place you. You and your pity party." He chuckled, shouldered a battle axe, then slung one of the bigger guns across his back and tucked another in his waistband.

Dracula led the way, with Neil just beside and behind him to navigate. Malcolm after that, then Siri, then Brian and Cammy, then Akerman at the back, snorting and sighing all the way. Cammy wasn't sure where Aki had gone. Under the trees it was still really dark. She stumbled on the shifting ground and nearly fell a number of times. Brian caught her so she didn't faceplant onto muddy rocks, at least. The trees were black shadows moving against the darkness of the soil. Another dark forest from a fairytale—the real ones, before Disney made them cute, she supposed. She shivered, and recalled her thought last year that life would be so much better once she knew about vampires and ghosts and monsters, how she would be like one of those characters in a fairytale or a story. She wished she'd never had that thought. But then, Heather might have killed her, and she'd have never understood what happened.

There was no going back, and there never would be.

They pressed on, climbing, some of them stumbling on the uneven terrain. The sky lightened, turning to gray and yellow and pink-orange. Clouds were rolling in, but it had been clear for a good portion of the night. The trees stood out blacker against the changing sky. As it grew lighter, Cammy's eyes could pick out the gray shapes of leaves and downed branches, and Aki's little form slinking up and over or under fallen debris. She decided she hated hiking. Her shoes were soaked all the way through, as well as her socks. Her leggings were wet at the ankles. She shivered.

Now the morning light turned the clouds red, which was reflected in a gorgeous lake she glimpsed through the trees. The lake glowed red under the red sky.

The sun came up, and they still weren't there. Cammy's legs were screaming at her. She wasn't sure what she was going to do if she simply couldn't climb anymore. Get left behind? But maybe she'd have to. They had to make sure to stop Ocelotl.

"Well, sun's up," Malcolm commented. "We're gonna be too late to prevent the ritual from starting. It's gonna be fun once we get up there."

"Is this your only mode? Constant class clown?" Brian demanded.

"Is your only mode? Being weepy and a whining little bitch?" Malcolm snarked back.

"You're friends with this guy?" Brian whispered to Cammy.

"He works for Vlad."

"And now you're tattling to your crush. Man up, my guy," Malcolm told him. Brian glared at the back of his head.

Some sort of eerie, bone-chilling, teeth-grindingly awful sound whispered through the trees. As they drew closer to the summit, Cammy started to hear sobbing and screaming. She wanted to block her ears. The special ear plugs Dracula had gotten her were specifically for gunfire, so they were pretty good at letting other sounds in. She wished they weren't. She pressed her hands to her ears and saw Brian's look of commiserating misery.

They came across two men armed with rifles, and pulled to a stop.

"Neil! Weren't sure you were going to make it," the first rifleman whispered. "I'll let them know. We have a vest for you."

DRACULA'S DEATH

"Thank you. What is the situation?"

Rifleman glanced over the group, then replied, "We've got a perimeter set up. The target set up stone walls around the cabin up here. He's also got people tied up all around the walls. Maybe to stop us from getting ideas of blowing it up. We've got two choppers, but our research and Ophois both told us that some *yaogaui* have strong enough powers to down helis, so they're keeping distant. There is a small window for sniping, but there are civilians in the way, so the director is getting permission from the top to cut through."

Cammy's ears stung. Cut through... civilians? The people she and the others were there to rescue? She stormed forward, but Dracula thrust out an arm and pushed her back. He shook his head at her protests.

"But you heard what he said!" she protested. Everyone shushed her.

"He already knows we're here," Malcolm said in a tone of resignation. "He knows all these guys are around here." He crouched down and peered through the trees. They were very near a little clearing at the top, and sure enough, Cammy could see some stone walls. There was a bloody-looking pile of something disgusting lying in front that Cammy couldn't make out and didn't want to look at, and smoke rising behind the wall. A line of people were tied to each other by hands and wrists outside the wall, forming some kind of human chain. They were the source of some of the horrible sounds she had been hearing. Many of them were crying, others were hanging their heads in despair or exhaustion. From the looks of them, a good number had been outside during the rain. Mud-stained clothes, hair hung down, bedraggled and scraggly. Stubble. A tiger stood on its hind legs near the crowd.

"There's one of them!" Cammy pointed.

"No good," Rifleman said. "We sniped it. No reaction. Best bait we've ever seen."

It sure looked like one of those tigers. It even had that spear she'd seen at the diner grasped in one paw.

The screaming renewed, one voice rising in terror, shrieking "No! No! Stop! Please, no!" over and over. She couldn't see who it was. The screaming continued, then fell suddenly silent. A moment later, a human form was flung from an opening in the stone wall. The person rolled down a freshly-formed channel in the soil, partly formed from rain, partly dug out, so far as she could see. The channel ran deep and she quickly lost sight of the person.

"We need to go help him!" Cammy whispered. Brian's jaw was tight.

"Cammy," he said. "That person... didn't have a head."

She stared.

"Officer Warren," Dracula said over his shoulder. "Are you going to be able to concentrate with her here?"

Cammy could barely understand the question. Someone without a *head*...!

Brian gritted his teeth, but he nodded. Dracula shook his head a little and grumbled to himself. To the rifleman, "Do you have any further reconnaissance?"

"He's got a lot of critters inside that wall. We're not sure exactly what or how many. We were hoping the choppers could get a look."

"Aki, can you see what is happening in there?" Dracula asked. The fox nodded and darted forward. The grass thinned the closer to the wall she got, where the ground showed bare, but the fox pressed low and scurried to the stones. She leaped up the wall and peered over the top. A gun fired, and the fox tumbled backwards. Cammy felt her heart in her throat, but Aki came darting back as quick as lightning.

"He has the chain of humans leading to a large stone he has placed in front of a cabin," the fox reported breathlessly. "He has already slain a large number of people. I could not count the heads. Four yaogaui are within, as well as two nekomatas."

"No sign of a large, gray cat anywhere?" Dracula asked. The fox shook her head.

Cammy supposed that if nothing else, it was good that the ccoa wasn't around.

"I propose storming in," Dracula said. "Through that front opening. I will go first and try to pin down or slay at least one or two of the yaoguai."

"Nekomata are necromancers who can control the dead," Aki warned, reminding him. Dracula let his breath out through his teeth.

"None of the rest of us are heavy enough tanks for the yaoguai," Malcolm said. "And at least one of them has a gun."

"There are many guns," Aki confirmed. "And other weapons."

"Such as?" Dracula asked.

"Grenades."

"Grenades!" Rifleman and his partner jumped up. "Are they planning to start a war?"

"Of course they are. They intend to end the world," Dracula told them coolly.

"Suppose we try to destroy the whole little complex he has set up?" Rifleman's buddy said, speaking for the first time.

"An airstrike?" Rifleman asked. "We can try it. Call it in."

"But there are *people* over there!" Cammy shouted. Rifleman's buddy was already making a call on his walkie-talkie. "There are *people!*"

"There are American citizens over there," Brian said to the government guys. "Civilians who are in life-threatening danger."

"Call in to let the director know that Subject D also brought Subject B1 and a bunch of civilians and some sort of talking animal along," Rifleman told his buddy.

"Sir, what are you doing? We need to get those people to safety," Brian told him.

"Also tell them that he brought the Ophois werewolf along." Rifleman ignored Brian.

"Hey, what gives? It's a free country, I have a right to get myself sent straight to hell if I want," Malcolm told him.

"The target works for Ophois. The director wants to keep them out of this until we can determine to what extent they are involved. So none of them fielded out here."

"We need him," Dracula growled. "He is the best candidate to stop Ocelotl, if we can create an opening for him."

"He's not permitted to engage with the target," Rifleman asserted. "Orders from up top."

"*Give me that.*" Dracula snatched the walkie-talkie from Rifleman's partner. Another set of screams pierced the quiet morning air, and another body rolled down the channel while Dracula demanded to be put through to Boese.

"Guys, we can't just stand here arguing!" Cammy cried. "He's *killing people!*"

"You can't kill civilians," Brian backed her up.

"Gentlemen, surely ve can come to an agreement?" Siri asked, touching Rifleman gently on the back of the neck. His partner drew a handgun and aimed it at her.

"Don't do whatever it is you're thinking of doing," he warned.

Siri withdrew her hand.

DRACULA'S DEATH

Dracula was still trying to get through to Boese. A new person was already screaming and pleading for mercy. The blood pounded in Cammy's head. It hurt. It hurt *so* much.

Think! Think! Think! she screamed inside her mind. Louder than the screams she heard. Louder than her own heart.

"Wait a minute!" she said. "Wait! Malcolm said... there was intent, or something, right? Ocelotl intends to kill all these people! And... he said he wants a willing sacrifice, and he's a vessel of Tez-cat-god, right?"

Malcolm turned, his eyes wide as he realized what she was getting at.

"So we can't just kill everyone! Then we're doing what *he* wants! The Aztec god or Ocelotl or the demon or whatever, right? Whatever's possessing him *wants* these people dead, *and if he's the vessel or whatever, he's the main sacrifice,* so it can't be good to do that!"

All eyes fell to her. Malcolm swore.

"Gentlemen, it is with great displeasure I have to inform you that we are scuh-rewed," he said. "Officially."

"Then what do we do?" Brian demanded. "We can't kill him? We have to take him into custody, right?"

"Something like that," Malcolm agreed. "But he's not going to pay us the same courtesy. We have to fight with one hand tied behind our backs."

It was Dracula's turn to swear—in about three different languages. He threw the walkie-talkie into the trees.

"Devil take him!" he shouted. "Take him straight to hell!"

Rifleman pulled his own walkie-talkie.

"All units, report in."

"Beta unit, reporting in."

...

"Delta unit, reporting in."

...

"Zeta unit, reporting in."

Rifleman fidgeted. "Gamma, Epsilon, report in."

He waited. No response.

"Does anyone have visual on Gamma or Epsilon?"

"Negative."

Malcolm stood up, his eyes scanning the trees behind them. Cammy whirled around. Was there something out there?

"Go check on Gamma and Epsilon's positions."

"Copy that."

"Stop talking into that thing," Malcolm hissed.

Rifleman considered him, and also scanned the trees.

"What is it?" Dracula whispered.

"They've got us surrounded, I think. I just heard…" He pointed back the way they'd come. "Lots of movement. Also…"

He closed his eyes and sniffed the air a few times.

"Yaoguai. Close by. And blood."

"Where?" Dracula asked.

"Can't tell where. Gotta be upwind."

"Upwind? That's—"

Dracula whirled to his right. A great, big silhouette leaped through the trees, a sword flashing in one hand. Dracula raised his magnum and fired. Whatever it was glistened red and white and then fell awkwardly beside him. It was nothing but blood and bone and blood vessels, and when it raised itself to four legs Cammy realized it was a skinless tiger—armed with a sword.

The skinless creature made to flee, but Dracula fired again and the monster dropped. It groaned in pain, so Dracula beheaded it with his sword.

"The bait!" Malcolm breathed. "He took his skin off to trick you all!"

Dracula's Death

"We're surrounded?" Dracula checked with Malcolm. Cammy couldn't peel her eyes from the gore at his feet.

"Sounds like it. I think he's got his vampires or his undead all around us. Way to set up a perimeter, guys."

Rifleman glared at Malcolm.

"You" —Dracula singled out Rifleman and his partner— "lay down cover fire. I'm going to draw fire from those in the enclosure. Have your men shoot anything that pops up, do what you can to distract the enemy and draw them off of us. Siri, can you distract them?"

"Not vithout distracting you all together."

Dracula growled to himself.

"Then help keep all those out there at bay."

"What about us?" Cammy asked.

"You do what you always wish to do." Dracula pointed to the people tied in a chain across the little summit and the clearing. Then to Brian, "As a police officer, your duty should be to protect those people. Do so. Officer Akerman, you do the same."

Brian sucked in his breath and nodded. He grabbed Cammy's hand.

"Hold up, there's more going on out there," Malcolm said.

"What now?" Rifleman demanded.

Malcolm chuckled. "I hear Latin. I think Vlad's friends are the cavalry coming to save our bacon."

"Those Catholic knights?" Rifleman asked. "We stopped them from getting up the road."

"Sounds like you didn't," Malcolm told him with a grin. "Thank God, I guess."

"Excellent," Dracula clapped him on the shoulder, "that you finally understand."

Malcolm made a face at him.

Cammy could see people moving through the trees. Some looked like normal people, others were moving oddly, with limbs that did not bend as they should, shuffling across the ground like grotesque spiders, making her skin crawl. Behind them she could see others wearing what looked like tactical gear.

"There!" she heard from her right, towards the lake. One of the men in tactical armor, carrying a semi-automatic strapped to his side and a sword in hand, came hurrying as quickly as he could over the crumbly, muddy terrain.

Dracula greeted him in what she guessed was Latin, and they exchanged some hurried greetings.

"This is Father Sebastian," Dracula hurriedly explained. "The support I requested *was* intercepted on the road, but they were able to mobilize some members of the Order of St Jeanne d'Arc who were in Forks. We have some of them, as well as a few from the Order of Saint Michael. I need to bring you up to speed."

He related all that they'd discussed, as well as the threat of an airstrike. Father Sebastian's face soured.

"There are all manner of...unspeakable undead crawling out of the mountain now. We are pinned down and can't come up here in force."

"Keep fighting them down there. Any men you can spare, send up here. I will start drawing fire. Everyone else"—he met all their eyes—"the same as before. Go!"

Cammy heard another heart-rending scream. Akerman thrust a bag heavy with ammo at her. She slipped the strap over her shoulder, then ran with Brian, who had been given ammo and a shotgun as well. He grasped her hand and they began to sprint over the uneven ground. He was going around the front of the walled-in cabin. The way looked steeper and more treacherous behind and away from the trench and cabin, so this was the best route if they wanted to hurry. Akerman came behind them.

Dracula's Death

She heard the *crack! crack! crack!* of dulled gunfire as they ran, and was grateful for the earplugs. Brian covered his ears. She felt for him. When she risked a glance towards the walled cabin, she saw four Draculas walking out into the open. Four? Was that Aki's illusion? Where was the real Dracula, or was he one of them?

They came around to the channel cut into the mountain. It must have initially started as a natural mudslide that had been dug out and made deeper. At the base of the mudslide was a pile of headless human bodies. Cammy screamed at the sight, and Brian pulled her close to him.

"Don't look at it," he told her. Akerman came around her right side—to block her view, maybe. Brian ducked down when they came to the trench. Cammy whimpered to think of what had come rolling down it. She glanced to her left. There was an opening straight through the stone wall that she had not been able to look through before. Behind and between more people tied in place, there stood Ocelotl, dressed only in the jaguar skin, his face still painted. She could see some sort of tattoos all over him. Someone was lying on their back on the stone slab in front of him.

He looked right at her, and grinned.

They jumped as far over the trench as they could, but only Akerman was able to clear it; he turned to help them both climb the other side. The muddy ground slipped out from under them. Cammy ended up face down in the chill, wet grass, and scrambled back to her feet. Brian and Akerman helped her up. It shouldn't be too hard to get to the tied-up people now.

Something *exploded*, and she felt the air slap at the back of her neck. When she turned, she saw the four Draculas moving away from a rising column of smoke. She had never felt so cold, realizing that she really *was* in a war zone.

"I call on you, the Lady of Terror! She Who Brings Death!" Ocelotl's voice carried over the brief silence that the explosion had bought. Everyone, even the tied-up civilians, had been cowed by the sudden outburst.

Brian pressed on towards the civilians, so Cammy and Akerman followed. Movement near the walled-in cabin drew her attention and she turned to look. The bloody pile she hadn't been able to identify boiled and bits jumped up and piled atop other bits, the whole mass rising until it took a recognizable form. Humanoid, feminine, with a feline-shaped head. Thirteen feet tall at least. All made of the corpses of slaughtered cats. Blood dripped down the matted fur, running down the ill-formed legs. The eyes were gaps formed by the broken bodies.

An Egyptian goddess made of the bodies of slaughtered cats. It was a sick joke.

Sekhmet swung a great arm at the nearest Dracula, and her fist passed right through him. She spat out a stream of flame like napalm that swept the others. Cammy felt the heat from all the way on the other side of the summit.

She and Brian and Akerman had reached the civilians. Men, women, even some teens and children. Cammy was aghast.

"Please, help us!" one woman pleaded.

"Please stay calm, ma'am," Brian told her, setting down the bag of ammo and the shotgun. "I'm a police officer."

He pulled out the sword, then stared at it like he had no idea what to do. Cammy dropped her bag of ammo too and offered the dagger, but it didn't seem very good for cutting ropes. Akerman passed over a Swiss Army knife.

"Never know when it'll come in handy," he said, then drew his handgun and swept his eyes over their surroundings, his finger beside the trigger.

Dracula's Death

Brian sawed at the rope connecting the group nearest to him.

"Once I cut you all free, work to untie yourselves," he advised, "and move away, down toward the lake. There should be a road on the other side."

"Hurry!" five of the civilians urged him. The rope tugged, and Cammy realized that they were being hauled slowly toward the walled-in cabin. One at a time. To take their place on that dreadful stone. Brian tried pulling in the other direction, but his feet slid in the mud and he was dragged with it. The pulling stopped. Ocelotl had what he needed.

Cammy was crouching about fourteen feet from the opening. Should she run to it? To do what? She didn't have her pepper spray anymore. It was lost in the woods outside Dracula's estate somewhere. It might have actually been able to save the day here. Or maybe not. There were *yaogaui* with guns and grenades in there; she'd have a hard time getting close enough to spray anyone, and she didn't think she'd be able to stop them all before.... She gulped at the thought. Her throat was so dry.

"Through!" Brian announced. Something like twenty people came loose from the others. They tumbled over each other in a scramble to get away. "Stay calm!" Brian admonished. "Go carefully, the ground is very shifty! Help each other along."

"Try to untie yourselves," Akerman told them. "Careful!"

But they weren't listening. The whole group was moving, mindlessly, arms and legs scrambling for escape, pulling on each other. Finally, moving towards the lake. A woman got knocked onto her back and she screamed as the others dragged her along.

A tiger jumped down onto Brian.

"Brian!" Cammy raised the gun she'd been handed. The tiger saw it, snarled, and batted the gun out of her hands with a swipe of its paw. The weapon flew off to the side and was lost in the tall grass.

Just as the tiger returned its attention to Brian, the nicker kicked the tiger with both back hooves and sent it flipping backwards through the air. Brian sat up, bewildered and gasping for air. He looked to Cammy and Akerman, and nodded. He picked up the shotgun and aimed at the tiger.

It leaped up to the top of the stone wall, and Brian pulled the trigger. Red burst from its flank, and the tiger roared, then pounced on the horse's back. Akerman rolled backwards from the impact, his legs and hooves flying in the air, whinnying in pain or terror. He lurched to his feet, but the tiger jumped once more onto his back and sank its fangs into his neck. Brian picked up his handgun to shoot at the tiger, but hesitated, probably afraid of hitting Akerman by accident. The nicker bolted through the trees, carrying the tiger with him.

"Akerman!" Brian shouted.

The nicker was gone. The air burned hot, and Cammy flinched, turning to see Sekhmet spraying flame across the summit. Flames blazed across the mud, sputtering and going out. Another grenade detonated, throwing mud and rocks high into the air and raining down across Cammy's head and shoulders. Sekhmet let out a roar that was nothing like any animal could make. It scraped against Cammy's nerves and made her queasy, it cut straight past the ear plugs. The sound felt like fire in her brain. Like suffering.

She heard the crack of more gunfire, and blood sprayed from impacts in Sekhmet's horrifying body. Bits of fur, blood, and skin flew off her, but the bullets seemed not to bother her at all. She scanned the summit for targets and stepped forward.

Dracula's Death

Cammy spotted a cloak burning on the mud, and near the trench, a little yellow fox trapped within a circle of flames.

"Aki!" Cammy called.

Hearing her name, Aki stood up a little, her ears fixed on Cammy's position. The fox calculated the distance and the height of the flames all around. She darted forward, leaping over the fire.

Crack!

The fox flipped sideways, disappearing over the edge where the summit fell away towards the mud slide and trench.

"Aki!" Cammy screamed.

"Cammy! Come here and help me!"

Cammy turned around. Brian was sawing at the rope, but looking up at the wall. Another tiger perched up there. How many yaogaui did Ocelotl have? Brian dropped the knife and raised his gun. He fired. Cammy dove to grab the knife and continued sawing at the rope. Brian stood over her and fired again. He swore.

"How fast *are* these things?!" he demanded.

The rope parted.

"Run!" Cammy instructed the civilians she'd freed. The same panicked, haphazard escape repeated, with people not knowing where to go or how not to trip over each other in their panic to get to safety. Some of the people did their best to help those who were less able—two elderly men, and a tween, but most of them just panicked.

Where was the rope closest to the wall? She ought to go for that next. It would release the rest of them into a big pile-up, but they couldn't be dragged along for the sacrifice.

The rope pulled someone else in.

"No!" But screaming wouldn't help. She had to find a better place to cut.

"Cammy, hurry up, I'm almost out!" Brian told her. Out of the corner of her eye she saw him drop to one knee and wrestle with the bag of ammo.

Her palms were sweaty, but she ran towards the wall closest to the enclosure. Now she could see there were people tied to each other all around the wall, and a separate group tied up inside. She grabbed the rope at the very corner of the wall. She had to do the best she could.

A thunderous *WHUP WHUP WHUP* noise preceded a wind blowing in her face. She looked up. Coming from the direction of the lake was a helicopter. She felt like it was trying to sneak up behind the walled in cabin, though the idea was ridiculous. A helicopter sneaking up on *anything* was ridiculous.

"Cammy! Get down!"

Brian tackled her against the stone wall, then dragged her out of sight of the helicopter. One of the stones popped, raining splinters of itself through the air. Streaks of light punctured the ground beyond her.

"They're using a Minigun?!" Brian seethed. "Don't they *care* that there are people down here?!"

A loud, sharp, short hiss, then a tremendous *BOOM*. A glow against the summit and the trees, even in the daylight. The screech of tortured metal, the snapping of branches, something smashing below and behind them.

"And these guys have some sort of RPG?" Brian realized. "How are we supposed to *stop* these monsters?!"

"By rescuing everyone," Cammy muttered, looking towards the tied-up people. Her hands were shaking, but she and Brian crawled back to the wall. Some people had been shot and were slumped against the wall, some were sobbing, some were praying.

Dracula's Death

Where was the knife? She'd dropped it when Brian tackled her. She fumbled on the ground of packed mud and stones until she found it.

"Cammy! Watch out!"

Something heavy slammed her face-down into the dirt, then lifted her up, up, up. She couldn't get her bearings. The sky was below her, the ground and the flames all above her. Like falling headfirst into fire. She thrust out her arms for balance and to grab hold of a*nything*, but there was nothing but open air.

Then a dizzying fall into shadow, and being shoved down onto her face. The smell of smoke and some kind of incense. The metallic tang of blood in the air.

"There you are," Oceoltl's voice greeted cheerily. "You look like a volunteer!"

"No!" She was lifted off the ground. A tiger had hold of her arms, its paws like those iron-grip hands from last year. She tried to kick backwards at it, but her heels connected with nothing. Dracula had said he wouldn't come save her.

"No!" she repeated, her throat burning from the strain and the smoke and whatever else Ocelotl was burning beside him on a large stone. "Let me go!"

"Bring her here," Ocelotl instructed the tiger. His eyes blazed as though a fire was lit behind them. "Oh, yes! *Her* next!" He actually cackled. Like a hyena or a jackal.

"No! Help! Get off me!"

The tiger effortlessly pushed her forward. Her heels bit into the dirt, digging little trenches of their own, but she could not overpower the creature. There were five of them inside the walls, and two enormous house cats, each with two tails. The house cats leered at her, their faces twisted and hateful, like that white cat that had tried to kill her. There was one tiger holding the rope that connected to the victims outside. It dragged both the rope and the victim who would have been next to one side to make room for Cammy. How was it strong enough to pull on dozens of people like that? There was a man kneeling and crying beside the large stone with a flat top, which was absolutely soaked in blood. Cammy kicked at it to stop the tiger lifting her up and placing her down on her back.

She stiffened her legs against the stone, but the other tigers came forward and grabbed hold of her, pressing, and then she couldn't move. The tiger who had thrown her down offered her hand to the crying man, who hugged himself and shook his head.

Ocelotl nodded to the crying man. He received another frantic head shake in answer.

"Oh, now you cannot do it?" Ocelotl asked.

"Please stop. Please stop!" the man sobbed. He wore his hair in a messy man bun that had half-come out. "I can't do this anymore..."

"If you don't, then you are next."

"Please, no!"

"He's next," Ocelotl told the tiger.

"No!"

When the man tried to bolt, the tiger holding Cammy's arms let her go, grabbed him and pushed him down into the dirt. She sat up, but couldn't escape with the other two tigers holding her legs. She clawed at their paws, but couldn't pry free. From here, Cammy could see there was a little stash of weapons inside the cabin—they were definitely prepared for a fight. A gory pile of human heads was placed against the stone wall farthest from her. The tiger behind her stepped on the man with the man bun, then took Cammy's arms and pulled her down onto her back again.

Ocelotl's hands were slick with blood almost up to his elbows. The tattoos on his chest looked like hieroglyphics. He

Dracula's Death

gripped an obsidian knife in one hand, and with the other he ripped open her shirt. She screamed.

"Wait! Stop!"

Brian was at the opening in the stone wall, at the head of the trench.

"Wait, stop. Hang on!"

"He's next," Ocelotl pointed at Brian.

"Wait, you want willing sacrifices, right?" Brian yelled over the wailing and the chaos outside. Ocelotl narrowed his blazing eyes at him. Brian held up both hands. "You can take me, and let her go."

"No!" Cammy tried to kick free again.

"I mean it. Let her go, and you can do whatever you want with me."

The tigers leered greedily at him, and the two giant cats lashed their too many tails. But they all looked to Ocelotl to see what he would say.

"Brian, don't! Get help!" Cammy protested. She didn't want to die, but she didn't want Brian to die, either.

"Let her up," Ocelotl told the tigers. The one holding her arms yanked her up off the stone and drew her away to one side. One of the others approached Brian. He held both his hands forward, as though awaiting a pair of cuffs to be slapped on them. The tiger seized him by one arm and the neck, while another tore off his shirt. The first dragged him toward the stone, while the second hurried to the cabin and emerged with a bucket of what looked like blue paint. It dipped its paw into the tincture and smeared the color all over Brian's face and skin. Another explosion sent blood and fur and wet dirt raining across them all. Ocelotl looked up into the falling debris, calmer than he had been. A few large drops of blood splattered across his cheeks and dripped down like tears.

Cammy heard that unnatural Sekhmet roar again, and covered her ears despite herself. The tiger dragged Brian to Ocelotl.

"Go!" Brian told her.

She had to find help before it was too late. She tried for the opening, but the tiger who had picked her up gripped her again and held her fast.

"Let me go!"

"You said you'd let her go!" Brian protested.

"I did. And now I've captured her again," Ocelotl told him. "However, I do thank you for your sacrifice."

Brian swore and spat in his face. Ocelotl only grinned, that manic grin returning and burning away that brief calm. The grin looked wrong. Painful. Too wide, too broad, too eager. Like something under his skin was pulling his face into some grotesque semblance of giddy joy.

Cammy yanked her arm. She could not get free. Brian couldn't tear himself away from the tigers who pressed him down on that horrible stone.

"Let him go!!" Cammy screamed.

Ocelotl raised the obsidian knife.

"Cammy!"

Emet came charging in through the opening, waving a gun. He fired once—thankfully hitting nothing with the totally wild shot—then took a panicked look around at the enemies within. He was visibly trembling, but the gun in his hand was now pointed at the were-tiger holding Cammy. For several moments, no one moved; everyone was too bewildered by this development. Then one of the yaogaui raised his gun.

"Wait!" Ocelotl pointed to the yaoguai, then swept his finger towards Emet. "That necklace..."

Dracula's Death

"Let everyone go!" Emet shouted, and aimed his shaking gun at Ocelotl.

"Stop, Emet! We can't kill him!" Cammy shouted. Emet turned towards her. This afforded the *yaogaui* to his other side the chance to grab his hands and yank him up into the air. Emet yelped with pain. The tiger stripped him of his weapon and opened its mouth, baring its teeth.

Ocelotl shouted something at the yaoguai, and it stopped. Ocelotl fixed his finger at Emet again.

"Your necklace. Is that just for show?"

"Yes," Emet admitted. "I just...wear it to...to show off..."

"You said you were going to take your faith seriously," Cammy reminded him. Ocelotl studied her, then returned his attention to Emet.

"Which is it? Fashion, or faith?" Ocelotl grabbed the guy with the man bun by his hair. "This man wore his faith like fashion. That's why he's so weak and spineless."

"Please let me go! I can't anymore!" the man bun guy pleaded.

"You will still serve," Ocelotl told him. "One way or the other, you *will* serve the gods."

"No, please, no—!"

Ocelotl yanked hard on his hair and leaned down to snarl into his ear. "If you have no faith of your own, I will provide mine to you."

The guy with the man bun started sobbing. Ocelotl shoved him aside, and he collapsed on the mud in a quivering heap. He returned his attention to Emet.

"Which is it? Faith or fashion?"

Emet's jaw tightened and his empty hands shook.

"I am trying to make it faith."

"Trying. I see. Let us test that." Ocelotl set down the obsidian dagger, and Brian tried to wriggle free, or perhaps knock the knife off the altar, but the tigers held him fast. Ocelotl pulled a gun and aimed it at Emet.

"If you recant, I will let you go. If you don't..." He fired. Emet jumped and cried out. After a moment, a trail of red spilled down his shirt. He's been shot beside his right shoulder. Ocelotl's eyes burned like molten metal. "I will take you apart, piece by piece."

Just then, a tiger wearing bandages around its throat came charging in through the opening in the stones, and Ocelotl fired at it next. The tiger jolted a little to one side, and staggered. Its tongue lolled and it panted, its head hanging down.

Masayu! Cammy realized. The tiger did not seem to notice her, but caught her breath, then stepped between Emet and Ocelotl. Ocelotl took stock of his minions. They all more or less had their hands full. He squinted at the tiger, and aimed with the gun.

"No!" Emet shouted. "Leave her alone!"

"Faith or fashion?" Ocelotl demanded again, his eyes blazing like twin comets. He raised the gun and fired again. Masayu tried to leap up to take the bullet, but could not quite do it. Emet tried to reach down, but the yaogaui held him fast, and now a second stream of blood dripped from the side of his neck.

"I won't abandon my beliefs," Emet told him, though his hands still shook. "I have done so for too long."

Ocelotl's blazing eyes tried to burn away any lie, and at last he lowered the gun.

"A man of faith," he said. His tone sounded like praise. "Very well. I will grant you a violent death. The most glorious. But not this"—he indicated the altar—"You serve your own god. You are helping to maintain the order of the world, and you should be rewarded. Once we have finished here, I promise you a violent death."

He nodded, and the tiger holding Emet dragged him to one side where there lay a pile of rope. Masayu growled and leaped, digging her claws into yaogaui's shoulder. It roared and knocked her violently back. She collapsed on the mud, panting desperately, but struggled to her feet. By the time she'd stood up, the yaogaui had finished binding Emet. It turned back and stepped on Masayu's neck and pinned her to the earth. She could not rise. The bandages around her were peeling free, and blood was seeping down her sides from her wounds. Her claws dug weakly at the mud. The *yaogaui* reached down and effortlessly dragged her towards Emet by her throat. Once done, he looped a rope around her neck and left her there, panting, her side rising and falling rapidly, her breaths desperate. Emet hugged her around the neck.

Ocelotl took up the obsidian dagger again, loomed over Brian, flexed the fingers of his other hand, grinned at the sky, and raised the knife. Brian tried to pull free, but he could not escape the yaogaui.

The blade shattered into stardust and Ocelotl's hand jolted. The fingers trembled with pain and shock.

Dracula walked in through the opening, a rifle trained on Ocelotl. Ocelotl's blazing eyes took him in with awe and anticipation.

"But can you kill me?" he asked, and opened his arms, inviting the bullet.

Dracula aimed the rifle instead at the nearest *yaogaui* and fired. The tiger roared in pain and fell backwards, its tail lashing and claws scouring the slick, bloody mud beneath it.

One of the nekomata leaped forward, up and over Dracula's head as he fired at it. The nekomata let out a laugh that sounded like mewling, raising its paw as though dangling puppets on strings. Its sharp teeth gleamed and its red tongue passed across them hungrily. Its front paws twitched, and suddenly Dracula collapsed to the bloody ground.

"They can control the dead," Ocelotl explained. He turned and entered the cabin, emerging with another obsidian dagger in hand.

"One never knows what may happen while traveling," he giggled. Actually giggled. "Ah, yes, euphoria. We are almost there."

"We let a lot of your prisoners go," Cammy told him. "So no, you're not."

He chortled in response, his mouth still drawn too wide for any natural mirth. His eyes burned in his face. He spotted a silver chain around Brian's neck, and reached down to inspect it.

"A crucifix?" he asked, and giggled again. "How wonderful. Wonderful!"

He yanked on the chain and broke it, then hurled the necklace and the crucifix up over the stone wall.

"Tezcatlipoca is your god, now!" he announced.

"You're a liar and a monster!" Brian snarled at him.

Ocelotl grinned. "Oh, I know I am."

Once again, his eyes were drawn out beyond the opening, and he hesitated. Cammy hoped it was someone to the rescue. Those Catholic guys Dracula had managed to call in, maybe. They ought to be able to help.

Instead, Neil was standing outside the opening, his arms held wide as though shielding those inside from a coming threat.

"If you shoot, you'll only power his ritual!" Neil shouted into a walkie-talkie. He wasn't wearing a vest. His government buddies had never gotten it to him, apparently.

Dracula's Death

"Stand down, Neil!" came the response over the walkie-talkie.

"Ophois uses magic to stop bullets anyway," Neil countered. "There's no point."

"Take the shot."

That sounded like Boese. Cammy's blood ran cold. She looked to Ocelotl, who straightened up and waited in eager anticipation.

The back of Neil's head exploded and he crumpled, collapsing forward into the bloody trench. Cammy screamed and covered her face. Her blood was screaming in her head. Suddenly, the tiger let her go and she nearly fell forward, but caught herself on the stone wall. When she turned, she saw the other tigers leaping up over the wall. The two-tailed nekomatas followed.

Ocelotl was grinning with self-satisfaction, and sunlight reflected off the bits of jade in his teeth. The blazing light died out in his eyes, and he fell gently backwards. A single line of blood trickled down his chest. He'd been shot right in the heart.

Dracula rose from the ground. His cloaks were gone, but other than mud and blood staining the armor, he looked whole and unharmed. He took Cammy by the wrist and pulled her upright.

"Damn that man!" he seethed at the gap in the stones, then turned to glare down at the corpse. Even in death, Ocelotl wore that manic grin like a delighted grimace. Cammy's legs gave out from under her. Dracula caught her with one hand and hoisted her up by her waist.

As Dracula held her, his searching gaze took in Emet and Masayu. "What are you doing here?" He demanded.

"I... thought I should come," Emet explained, his breath shallow. Blood was running down from his neck, and from the wound in his shoulder. "I...I couldn't be brave before, but

I also couldn't let everyone else do what was necessary while I stayed behind. After you left, I made to follow.... Masayu wouldn't let me go without her. So we drove after you. She was able to track you all up here. But there were so many... monsters out there. We fought the ones we couldn't avoid. There were, they looked like army men, but they had swords and shields too, fighting...." He touched his forehead to Masayu's.

"Wait there," Dracula told them. "I will see how matters are proceeding. You are both badly wounded; do not move too much. And put pressure on your wounds. I will see about your care once we have located the rest of our companions."

Emet nodded and obeyed, though he grimaced, baring his teeth as he put his fingers to his shoulder, and pressed his other hand over one of Masasyu's more copious leaks. Brian was tearing strips of cloth from his ripped up shirt to serve as makeshift pressure bandages. He handed these to Emet, then followed Dracula and Cammy.

*****

Dracula guided Cammy out of the slaughterhouse that Ocelotl had made of the enclosure. Now that he'd seen it, one mystery was cleared up. Yaoguai and nekomata liked to eat humans, and that building could not have been erected quickly: the stones had to be quarried and brought to this location. The were-tigers must have been providing meals to the other monsters while Ocelotl put his plan into action.

The column of smoke from the downed helicopter rose high above them, casting the summit into deep shadow. The grotesquerie of mutilated cats stitched together twitched and writhed on the ground; he had managed to damage it with one of the grenades the enemy had lobbed at him. However, it would require something other than physical damage to

Dracula's Death

banish whatever wore those corpses as a skin. He could see the clumps of fur and broken bones rippling like a treacherous sea.

Cammy was sobbing. This had been far too much for her. He would not have let her come but for the fact that she had shown herself partly capable of defending herself, and Dracula had expected more support on the ground providing protection for his allies, and thus less need for her to try directly to stop a madman from ending the world. As it was, she and Officer Warren had slowed the bloodshed. Their efforts might even have been enough to derail the ritual, if some idiot hadn't completed it with that too-well-aimed bullet.

He stepped past Neil's corpse, drawing Cammy and Brian back towards the trees.

"Wait here, we need to coordinate with Malcolm and the others," he instructed Officer Warren. He strode back to the wall. The summit afforded him a better view of the surroundings, while also making him more visible if there were any allies looking for him. The remaining captives had filed hesitantly out of the slaughterhouse, but they milled about aimlessly, uncertain of where to go. Their rescue was best left to Special Services; Dracula could not direct them anywhere, nor transport them all.

The young man, Emet, was badly wounded, and Dracula was not certain several hours' drive back to his estate would help the young man's chances of surviving his wounds, so he also intended to get one of Special Services to call in one of their medics. If he explained that the young man already knew about the supernatural, then they might be willing to help what they ought to view as a potential asset. Dracula did not think an ambulance would be allowed anywhere near the area, and doubted that one could arrive in a timely manner even if it *could* arrive, but Special Services still had one helicopter in the area. If Special Services resisted his attempts, then he would take Emet and to the nearest town and try for an ambulance there—though the tiger would be forced to brave the journey back to his estate for care. As a stopgap measure, the Orders of St Jeanne D'Arc or St Michael might have medics; he intended to ask for their help also if he came across any of them.

He surveyed the carnage below. Dead Special Services agents, mutilated undead—some of which had indeed been stitched into a semblance of wholeness—some members of the Orders also dead.

"Yo!"

Malcolm came through the trees towards him. He was limping a little. He supported Siri, one of her slender arms draped over his shoulder. Blood poured from her other shoulder, down her blouse nearly to her waist. That would require tending to. As with the tiger, she would have to endure the hours-long drive back to his estate.

Dracula considered Neil lying dead at his feet, and knelt. He turned the man over. Though the back of his head was a ruin, his face was intact save for the entry wound; his body was dirtied by the blood and mud into which he had fallen. Dracula did his best to wipe the face clean, then shut the eyes. He laid the man beside the stone wall and folded the arms across the chest.

Malcolm waited while he said what prayers he could for the fallen.

"Sorry about him," Malcolm said.

"He gave his life trying to stop Boese from making a grave mistake," Dracula said. "He deserves what honors I can give him."

Some members of the two Holy Orders came out of the trees and made their way up the summit.

Dracula's Death

"God rest him," said one, seeing Neil.

"What has become of the other undead?" Dracula asked.

"Quite a few simply collapsed," the priest answered.

"When the nekomatas scattered, I guess they stopped controlling them," Malcolm mused. "Any still moving are on their own power. Some are old school strigoi. That sure gave me a surprise."

"Don't let them wander off," Dracula instructed, and pointed to the civilians still tied to one another. "And release these poor souls. Do you have any medics with you?"

"One, a little way down the mountain. We radio'ed that he can come up."

"There is a young man within" —Dracula nodded at the walled in cabin— "who is badly wounded, and I do not yet know whether Special Services will assist him. If you are able to help him, please do. There is some sort of tiger creature with him who has helped to fight against the other monsters."

The Catholic knight, dressed in modern tactical gear decorated with emblems of the faith, nodded and pulled a walkie-talkie to call in the request. Then he entered the opening in the wall to see to Emet.

Dracula guided Siri and Malcolm over to Cammy and Officer Warren. He saw no sign of Aki, but she was small and could easily have escaped notice. However, she had stopped casting illusions shortly after the Egyptian goddess appeared. Dracula doubted he would find the fox in good condition. He went to help hunt down any remaining monsters and look for Aki.

A growing rumble that rose to a roar alerted him of the arrival of the other helicopter approaching. The column of smoke bent back, twirling around the new disturbance.

Agents of Special Services were running around. Several had scrambled down the slope to the pile of bodies at the bottom of the trench and were pouring some flammable fluid over it. Others were bringing the damaged or killed undead to add to the pile.

"We have priests here. There is no need to treat with them so shamefully," Dracula told the agents.

"Orders. This is all standard procedure," one called back.

You cretins.

The helicopter was now overhead, so he looked up. Someone was getting lowered on a ladder. Dracula guessed who it would be.

Boese was still able to move around fairly nimbly, despite his age. Descending one of those ladders was no easy task. The director dropped the last two feet or so, nearly falling backwards but managing to keep his feet. He took stock of the carnage all around. He grinned and spread his arms.

"Director, you have nothing to celebrate. You should be repenting in ash."

"For what? Finally putting an end to this madness?" Boese peered down at the pile of bodies and scowled. "Ophois is going to pay. They're going to pay through the nose. Soon as I make a call. I'll have whoever it takes out in force and hunt those rats down their little holes—"

"Director, it has obviously escaped you, but you gave that warlock exactly what he wanted!"

Boese glared at him.

He turned towards the slaughterhouse and stormed up to it. Dracula went after him.

Boese stood just inside the opening, his hands on his hips. He ignored the two members of the Catholic Orders giving Emet and the tiger first aid.

"Unbelievable. Lunatics," he grumbled, and strode towards Ocelotl's body. The dead man grinned to see his ally drawing near. Boese stepped over the body and peered into the cabin.

"Looks like I stopped them before this got way more out of hand," he observed.

"You helped power devils and demons—!"

"And *guess what??*" Boese demanded, whirling on Dracula. "We're all still here! The world didn't end, you superstitious, old fossil! You pack of Medievalists would have let him keep up this little black mass and have the rest of us sit on our *hands!*"

Boese kicked Ocelotl's foot, and the dead man's head rotated, the dead eyes settling on Boese, unnoticed.

"Maybe I'll take the corpse down to the lab. We've never managed to get full access to one of Ophois' front-liners. Just your little buddy, and only for a few days. Let's see what makes them tick. Get all his guts in beakers and his head in a jar and find what we can find. How's *that* for magic?"

Dracula gripped his sword.

"You do absolutely *anything* with that, and I'll feed your pet to something nasty I have down at the lab. Try me. I'm king of the world right now. I just saved the entire planet from some maniac and his so-called gods."

"You have too literal a mind, Director," Dracula seethed. "You completed what he started, and you will see what comes to pass. The fuse is, as they say, lit."

"Cry me a river. You don't think I dotted my magic i's or crossed my magic t's?" He flicked his hand as though signing a flourish in the air, then pointed out the opening again. "Raw manpower, ballistics, and basic tech just saved the day. You people need to get out of the Dark Ages. We'd already run the numbers on the outcomes here. Had all the contingencies figured out."

"Director, you have no idea what you have unleashed—"

"Can it. I've had enough of old wives' tales. Out of my way." Boese pushed past him, never even noticing Neil lying to one side. He surveyed the slopes, his men and the members of the Orders scrambling to put a stop to the remaining vampires. "We got people chasing down those rats that got away?" Boese called down to one of his men.

"We've got a few units after them. But they're fast."

"I don't want to hear how fast they are, I want to hear that we've got some samples for the lab," Boese shouted back. "Get on that. Where are the other civilians?"

"We've intercepted them. Bringing them back now."

"Fine, fine." Boese caught his breath. It was a little shallow. He winced, and pressed a hand to his side.

Too much exercise for a man his age after all? Dracula considered beheading him right there. It would be very easy. Just above the collar, where the shaven head met the neck.

He walked past Boese towards Cammy and the others.

"Has anyone seen the nicker or the fox?" Dracula asked. Officer Warren, Malcolm and Siri shook their heads. Cammy was too busy sobbing to answer. Dracula's cloaks had been burned up by the Egyptian goddess, so he motioned for Malcolm to give up his jacket. Malcolm obliged, and Dracula passed the jacket to Cammy to cover herself.

"That all of them?" Boese shouted from behind.

"This group, yeah. ETA on the other is two minutes. Maybe more, the fire is spreading."

"Tell them to hurry; we have a lot to clean up here," Boese instructed. He gasped a little for air. His face was paler than usual.

One of the groups of people Cammy and Officer Warren had cut free was being led back up to the summit to join those who had not yet run. Dracula had a certain suspicion—especially after what happened at the Space Needle last year. He turned to Officer Warren.

Dracula's Death

"Take her to the vehicle. *Now*," Dracula ordered him. He turned to hurry towards the walled-in cabin to help evacuate Emet and Masayu. He didn't want to draw too much attention, so he did not sprint, but instinct told him he needed to make good time, so he did what he could to satisfy both prudence and expediency.

When he came to the opening, he urged the men, "Get them out, now. I think the director has ill intentions towards the civilians here. I suggest saving anyone you can."

One of the Catholic knights considered his serious expression, then nodded. Masayu had recovered enough to change back to her human form, and was leaning on the second man. They made it out through the opening and Dracula directed them towards Officer Warren and the others, who had already reached the tree line. He turned to see who else he might be able to warn.

The people that Cammy and Officer Warren had freed had been brought back up the hill, rounded up and herded by agents. Boese nodded at them. His agents raised their weapons and took aim. Cammy's mouth dropped open at the sight.

"*No!*" she screamed.

The agents opened fire.

Cammy convulsed and shrieked in horror.

"Officer Warren!" Dracula shouted. "Take her to the vehicle!" Two bullets clanged off his armor, but did him no harm. Someone must have fired at him instinctively, or else was a very bad shot and had missed Emet, Masayu, and the two Catholic knights helping them. Others did not miss their shots, and the four retreating figures dropped. Screams filled the air once more, this time high and sharp.

Men, women, and the young screamed as they were gunned down. Too many witnesses to manage. Too many to keep track of. It was simply easier to leave them classified as "missing". Boese had run the numbers.

A member of one of the Orders ran forward to shout at Boese, demanding he call a stop to the slaughter, only to be gunned down himself when he refused to back away. The agents kicked him towards the new pile of bodies. The other members retreated into the tree line.

All at once, it was over. Silence descended on the summit, and it rang in Dracula's ears after the excruciating cries and screams of misery and fear, the roars of an Egyptian goddess, the weapons of war, and helicopters. Booming, deafening silence. Another agent was climbing the hill, and stooped. He picked up the limp body of a yellow fox. Red stained the fur from the throat to the shoulder. The agent carelessly tossed the fox onto the burning pile of bodies behind him.

Two pillars of smoke rose into the air, the scent of cedar and soot and burning flesh all mixed together. Boese watched it all, and waved as he ordered his men to perform some other heinous duty he deemed necessary. The cold, calculating, impersonal face of the modern world. A warlord might have felt something while ordering his men to slaughter a village or town. He might have relished it, or felt the weight of his duty, or had the decency to hate the people he had cut down or tortured before him.

Even the sultan Mehmet had shown some reverence and awe when entering the Hagia Sophia after his men took Constantinople. The modern man pressed a button from miles away, or signed an order. He calculated only "acceptable losses" and financial and logistical costs. Human life had become so cheap.

Boese bent forward, and winced. Then he fell to one knee and clutched at his chest and his side.

Dracula walked into the trees after the others. Siri was in grave danger unless someone saw to her wound soon. And Cammy... she might never recover.

Dracula's Death

EPILOGUE

Brian checked on Cammy. She hadn't gotten out of bed for days.

"Hey, there," he greeted her. The gray daylight suffused the room with a cold glow.

Cammy curled tighter underneath the covers. Her hand drew up to her chin. She squeezed her eyes shut. Brian wished he knew what to say. She'd cried the entire ride back. She'd cried while Dracula did his surgery on Siri in the kitchen when they got to the mansion.

And she hadn't left her room since she got back.

"I'll get some coffee," he offered.

"I wanted to help," Cammy whispered. "I wanted to *help*."

"I know." Brian took her hand. Her fingers felt cold. He squeezed her hand gently.

She reached out and hugged him and sobbed into his shirt. All he could do was hug her back. He had never felt so helpless.

When Cammy finally ran out of tears, he told her he'd bring her some coffee and food. She hadn't eaten in days.

Downstairs, there was some woman who he'd heard was an Icelandic elf cooking in the kitchen. A young boy was trying to peer into the pot she was stirring.

"Trausti!" the woman scolded, then sent him away. The boy darted past Brian, then hesitated at the back door.

"Will Miss Cammy be all right?" he asked.

"I don't know," Brian told him. The boy cast down his eyes, then let himself out and darted over the gravel and disappeared—literally, not figuratively. Brian blinked, then went to the fridge.

"The master said she should eat soups," the woman told him. "She is wery unwell."

"Yeah," Brian agreed.

"I almost have something ready for her now," the woman said. "And some wery nice tea." She pointed to an unmarked bottle on the counter. "And there is some medicine."

"What is it?" Brian asked.

"The master said it was for her."

Brian walked out into the light drizzle to look for Dracula. Brian had gotten the whole tour the day before, even out to the vineyards and the lake. On a hunch, he walked out towards the vineyards now.

Sure enough, he found the Impaler out there, kicking at some of the piles of downed vines and surveying the damage. Dracula shook his head every so often as he walked through the nearly naked trusses, his hands in his pockets.

"Officer Warren," he greeted. "Good morning."

"What's that stuff you're giving Cammy?"

"Laudanum. She is in a very bad way."

"*Laud...* you know we're not living in the Victorian Era, right?"

"People haven't changed since the dawn of time," Dracula told him, sounding frustrated by the necessity of having to justify himself in the face of what he clearly viewed as the stupidest protest imaginable. "She has a very sensitive constitution."

"You know she's missed all her midterms, right?"

Dracula's Death

"Yes. I doubt she will be in any condition to resume her education before next semester, at the very earliest. She needs rest, and time."

"You didn't have to bring her along."

"Officer Warren." Dracula looked up at him, his eyes unfriendly. "I told you to come get her half a year ago."

Brian glared at him. "I was... you didn't tell me what was going on."

"You didn't ask."

"How could I have asked?!?"

"By *asking*, Officer Warren. I would have told you, had you been straightforward. I don't reward cowardice."

"*Cowardice?*" Brian seethed. "Because you didn't tell me anything, I was coming up here to *kill* you. *That* could have ruined your trying to stop Aztec Crazy Guy."

"*Ha!*" Dracula grinned with amusement and turned away. Brian thought he was chuckling to himself. Brian felt his blood hot in his head.

"So what now?" he demanded.

"Now?" Dracula cleared his throat, turned back, and shrugged. "Now we must see how matters play out."

"The world still seems to be here," Brian observed. Dracula shook his head and cast his gaze out through the trees, towards the city.

"You modern men. How did you come to be so ignorant and so blind? There are many ways for the world to end. The atom bomb ended the world."

"What? No, it didn't."

"It ended the way the entire world wages war," Dracula told him. "Nothing was the same afterwards. Now countries must wage proxy wars through smaller, weaker countries. No longer do you have to spill your own blood. Now you can force others to spill theirs against the minions of some other nation. War is at the same time too costly to wage, and too cheap not to engage in. Your vision is too narrow." Dracula sighed. "Time will reveal to what degree Ocelotl succeeded."

Brian looked out at the city. The buildings were faint smears through the cloud cover and the drizzle. Then he noticed something swinging just a little from a tree at the far corner of the vineyard. He let his eyes focus on it. Some sort of corpse hanging from the limb of a tree. He covered his mouth.

Dracula noticed that he had noticed, and nodded.

"One of the satyrs threatened Cammy. I have him up there as warning to the others. I won't have them molesting my guests."

He was sure living up to his reputation. He wasn't much less bloodthirsty than the lunatic they had all fought to stop. Brian would have to talk Cammy out of staying here. He turned back.

On the way, he spotted a girl sitting under the big tree which overshadowed the mansion. There was a little puppy or maybe a fox in her lap. She was stroking the little animal, which rested its chin on her knee, but its eyes were watery and listless.

Brian made it back up to Cammy's room.

"I have to head to work. Let me know if I can bring you something?"

Cammy shook her head. As he straightened up to go, a text came through on Cammy's phone. She didn't reach for it. He couldn't help but sneak a peak in case it was important. It was from her father.

Cammy, please call me. It's about your mother.

He couldn't delete it. He'd need her thumbprint to unlock it. Instead, he turned the phone over and pushed it further out of reach. Whatever that was about, Cammy didn't need it right now.

Dracula's Death

*****

Kenzie huffed and checked her phone again. Her sister sure was taking her sweet time getting out of whatever after school club she'd joined. *Please let it not be drama class; rehearsals take forever.* She'd already texted to say she was waiting, but so far, no response.

Kenzie kicked the curb. It wasn't fair. One of her roommates, Billie, had decided to move out, so Kenzie needed money more than ever. And her mother wanted her to take even more time off work to keep an eye on Raquel, all because some other parents couldn't keep an eye on their stupid kids.

The hail and ice storms had stopped, and it was back to mostly cloudy with occasional rain. A tree in front of the middle school had lost a branch, which lay on the wet grass, now sawn into smaller pieces. Leaves lay plastered to everything. The grass was dead in patches from the pummeling it had received, and there were two broken windows in a building across the street that had been boarded up. At five p.m. there weren't a whole lot of parents waiting to pick up their kids, not even from the after-school clubs, so it was just Kenzie standing on the sidewalk to make sure her sister got home safe. Her mother was being paranoid.

A couple walked slowly towards her from the other side of the school entrance. Some middle-aged businesswoman and some black-haired, tall man in a jacket. Kenzie assumed they were parents, but the man with the black hair and beard came to a stop before the school entrance and cast his black eyes over the building, while the redhead kept walking. Kenzie squinted. They *felt... odd.*

"Can I help you?" she called out, when it was clear the redhead was coming straight for her. The woman's red lips pulled into a friendly, eager smile.

"Hello there," she said. "You work at the Mindful Bean, don't you?"

Kenzie narrowed her eyes. This lady had a "Dracula" accent—the Lugosi kind. She was sure if any customer had come in talking that way, she'd have noticed it.

"Yeah?" Kenzie laced her reply with plenty of annoyance. She wasn't on the clock, and she wasn't being paid to be nice to random boomers. And judging from this lady's clothes, a rich one.

"You are the one who likes horror movies?"

"Are you stalking me?" Kenzie demanded. "I know a cop. I can call him."

"No," the woman shook her head. "But you do know a man I am interested in keeping an eye on."

Kenzie pulled her phone and made a show of pulling up Brian's contact.

"And you like vampires," the woman continued. "Enough to want to be one?"

Kenzie glared at the stranger. There was some strange scent on the air. Alluring and sweet on top, something like death underneath. She crinkled her nose and rubbed it.

"Is there some sort of point you have to make? 'Cuz I actually have stuff to do," Kenzie told her.

"What do you think about the man named Dracula? Who knows your friend? Cammy?"

Kenzie glared at her, scrutinizing that fixed smile, the immaculate red nails. Her eyes drifted to the guy with the black hair behind her. Big, thuggish-looking guy. His face seemed familiar. Kenzie couldn't place where she'd seen him before. Maybe the beard was thicker and longer than the image that couldn't quite surface in her mind. But where had she seen him...? Come to think of it, the redhead seemed familiar, too. But she felt certain she'd never seen either of these two weirdoes before. Or at least, not *met* them. They'd have left a big impression.

"You do know that vampires exist?" the businesswoman prompted with a little laugh.

"Of course," Kenzie snarled at her. "Who *are* you? What do you want? And the king of creeps back there? He's going to end up on a registry if he keeps salivating in front of middle schools like that."

The businesswoman cast a glance over her shoulder at her companion. He noticed her look, and she flicked her eyes for him move away. He crossed to the other side of the street. The woman returned her attention to Kenzie.

"I think you will have heard of me," she said, "so I will tell you my real name. I am Countess Báthori Erzsébet. Elizabeth Bathory, rendered in English. You needn't curtsey."

"Wasn't planning on it," Kenzie snarked. She squinted at Bathory's face. Now she thought she could place where she'd seen her before. Paintings. She could see the resemblance. Kenzie considered Bathory's companion back there. Maybe he looked familiar because she'd seen a painting of him? Meaning he ought to be somebody she'd looked up before. But who?

Bathory seemed to be waiting for a reaction. Kenzie made a point of looking her up and down.

"Let's assume you are," Kenzie said. "You're a long way from home. What are you doing here, and what do you want?"

The corner of the smile twitched. Maybe the redhead was offended. Whatever. Kenzie wasn't on the clock, and if this woman was legit, she needed to prove it. If she was like the other vampire in town, Kenzie wasn't sure she wanted to be friends, vampire or not. She'd asked *him* to turn her, and gotten socked in the face by way of an answer. She ought to have figured that some guy from the 1400s was a raging misogynist, but *still*. Bathory... Maybe she'd be better? Assuming this woman was legit.

"I was hoping you'd be willing to get me information on the man named Dracula," Bathory said.

"You mean, you aren't already acquainted?"

"We haven't crossed paths, no," Bathory explained. "I have a proposal for him, but he has quite the history of... aggression. I don't wish to approach him openly until or unless I know that he may be receptive. And I prefer to arrange the meeting at a place of my choosing. In the event that he proves... not receptive."

"He doesn't like women," Kenzie told her.

Bathory smirked.

"Perhaps not. But his predilections towards women are irrelevant with regards to my proposal. I have come to ask your aid, and to pay you well in exchange for your service."

"You'd have to prove you are who you said you are," Kenzie told her, casting a glance at the black-haired creep lurking across the street. "Before I agree to anything."

"Of course," Bathory said. "Though I don't think this location appropriate. If you *are* interested in what I can offer, then suggest a time and place. I can do a great many things for you. I have... abilities."

The mixed smell wasn't so off-putting now. The smell of death seemed less strong, or maybe Kenzie'd gotten used to it. She spotted Raquel's hot-pink dyed hair bobbing out of the front doors. *Finally.* Clubs were letting out. Kenzie waved to her sister. Raquel came trotting over, and eyed Bathory up and down. Bathory smiled at her.

Dracula's Death

"You know where I work," Kenzie told her. "Drop by sometime. We'll work it out then. Or if you're legit, get me on the cover of *Fangtasmagoria*. That would be cool." She wrapped an arm around Raquel's shoulder and drew her away. She pulled out her phone to order a ride for them both.

"Who was that?" Raquel asked.

"Dunno," Kenzie said. She glanced back. Bathory was watching them leave. If this woman was for real, and her offer was for real, she'd just been handed the best way to get back at the Impaler and Cammy for keeping all this secret from her.

*****

Dracula made his way up towards Andrew's farm. He had visited several times since the *draugr* rampage, and spoken with the young man about how his family ran the business. The bad weather caused by Ocelotl and the *ccoa* had wreaked havoc on farms; even now large branches lay piled up on the side of the road. Some of the little houses had damaged roofs from trees coming down, or from the relentless hail. He spotted cracked windshields in driveways as he went.

Soon the little farmhouse appeared through the gray, and he pulled into the driveway. During the day the family members sold eggs at various markets, but someone ought to be home to care for the animals, so Dracula made his way to the front door. Some of the lawn decorations were lying flat in the mud.

He knocked on the door and took stock of the damaged roof shingles. After a few moments, Mr. Swindelhurst answered the door.

"Oh, hello," he ventured. He, like his wife and son, had been introduced to Dracula half a year ago, and knew that the supernatural lurked in Seattle's shadowy corners. "My wife should be back soon. I don't know if she'll have any leftover eggs, though. I'm afraid the weather wiped out almost everything. Andrew and I tried our best, but we're just going to have to see what survives."

"I'd like to buy your farm and hire you to work on an even larger one," Dracula told him. Mr. Swindelhurst blinked, confused.

"You'd like to what?" he asked, with a nervous chuckle.

"To buy your farm, and to pay you and your family handsomely to expand."

Mr. Swindelhurst pulled his glasses from his nose and wiped them on his checked shirt.

"I... really don't know what to say to that. We have our hands pretty full here, and while we're not getting rich, we are getting by."

"It is a straightforward offer," Dracula told him. "I wish to employ you. I have a good many resources which you could use—not the least of which is a great deal of capital. I wish to grow a great many crops."

"I, well, that is quite an idea," Mr. Swindelhurst said, and replaced his glasses. "And I wish you the best on that. But I think we're pretty happy where we are. If that's all you came to say, then I think I'll be heading back to the beds. Got lots of dead plants to pull up." He swung the door gently shut. Dracula caught it and forced it back open.

"I was not precisely *asking*, Mr. Swindelhurst," he said.

*****

Brian added more weight to the bar.

One.

He had no idea what to do now. Cammy was staying with a bloodthirsty warlord from hundreds of years ago, who nevertheless *maybe* wanted to protect the city and maybe even her, in some strange way.

Two.

His sister was dating a horse. Or at least, had been. Brian didn't know what had happened to Akerman. He hadn't shown up to work.

Three.

The US government had shot dozens of people, and he had witnessed it. Odds were good there were going to be consequences for that. He just didn't know what they were yet.

Four.

There were monsters and crazy people who used magic or spells or gods to try to affect the world, and they were getting bolder. One year ago it had only been Dracula, and he'd only revealed enough to make Brian question who—or what—he really was. Then it had been an undead wrestler destroying tourist traps. Now some crazy Aztec wannabe with nightmarish delusions of godlike grandeur. What next, Godzilla?

Five.

His shoulder twinged in intense pain and the weights dropped on that side. Someone caught the end before the bar fell on Brian's chest.

"Akerman!"

Akerman helped lift the bar onto the frame and Brian sat up. Sure enough, Baby Face was here, and whole. Brian got to his feet and hugged him. It was Akerman's turn to wince. Then Brian punched him.

"That's for lying to me and dating my sister, you asshole," he told him. Akerman rubbed his shoulder. He was wearing his police hoodie, but Brian could see a bandage across the side and back of his neck. "What happened?"

"The yaogaui made a mistake when it jumped on me," Akerman explained. "I can drown anything that gets on my back. I ran down to the lake and jumped in. And drowned 'im."

"Why didn't you come back?"

"It is a whole lot easier to run down the side of a mountain and hop in a lake than it is to climb back out of the lake, back up the mountain, through a small forest fire, past vampires, and then to the top," Akerman told him.

"So where have you been? I haven't even heard from you for days."

"They wanted me... at their headquarters," Akerman explained, and hugged himself. "To explain what I was doing up there."

"About your bro—"

Akerman shook his head furiously. "They're going to transfer me to a different precinct soon. I've been here too long." He gestured to his face. "I can either look like this, or like an old man. I can't age like normal humans."

"Right," Brian agreed. It was pretty hard to believe that anyone past thirty could look that young. "That means you're breaking up with Melissa?"

"Breaking up?" Akerman repeated. "No way. She's the nicest girl I've met."

"Akerman. I am not letting a horse date my sister."

"Sea horse," Akerman corrected with a little smile.

"Any kind of horse!" Brian insisted. "You're not even human. What are you *thinking?*"

One of the other officers made a face at them, but went back to his own reps. Akerman shook his head at Brian. "I also wanted to warn you that they'll probably come after you," he said.

"I figured as much. But I have no idea what to do about men in black coming to get me."

Dracula's Death

Akerman blew out a deep sigh. "I tried to warn you. And I tried to buy time." He shook his head. "You could run," he suggested. "Some monsters or humans make it to Canada, from what I hear."

"I'm not running anywhere," Brian told him. Akerman nodded, but he looked miserable. He clapped Brian on the shoulder.

"I guess I'll see you around," he said.

"Yeah," Brian agreed. "See you around."

"I have to clock in," Akerman told him. "We should catch a drink one of these nights."

"Only if you break up with Melissa."

"Not going to happen," Akerman told him, then turned and hurried off.

That was definitely something Brian would have to figure out. He'd only come to work out a little to clear his head, so he headed out to the parking lot and ordered an Uber. The car pulled up and he got in the backseat. So did another guy, from the other side. Brian took half a second to assess the man and why he'd hop in Brian's ride before he opened the other door to get out. Another T-shirted man was standing outside, waiting for him to do just that. He had a taser at the ready.

"Relax," he told Brian. "We just want to talk."

Brian moved to the middle as the second T-Shirt guy slid into the righthand seat and shut the door. The driver was also wearing a T-shirt. Another guy opened the door and got in the passenger seat. Brian glared at them all.

"First, put this on," said the man with the taser. He held up a cloth bag.

"I am not going to—"

The man with the taser threw the bag over his head, then the two guys on either side grabbed his arms when he tried to resist.

A car and elevator ride later, he found himself dumped into a metal chair in a metal room with harsh, white lights glaring down at him. There was a metal table in front of him, and a thick metal door that swung shut behind the T-shirts who had dumped him down here. Brian spotted a camera in a ceiling corner, pointed down at him. Across the table was some sort of television screen on rollers.

He was about to hear something he didn't want to hear, or else find out what the inside of his head looked like.

The screen turned on, and the image of a bald man with scars notching from his cheek back into his ear popped on. It was the guy who had flown in on the helicopter and ordered that massacre. The guy who had stalked Cammy to Heather's grave to harass her. Brian glared at him.

"Hello, Mr Warren," the man said. He flipped through a manila folder. "Twenty-two years old, with an older sister, Melissa Walenta-Warren; a little sister, too."

"I've met her once," Brian informed him. "Mom's on her third marriage."

"So I've read," the bald man agreed. "Mother's name is Barbara, maiden name...*Mendoza?*"

"Problem with Mendoza?" Brian growled.

"You're the whitest Mendoza I've ever seen."

"Spaniards, not Mexicans," Brian informed him. "Very Catholic. Mom was disowned and hasn't bothered being 'Spanish' for ages. Third marriage and all."

The bald man grunted. He closed the file.

"I hear you were helping to manage the civilians up there and kept a pretty cool head in all that chaos."

"I hear you had dozens of people shot," Brian retorted.

"We'll get to the why on that later. I just wanted to congratulate you on doing a pretty fine job, considering you didn't know about any of this before. And you didn't, right?"

Dracula's Death

Brian glared at him. He thought the man's low collar looked a little like a hospital gown.

"Nothing at all," Brian told him.

"Good," the bald man smiled coldly. "Since you can keep a secret, I just wanted to let you know I have a nice position available for you. Wouldn't even change your work schedule."

"No thanks. I'm a cop to protect people. Not shoot them."

"You wouldn't be a specialist," the bald man told him. "Don't worry about that. Hardly anything about your life would change. Except the paycheck, and the benefits. You'll like those. I just need you to report back to us if you see or hear anything... untowardly suspicious. You know the sort of thing I mean. That's all."

"No thanks," Brian told him, and kicked himself up from the table. He went to the metal door, but it wouldn't open.

"Son," he heard the bald man's voice say behind him. "I am not *asking* you."

The End

Amaya Tenshi

To be followed by:

Dracula's Minions
Dracula's Daughter

DRACULA'S DEATH

AUTHOR'S NOTE

Greetings, dear reader, and thank you once again for finishing another installment in this silly series of mine. Allow me to address a few details with regards to this book. Some may notice that the magic included in this book is a bit "theatrical". That is on purpose, as I do not intend to write a grimoire, so not everything that I mention will be based on folklore or other sources. While that will muddle some of what otherwise feels "anchored", it is not my intention to focus on magic specifically. Ocelotl is not quite Aztec or Mayan, but a blend of both, as evidenced by his teeth—more Mayan—though he generally has more overt Aztec influence. I did rely on my reading of the *Popol Vuh* for his appearance (as well as some Egyptian theology, as the Order of Ophois has strong Egyptian influences). His use of the phrase "My beloved son" is a reference to a practice of the Mayans when taking slaves: they would capture someone by the hair and say this phrase specifically. His revulsion at sexual immorality (as evidenced by his insulting the girl in the opening for her choice of dress) is also very Mayan, as they had a horror of and disgust for sexual immorality. Moreover, Mayan priests would have to avoid contact with women for certain ceremonial purposes. Ocelotl has a few other quirks or behaviors to reference Tezcatlipoca (of the Aztecs, *not* the Mayans), such as his playing the flute and the makeup he wears to make his video.

On that note, the ritual which Ocelotl uses is not meant to specifically reflect or correlate to a real-world religious practice either. However, my mention of religious persecution was meant to draw some attention to such practices happening today: in China against many different believers including Uighyrs, and to Armenians trapped in Azerbaijan, to Buddhists in Malaysia (Masayu is a nod to this), Christians in Nigeria and other locations, etc. Including Emet was a reference to the persecution Zoroastrians undergo and underwent in Iran, although he is a Parsi, and comes from India. I had wanted to find an organic way to include a beautiful story of how the Zoroastrians came to settle in India. When asked why they should be allowed to immigrate, a full jar of milk was held out to illustrate that there was no room for the newcomers. The Zoroastrian leader took the jar, and, depending on the telling, dropped either some sugar or a coin inside, and said that his people would be like the added thing, only improving the milk. Alas, I could not find a home for this in the narrative, so I have shared it here. Emet also explains in this novel that what he is wearing to show his faith (his necklace) is not what he is supposed to wear. To my understanding, Zoroastrians are to wear something called a *sudreh,* which is a shirt-like article of clothing, and a *kushi,* which is like a belt. If I have erred in this, it is unintentional. Emet mentioning that he had tried dating a Hindu girl was also a small reference to the increase of interfaith marriages for Parsis. A final note about Zoroastrians and their practices: it would be unthinkable for a Zoroastrian to burn a body, as this would be viewed as introducing impurities into fire, hence their unusual form of burial (which does not place a body into the ground either, for similar concerns about introducing impurity into a substance).

As a small aside: while it is the case that four women specifically were sacrificed along with Tezcatlipoca's avatar, the number four is considered unlucky in both Japanese and Chinese culture, given that the word sounds like the word for "death".

On the topic of stories that did not make it into this book, or into the previous book where it belonged, I do wish to address that there is a very famous story of Vlad the Impaler where he burned alive numerous of the poor of his country. As yet, I have not been able to address this, and though I wished to bring it up in *Dracula's Match* I have not yet found a home for this historical anecdote.

One of my beta readers was confused by the title "priest monk," assuming it to be redundant. As Orthodoxy is not well-known in the West, I should note there that this is a distinct title: a monk who is also a priest. Not all monks are.

I refer to Akerman as a "nicker" as that seems to be a generic name for a creature or family of similar creatures in the legends of many countries, from Denmark to Iceland. Since he is from Sweden, he probably would say something more like "näck" or "necken". Undoubtedly, members of Special Services have been referring to him by the general term long enough that he has decided to simply go by it. Moreover, as "nicker" is a word to describe a sound horses make, I thought it appropriate on that level as well. Akerman is still a bit of a blend of the various versions of this mythical creature, rather than being *specifically* the Swedish type, which is in keeping with the rules for this series as I have laid them out. Anyone wondering whether, given what he is, Akerman can play the violin will have to wait for later installments to find out. And while characters have joked about him being a "sea monster" or "sea horse", he is a freshwater dweller.

The huli jing may be a creature familiar to some readers as similar to the nine-tailed foxes of Japanese mythology. If so, they may wonder why she only had three tails. Huli jing acquire more tails and powers with age. The one presented in this story is quite young, and so she only has three tails. Boese also briefly referenced "newspaper articles" when discussing tanuki with Cammy. I was referencing an article in *Too Nippon* published in 1889 about a tanuki, as well as a 1923 article about a kitsune from *Japan Chronicle* relating the events of the animal being deified. I should mention there are stark differences in beliefs about shape-changing foxes in China compared to Japan (or even Korea, for that matter).

On a related note, Tsuki, Yui and Chou, the cat women who work at the noodle shop, are not vampire cats like the large white ones, but are instead a reference to a type of shape-changing cat in Japanese folklore and mythology who would take the form of prostitutes, called bakeneo yūjo. I use several terms for the supernatural cats in this book. *Henge* refers to shape changing creatures in Japanese mythology and folklore, while kaibyō refers specifically to supernatural cats. For those wondering why her tongue was so badly injured when Dracula and Cammy encountered her late in the novel, this is a reference to ritual bloodletting by the Mayans. Women would often pierce their ears or tongue as a means of bloodletting. In this case, the huli jing had this done *to* her to pay for her sins before she escaped.

Maat, the Egyptian Mau cat is only a Mau because of the modern-day connection. I do not know if there is direct evidence of the breed's origin in Ancient Egypt, though this is popularly believed to be true.

Early in the book, a female were-tiger refers to Dracula as "vetala". This is because I had conceived of a Hindu, Buddhist, or simply Indian origin for her family. However, I found out about other creatures from other locations, so the

DRACULA'S DEATH

were-tigers all have Malaysian names. I am not aware of any Malaysian vampires that correlate even remotely to the strigoi, so I still have her use the Indian word. I do not think it too much of a stretch that supernatural creatures would be aware of other creatures inhabiting regions close to where they live. Strigoi and vetala are not the same creatures, but I thought the character might find enough similarities to apply the title to something she encountered if she did not know the actual name.

The title of this book might seem provocative to some readers. When I first conceived of the series, each title was supposed to reference another "Dracula" work. *Dracula's Guest* is an obvious reference to Bram Stoker's previously unpublished first chapter to his famous book. For various reasons, the second in the series had its title changed from *Dracula's Gauntlet* to *Dracula's Match*, and as far as I know it no longer references any other work. This book's title is a reference to a piece of Hungarian lost media, a silent film titled *Drakula Halala,* or *Dracula's Death*. Not all subsequent books will be titled after existing works, but at least one more will be.

This, though the third in the series, is actually the first book I wrote. When I originally conceived of this series, it was intended to be a television show. In that format, it had a slightly different overall plot and focus. Different characters survived to the end, and different ones did not. This book was my first attempt to adapt my story to novel form, and though I have gone over it, I still feel a bit of the roughness remains, despite my attempts to match it to the other novels. Additionally, this book was substantially darker in its original form, and I have gone to some length to try lightening it. (Yes, it was darker, though there were fewer character deaths.) Originally, Emet and Masayu both survived and fled to Canada, so they could have returned to the series. When this series was a television show, having characters who could return if fans liked them—or not—would have been useful. It was not precisely that I had any particular plan for them in the long run. I debated with myself about their fates, but ultimately felt that their deaths —martyrdom, in some sense—fit thematically and symbolically better than their survival. I went back and forth about this decision for some time, as neither their survival nor their deaths were 100% pleasing to me, for assorted reasons. I did not choose to kill them in order to manipulate readers. I do hope that their deaths are felt as tragic—they are meant to be—as well as thematically and emotionally appropriate for this turning point in the series. It was a shame to lose such nice and wonderful characters, but their deaths ultimately fit into various pieces of foreshadowing, as well as giving a face to the otherwise indistinct grouping of Ocelotl and Boese's victims.

The "historical" prologue of this book is, I hope obviously to readers, almost entirely fiction. I have taken inspiration from a folktale or legend in which Dracula—near his end and before the Ottomans killed him—had his gold moved (probably from Snagov, where he was said to keep some of it) to some unknown location, and then slew all the men who had moved it, in order for it to remain hidden. Then, of course, he was killed. It is silly to think that Dracula and his men would have ridden twenty-two miles to the monastery to perform this action with an army marching against them, given that it would be something like a full day's ride there and back (they could not have galloped the distance). It is totally my imagination to have him dump his gold in Snagov Lake; there is no evidence that I am aware of that any such thing happened. I chose to write this imagined scene for

Dracula's Death

narrative purposes. However, it would have been in keeping with Vlad's strategies for him to have attempted to lure his enemies into the marsh by the Snagov Monastery in an effort to weaken them. And it does seem he was killed a fair distance from Bucharest. I also had Dracula think that St. Ștefan's men had all perished in the battle. Historically, ten survived and returned to Moldavia to sadly report the events, but given that the narrative was from Dracula's perspective, I thought it reasonable that he would not be able to tell what had happened, it simply appeared to him that they had all died.

There are rival claims that Dracula's decapitated body was found either in the marshes near Snagov or Comana Monasteries. Both locations are about equidistant from Bucharest, but in opposite directions. I have chosen to open this story in Snagov Monastery, as that was the one I came across first in my research as the final resting place of the famous Impaler, as well as because I have been to the tomb where he is reputedly laid to rest. No longer hidden in a wall, and no longer full of animal bones, supposedly the Impaler himself lies in a tomb in the floor, which can be visited. Fans interested in history may really enjoy taking a trip to the location. Snagov Lake is a beautiful place, should any of my dear readers wish to visit, and the Snagov Monastery honors the (reputed) remains of Vlad Țepeș Dracula. I should mention that this is an active monastery, not a tacky tourist trap, and religious services are held there. If you do visit, please be respectful.

A small historical note: I had Dracula call the Byzantine Empire the Roman Empire despite "Byzantine" being more readily intelligible to modern readers. This is more accurate for the time, as people living at that time would have simply thought of Constantinople as part of the Roman Empire. The term "Byzantine" was coined later, and subsequent to the fall of Constantinople. Moreover, the use of this word is hopefully historically evocative, as it may surprise readers to think that the Roman Empire only ended as recently as 1453! Joan of Arc had died almost exactly twenty years prior to this event, and the Magna Carta was written about two hundred years prior. The United States formally came into existence about three hundred years after. The distance between the modern day and the United States Civil War is about the same distance as between the writing of the Magna Carta and the Fall of Constantinople (making use of very loose rounding). History is always nearer than we think.

    I have continually tried to update the historical facts as I find small (but important) errors here and there in my books; hence readers should be prepared for some details to not quite line up with the modern scenes. I have been a going back and forth as to whether Dracula was born in 1430 or 1431, for example. I had originally decided on 1430, but at the opening of this book I indicate he was 45 when he died, which would require the 1431 date. I may continue to flip-flop on this, I'm afraid, until one date strikes me as the "best" for narrative purposes. I also was not certain whether to refer to Wallachia as Muntenia, which is the Romanian word for Greater Wallachia and often used to encompass the entire country, though I have also seen Valahia as a name. Because I could not pin down the proper Romanian version of the name, and using one would probably have confused readers in any case, I opted for the more commonly used exonym instead. On a similar note, I had referred to St. Ștefan the Great as "his Majesty" because I am not certain what the proper form of address would actually be for a man who was both a voivode and styled himself as a "lord"—a rank he seems to have held as more authoritative than that of voivode. As the leader of his country, I opted for "his Majesty."

As I am not certain this was clear, when Dracula thinks that history might have been repeating itself with regards to his country, I did not mean that Romania had been occupied by Russia before, but that he was concerned the country would be occupied again. Dracula mentioned Zalmoxis, which is unlikely to be familiar to readers. This is the name of the founder of an ancient cult in Romania, but his name is often conflated with the deity of the religion. Dracula has also committed this error, as he is not an expert on this ancient cult.

ABOUT THE AUTHOR

AMAYA TENSHI

Amaya grew up on mythology: Greek, Egyptian, Norse, and of course fairytales from Europe and Japan. She has spent years amassing a nifty little collection of fairytales and legends from as many different cultures around the world as she could find: China, Vietnam, India, Africa, and more. With interest in subjects like history, theology, folklore, philosophy, and humanity itself, she earned two BAs which have been entirely useless since graduating college.

When not reading hard to find history books or trying to decipher a rare tome in yet another language she doesn't speak, she writes, produces media content, some of which can be found on her website: amayatenshi.com, spends time with her cat, and attends the occasional media/SF convention. She also designs illustrations for an indie comic book, and collaborates with writer Molly Blake in several supernatural crossover stories that involve Dracula in Molly's series: *Vampire Mall Cop*.

Dracula's Guest

By

Amaya Tenshi

Vlad Dragulya--Vampire Hunter???

When Cammy, Seattle hipster, part-time barista and college student, survives an attack by a pack of vampires, she resolves to learn more about what is going on in the shadows of her city. What she discovers is that none other than Dracula himself is involved in vampire abatement efforts. She asks to join forces, and refuses to take "No! Absolutely not!" for an answer. So Cammy ends up moving in—minds out of the gutter about that, folks, this isn't that kind of story. The unlikely duo bring their disparate skill sets together in an effort to put down a mysterious horde of Hollywood-style vampires, and to find out where the bloodsuckers are coming from. A friendly werewolf-for-hire tags along to help out as little as possible.

Dracula's Match

By

Amaya Tenshi

Cammy and Vlad are back! Cammy is still grieving after violent death of her friend Heather, but her life is about to get way more complicated. First, there's the appearance of children who can turn invisible; then a stalker huldra — a magical creature with a tendency to kill her lovers — follows her to her place of work; and there are all the unanswered questions her friends keep asking her.

But it isn't just Cammy having problems; Vlad must deal with a formidable adversary. A draugr is loose in Seattle and is destroying Seattle tourist hot spots, killing anyone unfortunate enough to get in his way or run across his werewolf buddies. Even Dracula cannot subdue him, and a draugr is even harder to kill than a vampire.

Unless Vlad and Cammy can figure out a way to stop him, her friends will be in danger, not only from supernatural monsters, but from government agents increasingly desperate to keep the supernatural secret.

PENMORE PRESS
www.penmorepress.com

The Sorceress and The Skull
by Donald Michael Platt

San Francisco 1946: A Confrontation of Sorcerers and Seers

For the first time in almost 400 years, Michele born in 1932, a direct descendant of Nostradamus, will have all his gifts of precognition and even greater powers, but they will not be fully manifested until after she enters puberty. More than one secret society has been obsessed with finding and controlling Michele, to learn from her where Nostradamus' unpublished prophecies have been sequestered. Hidden since birth, protected by aliases, an aunt, and a gargoyle, Michele at age 13 has become a fugitive, fleeing across Europe and Canada before finally arriving in San Francisco.

Around Michele deadly forces are closing in, but a new ally, *Le Crâne*, the Skull, has also appeared, coming to the aid of the young seer. Who will hold claim to Michele's powers and at what price to her? And who will succeed in acquiring the hidden secrets of Nostradamus?

A Gothic Horror Novella from Award Winning Author Donald Michael Platt

PENMORE PRESS
www.penmorepress.com

Amaya Tenshi

Penmore Press
Challenging, Intriguing, Adventurous, Historical and Imaginative

www.penmorepress.com

www.ingramcontent.com/pod-product-compliance
Lightning Source LLC
LaVergne TN
LVHW040131080526
838202LV00042B/2865